"SO YO

Katherin
teeth. How
would fuse his boots to his feet.

"Hang on to your hat," she growled, and stepped forward again.

Lightning struck her lips as they touched his. A trail of flame sizzled down her neck, crackling along her arms to burn at her fingertips. His hands had somehow settled around her waist, heating her body with inexplicable fire as his lips moved across hers.

He smelled of wide open places and leather. His tongue touched her lips, and suddenly her mouth was open, too, allowing her own tongue to taste him in heated, first-time exploration.

For the first time in her life Katherine was fully alive, each fiber of her body alert, every nerve vibrating with awareness. So this was a kiss!

My Desperado

Lois Greiman

DIAMOND BOOKS, NEW YORK

This book is a Diamond original edition,
and has never been previously published.

MY DESPERADO

A Diamond Book / published by arrangement with
the author

PRINTING HISTORY
Diamond edition / October 1994

ISBN: 0-7865-0048-4

Diamond Books are published by The Berkley Publishing Group,
200 Madison Avenue, New York, NY 10016.
DIAMOND and the "D" design
are trademarks belonging to Charter Communications, Inc.

PRINTED IN THE UNITED STATES OF AMERICA

10 9 8 7 6 5 4 3 2 1

Dedicated to:

Mary Vigoren, a God-sent friend,
who is never too busy to listen
or too rational to understand.

Chapter 1

Silver Ridge, Colorado

"Dead?" Katherine bolted upright in bed, her eyes wide, her mind still dulled with sleep. "What do you mean dead?"

"Dead!" Daisy squeaked hysterically. "Dead as me shoe."

"But he can't be dead," Katherine denied, gripping the bed sheet painfully in clenched fists. "How could he be dead? He was alive when he came in!"

"Course 'e was alive," moaned Daisy, wringing her hands. "You think I'd diddle a . . ." She halted in mid-sentence. It wasn't nice to shock ladies like Katherine Simmons, and it certainly wasn't smart, especially since Katherine was her employer—at least for the moment. "'E was alive as you and me is," she assured. "Livelier."

"Then, did he fall?" Katherine questioned, desperately trying to make some sense of it all. This couldn't be happening. Her life had always been so serene. So wonderfully predictable. Boring even, she'd thought three weeks ago when she'd been young and foolish. Now, however, boredom seemed to be nothing less than a synonym for heavenly. She shook her head, feeling as if her brain were rattling inside her skull like dry seeds in a pod. "Was he ill?" she asked weakly.

"No. No," exclaimed Daisy impatiently. "George was always 'ealthy and raring t' go. If you take me meanin'."

"Then how . . . Ohhh!" Katherine deduced dizzily. Daisy was merely pulling her leg. These westerners had a strange sense of humor. The little English tart may have a heart of

1

gold, but she couldn't quite control her penchant for practical jokes. That was all there was to it. She was merely jesting. "Don't tease me, Daisy," Katherine whispered hopefully, but the other's face was as solemn as a dirge.

"I ain't teasin' y', Miss Katherine. 'E come late, as was 'is way. And we . . . " Daisy shifted her gaze and pulled a face, trying to spare her new employer's sensibilities. "Well, we done it right off," she continued nervously. "Then 'e asks me t' wake 'im four hours after midnight. Said 'e 'ad 'im some important business t' see to. George, 'e liked t' feel important," she said, wringing her hands again. "So I always fussed over 'im, 'y know. 'E was such a 'armless old gent. Drank a tad too much, 'e did. But . . . But I didn't mean t' . . . t' . . . Ohhh!" she wailed, grasping for Katherine's hands. "What am I gonna do? I didn't mean t' . . . I never thought 'e'd . . ." she stammered, not quite able to complete a single sentence and squeezing Katherine's fingers even harder. "'E woke up early. In a frisky mood, 'e was, and wanted to 'ave another go at it. And I didn't know. I mean I ain't never . . . I ain't never *killed* any of 'em afore!" she wailed in quiet terror. "I ain't never. But just after we finished, 'e . . .."

Daisy paused, eyeing Katherine's ghostly pale face in the darkness of The Watering Hole's largest bedchamber. "Y' don't look so chipper yerself there, missy."

"I'm fine." Katherine's voice sounded as if it came from the far end of a narrow tunnel. Her eyes were focused on something indiscernible, and her heavy dark braid stood out in sharp contrast against the bleached whiteness of her modest, buttoned-to-the-chin nightshift. "I'm just fine," she intoned ghostily. "We Simmons are heartier than we look."

Daisy eyed her dubiously in the darkness and sincerely hoped it was true, for Katherine Simmons looked about as hearty as a crushed leaf in a windstorm. There was little time to worry about her, however, when there was an unsightly corpse lying nose up on the next room's bed linens.

"What am I gonna do?" Daisy whispered frantically. "What if they say I murdered 'im? What if they lock me up? I'll never 'ave me own little 'ome with the picket fence. I'll never 'ave me a man to call me own. No little ones to love. Me 'ole life will a been fer nothin', just like me old pap always used to say. Ohhhh," she moaned. "They're gonna 'ang me. I know they is."

"Now don't panic!" Katherine gasped, dropping the bed sheet to grasp Daisy's wringing hands. "They're not going to hang anyone."

Daisy sobbed, her half-bared chest heaving above her hastily donned gown. "What am I gonna do? I'm too young t' die. I ain't never 'urt nobody. Least ways I ain't tried. Ohhh, Miss Katherine, I don't want t' be 'anged. It'd be so 'umiliatin'—gaspin' and swingin' and—"

"Shush!" admonished Katherine, feeling her consciousness waver and desperately grappling for lucidness. But emotional shock and lack of sleep conspired against her. Silence entered the room as her brain scrambled for sanity, then, "We'll take him outdoors."

Daisy's mouth fell open, her eyes enlarging. She mouthed a few words, which failed to be audible, then gasped, "But 'e's dead!"

"I know he's dead," Katherine hissed in return. "That's why we have to get rid of him."

"But Miss Katherine. 'E's . . ." Daisy leaned closer, whispering furtively into the other's pale face. "'E's bare-assed naked."

Katherine's hands fell away, her eyes looking glazed, but Daisy's low, piteous moan returned her to reality.

"Ohhh, I'm gonna be 'anged and fer nothin' worse than givin' a man pleasure."

Katherine refocused her eyes and brain with an admirable effort. "Now quit that," she ordered. "No such thing is going to happen. We're going to . . ." She closed her eyes for a moment, her hands shaking like aspen leaves in a northerly wind. God save her immortal soul. "We're going to get him dressed and take him out onto the street."

"The street?" Daisy leaned close again, her eyes round.

"It'll appear as if he simply died of natural causes," Katherine whispered.

"It *was* natural." Daisy nodded, causing her blond,

disheveled ringlets to bob against her plump bosom. "Ain't nothin' more natural than—"

Her speech stopped with Katherine's palm firmly plastered to her mouth.

"Please," Katherine whispered hoarsely. "Don't talk. Let's just do what needs doing."

In a moment the two were slinking side by side down the night-silent hall. Dusky wall flowers nodded to them from the faded paper as they crept past, holding on to each other as if they would collapse without their partner's support.

Daisy's bedroom door creaked open. The women entered with trembling timidity, clinging together like wilting vines.

A small flame flickered from an oil lamp, casting wavering light across the bed. Katherine stole a glance in that direction. The corpse was blessedly covered with a wrinkled sheet, leaving only his balding head exposed. His complexion was a pallid gray, and on his face was a smile.

Katherine snapped her frantic gaze from the corpse to Daisy, who shrugged apologetically, easily reading Katherine's thoughts.

"It was just after." Daisy nodded solemnly. "'E was feeling fine."

"God help us," Katherine whispered shakily.

"Amen," responded Daisy.

Katherine nodded jerkily toward the floor by the bed, still holding Daisy's hands in a petrified grip. "Those must be his clothes."

"Yes, 'um."

"Daisy . . ."

"Yes, 'um?"

Katherine's haunted eyes lifted to the other's face, her knees going weak and her stomach flip-flopping fishily. "I can't do it. I've never . . . I've never . . ." She gulped.

Daisy scowled for a moment before comprehension dawned, and her eyes widened. "Y' ain't never seen a bloke naked afore?"

Katherine shook her head, and Daisy straightened somewhat, feeling rather maternal with her superior knowledge. "There now, miss," she said, pulling one hand free to pat

Katherine's and share her worldly wisdom. "If the truth be told, there ain't that much t' see."

That knowledge imparted, Daisy studied Katherine's face for signs of relief but realized with a scowl that her employer looked only marginally healthier than poor George himself.

"Now, now, Miss Katherine," she crooned, feeling stronger by the minute. "I'll do the dressin' of 'im. You'd best sit for a spell."

"No!" Katherine shook her head in vehement refusal. There was no way on God's green earth she would be seated in the same room with a smiling corpse. Her eyes strayed foolishly toward the bed, but she shuddered and withdrew her gaze before it reached its awful destination. "I'm fine." She drew a deep breath that rattled down her throat like an overloaded freight train. Remembering her father's words of wisdom, she swallowed hard and closed her eyes. "Adversity is good for the soul."

Daisy scowled. "It may be good for the soul, Miss Katherine," she theorized with a singular shake of her head. "But it's 'ell on the pocketbook. The mayor 'adn't even paid—"

"The mayor?" Katherine whispered, her eyes wide with shock and disbelief. "You killed the mayor?"

Daisy nodded nervously. "'E wasn't much of a mayor, but 'e tried, specially since the last sheriff run off." She shook her head, gazing kindly at the balding man. "'E was right lively in the sack."

Katherine's knees buckled, and she dropped weakly into a chair.

"Now, Miss Katherine, we ain't got much time for swoonin'. P'raps y' could gather up 'is things now and swoon later."

"Things?" Katherine lifted her head to look at Daisy. "What things?"

"George always 'ad 'im a walkin' stick and bowler 'at." Daisy turned to scoop the mayor's clothes from the floor. "But t'night 'e 'ad 'im a satchel along, too. We'd best take it out with 'im, I spect."

"I suppose," Katherine intoned weakly. Daisy was lowering the sheet, her movement quick and efficient now.

"Where're we gonna put 'im?"

"I don't know," Katherine said, then stood and left the room to think without the distraction of the naked mayor.

How had this all come about? She'd only recently learned she'd inherited The Watering Hole from her aunt and had no intention of staying. But she couldn't simply throw the girls out of work, and so she'd remained in Silver Ridge while seeking a buyer for the saloon.

Who would have thought she'd be dragging a corpse out of her establishment only three days after her arrival there? She obviously was not cut out for this line of work. She'd have to sell the place and leave town, especially now. But the bright mineral that had inspired both the community's rapid growth and its name was rumored to be running low, leaving the citizens uncertain of their futures. There were no prospective buyers for a saloon in a waning western town, and the fact that public officials were dropping dead in the place was not likely to heighten interest in Katherine's property.

If she couldn't make some kind of profit off the place, she wouldn't have sufficient funds to return east. It seemed her employees hadn't been paid in over a month, and since Aunt Dahlia's bank account was notably emaciated, Katherine had felt compelled to pay bills from her own pocket, leaving her frightfully impoverished.

"God help me!" she whispered weakly.

The West wasn't merely a bold challenge, as the little novels had said. It was wild and unpredictable and scary and . . . exciting. It was true. The place was exhilarating and stimulating, but she did not belong here. She belonged in the security of a Boston schoolroom. But in order for her to go home, she had to first sell the saloon, and she could hardly sell it with a smiling corpse as bedroom decoration.

Katherine drew herself straighter. She'd simply have to take things one step at a time, as she'd always taught her schoolchildren. And the first step was to find a temporary resting place for poor George.

Taking a deep shuddering breath, Katherine returned to Daisy's room. "Are you finished?"

"Yep." Daisy nodded, scowling at her handiwork. "'E's decent. Or decent as a man can be. Probably more so cuz 'e's dead. What now?"

"Across the street in front of the mercantile one of the steps is loose," Katherine explained. "We'll leave him there. It will look as if he fell and hit his head."

"Coo, that's a right good plan, miss. I knew you was a thinker, I did."

Katherine cautiously eyed the now dressed and grinning mayor. "How do we get him there?"

"Oh that," said Daisy with a dismissive toss of her hand. "Not a problem that. I been draggin' blokes about since me brothers got their first taste o' ale. Couldn't 'ardly leave 'em lyin' facedown in the mud, so I'd drag 'em off t' bed." Placing her fists on her hips, she eyed their burden. "Course, they weren't so 'eavy like. But . . ." She shrugged as if she was considering nothing more serious than an overloaded sack of flour. "You take his feet. I'll take the other end."

They did just that, lugging poor George from the bed to plop him to the floor. Already they were breathing hard. Each woman now took a booted foot as they prepared to drag their burden out of the room, but suddenly Katherine remembered his possessions.

"Right again," Daisy said, then hustled off to retrieve the good mayor's belongings. The satchel was placed on the man's chest, the hat crammed onto Daisy's own riotous curls, but the cane was an ungainly nuisance. She grappled with it for a moment, then finally bent to thrust the thing beneath the waistband of the man's baggy trousers. It skimmed beneath his pant leg, settling solidly against his thigh, and Daisy gave a single nod before straightening with satisfaction.

Katherine, however, was shocked to immobility.

"Daisy!"

"What?" asked the other with a squeak and a start.

"You can't put it there," Katherine whispered nervously. "It's indecent."

"And diddlin' 'im t' death ain't?" Daisy scowled, pragmatic to the last. "But any'ow, 'e's dead. 'E don't mind. And we're in a bit of a rush, aye?"

The reminder was as subtle as Daisy could be and was the perfect means of jolting Katherine into motion. They heaved together, dragging George through the doorway and standing red-faced in the hall, drawing breath in deep gulps.

"George," Daisy explained laconically, "'e liked 'is pleasures."

Katherine could only assume the other was explaining the mayor's rather ponderous form, but she couldn't help blushing nevertheless. After all, if old George had employed a bit more discretionary self-discipline, they'd all be a sight better off.

They heaved again. The hall was runnered by a worn scarlet carpet, which muffled the sound but did nothing to speed their progress. Eventually they arrived at the steps.

Katherine eyed the descent and grimaced. He was far too heavy for them to carry. They'd have to drag him. She closed her eyes with a silent apology. She'd come from a conservative Protestant family, where speaking ill of the dead was considered a sin. What would they think of dragging the same down a flight of stairs by his heels? She shivered, prayed again, and took a step backward, refusing to look as poor George's head bumped against the top step.

After a grizzly eternity the threesome was outside. The street was still quiet. A grinning full moon sliced out from behind a dark, bubbling cloud, casting its spooky light upon the shadowed town. The women shuffled backward down the boardwalk, crossing the hard-packed clay of Silver Ridge's main thoroughfare and reaching the broken step with a lurch and a groan. Their breathing was labored, their muscles aching, but they'd reached their destination.

"We've done it." Katherine paused, still trying to catch her breath. "Now we have to make it look like a natural fall."

"Right-oh." Daisy grasped the walking stick to pull it from George's pants. Katherine shuddered and snatched his hat from the tart's head, placing it just so, a short distance from the corpse.

The satchel, which had caused them a good deal of

difficulty by insisting on sliding from the sloping plane of George's chest, was now placed just out of reach of his hand.

The women stepped back a pace, studying their handiwork in the waning light of the moon.

"What do you think?" Katherine asked, nervously twisting the heavy black braid that had fallen over her shoulder.

"'E looks right peaceful t' me," Daisy whispered, hands on hips. "Y'd never know 'e was drug from there t' 'ere."

"You think not? Maybe we should turn him over. Maybe—"

"Maybe," a deep voice from the shadows suggested, "you should wipe that grin off his face."

Chapter 2

The two women gasped in unison, clutching each other with frantic fingers.

"Who are you?" Katherine demanded in a whisper not loud enough to shake the dew from a dandelion puff.

Silence held the street in its chilly grip, but finally was broken by a smoky voice. "Can I give you ladies a hand?"

Katherine mouthed an inaudible response, found her voice with great difficulty, and squawked, "This isn't at all as it appears."

The shadow's head tilted, proof he was looking at the corpse, then straightened again. "And how does it appear?" he asked in a tone deep as the night.

"Well . . ." Katherine could feel herself tremble. They'd been caught dead to rights. God help them! And she was barely able to raise her voice above a murmur in her own defense. "Well it might look as if . . ." She was completely out of her depth.

To date, her most traumatic experience had been when little Johnny Tensel had put the toad in her coat pocket and the entire classroom had erupted into howling chaos when she'd fainted dead away.

She wished she could faint now, but her consciousness was stubbornly intact. "It might look as if . . ." she began again, swallowing hard and glancing, against her will, at the ghoulish corpse. "Well . . . How *does* it look?" she sputtered suddenly.

If she wasn't mistaken, the shadow chuckled, the sound

11

so deep and quiet she had to cock her head to catch just a whisper of it.

"It looks like he's dead," came the response finally. "Real dead." The shadow approached a step, causing the women to retreat cautiously backward, still gripping hands in desperate terror.

"Oh!" Her mother had been right, Katherine thought in frenzied retrospect. She should never have read those dime novels about the heroes of the West. She should have married Edgar Winston when he'd first asked and should never have left Boston. "Well yes, actually," she admitted with a spasmodic nod. "He is dead. Quite dead, I'm afraid. But we aren't responsible." She was breathing hard and wishing she'd had those twelve babies of Edgar's, even though he was potbellied and holier-than-thou.

There were worse things than being married to a sanctimonious stuffed shirt.

Being hanged for instance. Being hanged was at the very bottom of her list. "I mean," Katherine continued, "we *are* responsible, but we didn't mean to do it."

"Looks like he died happy," said the dusky voice from the darkness.

Katherine scowled, canting her head again and wishing to God she could see his face. "I beg your pardon."

"He died happy," the shadow repeated. "I can only assume one of you two should get the credit for that."

Daisy and Katherine turned face-to-face, seeing the identical mixture of horror and confusion in the other's expression.

"Which of you was it?" he asked quietly.

The women's eyes widened to an even greater extent.

Daisy moaned in silence. She'd never see that picket fence, never have babies and give them a better life than she'd known.

Poor Mother, lamented Katherine in anguish. She'd die of shame when she learned the truth of her daughter's demise, but it had been Katherine's decision to accept the saloon as her inheritance, and with that decision came the responsibility of looking after her employees.

"Me," they said in squeaky union, each courageously trying to save the other.

"Who?" The stranger's tone was mildly surprised, and the two women turned inward, each telepathically ordering the other to silence before staring at the shadow again.

"Me," they echoed a second time.

"Riding double?" intoned the stranger, taking a step forward and seeming to grow in size as he nodded briskly toward the corpse. "He was a lucky man."

The women squeezed closer together, backing away, with Daisy moaning a bit in utter mental anguish. She'd held so tenaciously to the hope of a better future.

Katherine felt Daisy's emotional agony like a stab in her conscience. Her own life had been so uncomplicated that she'd fantasized about enduring and miraculously overcoming the hardships of the West. While Daisy, on the other hand, had never been given a chance at a decent life. It wasn't fair. It wasn't right, and Katherine couldn't bear to have her take the blame for a death she hadn't meant to cause.

"It was my fault," Katherine blurted. "All mine. But I didn't kill him."

"'E died o' natural causes," chimed Daisy. "Real natural."

The stranger tilted his head slightly. "There's nothing more natural than—"

"Please, sir," interrupted Katherine, frantically hoping not to hear the word he was about to say. "There's been no foul play here. I promise you I—"

"It ain't none of my concern."

Utter silence gripped the place, then, "What?" both women questioned numbly.

"I'm in town to conduct business and get out. What you ladies do to entertain your friends is none of my affair," assured the whiskey-voiced stranger.

Katherine knew she should be grateful. She knew God had saved her foolish skin, and she should chant salutations of praise and promise everlasting holy servitude. "But he's dead," she said abruptly, somehow appalled by the man's callous acceptance of the situation. "Dead."

"Looks damn dead to me," remarked the shadow dryly. "So if you ladies will excuse me, I'll leave you to your diversions and see to my business." He turned slightly, ready to leave.

Katherine was shocked speechless, while Daisy, made practical by circumstance and a strong desire to survive, pulled her hands from her employer's grip and took a pace forward.

"That's specially kind of y', stranger," she called, smoothing a hand down her waist to her hip. "P'raps I can repay the favor."

The man stopped, pausing a moment before tipping his hat. "I appreciate the offer. But I only have a couple of hours before my business appointment, and I can see a woman like you would deserve more time."

Daisy, flattered by the words spoken in a gravelly, seductive tone, straightened her back. "After yer business?"

"It's unfortunate, but I'm meeting a man and then I leave."

"Cooo." Daisy cocked her hip in open invitation. "Seems a pity. But maybe at a later time. What's yer name, stranger?"

Quiet held the street.

"Ryland," he answered. "Travis Ryland."

"God save us!" Daisy's sudden desperate plea was no more than a whimper. "Y've really come, then. God save us!" She stumbled backward, but Katherine caught her about her hunched shoulders.

"Daisy. What's wrong? What is it?"

"Ryland!" the woman whispered, raising a limp hand toward the towering shadow. "It's really him! The one they calls The Ghost."

Katherine had never heard of Ryland, The Ghost, but could guess by Daisy's response that his presence there was not good news for them.

The large shadowy figure had gone perfectly still.

"Don't 'urt us," pleaded Daisy.

The shadow flexed. "I've sworn off eating helpless little soiled doves," he said.

"What do you want here?" Katherine whispered.

"It's none of your concern. My business is with the mayor."

It felt as if Katherine's very life was seeping from her body onto the darkened street. Daisy was slumped beside her like a broken doll.

"Mayor?" Katherine's voice was so squeaky and weak that Travis had to step forward to hear her, and it was with horror that Katherine learned she had no strength left to retreat. "You're here to see the mayor?"

Ryland loomed closer, towering over her. She saw his face was bearded, and his eyes shone down from just below the rim of his hat.

"Do you *know* the mayor?" he asked, his voice slow, dramatically deep, and cautiously quiet.

"Know him?" Katherine asked, hoping to buy some time. "In what sense do you mean?"

She doggedly refused to allow her gaze to stray to the smiling corpse. Sweat had suddenly appeared on her shaky hands, and a quiver shook her voice. She didn't want to die on a dusty street so far from home. Maybe she'd been all wrong about adventures. Right now her once thrilling dreams seemed frightful, terrible things that made her quake from the inside out.

"Do you know him?" repeated the stranger. "Biblically or otherwise?"

Katherine's mouth opened to respond but she could think of no clever lie.

"No." She shook her head. "No, I didn't know the good mayor."

"You didn't know him?" The man took a step nearer. "You *didn't* know him?"

"I mean . . ." Katherine failed again to back away, though Daisy had slipped behind her and was tugging weakly at her nightshift. "I mean . . . I *don't* know him. I *don't*!" She shook her head again. There'd be no need for him to shoot her. She was going to die of sheer fright right here on the spot.

The moon eased from behind a silver-gilded cloud,

laughing at such human melodrama and casting just a
glimmer of light on the deadly stranger. But the illumination
gave Katherine no added hope, for his shoulders were
double the width of her own, and his body looked huge and
hard, awaiting action.

"You killed the mayor?" he asked now, his voice still
even. "You humped the mayor to death?"

Never in all her days had Katherine imagined she would
hear such a question addressed to her. She'd been known to
blush at the mention of a body part as innocent as an elbow.

Her mouth fell open, her lips moving hopelessly, her skin
burning.

"Is the money in the bag?" he asked in a gruff voice.

"What money?" Katherine asked, but Ryland was already
lifting the satchel from the dirt. "You can't do that," she said
weakly, her sense of decency immediately offended. "It's
not yours."

"He brought it for me," countered Ryland darkly.

Katherine's overdeveloped sense of fairness was absolutely affronted now, allowing her to raise her voice above
a whisper. "How do you know it was meant for you?
Perhaps it contains his personal . . ."

Daisy's gasp stopped Katherine's words. From the satchel
the stranger had drawn a tidy stack of rectangular papers.

"Coo," breathed Daisy as she peeked over Katherine's
shoulder. "'E's Ryland all right. But 'e ain't no ghost.
Leastways, if 'e is, I can't tell. 'E's come t' croak Dellas fer
stealin' them miners' wages, and there's the bills t' pay 'im."

Deftly Travis Ryland removed the bands of rubber to fan
the papers, then shifted his gaze to the women. "Where's the
rest?"

"The rest?" Katherine gulped, hearing the threat in his
gravelly tone.

"I was promised a goodly sum," said Ryland. "This . . ."
He lifted the bundle. "This is only two bills at the ends
of blank pieces of paper. And I'd like to know where the
rest is." He took a step toward them, and they stumbled
back in unison, with Daisy's small form pulling Katherine
along.

"We don't know anything about the money!" declared Katherine quickly.

"I want to know where it is," exclaimed Ryland evenly. "I don't mind killing Dellas," he said in a midnight voice, "but I expect to be well-paid for it."

Katherine could feel her heart thumping against her ribs. "I don't know anything about this. Honestly."

"But you were the one who humped him to death," he reasoned.

"No," she wanted to scream. She'd never even met the mayor. Never laid eyes on him before an hour ago. But Daisy hadn't taken the money. Katherine knew it in her soul. "That's such a crude way to refer to it," she said.

Silence.

"You're the damnedest whore I've ever met."

"I see no reason for you to be rude just because I'm . . ." Katherine sputtered, flapping her hands as she searched for the proper term.

"You're the one who loved him?" Ryland asked abruptly, toning down his speech for the girl's apparent sensibilities.

She'd hate to claim to have loved the man. Indeed, she'd never actually seen him alive. "Well he seemed like a nice enough gentleman, but I wouldn't say I actually *loved*—"

"Goddamn it, woman, did you sleep with him or not?" Ryland gritted, stepping up close to her in one fluid motion.

Katherine's jaw dropped. "Yes, I did," she whispered faintly.

"Then he must have paid you." The giant man was bent over her, growling into her face. "Did he take the money from the satchel?"

"Pay?" Katherine squeaked. The moon had probed beneath the brim of his hat, faintly lighting his face. It was bearded and hard-looking.

"Did he pay you from the satchel?" he asked again, his voice dropping another notch.

"Ahh." Katherine glanced over her shoulder at Daisy's paled face. "Ummm . . ."

"Not till after," Daisy squawked suddenly.

"What's that?" asked Ryland.

"The gents—they pay after."

Absolute stillness held the street, but suddenly Ryland grasped Katherine by the front of her nightshift, lifting her to her tiptoes. "That's just as well," he growled, "since you'd already taken far more than your share." He shook her lightly, and she felt like an abused rag doll.

"I didn't," Katherine managed. "I promise you I didn't."

For a moment she was sure she would die, but his fist loosened as he settled her back to her feet.

"Ladies," he said quietly. "I don't mean to be unpleasant, but there's a happy dead man lying in the street, a dead man who seems to be short about six thousand dollars."

"But we didn't take it," Katherine breathed, to which Daisy shook her head in emphatic agreement.

"Then where might it be?"

"I wouldn't know," piped Katherine.

"Listen, ladies. I learned a few things a long time ago. The first is never to draw a gun when the sun's in your eyes. The second is that generally folks are mostly understanding about murder in this sort of town." He shifted his weight slightly and wiggled his gloved fingers near the butt of his holstered gun. "But take their money . . ." He shook his head slowly. "Take their money and they'll hound you till you're dead and damned. You catch my drift?"

No answer.

"Do you?" he snapped.

Katherine jumped, gasped, and shook her head.

"I'm saying the good folks of Silver Ridge scraped their money together to pay me to kill Dellas," Ryland explained patiently. "Now the money's gone. The mayor's dead and Dellas ain't. Who do you think they're going to blame?"

"You?" Katherine guessed timidly.

"No." He shook his head again, more slowly yet. "Not me. I've done enough deeds to damn me without taking credit for things I didn't do." He stood quietly for a moment, then dropped the stack of papers into the bag and tossed the thing to the ground. "Good luck, ladies," he said, and turned away.

"Where're you going?" Katherine gasped.

He stopped for a moment, looking over his shoulder. "Where does Thomas Grey live?"

"South side of town. On Aspen Street. Big white house with green shutters," Daisy babbled.

He turned again.

"Who's Grey?" Katherine asked.

Travis didn't answer, for his long strides were already taking him quickly down the darkened street.

"Thomas Grey," Daisy whispered. "'E's a rich duffer. They say it was 'is idea t' 'ire The Ghost. But I didn't think they'd really dare. Not 'im!" She nodded toward Travis's broad retreating back. "'E's killed more men than the plague." She shivered. "I didn't think they'd get 'im."

Katherine's mind spun. If there had indeed been more money in the satchel, someone would be accused of theft, and if Ryland convinced Grey he was innocent, she was likely to be accused.

"We can't let him go," she whispered.

"What?" breathed Daisy in shocked disbelief.

"If he tells Grey about this . . ." Katherine's words quivered to a halt. "Wait!" she called to Travis.

"Miss Katherine," gasped Daisy, gripping her arms from behind. "Are you off yer crumpet? What're you thinkin'?"

"We have to convince him we're innocent."

"Convince The Ghost we're innocent?" Daisy whispered dazedly.

"Don't you see? If he tells Grey what he saw, it'll seem as if we killed the mayor and took the money. We have to stop him. Wait!" she called a bit louder, stepping forward to follow Ryland, but Daisy now gripped her nightgown in a tenacious hold.

"No, Miss Katherine! Don't go!" Her bare feet were planted on the outsides of Katherine's as she was dragged along the dirt course. "No! 'E's a mindless killer. Kills just fer fun. Y' make 'im mad, 'e'll croak y' without even blinking."

"But we're innocent."

"I know we's innocent, but let's not be dead," Daisy pleaded, dragging along behind. "Please, Miss Katherine. I got me some friends. We can 'ide out in New Prospect. Work at the Red Garter till I make 'nuf money t' send you back east. Please, Miss Katherine."

"But we're innocent!" cried Katherine, and suddenly she broke free of Daisy's grip and was sprinting down the street, her bare feet pattering like raindrops beneath the hem of her uplifted nighshift.

Chapter 3

"Wait!"

Ryland had already mounted his horse when she reached him.

"Wait," she gasped, coming to a halt a safe distance from him. "Mr. Ryland. Please. I didn't mean to kill him. And I didn't take the money."

"It's not my problem, lady." At his nudge the horse turned away.

Katherine watched him. What was she to do with a satchel of paper bills and a smiling corpse? "Mr. Ryland!" She scurried after him, running to keep up with his mount. "I tell you I didn't do it."

He refused to look down. "And I tell you it's not my concern."

"But . . ." She was panting slightly. The horse had begun to trot in long, smooth strides, and Katherine reached out, grasping Travis's pant leg with desperate strength. "If he asks who killed the mayor, what will you tell him?"

"I might try the truth."

"Then he'll think I killed him. And he'll think I took the money."

"Better you than me, lady." Ryland clicked to his mount, and Katherine's grip tightened as panic overcame her.

"But I didn't do it," she yelled, desperate to convince him of her innocence.

"Life's hard." The horse shifted into a slow lope.

Katherine was running full tilt now, her night rail billowing behind her. "You can't do this."

His leg was pulled from her grasp, but desperation made Katherine clutch frantically for a new hold. Her fingers found his stirrup leather and wrapped tenaciously about the thing. Her legs pumped wildly, and she gasped for air. "I'm . . ." she rasped, but suddenly she stumbled, half falling beside the loping stallion, but refusing to loosen her grip as she was dragged along beside. "Oh! Oh!" she shrieked.

"Damn it, woman!" Travis gritted, hauling his mount to a sliding stop. "Who the devil are you?"

Katherine scrambled for footing, then grappled her way up his leg, struggling to an upright position and drawing in shaky breaths. "Katherine." She brushed away the wisps of midnight hair that had come loose from her braid and tried not to tremble. "Katherine Amelia Simmons."

Despite her fear there was a hint of pride in her tone, and Travis bent slightly nearer to stare down into her upturned face. "Katherine Amelia Simmons," he growled, "you're the biggest nuisance of a woman I've ever met."

She blinked twice. The tears came nevertheless, squeezing from beneath heavily forested eyelids. "But I didn't kill him," she choked, her voice rising into hysteria.

"Quiet!" he ordered. Hysterical women made him nervous, and this one was blubbering herself toward a real fit. "Hush."

"I didn't e-even know I was inheriting . . . I mean, how was I supposed to know? And then all the girls . . . and then poor G-George expired, and I was just trying to . . . to . . ."

"Hush. Hush." Travis's voice had softened as he glanced nervously about. "Shhh."

"I didn't know what to do," she babbled. "I couldn't abandon the girls, and Mother would die if she knew and—"

"Lady," he whispered, seeing a flame flicker to life in a nearby window and thinking it would look bad for him if poor George was found toes up on the street while he was being screamed at by a hysterical woman dressed in a flimsy nightshift. "I ain't saying you killed him. But I sure as hell didn't kill him either."

"But Mr. Grey will deduce that I did. After all, it might seem somewhat suspicious, what with Daisy and I dragging him out into the street and the money being gone."

"You think so?" Travis asked wryly.

"So I have to go with you to prove my innocence."

"I ride alone, lady," he said, straightening slightly and nudging his horse.

"But Mr. Ryland," she pleaded, walking again as she found her former hold on his pant leg, "who knows what the townspeople will think? I need to talk to Grey—tell him the truth."

"The truth?" he scoffed, not looking down at her. "Like you told me?"

"I *did* tell you the truth," she said, her voice squeaking again as it always did in a lie.

He lowered his face now. She could feel his hot gaze on her.

"Sure you did, lady," he said, and clicked to his stallion again.

Fresh panic showed in Katherine's face, but Travis Ryland knew far better than to care. Caring for another human being was the single most efficient way to get oneself killed. He pressed his horse into a canter.

"Mr. Ryland," she gasped, running along again. "Just listen!"

They were picking up speed.

"Let go!"

"Mr. Ryland!"

"Let go!"

Her legs were giving out. Still holding on, she yelled out to him, desperation forcing the words out on a windy gust. "I'll tell them *you* killed him."

The horse skidded to a halt, nearly plowing over Katherine's legs, but suddenly Travis reached down, grasped her by her nightshift, and snatched her effortlessly across the pommel of his saddle.

"All right, lady," he gritted. "You want to go. We'll go."

The saddle horn burned like fire as it dug into Katherine's abdomen, but it was the humiliation of her present position, with her bottom wriggling practically in his face, that made her gasp. "Wait. I can't go like this. Not in my nightshirt. It's indecent."

The big horse shifted into a trot, a pace which Katherine was certain would cause her death.

"Let me get this straight. You say you sleep with men for a living. Only this time you were a bit too enthusiastic and your customer wound up dead. So you dragged him out in the street by his heels, and now you're worried that going around in your nightshirt is indecent?" He shook his head, steadying her with a large hand on her bottom as he shifted the buckskin into a lope. "Lady, you're about one bean short of a full pot. You know that?"

He heard her grunt of pain as Soldier jolted ahead and with a mental sigh eased her over the horn until she was pressed against his abdomen for safekeeping. The nightgown had crept upward a bit, he noticed, revealing slim, pale legs that kicked rhythmically.

"Let me down," she demanded.

Travis had to admit that she sounded as if she was nearly ready to die from sheer embarrassment, and he knew without looking at her that she was blushing from head to toe.

"You said you wanted to come, lady."

They jolted into a rut in the road, jamming her sharply against the most private part of Ryland, which Katherine absolutely refused to contemplate. "I can't go like this. I can't!" she insisted. "Take me back. It'll only take me a minute to dress. We can talk about this like adults."

Her bottom was round and soft beneath Travis's hand, reminding him just how adult she was, despite her childish antics. "Lady," he said, his tone harder than he'd planned. "If we go back, I got me a whole helluva list of things I'll do with you before we talk."

Katherine could only be grateful he couldn't see the hot blush that infused her face. They hit another hole, but she swallowed her grunt of pain and hoped she'd faint before she had to face him again.

*   *   *

It seemed like hours before they finally stopped. Katherine's feet were numb when they hit the ground, and she tumbled backward, her bottom striking the earth with a thud.

"It looks like we're here," Travis said, throwing his leg over the cantle to dismount with more dignity than she.

Katherine wanted to glare at him, but first she had to make certain her nightshift covered all the essentials.

"Are you sure?" She scrambled to her feet, staring at the house. It was huge and somehow seemed foreboding, with the windows looking like large eyes watching them with malevolent curiosity. "Are you sure?" she asked again, but in a whisper now.

"I'm sure, lady," replied Travis, reading her fear with ease, for he himself felt the same apprehension as a nagging pain ground at his ribs—a pain he'd like to believe was nothing more than the scrape of an old pellet against his bones. He had no use for premonitions. "So you just march yourself up to the door and tell Grey how the good mayor died."

Katherine took an involuntary step backward, her hand fluttering to her chest. "Alone?"

"You wanted to tell him how you killed old Patterson. Remember?"

Katherine's bravery was ebbing away, and the small hairs along her arms stood on end. The truth was she didn't know how poor George had died. And she had no wish to try to explain that to anyone who would live in the looming mass of that darkened house. "I've been thinking," she said. "There'd be no reason for me to speak to Grey if you'd promise not to—enlighten him about my part in the incident. You could simply say you found the mayor on the street. That he must have tripped on the broken stair. Bumped his head. Died naturally," she suggested quickly.

"There's nothing more natural than—"

"Please," she whispered. "Don't tell."

Travis stood perfectly still. He couldn't see her clearly in the darkness, but could tell she was a pretty thing. Her hair was dark, long, and braided, her eyes huge and luminous.

"You might have guessed I ain't the kind of man who does something for nothing," he said quietly, not moving.

Katherine grasped her frazzled braid in a clammy fist, a nervous habit from childhood. "What do you want from me?"

Travis smiled. She had the throaty voice of a born seductress, but her eyes were wide with innocence. Stepping nearer, he noticed how each lace of her nightshift had remained tied, making it seem as if she'd done nothing more than step out for a breath of fresh air. Her braid, however, was coming loose, fraying away from confinement as if in testimony to the ordeal she'd come through. He noticed the set of her shoulders, her stiff stance, and passed her by to circle behind.

There was a light breeze blowing out of the east, and it flattened the woman's nightgown against her tidy body, outlining it perfectly. She had a sweet little bottom, Travis thought with a mental sigh of longing, knowing, no matter what she said, that she was out of his reach. "What can you give me?" he asked, nevertheless.

Katherine's mind spun. "I don't have any money with me," she whispered.

Ryland shrugged. "Bartering's a time-honored tradition in these parts."

It took her several seconds to realize his implied meaning. He was referring to personal favors, she thought in fresh panic. She didn't . . . She wouldn't . . . Well, she just couldn't! Could she?

But her choices were so few and very unfavorable. "I could . . ." she began, but found she didn't even know the right words to say.

"You know, lady," Travis said, stepping casually before her again, "most doves I've known have been real bold talkers. Have you always been so tongue-tied?"

"I'm not tongue-tied," Katherine denied, offended. "My diction is exemplary."

He was silent for a moment, then, "Right. What's your offer?"

"A kiss!" she spat out before it could catch on her tongue. He laughed. "A kiss?"

"Yes."

Her mother would simply die if she knew what her

daughter had come to, but her mother wouldn't be particularly pleased to learn Katherine Amelia had been hanged for murder either. "But just one . . ." She held up a singular finger.

"A kiss?" he repeated, and shook his head as if unable to believe he'd heard properly.

Have I been too forward? Katherine wondered dismally. Had she shocked him? "I've got no money," she whispered.

The street was as silent as death.

"Is it a deal?" Katherine breathed, feeling all her blood had drained to her feet.

"It'll depend on the kiss."

"No!" she said, knowing she couldn't kiss worth a hoot, for in truth, she'd never tried, and did not wish to be hanged for lack of ability in that arena. "You have to agree first."

He tilted his head sharply. "It seems to me I got the upper hand in this bartering business, lady. You'll have to kiss first. I'll decide if it's worthy."

She had no choice, Katherine thought dizzily. She'd have to go through with it.

The distance between them seemed the longest she'd ever traveled. Her knees felt weak, her head light, and when she reached him, he seemed to tower above her like a mountain.

She hesitated for a moment, and then, using every ounce of willpower she possessed, she rose to her toes, brushed her lips to his cheek, and jumped back.

Travis Ryland remained perfectly still. Katherine waited, breath held.

And then he laughed, the sound floating out in rich, deep timbre from the massive breadth of his chest.

"What are you laughing at?" Katherine scowled, knowing he was making fun of her and worrying what the consequences of a bad kiss would be. "What's so funny?"

"Nothing," he said, unable to control his chuckles.

Her scowl deepened, and she placed her fists on her hips, thinking him quite rude, even for an outlaw. "Then is the bargain met?"

"Lady . . ." He chuckled again, lifting a hand and seeming to wipe at his eyes. "If your worst crime was spreading gossip about the preacher's wife, I might consider that little chicken peck enough to buy my silence." He shook his head, finally attempting to still his laughter. "But the mayor was . . . Well he was loved to death, and I'm afraid you ain't got what it takes to keep me quiet about *that*."

"Well!" Why she was so offended Katherine wasn't certain, but apparently this oversized lout was insulting her feminine appeal—something she'd spent very little time worrying about in the past. "So you think I can't kiss?"

"No," he said quickly, lifting a hand as it to ward off any zealous advances. "It's just that I thought old George was overstimulated. But now I see he died of boredom."

Katherine narrowed her eyes and ground her teeth. Died of boredom, indeed! How dare he! She'd give him a kiss that would fuse his boots to his feet.

"Hang on to your hat," she growled, and stepped forward again.

Lightning struck her lips as they touched his. A trail of flame sizzled down her neck, crackling along her arms to burn at her fingertips. His hands had somehow settled around her waist, heating her body with inexplicable fire as his lips moved across hers.

He smelled of wide open places and leather. His tongue touched her lips, and suddenly her mouth was open, too, allowing her own tongue to taste him in heated, first-time exploration.

Her head swam. The world shifted, and she lifted her hands, steadying herself against his chest.

His beard tickled her chin, and his hands moved upward slightly, blazing a trail up her back as he pulled her closer.

For the first time in her life Katherine was fully alive, each fiber of her body alert, every nerve vibrating with awareness. So this was a kiss! Her tongue touched his again, shocking her with a new jolt of sizzling excitement. So this was why George was smiling.

George! The memory of him blasted through to Katherine's brain. The mayor! She drew away, pushing on Travis's chest with trembling hands and trying to remember her mission.

"Well?" she asked foggily.

He was absolutely quiet for a moment, then, "Any other

sins you'd like me to keep quiet about?" he asked, his voice hoarse.

"No." She shook her head slowly, her lips parted and burning. "This is my first."

"Lucky George."

"He's dead."

"It might be worth it."

She blinked at him, not comprehending his words.

"See that grove of trees?" Travis asked, not raising his eyes from hers. "I want you to take Soldier in there with you. Wait ten minutes. If I don't come out, you get on Soldier and you ride back to wherever it is you came from."

"But I can't go back to The Watering Hole."

"Lady!" His fingers tightened against her back. "I ain't talking about the saloon. You ride east till you can't even remember Colorado in your dreams."

"But what about—"

He shook her slightly, stopping her words. "Promise me!"

"But what about you? What are you doing to do?"

"I swear to you, lady, if you don't hightail it, I'll make them damn rumors come true and haunt you for eternity."

Her mouth fell open as she realized the implication of his words. Not only was he expecting trouble, he was expecting *big* trouble. "But I can't ride, " she whispered.

"You can't ride?" He glowered into her face. "Then what the hell are you doing in this kind of country?"

Tears formed without warning and she sniffed. "I inherited—"

"Don't!" He changed his mind about hearing her explanation and held a hard palm toward her. "Don't tell me. Just remember. Ten minutes. If I'm not out—head east." He stepped back. "And . . ." His voice dropped a notch. "Take care of old Soldier."

Panic tasted bitter. "You'll be back."

His ribs ached. "Promise me."

She hesitated wondering which way was east, then nodded.

He was gone in a moment, swallowed by the darkness.

Within the quiet copse, the horse nibbled at nearby leaves

as Katherine fidgeted. Five minutes passed, then ten. Katherine tightened her grip on the reins, glancing at the big animal. Ryland would be back. She was sure of it. What could happen? He was innocent of George's death.

She waited as ten more minutes dragged by. Her heart cramped within her chest. A long gun lay nestled in its leather case near the back of Ryland's saddle. How far could that gun shoot? Which way was east? And if she called for help, who would come? Daisy had said Silver Ridge had lost its sheriff.

A clatter of hooves sounded. Katherine spun about in her leafy enclosure but could see nothing through the foliage.

"Mr. Grey!" The words split the night as running footsteps thundered toward the house. "Mr. Grey! George's been killed. Stabbed—clean through the heart."

Chapter 4

Travis's first conscious thought was that his hands were tied behind him. He was laying facedown on a hard, cool surface, and when he tried to move, his skull protested with loud clanking throbs that sent pain echoing through his entire being.

He lifted his head, nevertheless, and the pain increased. He closed his eyes to the ache and found the room was no darker with them shut, which had to mean there was no window nearby.

Pieces of memory floated through his mind like milkweed seeds in the wind, with none of them settling long enough for him to grasp a firm hold. Rolling over slowly and pushing himself to a sitting position, Travis tried to concentrate.

The woman! Her shadowed face appeared to him through a haze of pain and darkness. The girl with the soiled dove's voice and the lady's speech. He'd kissed her. Where was he? Facts filtered back quickly now, slamming into his stunned brain with painful impatience.

He'd entered Grey's house, had spoken hardly a word—then darkness. His revolvers were gone. He must have been dragged into this room. How long had he been unconscious? Had the woman fled? Had she taken Soldier? She didn't seem like the kind to take orders well. What if she had stayed? How was she connected to Patterson's death? Why was he tied?

Questions crowded in, increasing the ache in his head, but the only answers he could imagine were horrid and immobilizing. So he shoved the thoughts from his mind and rose unsteadily to his feet. The room swam. His ribs ached.

Turning carefully, he searched for a way to escape. Off to his right there was a faint line of light that seemed to outline the bottom of a door. He stumbled toward it trying to be quiet, but the sounds of his own footsteps seemed to clatter loudly in his ears.

Reaching the portal, he leaned against it for a moment, listening. Travis could hear voices, but couldn't discern the words or guess who spoke them.

Perhaps he should just wait. For a moment weakness overtook him, and his knees buckled, threatening to spill him to the floor.

But he willed his legs to hold him steady. Whoever had trussed him up like a Thanksgiving goose was not planning a pleasant Sunday social, and he needed to escape immediately. Clumsily turning his back to the door, he tested the latch. It refused to move beneath his numbed fingers, and he silently swore. It was locked and his hands were tied, literally and figuratively.

First things first. Free his hands, then contemplate his next move. Straightening, Travis tested his legs again. They were a bit steadier now, his steps more true. He walked carefully back in the direction from which he'd come.

It was like blindman's bluff with no hands to feel his way and a splintering ache in his head. His boots tread on something softer now. A rug. He slowed his steps even more. His thigh thumped against the hard edge of something and he turned. There was little enough mobility in his arms, but he stretched them as far back as he could, feeling along the surface of what he figured to be a desk.

Papers. Several books. An inkwell and . . .

His hands brushed something hard and cool. He felt it topple and jerked to catch it, but he was too slow and it crashed to the floor.

Travis sucked air through his teeth and waited. Surely the noise would alert someone, but no footsteps came, and he realized in a moment that the object's fall had been blessedly muffled by the carpet.

Kneeling with some difficulty, he skimmed the floor with his fingertips.

The broken globe of the lamp sliced the pad of his right index finger before he had time to ascertain what the object was. He drew his hands away, stifled a curse, and realized in a moment that this was the answer to his most pressing problem. Finding the curved glass, he steadied a large broken piece beneath the heel of one boot and thrust his hands over the shard. It cut his wrist immediately, but he ignored the wound and shifted his position.

Hemp scraped against jagged glass. Back and forth. Back and forth. He could hear voices again and wondered if they were getting nearer. Travis sawed faster, hoping he was making progress.

A shout sounded from outside. He pushed harder against the glass. It broke and he swore, aloud this time. He winced, waiting a moment.

From somewhere in the house a door swung open, allowing the harsh swell of many voices to reach him. Travis hurriedly shifted his weight, settling his heel against a smaller piece of glass and sawing with increased speed.

Something was afoot. Something that boded ill for his continued survival. He could tell by the cramping ache in his ribs.

"Dead?"

That one word sounded loud and clear as day. Ryland gritted his teeth, knowing what this meant. Patterson had been discovered and the townspeople had arrived. But why? Wouldn't they assume the mayor had died from a fall?

He needed more time. Just a bit more, but footsteps were coming toward him. Travis shifted again, pushing the lamp away, hoping it was hidden below the desk. Falling to his side, he lay still and closed his eyes.

A key turned in the lock. The door was thrust open.

"But please, my good people. He deserves a fair trial."

"Trial! The money's gone and George is dead!"

Travis opened his eyes to the glaring light and blinked. He had no need to see the faces that crowded around the upheld lamp. He'd seen lynch mobs before.

"We're just lucky Red here apprehended him before he

got out of town." The speaker had a walrus moustache and narrow eyes. "What'd you do with the money?"

Travis remained silent, waiting.

"He killed George."

"Deserves no better hisself."

"But where'd he put the money?"

"Please, people," interrupted a man with silver hair and brocade robe. Thomas Grey, Ryland deduced. "How do we know it was he that committed the murder?"

"Know? Red here seen him do it," said a gritty voice.

"Is that true, Red?" asked Grey, his expression as concerned as his tone.

The man called Red shifted nervously. He was narrow and tall, with fire-bright hair. "It was dark. But I seen it all." He shook his head as if still stunned by the horror of what he'd witnessed. "George. He was such a harmless gent and . . ." His words faltered.

Travis's mind careened along. The man was lying, and he was damned good at it. But why? And what about Grey? Was he trying to sound like a good peacemaker for the sake of the townspeople? Had he been the one who had hit him?

"You saw George stabbed?" Grey asked solemnly.

Stabbed? Every muscle in Ryland's body wrenched. Patterson had been stabbed? But why, when he was already dead?

"I seen it all, Mr. Grey," said Red, and shuddered.

"God help us," Grey murmured, shaking his head miserably. "And the murderer—you're sure . . ."

"It was him!" Red raised two fingers abruptly toward Travis. "But I couldn't catch up to him right off. So I followed him. Only I lost him in the dark. Then all of a sudden like, there he was—right in front of me. I didn't want to shoot him. It all happened so quick—wasn't sure who he was. So I just swung with my rifle."

"And you're sure? You're sure it's the same man?"

Red nodded grimly. "He's the one. He killed George."

There was an angry swelling of sound, like incensed bees, and then the men poured into the room, undeterred by one frail voice that still questioned the whereabouts of the money.

There was nothing Travis could do. His head swam as he was jerked to his feet. The walls dipped and blackness threatened. His feet faltered, but there was no need for him to walk, for he was being carried along by his still bound arms.

The mob swarmed outside with him, bubbling about in seething rage.

The fat yellow moon leered down on him, granting just enough light for Travis to see the rope.

From the dark, hidden copse, Katherine grasped a branch in each hand and peered through the unfolding leaves. What was happening? Had the world gone mad?

Ryland stood in the center of a rumbling crowd. She could just make out his head above the others', but it was the rope that drew the gasp from her.

This couldn't be happening! He was innocent! And she knew it!

The noose swayed from the branch of a nearby scrub oak, stiff and waiting. The mob pressed toward it. Katherine watched the madness unfold as if each part was played with no more consequence than if they were but actors on a stage.

"Hang him!"

"No." She found she'd only whispered the word.

The noose was pulled downward. Ryland was pressed nearer, and suddenly the horrid reality of the situation broke through to her senses. She was beside the huge horse in a second, her hands on the long gun behind his saddle. She pulled it free with some difficulty, and then she was running through the undergrowth toward the mob.

"No!" she screamed. "Don't!"

The crowd took no notice. There were angry shouts all around. She felt small and helpless. Her hands tightened around the rifle.

Never in her life had she fired a gun, but she'd seen it done, and desperation made her act. Cocking the thing with shaking hands, she tilted the muzzle toward the inky sky, and fired.

Her buttocks hit the ground with numbing force. The rifle fell from her stinging fingers, but she scrambled to her feet, only noticing the quiet that had settled in like a wet blanket, chill and uncomfortable.

"He didn't do it!" Her voice sounded weak to her own ears. Every face was turned toward her.

There was a moment of silence, then, "How do you know?" A man in a robe stepped away from the mob.

"I was . . ." Katherine stumbled on her own words. She needed to save Ryland, but to condemn herself was more than she could do without blanching.

"Who are you?" The robed man stepped closer.

Katherine pressed her palms to her nightshift, suddenly remembering her shameful state of undress. Before she could explain, there were shouts of outrage and shock. Bodies near the center of the crowd toppled like toy soldiers and then a man careened away from the mob.

"Run!" Travis shouted, but Katherine was stuck to the ground like a great tree root as she gaped at Ryland's galloping form. His arms were unbound, and he yelled again, something indiscernible, as he sprinted toward the trees. She watched him go as shots rang out mingled with shouts. Bullets whizzed their high-pitched threats of death.

Ryland jerked once and faltered, but he collected himself and sped on, finally diving through the screen of trees and out of sight.

Katherine had no time to think. Men were screaming. People were running toward her. Hoofbeats thundered behind her, and she turned dully.

"Come on!" Ryland was aboard the giant horse and racing toward her. "Come on, woman!" he shouted again, but Katherine could not yet fathom the vulnerability of her own position.

"I'm innocent," she whispered numbly, still believing in justice with fanatic childishness. "I'm innocent," she said more loudly, and turned to declare that fact to the men behind her.

A gun exploded close at hand. The bullets twanged between her legs. Katherine bent, staring at the hole bored cleanly through her nightshift. Then, lifting her head with numb slowness, she reached abruptly for Ryland's outstretched arm.

The stallion never stopped. The momentum of his power aided by Ryland's strong grip whipped Katherine up behind the saddle.

Bullets shrieked past. Katherine wrapped her arms about Ryland, pressed her face into his back, and prayed, her eyes closed.

The sound of bullets became less frequent, but hoofbeats could still be heard. Katherine refused to open her eyes and prayed more fervently, gripping Ryland with petrified fingers.

Soldier's hoofbeats echoed down a hard-packed street. He took the corner with the litheness of a huge cat, and Katherine nearly fell, slipping dangerously down the horse's side and feeling a scream rip from her throat.

Ryland's hand clutched her thigh, holding her steady as she clambered upright again.

They were going back toward Grey's house! Why? Was he insane? Every able-bodied man in Silver Ridge was waiting to send them to meet their Maker.

Soldier turned slightly, and his hoofbeats were muffled on grass. Their passage was barely audible here. Finally understanding Ryland's plan, Katherine prayed their pursuers had continued on in their original direction.

The clamor of town was left behind. No more gunshots. No hoofbeats followed as far as Katherine could tell, but her heart raced along on such a noisy course that it was impossible to know for certain.

They seemed to ride forever. Blackness turned to gray around them, and still they continued. The terrain was never level, but tilted up and down dramatically, throwing Katherine from side to side.

Trees whizzed by as ghosts of shifting shadows. They hit a downhill slope at a gallop. Soldier barely slowed, but set his big haunches and slid, dodging trees with breathtaking agility. He leaped. There was a sensation of being airborne, and then they splashed into water that suddenly rushed around and past.

It sprayed upward, soaking them all as Soldier struggled to keep his footing amongst the moss-covered rocks.

Miles sped by in jolts and jerks, but finally the stallion

stumbled to a trembling halt, his breath coming hard and fast.

"Are we stopping?" Katherine asked, turning her head to skitter a glance behind. "Shouldn't we hide? Mightn't they still be following?"

Travis Ryland said nothing. His shoulders slumped as, without fanfare or warning, he fell from her grasp into the roiling water.

Chapter 5

Katherine stared silently down at Ryland's sinking body.

"Dear God," she whispered, gripping the wet cantle. "Mr. Ryland!" she screamed, but Ryland failed to answer, for he was unconscious and drowning.

She half fell from the horse, floundered in the rolling stream, then struggled after Ryland's gently floating body. She grasped him with stiff fingers, turning him faceup.

"Mr. Ryland," she whispered shakily. The water was turning pink around them. Nausea turned her stomach. She wasn't good with injuries. In fact, splinters were known to make her light-headed.

She swayed woozily, then closed her eyes with a snap. If she fainted, she would drown, she thought with unexpected common sense, and opened her eyes to find the source of his lost blood.

"Don't panic," she said aloud, then shifted her eyes to find the bullet wound in his arm. It was half hidden by his tattered sleeve. With a shudder she continued to search for wounds and stopped at the sight of his right thigh. He'd been shot at least twice. Katherine loosened her grip and lifted a hand to cover her mouth.

His big body slipped sideways, tugged languidly downstream.

"No!" she cried, grabbing him again. This was no time for hysterics she told herself. No time for fainting. No time for anything but coolheaded action. But at the moment she didn't want to be coolheaded or active. She wanted to sleep, to curl up into a ball of forgetfulness and wake to learn it

39

was all no more than a bad dream. But even in dreams one must do what needs doing. She bit her lip. "Hold on," she whispered, and rose awkwardly to her feet, keeping a splay-fingered grip on Ryland's saturated shirt.

The current wasn't fast, but was strong enough to make maneuvering difficult, even without her soggy burden.

Eventually Katherine tripped over the final rock and fell with a splash atop Travis for the fifth time. Her breath came in deep gasps, and she stayed as she was for a moment, her chest pressed over his as she rested momentarily. "Made it," she croaked.

Something touched her back. She squealed in terror and jerked about.

Soldier nuzzled her again, his big eyes wide and sorrowful.

"Don't panic," she advised him shakily, wanting to pat his nose reassuringly but lacking the strength. "He'll be all right." She pushed herself doggedly to her feet, then staggered backward, dragging the man's limp body by his uninjured arm.

The struggle onto the rocky bank of the river was the most difficult yet. Ryland seemed to have doubled in weight and refused to budge once the mass of his large upper body was free of the frigid water. Katherine pulled frantically at him, but there was no strength left in her trembling arms. She was at the end of her reserves.

Soldier shuffled an apologetic step forward, leaning over his master with doglike devotion.

Katherine's head ached with fatigue, but the fear that their pursuers still followed made her press on. "Got to hide him," she murmured to the horse, her gaze skimming his dragging reins.

That was it!

Katherine grasped the thick ropes of braided leather. It took several minutes to untie them from the metal bit. Slipping the first saturated rein beneath Ryland's body, she tried to avoid his wound as she pried it under his arms to tie it securely over his chest. The second rein was tied to the first before she tripped forward.

Jabbering soothingly to the horse, Katherine led him by

the bridle, stopping him with his hind feet just inches from his master's head.

She hurried back to Ryland and, finding no better way, tied the second rein to an empty stirrup.

It took several moments for her to convince the horse to drag Ryland up the slope, and Katherine winced as the man's body scraped over the sharp underbrush, for surely it cut his back as badly as it did her bare feet. But the torturous journey didn't last long, for the answer to her prayers appeared in the form of a deep ravine. It was neither long nor wide, but large enough to hide two people and a horse.

Ryland was dragged as close to the slope as possible, and then, with some difficulty, Katherine untied the rein from the stirrup. Biting her lip and employing every bit of her ebbing strength, she pushed at his inert form, finally prying it from its spot and over the edge of the small fissure.

He slid crookedly, and then, gaining momentum, toppled down the short, rocky slope to bump limply to the bottom.

Katherine scrambled after him. "I'm sorry," she said bending down, not noticing the scrapes and oozing bruises that troubled her own body, and touching his throat where the pulse was weak but discernible. "I'm so sorry."

His bearded face was pale, with a smear of blood on his temple. She wiped it away with unsteady fingertips.

"You're going to be fine," she whispered. "Just fine." Tears swelled in the tide of her terror. What if he died? He could have escaped more easily without her. Her gaze strayed to his arm. It was bleeding, as was his leg, and she knew she must stanch the flow.

Tearing the hem of her nightshift with her teeth, she ripped it upward, then sideways, until she had a long, frayed strip of soft once-white fabric. His arm was limp and heavy, his thigh as thick as a tree trunk. She tied the cotton carefully around his upper leg, praying it was not too tight but just tight enough.

That task done, she settled back on her bare, raw heels and cried.

She cried for Ryland, who would probably die trussed up in a rag from her nightshift. She cried for her mother who would be heartbroken when she learned of her only daughter's fate. She cried for Soldier, for Daisy, for Patterson, for her deceased aunt, Dahlia, and finally, and most loudly, she cried for herself.

Crying turned to sobs, sobs turned to chest-heaving gasps and finally to hiccuped wails.

"Can I take this to mean things ain't going good?"

Katherine jumped at Ryland's words. "You're awake!"

"Am I?" Ryland's voice was tortured and weak as he winced. "I was hoping it was only a dream."

"No!" She shook her head, taking his words at face value. "It's not a dream, Mr. Ryland." She scurried closer. "We're in a great deal of trouble. They think you killed the mayor. You were shot." She hiccuped, swiping at her tear-streaked face. "Twice. We got to the river but nearly drowned. We have nothing to eat, you need a physician, and I'm lost." She paused for a breath before continuing, but noticed with a fresh spark of horror that his eyes had fallen closed. "Mr . . ." She touched his arm gently. "Ryland?" she said softly. "What do we do now?"

No answer came, and she felt a sob jerk at her chest. "Mr. Ryland?"

His eyes opened groggily. "You been flaying me with an oak sapling?"

She winced, her hand still on his arm. "I'm sorry," she whispered. "You were too heavy for me. I had Soldier drag you into the woods."

Travis bent his neck slightly, noting the wet leather still tied about his chest like an instrument of torture. His brows rose, and he leaned back again, his mouth turning up in a shadow of a pained smile. "Always were," he whispered, lifting a hand weakly to touch Katherine's cheek, "a clever girl."

The afternoon stretched on interminably. Fear and fatigue battled in Katherine's shocked system. It was cold in the shadowed ravine, and she shivered. It had taken a bit of doing to get Soldier to join them, but he stood now, chomping on the dried grass she had gathered for him, his bit rattling quietly as he chewed.

Ryland was covered with his thin bedroll, which was

slightly wet but better than nothing. He moaned in his sleep, and she moved nearer.

Perhaps she should try to wake him again, but her previous efforts had been to no avail and only seemed to increase his pain. And even if she managed to wake him—what then?

Katherine studied Ryland's face. It was broad at the cheekbones, then narrowed in gaunt lines to be hidden under the mass of his beard, which was trimmed and similar in color to the weathered leaves that covered the forest floor. His nose was straight, his eyebrows sun-bleached, as was his long, unkempt hair, which had dried and remained swept back, away from his forehead. She found herself wondering at his heritage. Scandinavian perhaps. There was something about him that reminded her of the Vikings she had studied with her schoolchildren not so many months before.

A scraping in the woods above scrambled Katherine's thoughts, causing her breath to freeze in her aching chest. Seconds stretched her nerves into raw bands of tension as she watched the slope above.

A squirrel scurried over a log and into view, jumping at the sight of them before settling down on its haunches to scold her for its fright.

Katherine drew a deep, quivering breath of relief, but could not still the thundering of her heart.

What if it had been something more treacherous than a squirrel? What if it had been their pursuers? Eventually they would find them, wouldn't they? She'd read stories about these western trackers. Men who could follow week-old trails in the dark. But perhaps the stories had been embellished. Or perhaps not.

Should she venture from their relative safety to hide their trail? She glanced at Soldier, who seemed to have no opinion, then, scowling worriedly, she pulled Ryland's blanket higher on his chest and scurried up the slope.

It was dark! Katherine's heart thumped against her ribs, and her feet felt numb from the cold. Perhaps she had slept for a moment. Fragments of details filtered back to her scrambling mind. She'd come to Colorado to inherit Aunt Dahlia's business.

Patterson had died.

Ryland had appeared.

There'd been shots.

Water—cold as ice.

A branch snapped up above. Inches away, Soldier lifted his head, the black points of his pricked ears hidden in the darkness. Moonlight filtered weakly through the freshly leafed branches.

Nearby and above a horse nickered!

Katherine's chest ached from lack of breath. She was on her knees, her frigid fingers reaching pleadingly for Soldier's nose, entreating him to be silent.

"Red! You scared the shit outta me."

"Find anything?"

The men were close enough for her to hear their horses restlessly shuffle their feet. Katherine remained frozen, too afraid to do more than pray.

"No, I ain't found nothin'. It's blacker than hell. We ain't *never* gonna find nothin' in here. And anyhow, I'm tellin' y', I blasted him clean through the chest. He couldn't a made it this far nohow."

"Then where's the body?"

"How the hell should I know? I'm just tellin' y' he's dead, is all. Unless you're believin' them stories 'bout him being a ghost."

"Shut your damn mouth. Ryland's just flesh and blood. Same as me."

"Same as you, only dead," corrected the other. "We might just as soon head downriver to New Prospect. Have us some whiskey and a soft—"

"You ain't gonna rest your sorry ass in Prospect!" growled Red. "Y' hear me? I done too much work already to stop now. We ain't quittin' till we can drop Ryland's bloody carcass on Grey's doorstep."

"And the girl?"

Katherine's lungs ached.

"Grey wants her . . . pronto."

"I'd think we could at least—"

"Grey don't pay y' t' think, Cory." The horses shuffled about again.

"And he ain't payin' me enough to be riskin' my hide out here in these goddamn woods. Why ain't Dellas here doin' the dirty work?"

"I told you before," Red snarled. "I don't need that old man doin' my job." He paused. "You say you got Ryland in the chest?"

"Yah."

"And I hit his leg—or maybe his horse." He paused. "They couldn't a made it this far. Come on." Hoofbeats moved away. "We'll head upstream."

The voices faded off in a rustle of leaves and underbrush.

Time slipped away unnoticed. Katherine's muscles felt cramped. Her knees hurt from the pressure of the rocky soil, but her hand remained pressed tightly to Soldier's dark muzzle.

She eased back on her heels, her chest aching from the breath she'd held too long, her gaze falling to Ryland's face.

His eyes were open, his body still as a rock. "It ain't going to help to swoon," he reasoned quietly.

"I'm not going to swoon." She spoke without thinking, her voice sounding distant and strange.

"Good. Then you better have a plan."

The world shifted. The dark edges of Katherine's consciousness tilted queerly.

"Lady!" His tone was sharp. "You better have a plan cuz I hurt like hell and I'm blamin' you."

"Me?" The single word seemed to roll down a long tunnel and echo quietly in the night.

"Yah." His hand caught her arm, jerking firmly. "So let's go."

"Go?" She stared at his hand. It was square and large. "Go?"

"Listen, lady, this is fascinating conversation, but I know you couldn't a been sitting here doing nothing the whole day. Not a smart woman like you. So tell me what you've figured out." He watched her face like she imagined a hawk would watch its prey, his eyes unblinking and sharp.

She said nothing, her mind wandering blearily, and he
jerked her arm again.

"Woman," he growled fiercely. "It's your fault we're in
this hole. Now get us out."

Reality snapped in place with a click and a start.
Katherine raised her nose, drawing her arm haughtily from
his grasp. The lousy ingrate. She'd save his worthless hide,
and he dared treat her like some mangy, stray dog!

"New Prospect," she said with hard finality, rising rapidly
to her feet. "I've got friends there."

Chapter 6

The town was quiet, the streets dark.

Katherine waited in the deep shadows of the pines, watching the Red Garter. She'd lied outright to Ryland. She had no friends in New Prospect. But Daisy did.

Stroking one grubby, scratched hand absently down Soldier's broad neck, Katherine wet her sun-dried lips. What now? It would be dawn in a couple of hours. Ryland was slumped over the stallion's neck like an overused rag doll, scraps of her nightshift tying him in place.

What if Red and Cory had come to New Prospect after all? What if word of Patterson's death had spread from Silver Ridge and the entire state was armed and searching for them?

Ryland moaned, the sound weak and eerie, and Katherine's hand froze on Soldier's neck. Her options were few. She'd made her best choice, had labored along the river's rugged wandering course for hours without end, and she had no strength to go farther. Besides, New Prospect was the only place the man called Red had said they *wouldn't* go.

"Stay here." Her hand slipped to Soldier's face, not realizing she expected him to understand. "I'll be back."

Moonlight cast its wavering shadow along her skittered course toward the dance hall. The back door proved to be locked when she tested it. Katherine bit her lip, glancing furtively about, looking for another way in and finding none.

There was nothing to do but knock. The rap of her knuckles against the heavy portal sounded ominously loud in the darkness, and Katherine squeezed closer to the door, hoping to be swallowed by the shadows.

No answer. She let her air out in a quiet whoosh, grimaced, and rapped again, slightly louder.

"We're closed, laddies. Go sleep it off elsewhere."

The voice from inside was husky and confident, laced with tired good humor, and staunchly Scottish.

Katherine straightened, hope stiffening her spine. "Please." Her voice sounded pathetic to her own ears. "Please. Open up." She leaned against the door, feeling weakness flood up like a consuming wave. "I need hel . . ." she began, but before she'd completed the word, the door opened with a snap and she was pulled into Daisy's hearty embrace.

"Miss Katherine. Oh, miss." Daisy hugged her tightly, stroking the wild mass of her tangled hair. "I was so worried, I was. What with you running after Ryland like you done. I was 'fraid I'd never see you again. But I says—she's smart, Daisy. What would a smart lady do? And then I remembered telling you about the Red Garter. And I thought you'd come 'ere, if ever you could. So I come straight 'ere, 'oping against 'ope that you'd be along—that you'd get away from that crazed killer and—"

"He's outside." Katherine could barely press the words past her overwhelming fatigue.

"Out—side?" Daisy pushed Katherine slowly to arm's length. "Outside?"

"Where?" asked another voice.

For the first time Katherine noticed the woman by the window. Her hair was just a shade brighter than the scarlet gown she wore, her expression harder than pressed steel, and in her hand she held a rifle with casual familiarity.

"Lacy. Lacy MacTaggart," Daisy explained with a pert nod. "A friend."

"Where is he?" asked the woman solemnly, her Scottish burr strong.

"Ryland?" Katherine asked, straightening a little to pull from Daisy's arms as she watched MacTaggart's taut expression.

"Is there someone else about that I might be speakin' of?"

Katherine's gaze dropped to the rifle, then lifted to Lacy's face, her hand still clasping Daisy's sleeve. "He didn't kill the mayor."

The room was silent.

"Daisy." Katherine turned her face desperately to the English girl's. "You know he didn't."

"But 'e killed plenty others, miss. 'E's dangerous, and—"

"Oh, hell. We know he's dangerous, Daisy. Now where is he?" snapped Lacy.

Katherine wondered if there was a bounty on his head. She'd read all about bounties in her novels. She backed against the door now, fatigue causing her knees to shake. She'd gone through a great deal of trouble to keep Ryland alive, and wasn't quite ready to see him dead yet. "He's well hidden," she said soberly. "You won't find him. He didn't do it." Katherine held Lacy's gaze, fighting back the swirling cloud that threatened to spill her onto the floor. "You won't find . . ." she said, but Lacy's face dipped and swerved. The floor bucked upward, and she fell, her dark hair spilling around her like a black tide.

The unearthly beauty of the music stopped, the melodious strains peacefully floating into darkness to finally become mixed and confused with screams of terror.

"Nooo!" Travis shrieked, clawing his way to the surface of reality, fighting back waves of memory and sleep. "No!" He jerked himself upright, frantically searching for a weapon.

"It's all right." Both Katherine's hands clutched his arm. Her face was close to his, her eyes beautiful in the flickering candlelight.

"Rachel," he breathed. "Rachel."

"It's all right." Her face was so solemn and sweet. Her hair loose and dark. "We're safe."

Travis could not lift his gaze from her face. She was just as she should be. Soft and sweet and strong. "Safe?"

"Yes."

"My leg hurts." The words were right. It was his *voice* that surprised him. It was deep and mature and confusing.

But, of course, if Rachel had grown, he would have done the same.

"They got the bullet out." Her tone was soothing and husky, having lost the girlish lisp she had had as a child. "You're going to be fine now. Lie back."

Her fingers were warm against the bare flesh of his arm as she helped him settle against the pillows. "Sleep," she ordered gently, but he could not. Awful things waited for him in the guise of dreams.

"You're safe?" he asked tentatively. His hand had caught hers.

"Yes."

"Not hurt?"

"No."

He nodded, loosening his grip with an effort. "So smart," he breathed softly. "You were always so smart." His head hurt, but he scowled and tried to think. "Soldier?"

"He's fine. Hidden where no one will find him," Katherine soothed. "He sends his love."

Travis nodded again. Rachel always knew what to do. Always knew. His lids drifted shut, but darkness threatened to take her, and he wrestled them open, shifting his eyes quickly to find her face again. "Rachel?"

"Yes? I'm here."

"I love you," whispered the small boy in the man's body.

Travis slid unsteadily from a dream, not sure whether to hurry from the disturbing remnants of slumber or hold to the dark images allowed by sleep. Past experience had proven reality to sometimes be worse than his nightmares.

He opened his eyes warily.

The ceiling was white. His arm hurt like hell, and his right leg was numb, but no ropes bound his hands, his ribs didn't burn, and it wasn't raining.

He'd learned to be grateful for the little things.

It was a woman's room. He wasn't certain how he knew, but he knew. There was a window to his right. It was curtained with lacy drapery, holding back the bright light of day.

He turned his head, drawing in his perceptions carefully.

In the past—however long it had been since he'd first met the lady with the seductive voice—he'd been bound, nearly hanged, shot, half drowned, and dragged by his horse over some godforsaken side of the Rocky Mountains. He remembered it all so vividly now that the images startled him, making him decide it might be wise to be cautious.

Examining the room further, Travis stopped his gaze as his attention snagged on a curled feminine form that slumbered by his bed. It was her! Travis closed his eyes and swore in silence. Why was she here? She should be long gone by now, halfway to Philadelphia, or wherever the hell it was she came from.

He opened his eyes. She was slumped in a nearby chair, close enough for him to touch her. Her hair was braided again, but coiled now atop her small head, which rested against the padded wing of the floral fabric.

Her pale, scathed hands were lax in slumber. Her dress was not noteworthy, but her face . . . There was something about her face that made his chest ache to look at it. It was heart-shaped, with a shallow, delicate dimple in the center of her chin, and a dark peak of hair extending just a smidgen of an inch down the middle of her forehead. Dark, thick lashes rested over her hidden eyes, and her strawberry-tinted lips were slightly parted, exposing small, even teeth as she exhaled softly.

"Rachel." He breathed the word without realizing, and the woman scowled, her hands fluttering gently as she drew herself quickly from sleep.

He knew the exact instant when she came fully awake, for her lovely, dimpled jaw dropped slightly and her eyes opened to enormous widths.

Her eyes! They were not honey brown as he'd imagined, but were an unearthly shade of silver-blue, like the mountain sky after a heavy rain.

"Mr. Ryland." She breathed his name almost like the prayers Rachel had taught him as a child. Travis felt the words quiver like a well-aimed arrow in his gut.

She was a dark-haired angel, like a faded memory so dear he dared not pull it out for scrutiny.

"Mr. Ryland." Her small hand touched his arm with gentle slowness. "You're awake."

Travis was unable to answer her for his insides twisted into knots of hopeless mush.

"I feared . . ." She stopped and studied him. Her delicate face was so close to him now, her hand feather-light on his hale arm. She smiled, the expression tremulous, making Travis feel as if he were falling like an axed lodgepole sliding toward oblivion. "But you'll be fine now. I know it."

He needed her. Like no one else. Like he hadn't needed anything for years. Her very presence spoke to him, begged him to be a better . . .

No! Travis squashed his soppish longings and remembered the school of survival with well-rehearsed practice. Never become attached. Never become involved.

"Where the devil am I?" he asked, his voice rumbling low and gravelly through his parched throat.

She blinked twice and drew her hand away, caution returning to her mesmerizing features. "We're in New Prospect." She stood slowly, her back straightening. "At Lacy MacTaggart's . . . establishment."

"A whorehouse?"

He felt her retreat, though she didn't move, and an empty place near Travis's heart twisted while his mind nodded in smug satisfaction.

"A dance hall," she corrected stiffly.

"How far from Silver Ridge?"

"I don't know. It took me all night to—"

"Why didn't you get the hell outta here like I told you to?" he snapped.

She watched him, speechless for a moment, and then, "I couldn't leave you," she whispered softly.

His heart wrenched at the words, threatening to spill him back into living nightmares, but he'd learned to survive and survive he would. "Why the hell not?" he demanded gruffly.

"Because . . . " She wrung her hands, her expression worried. "I just . . . couldn't."

"Damn it, woman! I told you to ride east, and if you'd had the lick of sense you was born with, you'd still be riding."

"You were hurt."

For an instant he could think of nothing to say, then, "Life hurts, lady," he growled. "And I don't need no woman to go getting me killed." He sat up. His head pounded and swam dizzily, but he ignored the swirl and swung his legs over the side of the bed.

One cotton sheet became tangled between his thighs, pulling all the blankets askew, so that they stretched out over his crotch and one hip, saving him from absolute nudity. "Where're my pants?"

Katherine's gaze caught on his bare legs, skimmed to his bare hip, skittered up his flat, bare abdomen, over the sloping planes of his bare chest, to fall on the relatively safe terrain of his face.

She could find no words.

His deep blue gaze latched angrily onto hers. "You told me you was a soiled dove! Don't look so damned shocked! You ain't even seen the best part yet."

She mouthed something inaudible and kept staring.

"Hell," he snorted. "You might as well have taken a peek at the rest of me so you could at least answer my questions instead of standing there like a beached trout."

Her mouth moved again, as if she were trying to speak.

He leaned closer, listening intently, but there was nothing to be heard, so he scowled, shook his head, and grunted. "Damnedest whore I've ever met. Worthless as tits on a boar."

"Worthless!" The word came out on a gasp of utter outrage. "Worthless!"

He watched the fire flood back into her eyes and felt the relative safety of her anger. Her dark brows had drawn down slightly over her unusual eyes, and her nostrils flared with righteous rage. "I brought you here at great personal risk. I could have been killed." She bent slightly at the waist, glaring at him. "Killed!"

"But you weren't, were you, lady?" he asked caustically, canting a look up and lowering his brows in an attempt to dim the throb in his temples. "And you might notice who took the bullets." He raised a palm to his forehead, trying to quiet the war drums there. "What the hell have you been doing to me? I feel like I've been doctored with a broad axe."

She stepped away one pace, taken aback by his stunning lack of appreciation. "You have the manners of a Mongolian warmonger."

"A . . . Mongolian what?" he questioned dubiously as the room tilted again.

"Ghengis Khan!" she snapped. "You and he would have gotten on famously."

"I take it that's an insult," he said weakly, not daring to look up lest his head split.

"It most certainly is!"

"Is that the best you can do?" he snorted, chancing a glance about the room.

Katherine drew herself up even straighter. "If I chose, I could scorch the hair right off your chest with my verbal assaults."

He was silent for a moment. "Why don't I have a shirt on?" he asked curiously, just now noticing that detail. "You women needing to see a real man? Not that I mind. But you needn't be sneaky about it. If you're interested, just ask and I'd be happy to—"

"You conceited, braying pain in the . . . the . . ."

"Out of the mood now, are you?" he asked, finally looking up and wincing at the pain in his temple.

"You . . . You . . ." She searched for the perfect insult, but it kept eluding her, though her hands were motioning now to assist her thoughts.

"What?"

"You . . ."

"Jesus!" he spat in irritable impatience. "I could die of hoof-and-mouth before you managed to come up with a single respectable curse word. And I'd like to wait around, lady. Really I would, but I don't have the time. Seems I got me a small army of men after me because of your stupidity. So I'm leaving!" He rose to do just that. The blankets fell away, baring him to her gaze.

But she failed to notice.

"Leaving?" she gasped.

"At least you can hear," he intoned evenly. "Where're my pants?"

"You think you're leaving?"

"God, woman, you're making me crazy." He turned, flashing her with his nudity and searching for his clothing. "Just get me my belongings and we'll . . ."

"Get back on the bed!"

Her tone sounded deadly serious, and Travis turned around slowly.

The open end of a revolver glared at him from the palm of her steady hand.

"Take one step toward that door and I'll blow your brains out."

"What the devil kind of nonsense is this?"

"I dragged you out of the river when you where drowning. I gave you the blankets when I was freezing and exhausted. I walked from here to nowhere in my bare feet so you could ride. I'm not about to let you get yourself killed now."

Travis scowled, trying to figure this new twist. He cocked his right leg to ease the pain in his thigh and laced his arms across his bare chest. "Let me get this straight. You don't want me to get killed, so you're threatening to blow my brains out if I leave?"

Katherine shuffled her feet, a bit uncomfortable with the inconsistency of her words and intentions. She bit her lip, shifted her weight, and considered her next move. "That's right," she said, deciding to go with her original statement.

"Lady." He shook his head. "You're about one bean short of a full pot."

He took a step forward.

The sound of the revolver cocking seemed loud enough to blow out the windows.

Travis froze.

Katherine smiled.

The door opened softly, and Lacy MacTaggart stepped in. "What's all this, now?" she asked quietly, placing her fist on well-padded hips and looking at Katherine.

"He said he was leaving. I said he wasn't," she said matter-of-factly, her lips pursed in anger.

For a fraction of a second Travis thought he saw the shadow of a smile on the older woman's hardened face. "So you thought you'd shoot him, Katy, lass?"

"He's an ungrateful—"

"Aye, I know, but most men are," Lacy shushed, then firmed her voice and turned her eyes to Travis. "You. Get back in bed."

"I ain't got no hankering to lie around till a lynch mob shows up. Funny thing about me," Travis growled.

"Can I shoot him?" Katherine asked grimly, wetting her lips.

"Not yet. Listen, Ryland," warned Lacy gruffly. "I've spanked better men than you, so get back on that bed before—"

The scream in the hallway immobilized the room for a fraction of a second, and then Travis was barreling toward Katherine in all his naked glory.

But before she could do so much as *consider* shooting, the gun was in his hand and he was flattened against the wall, staring at the door with the intensity of a wolf on the prowl.

The room was pitched into silence, then, "Bernard," Lacy called evenly, not taking her steely eyes from the naked man with the gun.

"Yes ma'am?" Bernard answered timidly from the far side of the door.

"Quit pinching Garnet."

"Yes ma'am" came the meek response.

Footsteps tiptoed down the hall. Silence came again. Lacy held out her hand, palm up. "You're under my roof only because Katy is a friend of a friend," she explained solemnly. "You make trouble, you'll find yourself out on your bare ass. Understood?"

Travis felt the sharp dip of the room. He knew he was in trouble, but held tenaciously to consciousness by the edge of his stubborn fingernails.

"Understand?" she asked again.

He nodded once, the movement almost sending him to the floor as he handed her the gun.

"Get him decent and get him to bed," Lacy ordered, holding the revolver casually as she turned toward the door. She stopped, hand on the door latch. "And next time, Katy, lass. Shoot first. Talk later."

Chapter 7

"I'm sorry, lass. It's Friday. All my girls will be busy tonight."

"Oh." Katherine stood like a small child, with her hands clasped behind her back, her collar buttoned primly to her chin. "Of course. I'll see to Mr. Ryland myself."

Lacy MacTaggart leaned back in her padded chair and nodded. "That'll need doing, too, I suppose, Katy. But it's not what I was speakin' of. We'll be needin' the beds, lass. Unless you're considering putting yours t' profitable use."

"Oh!" Katherine breathed, realizing the other's meaning. "No! I mean . . ." she sputtered, bringing her hands forward to wring them in front of her faded, borrowed gown. "It's not that there's anything wrong with what you do. I mean . . . what the girls do . . . Of course, maybe you do it too, but . . ." she jabbered.

"Katy, lass." Lacy shook her brightly dyed head. "Just say what's on yer mind."

Katherine bit her lip, drew a deep breath to steady her nerves, and nodded solemnly. "You've been so very good to me, Miss MacTaggart. I won't forget it. And I'll pay you back as soon as ever I can."

"Sounds like you're going somewhere."

Katherine nodded. "We'll have to leave."

"You can't move him yet, lass. Not if you want him to keep that leg."

"But I don't see what else we can do."

"There's space for the both of you in his room."

"*His* room!" Katherine gasped.

"It's all that's available."

"But then I'll have to take him—"

"He wouldn't last a day with one leg," Lacy said solemnly. "I've seen his kind before. He'd sooner die."

Katherine knocked once on the portal, hugging the bandages to her chest and holding the pitcher with one hand as she pushed the latch and stepped inside.

Travis was lying on his side, facing her, his expression grave. "How long have I been here?"

Katherine lifted her chin, feeling her heart thump repeatedly against the wall of her ribs.

"It's Friday. We arrived Wednesday morning."

He narrowed his eyes, his left arm curled beneath his head. It looked powerful and broad and naked. "Three days, two nights. More than enough time for the hungry wolves of Silver Ridge to find us."

Katherine bit her lip. "No one knows we're here."

"No one?" He raised his brows at her, his expression more than dubious.

"Just Lacy's girls."

"Just her girls."

"And Bernard."

"Bernard," he repeated flatly.

"And . . ." She winced, realizing, perhaps for the first time, how precarious was their safety. "And Daisy—of course."

"Of course."

His gaze bore into hers, which she dropped rapidly.

"I'm sorry." The words slipped out.

He said nothing, letting the music from below punctuate the quiet, then, "For saving my life?"

She raised her eyes with a snap. Although his shoulders were broad and powerful, he looked helpless and needy. "No." She shook her head, knowing her denial as truth. "For bringing you here."

Her words were little more than a whisper, a whisper he felt down to the very core of his soul. He knew he should draw back behind the curtain of arrogant sarcasm, but she looked so sweet and earnest. There were a thousand things he thought to say—not one of which he spoke. "You need to leave, lady. Head east. Before they find you."

She stood still, staring at him, holding that damned pitcher of water and neatly rolled bandages. "But I'm innocent. There's no need to run," she whispered.

Innocence. It was painted across her smooth features like the loving stroke of a gentle artist. Innocent she was, he thought, and not the one responsible for Patterson's death. He was certain of it and longed to hear it from her own lips. To hear she'd never touched the fat mayor, had not wasted her precious youth beneath the panting bodies of lecherous men. But he had no right to ask, and she seemed unwilling to explain.

"I fear I have bad news." She changed the subject and approached him slowly, feeling tense and uncertain.

"Bad?" he echoed. "And things been going so well."

Katherine set the pitcher and bandages on the commode beside the bed and noticed that he was smiling slightly, like a small boy who couldn't resist a practical joke. And yet it was difficult to compare him to a child, for when she put her hand to his arm, she felt his strength and power.

Katherine seated herself in the chair she'd occupied during those long hours before he had found consciousness. "Lacy said Dory will be needing her . . ." She stopped again, biting her lip and unwrapping the bandage from his arm. "You see . . ." She cleared her throat and gently tugged the last bit of cloth from his wound. It was oozy and red and ugly, but the embarrassing topic distracted her, and she dipped a towel in clean water before dabbing gently at his arm. "Well, it's Friday night," she said with finality.

His eyes never left hers, though his brows had lifted in question. "Friday?"

She gave a curt nod, but it had been a hell of a week for Travis, and the significance of the day was beyond his present understanding.

"Friday," he mused aloud, gritting his teeth as she carefully rebandaged his wound. "Friday . . ."

"She'll have company," Katherine explained stiltedly, then flamed a deep scarlet hue.

"Ohhh." Travis nodded sagely. "As in a gentleman caller."

She refused to look him in the face. Was he smiling that boyishly charming smile that had tripped her heart?

"And three in the room wouldn't be proper?" he asked quietly.

She tied off the bandage and stood abruptly, hurrying away to fumble about with the washbasin for a moment longer than necessary before returning, eyes downcast.

Travis watched her return. She was a lady. A true-to-life raised-to-marry kind of lady, and though he may be no better than slime on a pond rock, he wasn't low enough to mess with a lady.

"You have to leave," he said again, knowing his voice had dropped to a husky murmur. "Get to safety. Now."

"I won't." She sat and looked directly at him. "I won't leave, Travis Ryland, until you can leave, too."

His chest ached, as if there was insufficient room for his heart to pump, as if he'd been shot. Don't care, he warned himself. Don't care. But, damn it all, he did.

"I'll take the floor," he managed huskily. "The bed's yours."

"No. Please." Her hand touched the curved muscle of his biceps, barely covering half its circumference, and he could feel the heat of her spreading from his heart in all directions. "Lacy says you need to rest quietly. Please," she repeated, her tone deep and hoarse. "You'll need your strength."

For the first time since her girlhood Katherine wanted to touch a man. But her father had been beyond her reach, needing nothing more than his religion. What is it this man needs? she wondered raggedly. "Please," she whispered again, but now the word seemed a plea for something different.

He couldn't help but kiss her. Her lips were as soft as a dream, and her face, when he touched it, felt like satin, like the pure fine fabric Rachel had said their mother wore at her wedding.

Raw, aching need slashed across his senses, and he pressed into her kiss, curving his hand behind her delicate neck.

"No." She pulled away abruptly. "No. I'm sorry. This isn't right."

Her eyes were as large as a doe's, very close and deep and beautiful.

No! *I'm* sorry, Travis wanted to scream. He dropped his hand as if burned.

She looked confused and lifted her fingers to her mouth, touching the lips he just kissed. "I'll see to your leg." She reached out, but her hand shook and he caught it.

"It's fine." His voice sounded rougher than he'd planned, as if he'd lived too many hard years alone. "Just fine, lady. Please." He drew a deep breath and hoped she was as innocent as she seemed and had no idea what she did to him. "I think it's best to leave it be, or it'll only start bleeding again."

She stared into his eyes, only inches from her own. They were sky blue and filled with enough pain to last three lifetimes. "Yes." She drew away with a rush. "Yes. I think you're right."

The night seemed endless, though Katherine's spot on the floor was comfortable enough. The music from below had ceased, but other noises now intruded—laughter, deep and male or quick and high-pitched. And then the sounds from next door, the rhythmic groan of the bed's ropes, low gasps of breath.

It was intolerable. She knew Travis was awake, could sense it, though she couldn't see if his eyes remained open. The rhythm behind the wall picked up speed, the breathing growing louder.

"Lady." Ryland's voice was quiet and deep. "Were you singing—before I came to my senses?"

"I thought you couldn't hear," she said, feeling endlessly grateful for the darkness that hid the hot flush of her cheeks.

"Just a memory," he murmured. There was a gasp of primal pleasure from next door. "Sing for me, lady."

"I don't sing really."

"Please," he said huskily. "For both our sakes. Sing loud."

For the life of her Katherine could think of nothing but

hymns, and though the inappropriateness of those songs struck her as strange, the intolerable situation was more than she could bear.

Perhaps the walls of that establishment had never heard the haunting melody of "The Old Rugged Cross," but they heard it now, followed by every song Katherine could recall from church.

When the last note faded, utter silence held the place. Not a breath could be heard. Travis lay quietly, one arm covering his eyes. Her voice enchanted him—no matter what the words, the tone was soothing yet erotic.

Let this be a lesson to me, he thought grimly. Better to hear the moans and sighs of pleasure behind their very walls than be tortured by a single innocent note of Katherine Amelia Simmon's church-schooled voice.

Chapter 8

"Breakfast." Katherine wet her lips and pushed the bedroom door open. She supposed she should become accustomed to sharing his room. After all, they'd survived the week's end together, closeted up here, hidden from the world. Yet being near him was no easier now than it had been in the beginning. She knew that under those blankets he wore nothing more than a pair of battered trousers, conveniently cut off at the thigh to permit access to his leg wound. She kept her eyes on the heaping tray of food and tried to cover her nervousness. "Hungry?"

Ravenous was his first thought, but not necessarily for food. Travis sat propped against multiple pillows and watched her face as she entered. Spending the past three nights alone with her had almost killed him. He'd found himself wishing more than once that she'd left him in the woods to be decently consumed by a wolf rather than lie in the darkness and listen while others found the carnal satisfaction denied him. He couldn't bear her nearness much longer without losing his mind. The simple brush of her fingers against his was enough to send his imagination soaring and his heart thumping madly. God help him, he should leave, but he knew he lacked the strength. And when he went, he'd take her along, and would need his full health to get her to some haven of safety.

"Feeling better?"

She was sitting near him again, watching him with those wide, otherworldly eyes. Her hair was neatly coiled atop her head, showing the slight dip in the center of her hairline,

65

which aligned perfectly with the top button nestled just below her delicate chin.

Travis could do nothing but watch her and could think of nothing decent to say as she continued to chatter.

"Fresh air would be good for you, I suspect. But, of course, we can't chance it. Still, you've had so little time to recover, and you already look so . . . hale!" she finished, her tone sounding ragged. "You look hale already."

Despite himself Travis's nostrils flared. God help him—he looked hale, while she looked like something he could eat for breakfast. So sweet and tender that he kept his mouth firmly shut lest he be tempted to take a bite of her.

Katherine uncovered the tray. It contained nothing less than a thick steak—cooked rare—three eggs, two slices of bread, and steaming coffee. She shrugged as he eyed the platter in surprise. "I can get you some chocolate to drink," she said enthusiastically. "It's wonderful. Just as good as in the chocolate houses."

"I'm not one for chocolate."

Katherine's eyes went round. "No chocolate?"

"No."

"Oh." She fumbled for a moment, losing herself in his eyes and clearing her throat nervously. "Lacy says a man your size needs a good deal of food to fully recover."

Lacy. Travis could bet the old carrot-topped crone knew exactly what he needed. Why had she chased Katherine, the innocent, into his room like a rabbit into a wolf's den?

But, he reminded himself grimly, better his den than some other wolf's. His gaze fastened on the tray as he tried to ignore the full, gentle curve of her bosom behind it. Better himself, he repeated mentally. She was safe with him. Safe. He repeated the words like a mental chant, but when he reached to take the platter, his fingers brushed hers, burning on contact, scorching his senses.

"Do you need help with breakfast?" she asked, her husky voice causing the hair to rise on the back of his neck. "I can't imagine how you manage at all with your left hand." She shook out the linen napkin and leaned nearer. "I'm absolutely hopeless without my right." She bit her lip and placed the linen just so, partially covering the breadth of his bare chest. "I could feed you if you——"

"Goddamn it, woman!" Travis swore abruptly. His body quivered with explosive frustration. "Don't touch me!"

Her face, when he looked at her, held an expression of utter shock, her eyes wide and brimmed with tears.

"Oh, God," he moaned, covering his eyes with one hand. "Don't cry." He drew a ragged breath. "Please, don't cry."

She backed away a step, her hands shaking, as did her voice. "I'm sorry."

"Don't cry." His tone had become wheedling he knew. But he'd rather face a troop of first rate militia than cope with one crying female. Especially this female, whose very touch inflamed him.

"It's my fault," she said solemnly. "They'd never have accused you of murder if I hadn't forced you to take me to Grey's. My fault." She sniffled once.

He closed his mind, trying not to hear her despair. Trying to pretend he was elsewhere, tracking Yankees maybe. But there was no safe harbor. Without thinking, he set the tray aside and then slowly got out of bed.

"It's——"

Katherine felt his arms wrap around her, and his chest was warm against her cheek. She should draw away she knew. She should be ashamed of her weakness, of her thoughts—of his nudity. But God forgive her, the strong embrace of his arms felt like heaven, like a safe haven from the horrors that had found her.

"I'm sorry," she whispered to the taut muscles of his chest.

His left hand stroked her back, while his right simply cradled her against him. "It's not your fault."

"Yes." She sniffled, feeling a single tear slip from her cheek to be caught and spread between their bodies. His arms felt immensely strong, his body warm and firm. "If I hadn't been with Patterson . . ." She shrugged, remembering her need to save Daisy.

He shushed her again, noticing her ears for the first time. Fascinating, how tiny an ear could be. And how alluring. He touched it gently with his fingertips, then followed the curve of it downward. She shivered. He felt the tremble, trans-ferred from her lovely softness to his aching form.

"If I hadn't . . ." she began again, but her line of thought had been disrupted.

"Shhh." He stood a full head taller than she, though she was not a small woman. "Quiet, lady," he soothed, and kissed that ear ever so gently.

As a young girl, Katherine had seen fireworks. But never had she felt them. Never until now. They exploded at the lobe of her ear, sending light sparking off in every direction. She slipped her arms about the incredible width of his chest and pulled him closer now. "Mr. Ryland."

Don't let her speak, he reminded himself. He was teetering on the edge of no return, and if he heard that lovely molasses voice, he'd fall, taking her with him, down to his level.

She turned her face, finding his eyes. They were warm, deep-set eyes that said so much. "Mr. Ryland," she whis-pered again, failing to realize the incongruity of such formality with a nearly naked man clutched to her body in a death-like grip. Love me, she thought, but said, "I'm sorry," in that same way she used to in an attempt to gain her father's approval.

"Shhh." Travis closed his eyes, shushing her through his gritted teeth and feeling the deep burn of his shaft throb against her thigh.

"It's all my fault," she said, not certain why she felt such a scorching ache to hold him. Only knowing that her need was deep. "I should never have been . . ."

He drew her closer, smelling the fresh fragrance of her hair.

"Never have been there . . ." She pressed up against him, breathing hard. "With Patterson."

"Don't." He moved stiffly back a pace, taking her arms in his large hands. "Don't say you were with Patterson." His eyes bore into hers. "I know it's a lie."

Katherine stared at him in silence.

"I know it wasn't you who was with him."

Frustration welled within her. Never before had she been

held in the strong warmth of a man's arms, and she wished now to feel that warmth again.

"You weren't with Patterson," he said, shaking her slightly. "Admit it! It wasn't you. You're not that kind of woman."

All her life she'd been told what kind of person she was. What she should be. What she should do, and suddenly she ached to shock them all.

"I am." She stared at him, her body stiff, wanting for once to be accepted, shortcomings and all. "And yes, I was."

"No one would believe that," he gritted. "No one. Not with the way you speak. Like a polished lady. And the way you dress." He scowled down at her gown, and she returned his expression.

"What's wrong with the way I dress?" she questioned evenly.

He shook his head, trying to clear it, trying to find his discipline. "It's hardly the kind of thing a woman wears to seduce—"

"So you think I can't be seductive? Is that it?" She drew away stiffly, burning with an emotion she failed to identify.

He stared at her, thinking her the most beautiful woman he had ever seen. But her wrath offered some safety—from himself, from his need. "Yeah." He nodded bluntly. "That's what I think."

"Well, you're wrong." She said the words evenly, her back straight as a board, her face hot. "Others do find me attractive. You think I'm not that kind, but you're wrong." She shook her head, her mouth pursed. "You don't know how wrong you are."

"Katherine." He'd pushed her too far and reached for her now. "I didn't mean—"

She slapped at his hand. "Oh, yes, you did. You think I'm an old dried-up prune. But not everyone shares your esteemed opinion." She lifted her nose, and turned, heading for the door. "Don't expect me here tonight."

His hand caught hers in a hard grip, turning her quickly toward him. "Don't say that. Do you hear me? Don't say it."

She gasped, staring in shock, then laughed, perversely pleased that she had upset him. "Why? Because you don't want to be proven wrong?" She leaned nearer, eyes narrowed as she tugged her arm from his grasp. "Well you *are* wrong. How do you think I pay for this food? This bed?"

She paused, breathing hard. "Sleep well," she said, and twisted toward the door. "I'll be busy tonight."

"Over my dead body," he growled, grabbing her arm. "Goddamn it! We're leaving. And we're leaving now!"

"No!" she yelled and struggled against him.

Travis would never quite figure how it happened. But suddenly there were women everywhere, half-clad women draped by pairs on his arms, legs, and back. And not gentle, refined women, but strong, uninhibited women who yanked him away from Katherine.

"Get him down."

"Over there."

"On the bed."

He tried to get free. But every time he got a grip on something, there was an outraged shriek and numerous fists beating on his person. Confusion smothered him. Fleshy bodies buried him.

The long strips of bandages appeared seemingly from nowhere, and suddenly he found himself tied, bound to the bed's headboard like a rabid beast.

"What's all this?"

Noise subsided. Half-naked bodies moved aside as Lacy MacTaggart stepped through the mayhem, her brows lifting as her gaze fell on Travis's strapped body.

"Having a wee bit of fun, are we, lasses?"

Daisy stepped from the bevy, her wild hair scattered like a disrupted bee's hive. "'E was botherin' Miss Katherine."

Lacy's gaze skimmed silently over Travis, starting at his eyes and floating down over his short cropped and painfully revealing britches. "What kind of bothering?" Her voice was flat and threatening.

Travis pulled his bonds taut and snarled.

"'E's a dangerous one," Daisy whispered shakily.

"He pulled my hair," complained Garnet.

"I broke a nail," whimpered Julia.

"Quiet!" Lacy warned. A hush fell. She turned slowly, her

gaze falling on Katherine's pale face near the door. "Speak, Katy, love, or I'll give him to the girls for amusement."

Katherine wrung her hands. Travis Ryland lay stretched and tied on the bed, his eyes burning her face. "He tried to leave," she explained weakly.

Lacy's brows lifted dubiously. "And?"

Katherine wasn't sure how all this had come about. It had happened so quickly. "And he tried to take me with him."

Lacy shook her head and tsked. "Bad boy," she said. "I don't like men who try to *take* women against their wills."

There were a few snickers in the background.

Travis glared.

Katherine considered fainting.

Lacy turned. "Katy." She crooked a finger at the blushing girl. "I'll be needin' a talk with you."

Chapter 9

The room contained no frills. It was an office and nothing more. Lacy MacTaggart appeared absolutely at home there.

"This used to be a peaceable house," she said, leaning into the spindle back of the room's only chair and folding her hands atop her generous lap.

Silence enveloped the room, and Katherine shifted her weight, feeling very much like the knobby-kneed girl who had so often cringed beneath her father's disapproval. She stared down at her shoe, making a crescent pattern on the carpet with the toe. "He tried to leave."

"Uh-huh." One plucked brow was arched over Lacy's olive-green eyes as she waited.

"I thought we were getting on better." Katherine lifted her chin slightly. "He and I."

"But?"

"I just offered to help him eat." Katherine felt the now familiar blush rush to her cheeks as she recalled his bare, tempting chest.

Lacy's gaze held the girl in a firm grip, reading a great deal more than her words. "Offended was he?"

"How did you know?"

"Lass, what I don't know about men ain't worth learnin'," sighed Lacy. "In fact, most of what I *know* ain't worth learnin'."

They stared at each other, neither talking for a moment before Katherine bit her lip. "I think he's quite—"

Giggles emerged from upstairs, accented by a low,

threatening growl. The sound of scattering feet followed, and then the bang of a door thudding closed.

The blood drained from Katherine's face. "Upset," she finished weakly.

MacTaggart sat in quiet study, listening to the pattering feet, watching Katherine's pained expression. There was more here than met the eye. It was unusual for a man to scare a bevy of half-clad women from his room, no matter what the circumstances. And what were the circumstances exactly? People rarely surprised her anymore, but these two . . .

"He eats like a horse." MacTaggart said the words flatly, watching for the girl's reaction.

"I'll pay as soon as I'm able." Katherine had lifted her chin a notch, and something in Lacy's chest twisted at the sight. Her little Emily would have been that kind of a lady, had she lived.

"Do you have any money?"

"Not just now. But I'll earn it," assured Katherine.

"How?" Lacy asked baldly. "And when?"

Hoping to appear calm and confident, Katherine remained unmoving, but she looked worried and pale.

"I'll feed him and you," Lacy said, rising suddenly to her impressive height. "Best cuisine in town. We'll keep you hid. My clan's got secrets of their own. They won't mess with yours. Tomorrow morning I'll start up some rumors saying folks like the two of you have been seen some distance from here—heading east."

Katherine remained very still, her hands caught together in a deathlike grip as she stared at Lacy. "In exchange for what?" she asked quietly.

"Coo, miss, 'oo'd of thought you was 'iding so much bounty under them dowdy dresses?"

"Turn," Margaret said, pushing on Katherine's nearly bare hip.

"Look at her waist," complained Dory, taking another bite from a raspberry tart and moaning when a blob of the filling dropped onto her gown. "Damn near big as my arm."

She licked the sweet from her sleeve, ate the remainder in one large bite, and plopped onto her elbow.

Garnet looked up after she pinned the hem. "She'll look like a princess."

"Men'll be drooling on their tools."

"Beggin' t' pay just t' 'old a lady's 'and," added Daisy with a mischievous grin. "Lacy's a genius."

"We'll cut it down to there," declared Margaret.

"Where?" asked Katherine in shock. She had been prodded and turned and measured until her heart sat in a cold lump of dread in her throat and her face burned a permanent shade of scarlet.

"There," said Margaret, casually tugging her chemise a half inch lower. "Just above your nips."

"Just above . . ." Katherine gasped, her hands flitting upward to cover the twin globes that pressed into view.

"Now, miss," Daisy crooned, hurrying to take her hands. "You'll look like livin' 'eaven."

"And," proclaimed Margaret, hurrying behind, "we'll cut it down to here in back."

Katherine turned, trying to see where they pointed.

Margaret flung an arm around Katherine's shoulder to squeeze her tightly. "And the men'll love it."

"Begging for favors."

"Dyin' for more," chirped Daisy.

"And you'll just lean into their faces like this," added Dory, rising to her knees on the mattress and leaning forward to show every inch of bosom above her nipples. "So they're looking right straight into heaven."

"And if that doesn't work . . ." began Julia, then lowered her voice to a whisper.

In the next room, Travis gritted his teeth, yanked savagely at his cotton bonds, and tried not to hear the giggles. He'd lain in purgatory for hours now, listening to the women's chatter from next door and wondering what they had planned. Goddamn them all. If they soiled her, he'd drown every one of them in their own toilet water. He yanked again, but the bed did little more than groan a complaint. Damn them all to hell!

Footsteps sounded in the hall. Dinnertime?

Travis narrowed his eyes and waited.

A mattress moaned, voices mingled. Minutes passed. Finally a key turned in the lock, and Katherine entered.

Travis lay flat on his back, his arms stretched above his head as he watched her draw near.

She moved hesitantly, bearing a covered tray and showing by her expression that she'd not considered until now just how he would eat in such an unlikely position.

She stared at him in mute dismay. Silence stood between them.

"You gonna feed me?" he asked finally, "or just let me starve and use me as a paperweight?"

Katherine bit her lip. He looked mad enough to eat her alive, bones and all. Her hands were shaking, she realized, and hoped he hadn't noticed the tremble of the tray she held. "If I untie you—will you promise not to try to leave?"

He was silent—staring at her, then, "Lady," he said, "hell will freeze solid and the devil himself move out before I promise you anything."

Katherine's back stiffened and her hands stopped trembling as she lifted her chin in a characteristic gesture of fledgling pride. "Then I suppose I'll have to take measures to ensure you don't injure yourself further. Daisy." She needed to raise her voice only slightly, and in a moment footsteps pattered quickly down the hall and a blond head peeked in the door. "Daisy," Katherine said again, her mouth pursed, her gaze unbent from Travis's. "Mr. Ryland is being difficult again."

"And the sun still rises in the east," quipped Daisy. "So what's new?"

"It seems he's too stubborn to make a sensible bargain, so I'll need help tying him in a seated position."

"What's this?" questioned Margaret as she crammed in beside Daisy. "Our livin' ghost still breathing fire? Hey, girls," she called, "we got us some live entertainment. Come on."

In a minute there were two women holding each of Travis's arms while Katherine tried to loosen his bonds. He lay still and silent, staring past half-bare bosoms to glare at her as she worked. But the endeavor was hopeless for he'd pulled the cotton strips into an impenetrable lump.

"It's no use." Dory gave up first. "We'll have to cut the bandages."

"Then what?" Garnet questioned, scrunching her face into a frown.

"Ropes," Julia supplied quickly. "I'll get some ropes from the stable. You wait here."

She hurried away. Silence fell. Travis glared.

"Does he always look so mean?" Margaret asked, staring boldly down at his long, tight-muscled body as it lay taut and ready upon the narrow mattress.

"Always," said Daisy. "If 'e ever smiled, 'e'd scare the nose right off 'is face."

"I think it's the beard," stated Garnet. "Could be he's smiling the whole time. We just can't tell."

"And it could be if I ate coins, I'd pee dollar bills," said Dory. "Only I don't think so."

"Well . . ." Garnet pouted. "I think it could be he's a real looker under them whiskers. Don't you, Katherine?"

Katherine didn't answer, feeling the blush burn her senses.

"Don't call her Katherine," reminded Margaret.

"Oh, yes. Princess," Garnet giggled. "Don't you agree, Princess?"

"Oh, come now," urged Margaret. "Tell us the truth, Princess. He's not half bad to look at. Good nose."

"Great eyes," added Garnet. "Deep. All full of mystery. Me," she sighed. "I always fall for a man of mystery."

"You always fall for anything in britches," corrected Dory.

"Or outta them," countered Margaret.

Giggles twittered around the half circle of women, but Katherine remained mute, her eyes locked on Travis's.

"But I will say he's got all the right parts," admitted Dory with a nod.

"And big ones," added Margaret. "Shoulders like a buffalo."

"It's his chest. Don't you think, Princess?" asked Garnet. "It's his chest that's most . . . scrumptious. All that muscle and . . ." She hunched her shoulders and shifted her own plump chest. "Oooo. I always fall for a man with muscle."

"He's got a scar. Look." Margaret leaned forward, placing a palm to his ribs. Travis gritted his teeth, his before-mentioned muscles bunching to undulated hardness over his flat belly. "Ummm," moaned Margaret, raising her brows and watching his lean form, "how'd your man get this scar, Princess?"

Katherine's gaze was trapped on Margaret's small hand. She wanted to pull the woman away and perhaps would have if embarrassment hadn't rooted her to the spot. She took a deep breath. "He's not *my* man."

Every woman stared at her, brows raised in question.

"Then whose?" asked Margaret flatly.

"I wouldn't wish 'im on no one," said Daisy, shaking her frizzy head, "not on nothin' 'uman, any'ow."

"Well, I'd take him," sighed Garnet, then let her gaze skim his hard body and corrected, "at least part of him."

Laughter bent the women nearly double, causing Margaret to allow her hand to slip from Travis's side.

"And which part'd that be?" asked Dory lasciviously.

"I'd take whichever part's available," Dory said, grinning, and Katherine prayed for unconsciousness.

"I know what part I'd take," said Daisy, warming to the conversation.

"Dinner's waiting," reminded Dory. "Let's get him tied." She looked down at their prisoner and grinned. "After we shave him."

"Yeah."

"Let's."

A hubbub of excitement brewed. Voices tittered.

"Remove one hair from my head," threatened Travis, his bonds stretched tight as he strained toward the women, "and I'll see each of you shorn like so many sheep."

"Now, now," crooned Margaret, her pretty face petulant. "You're always so serious. Relax. Have some fun. There are a few million men who'd give their right arms to be in your spot."

"It's true," grinned Dory, dropping her chubby body to her knees to place a hand on the incredible width of his tight arm and press her bosom snugly against his side. "We can be lots of fun."

"You sure he's not yours, Princess?" asked Margaret.

Katherine's head felt filled with air while her gut was tied in knots comparable to the ones which held Travis straining against the headboard. "I'm thinking I should get him fed."

The room was silent before the women burst into uproarious laughter, falling against each other with their ready mirth.

"Not a 'yes,'" giggled Garnet.

"But certainly not a 'no,' either," added Margaret. "Come on girls—let's get this job done before Princess takes a knife to the lot of us."

He didn't struggle as they cut his bonds, helped him to a sitting position, and tied him to the bed with the ropes Julia had retrieved.

"His back looks like hell," stated Margaret, who'd caught a glimpse of it as she'd plumped his pillows, letting her fingers linger on his shoulders. "What'd you do to him, Princess?"

Katherine dropped her eyes to the tray and reconsidered removing Travis from the Red Garter, leg wound or no leg wound. "I dragged him into the woods," she admitted softly.

"Oooo." Margaret snatched her fingers from Travis's shoulder to clutch them together behind her back with a good deal of showmanship. "She drug a two-hundred-pound man through the underbrush all by her lonesome." Margaret nodded, brows raised. "Let that be a lesson to all of us until she decides just exactly who he *does* belong to."

The others took a step back, their faces determinedly solemn, and began to leave.

"Good luck," called Margaret, gliding to the door after the others. "Oh." She leaned in at the last minute. "And if you need any help with his bath," she winked, then whispered, "call *me*."

The door closed softly. Laughter floated back to Katherine's burning ears. She cleared her throat and tried not to look at Travis's chest, but below his chest was his belly, hard, and feathered with golden hair.

"Hungry?" she asked weakly. When he didn't respond,

she retrieved the tray in silence, finally turning back when she could delay no longer.

"Well . . ." she sighed, finding her nerves were nearing the breaking point. "This one wasn't my fault."

"Whose then?" he asked, glaring at her from beneath lowered brows.

"Yours," she proclaimed flatly. "If you would have simply promised to stay put . . ."

"Stay put!" He pulled his new bonds tight. "I don't care to lie here and become a whoremonger to save my own hide."

Katherine was silent, thinking his words through. So he finally believed there were men who would find her attractive enough to—to sleep with.

Well, good.

"What makes you think I'm doing it to save your hide?" she asked, seating herself near his left side. But she could not meet his eyes. "Perhaps I simply enjoy it."

"And perhaps I'll paddle your backside raw."

She drew her gaze to his with a snap, anger brightening her glare. "And that from a man who doesn't even believe I could attract another's attention."

Silence fell between them. Gazes held—silver blue on azure, speaking more honestly than voices as heartbeats sped along and breathing accelerated.

His loins ached and every muscle tensed to break free from the bonds that held him.

But there was no hope.

"Feed me, goddamn it!" he swore. "Or get the hell out of my room."

Chapter 10

"Rachel!" Travis screamed the word, fighting through the fog of sleep. "Rachel!"

Katherine scrambled from her place on the floor. The nightmare has returned, she thought groggily, and stumbled to his bed. " Wake up. It's all right."

"Rachel!" His bonds were stretched tight again, his body just as taut.

"Ryland." She grasped his arms, shaking him. "It's all right."

"No!" He came fully awake as the word left his lips. His eyes were wild, and he managed to sit, supporting his hard form on the heels of his hands. "Katherine." Her name gusted forth on the same breath.

Katherine stared into his face, reading the panic there, and wondered dismally what memories could terrorize a hard man like Travis Ryland.

"I'm here." She spoke softly and touched his face, for he looked so very lost and helpless. "All's well. You're safe."

There was a scar beside his right eye, and she touched it with her fingertips, tracing the tear-shaped pattern. "Go back to sleep." She knew she soothed him as if he were a young boy, but sometimes in the night he seemed to be just that—a large, gentle child, with haunted eyes and hushed, frightened voice. Sometimes in the darkness she could forget what she knew of him—that he killed for pay, that he needed no one, especially her.

"Katherine," he breathed again. "Where have you been?"

She smiled gently, smoothing the hair from his forehead

and so acting out a simple fantasy she'd harbored. "I've been here—the whole while."

He scowled, seeming still lost in the fog of his dreams. "I thought . . ." His words ceased, and he shook his head. "Untie me, Katherine."

Their gazes fused. "I can't let you leave," she whispered. "I can't allow you to die. It would be my fault. I couldn't bear the guilt."

Her fingers lingered just above his beard. He tilted his head closer to her hand and closed his eyes, as if capturing something forbidden—holding it for just a moment before lifting his head and stiffening. "Then go yourself. Now."

"I can't."

"Please." His plea was mournful and husky. His arms tightened to hard cords of knotted muscle above the carefully tied bonds. "You could make it back east if you rode at night. It's not you they want."

"What?" She drew her hand abruptly away. "What are you talking about?"

He stared at her for a moment, then closed his eyes wearily and shook his head. "I don't know. Who would have stabbed him—and why?"

"What?"

"Patterson," he explained. "Patterson died of natural causes. But they said he was stabbed. Who did it?" He leaned forward, his expression intense. "And why? Where was the rest of the money?"

"I don't know." She'd been so busy trying to stay alive, trying to live until the next day, that she'd failed to consider such things.

"Get out, lady," he rasped. "Before it's too late."

Her hand reached up of its own accord to rest on the hard, tightly muscled hill of his chest. "I can't," she whispered.

They were mere inches apart, living in a world of dark solitude with not another sound to penetrate the quiet.

"Why?" The question rumbled forth unbidden, wrenched from his gut.

Why indeed? Katherine stared at him in silent appeal. He'd said in very precise words that he didn't want her—had no desire for her presence—and yet she couldn't leave him. She couldn't bear to draw away until she knew he was safe. Perhaps it was simply her personality.

She'd found a stray dog once—a one-eyed mongrel who'd snarled a warning when she'd first seen him. Her father had wanted to shoot it. The neighbors considered it a hazard to the community. But Katherine had named it Prince and left food out for it each night for two years. It had never allowed her to touch it, but had taken the offerings sometime before dawn. "Because I don't think you'd bite," she whispered nonsensically.

Travis's brows rose slowly, but she had no better answer, and he sighed finally. "Lady . . ." He closed his eyes. "You're about—"

"About one bean short of a full pot," she finished for him. "I know." She scowled now. "We have to figure out who stabbed Patterson, don't we?"

"We?" He shook his head, his eyes hard. "We ain't doing nothing but getting you back home."

She held his gaze. "Maybe Colorado is my home."

"The hell it is! This is no game, lady."

"You think I don't know that?"

"I think you don't know Dellas." His voice was very quiet now.

"Then tell me," she urged.

"Word'll get out that I was hired to kill him." He nodded, the movement stiff. "He'll be after me."

She remained silent for a moment, watching him. "He's an outlaw, right? A murderer?"

"Yeah." Travis's jaw hardened for a second. "Yeah, he's that."

"Then maybe we can learn where he's hiding out and report his whereabouts to the authorities."

Travis jerked angrily against his bonds, his expression showing his sudden rage. "Don't stick your nose in this. Lady, you'll stay away from Dellas. Don't even *think* about him!"

Katherine had jumped at his abrupt movement, and sat now, her heart hammering in her chest.

"You hear me?" he asked again, his voice softer.

"Who is this Dellas?"

"He's death!" Travis said with finality, and lying back down closed his eyes and turned his face to the wall.

Hours later Travis lay in the quiet of the room, watching Katherine sleep. Why was she here? Why hadn't she fled? He closed his eyes miserably. Why were those damnable dreams haunting him again? And why did he wake like a snot-nosed boy whimpering in fear? He was a man fully grown. He was nothing if not independent.

Perhaps she had been misled by his nocturnal ramblings. Perhaps she thought she sensed some softness in him. But there was none. Any gentleness he had possessed as a child had died with Rachel. He was a killer now, and he *would* kill Dellas.

So she didn't think he would bite? Well, she was mistaken. He couldn't deny his attraction to her, but it was an interest she'd be sorry she'd awakened if she failed to stay at arm's length. Let her save her maternal instincts for another.

There is no softness in me, he repeated mentally as he watched the faint outline of her pale, heart-shaped face, watched her sigh and shift slightly in her sleep, and felt something near his heart rip painfully. "No softness," he said aloud, and pushed back that awful, longing ache to hold her.

Katherine clasped her hands together and prayed for divine intervention. Travis hadn't spoken to her in days, although sometimes at night he would awaken, calling another's name. Who was Rachel, and how had she touched the man's soul? When the nightmares occurred, Katherine felt she looked directly into the deepest recesses of his hidden spirit. And a soul he most certainly had. Perhaps it was dusty and forgotten, but it was there, lying hidden beneath his splendid layers of muscle and flesh.

There were times when she touched his skin that it seemed she could feel his soul burn cleanly through to hers. Like the time her palm had lain flat and cool against the bare flesh of his chest, or the time when he'd cradled her in his arms and she'd felt the hardness of his form sear her best intentions to nonsense.

God help her. The situation was insane. She glanced at the white satin of the newly finished gown. She was most definitely, without question, certifiably insane!

"I can't do it," she whispered as her gaze caught the shocking amount of bosom exposed above her pearl-white bodice. "I can't."

"Yes y'can." Daisy rose from where she'd been fluffing the ruffled and slitted front of her skirt. "Yes, y'can." Her hands reached for Katherine's shoulders, holding them in a tight grip. "We all 'eard y'. Y' sing like an angel. Like a princess. So you're gonna go down there and knock 'em senseless. Lacy's gonna pay y' good money, and you're gonna take it and go back home." She shook Katherine slightly, her expression sober. "Y' 'ear me?"

"But what about Ryland?" murmured Katherine softly.

"You're gonna forget about him. Y' 'ear? I seen 'is type before, miss. E's no good. A killer. 'E eats sweet young things like you for breakfast."

"I don't think so," Katherine whispered. "And I think I—"

"No y' don't," rasped Daisy quickly. "Y' don't. Don't even say the words. Yer gonna go back home. Yer gonna have yerself a house." Her voice softened. "With a picket fence. And yer gonna have babies. A dozen or so. And maybe . . ." She reached for the thick white veil to slip it gingerly over the waving, flowing mass of Katherine's ace-black hair. "Maybe ye'll even name one of 'em Daisy."

Katherine blinked through the white morning-glory pattern of the veil. "Don't make me go through with it. I'll faint. Really I will."

Daisy stared through the delicate lace for a moment and laughed. "Faint? Huh! Miss, I've seen y' drag George down a flight a steps by 'is boot 'eels. I seen y' gallop down the street after a killer big enough t' gobble you 'ole. I seen y' come back with that same fella on a leash. And . . ." She blinked blearily, swiping a hand across her turned-up nose. "And I seen y' say y' was somethin' y' ain't—just t' save my neck." Daisy sniffed loudly, then spontaneously clasped

Katherine to her chest in a tight embrace. "Y' ain't gonna faint, miss; yer gonna go down there and make them men 'ungry. And," she added, drawing away to waggle a finger beneath Katherine's nose, "'y' ain't gonna show yer face. That's the most important thing. Don't let 'em see yer face."

"Is she almost read—Ohhh," Margaret gasped, stepping through the door to clap her hands delightedly before her. "Princess Charmaine. You're stunning."

"Margaret," Katherine pleaded. "Don't make me do it."

"Not do it!" Margaret laughed, reaching for Katherine's hand. "Honey, Lacy's got every man-jack between here and California crowded into the dance hall, and they're about to tear the place apart looking for the princess they've been hearing about."

"Sweet heaven," Katherine whispered, honestly feeling she very well might faint.

"Just keep out of their reach," Margaret advised, leading her toward the door. "Keep singing. Show them a little leg." She cocked one of her own well-turned, fish-netted calves. "But don't show too much. Keep them begging for more."

"Begging for more," Katherine repeated, trying to prod her bodice up her neck and feeling a decided draft blowing down the scandalous back of the ungodly garment. "But there *is* no more."

Margaret laughed again as they stepped into the hall. "Don't worry so, honey. Want to stop in to show your man?" she asked, but even through the veil she could see Katherine's eyes go wide. "No? All right, but no reason not to tease when you got yourself a captive audience I always say. Still . . ." She stepped back a pace, eyeing each of Katherine's tightly bound curves. "You're probably right. There's only so much a fellow can bear, and I'd guess yours has just about had his limit."

The other women swarmed out of their rooms now, each dressed in a red, frilly garment that barely reached the top of their thighs, where it met the course weave of black fishnet stockings. Their faces were rouged, their arms bare, and Katherine tamped down her stomach and thanked God for her comparably decent satin gown.

Her wooden body was prodded down the hall. The

raucous noise from below swelled up toward her, seeming to blow her back a step, but the girls urged her on. Bernard's lively pianoforte music coached the erratic beat of her heart.

"Come with me," Katherine urged, but the others wagged their heads and hugged her efficiently.

"Lacy says you're to be all alone."

"You'll be fine."

"Splendid."

"Chin up."

Lacy hurried through the scarlet curtains at the bottom of the stairs. "Finally." Her voice was clipped and tough as usual, but her brows rose when her gaze stopped on Katherine. "Katy, lass," she said, then nodded once in self-satisfied certainty, "give 'em hell."

Back through the curtains Lacy went. In a moment Katherine heard her speak, but she could no longer make sense of the language, for her brain was scrambled with fright.

"Now."

"Go on," the girls whispered, and abruptly she was nudged onto the stage like a fledgling on reedy wings.

"Princess Charmaine," Lacy announced.

Katherine's stomach roiled like a storm cloud threatening destruction. Hundreds of faces stared up at her through the smoky dimness. Bernard picked up a melody she vaguely recalled.

Sing. Keep out of reach. Don't let them see your face. Her mind rumbled with advice. Bernard paused, and Katherine realized she'd missed her cue. Panic swelled anew.

"Picket fence," came Daisy's whispered reminder, and Katherine swallowed once, finding the words to "Sweet Genevieve" were still planted somewhere in her boggled mind.

Her voice came, creaking hoarsely on the first notes.

Above stairs, Travis heard the song and gritted his teeth. So it had begun. He'd known they were planning something, of course. But what about after the ballads? Clenching his fists, he sawed the ropes against the wooden bed frame again. He'd been left in relative solitude since morning, and by now the bonds were frayed and weakened.

He had little time. Half an hour—maybe less. Her songs couldn't last longer, and once the last husky note had faded, she'd be swarmed by the mob. He was certain of it, for what healthy man could hear that voice and not crave her?

He sawed harder. A little more. The rope gave way with a final snap, and he rolled quickly to his feet, the stiffened fingers of his left hand frantically working at the remaining knot.

Voices! He worked faster, jerking at the knot, but in his haste he bumped the bed against the floor with a muffled clump.

"What's . . ." The door swung open. "Oh! Girls! Help! He's getting free!"

They swooped down on him in a horde of feathered boas and jiggling bosoms.

He fought like a madman. A madman with a conscience—for they were women, after all, and not to be hurt.

Unfortunately for him, they failed to share his sympathetic view and grabbed roughly at his person, pulling him down.

"Don't let him get away."

"Princess will be crushed. Grab him!"

He bucked them off his scathed back. They tumbled to the bed and sprang lightly at him again, seeming to come from every direction, bumping his healing wounds and sending shivers of pain scorching through his system.

He growled aloud, tossing Margaret to join Garnet on the bed and yanking at his bound hand. Almost free. Almost. The rope was giving way, and once he was loose, there would be no stopping him.

The hemp slipped over his knuckles and . . .

Travis felt the crack of the pitcher's porcelain edge against his skull and twisted slightly. Daisy stood behind him, pitcher raised, eyes round as her reddened mouth.

He reached for her, clearing a path through the vacuum of darkness with his hand. Voices echoed in his head. Faces dipped, then he was gone, greeting oblivion with a curse.

Chapter 11

Men cheered, standing on chairs and tables to hoot their approval of her performance. Katherine disappeared behind the curtain and into Daisy's arms.

"You did good."

"Wonderful."

"Oh, Princess," crooned Garnet. "Just beautiful." She swiped a tear from her eye. "'Greensleeves.' So sad."

"It was lovely," Margaret said briskly. "But we had a little trouble."

Katherine's heart lurched. "Ryland?"

"He's fine," assured Dory, and Daisy bobbed a quick nod, though Katherine did not fail to notice her wince.

"What happened?" Katherine asked, not realizing the weakness in her limbs was now caused more by worry for him than terror over her just finished performance.

"Well, it just . . . It happened so quick."

"Like lightning."

"He tried to get away."

"So . . ." Daisy gulped and wring her hands. "I 'ad t' 'it 'im—with a pitcher. But it's just a—just a little bump."

"And then we . . ."

"Well, we . . ."

"We gotta go," chirped Daisy. "Bernard's playing our song."

"Yes," gasped Dory. "Gotta go."

And suddenly the small area was empty except for Katherine, who stood like a sun-dazzled quail, her mouth slightly opened as she tried to assimilate the facts.

"Ryland," she whispered, but no sound was heard as the girls kicked their slippered feet to the first notes of Bernard's music. "Ryland," she said again, and sped up the stairs to his room.

He was propped on his elbows when she popped the door open. His eyes were like daggers and his face was naked—and beautiful.

"Who shaved my beard?" His voice was low and threatening.

"I . . ." She turned her head woodenly toward the door, mouthing a silent response. "They . . ."

"Who?" he snapped, and she jumped, bringing her hands rapidly forward to clutch them to her nearly bare chest.

"Me!" she squeaked. "It was me."

One corner of Travis's sensual mouth lifted to a crooked angle. "Astounding how you can be everywhere at once, *Princess* Katherine," he said. "Almost unbelievable. Or could it be . . ." He thrust forward slightly, stretching his bonds tight. "That you're protecting someone else . . . again?"

She backed away a step, wondering frantically if he knew the truth about George Patterson. "You shouldn't have tried to get away. You could have gotten hurt."

"Could have gotten hurt?" he raged, glaring at her from beneath gathered, sun-bleached eyebrows. "The little English tart cracked me with a pitcher. You think the blow speeded the healing process?"

"I'm sorry." She literally wrung her hands as she paced quickly forward to gently touch the crescent-shaped bump on the side of his skull. "Does it hurt?" she asked quietly, but he failed to answer, instead remaining as he was, his gaze directed toward her person.

"What the hell are you wearing?"

Realization of her scanty attire blazed its way to her consciousness, bringing with it a warmth she could not account for—a warmth that crept from her fingertips to her breasts, where his gaze lingered.

History told her that the old Katherine Simmons would draw away, would retreat to a safe and respectable distance. But this was not the old Katherine, and she stood her ground, her body tingling with his nearness. "Margaret said men would like it."

His eyes had lifted to hers. His nostrils were flared again, his bare chest as hard and taut as a hunting beast's. She felt his emotions like a brand upon her senses.

"Do *you*?" she questioned softly. "Do you like it?"

The quiet between them stretched against the backdrop of the music from below, and her hand slipped, seemingly of its own accord, down the side of his skull to his shaven jaw, to the jagged scar that marked his chin.

She could see the quick pace of his pulse thumping a speedy rhythm in the center of his broad throat. Her fingers fell to that pulse point and then down, between the packed mounds of his chest.

Every inch of her felt warm and glowing. Every inch of him felt hot and feverish. She moved her hand to the right. His muscles leaped beneath her fingers, and she lifted her brows and found his eyes with hers. "Do you?" she breathed.

"Jesus!" he rasped hoarsely. "Don't toy with me, lady! You'll regret the outcome."

"Will I? Maybe I'm not what you think I am," she murmured. "Maybe I'm not what anyone thinks I am."

"And maybe I'm a saint," he retorted. "But I wouldn't bet my ass on it."

"Maybe you don't know what you are."

"Don't go looking for good where there ain't any," he warned darkly. "It's a fatal mistake."

"I think it's *your* mistake," she breathed, and then breaking every rule she knew, she kissed him.

His lips were firm and hungry. His skin beneath her fingers was hot, scorching her senses on contact.

For a lady, she could really kiss, Ryland thought raggedly, his body aching with unquenched need. Maybe he'd been wrong all along. Maybe she was indeed a soiled dove, but only a high-class version of the breed. Maybe she had done this all before. Maybe . . . Maybe, he reasoned blearily. Maybe it didn't matter. Maybe there was nothing he could do to hold back the desire he felt for her. Maybe she was entirely in control of the situation, and he had no need to fight the attraction—since he could not do so much as touch her. Her jerked at his bonds, half growling in aching frustration against her mouth.

"Untie me, Katherine," he rasped, realizing that for the first time he had no intention of dragging her to safety, but instead of doing the very thing he'd vowed not to do. "Untie me."

Reality slipped slowly through the cracks in Katherine's desire. Regret followed more quickly, and she blinked. "I'm sorry." She drew her hands away, staring at them dizzily. "I cannot," she murmured, and spun away, fleeing to the safety of Dory's room.

The night was long and slow. Katherine lay on the floor of Travis's bedroom and wondered what was happening to her. She had become as brazen as a hound in heat. Perhaps it was the atmosphere—simply being exposed to such blatant carnal lust that made her act as she did. And perhaps she should flee this place before there was no turning back. But what about Ryland? She could hardly leave him here—which meant she'd be traveling with him.

She closed her eyes, the truth obvious even in her bedazzled condition. It wasn't the environment that was affecting her so adversely. It was Ryland's raw sensuality. It was his size, his masculinity, his vulnerability. Sweet heaven, it was everything about him. And now, to confuse her already flaming senses, his face was fully exposed to her gaze. And he was beautiful.

Even though his face was scarred and weathered, there was a primitive appeal about him, something that called to the most basic of her instincts, that melted her good sense and ignited every primal need she'd ever denied having.

In the darkness Katherine lay in silence, listening to him breathe and knowing beyond a shadow of a doubt that he too lay awake and listening.

To her absolute surprise Katherine found her voice much easier on the second night. Every chair was taken, and remembering Lacy's urgings, she wandered down from the stage, keeping a careful distance from the men as she wound her way through the mob.

The songs that best suited her husky voice were sentimental ballads, which happened to be the same songs that now most suited her mood. She lost herself in the emotion, forgetting the crowd, to let the music lift her from her problems.

The end of her performance came surprisingly soon, and in a moment she was behind the curtain again. The other girls waited only a few minutes and then rushed onto the stage for their high-kicking line dances.

Katherine stood in silence, watching the performance from backstage, delaying her return to Travis's room. Being near him was becoming too dangerous. Too tempting. And yet she couldn't set him free, for he had vowed to take her away with him when he left, and the proximity of his person was the very thing that threatened her most.

There was only one thing to do. She must convince him it was her wish to stay. She must send him safely on his way.

She planned quickly, scowling down at her silver slippers and moving rapidly down the darkened hall, lost in thought.

The man came from out of nowhere. One moment she was hurrying toward Dory's room, and the next she was crushed up against a body that reeked of indistinguishable odors.

His hand covered her mouth, while her body was pressed back against his. "Hello, Princess," he crooned. "I've been waitin' t' meet you. Saw you last night. Couldn't wait no longer, and now I won't have t'. Look at that empty room just fer us." He had captured one arm behind her back and prodded her toward Dory's room.

Katherine felt panic rise like putrid bile in her throat. Dear God, no! Her legs felt like wooden spikes, barely able to bear her weight. Her heart pounded a chaotic message of terror.

"You ready, Princess?" her captor ground in her ear, and she whimpered, the broken sound escaping weakly between his filthy fingers.

"Can't wait, huh?" He chuckled wickedly. "Just a little longer." He pressed her toward the door.

Katherine's mind spun in a widening circle. There was no one to save her. No one but herself. His hand rose, clawing at her low bodice, and she let the weakness take her, feeling it rise like a cloud. Her knees buckled, her head dropped.

His grip loosened, just fractionally and only for a moment, but Katherine grasped the opportunity with frantic fervor. Raising her foot, she stomped her high-heel on his instep with all the strength she could muster. His hands dropped away, and she lunged.

Freedom swelled in her face, and she was running. But he was faster and stronger. His hands reached her, and she shrieked in muffled terror as her mouth was covered again.

In the bedroom, Travis heard the scuffle and quit sawing at the ropes to listen. Who was it? Katherine was no longer singing. Raucous music lilted from below. The girls would be dancing.

"Lady?" he called loudly, worry drowning caution.

No answer came, only the shuffling of feet.

"Katherine!"

His ribs burned with premonitory pain. Images of her struggling in the hall scoured his conscience. "Katherine," he rasped, but before the sound was out, he was ripping at his already loosened bonds.

A scream sounded from the hallway—cut short in mid cry, and Travis lunged. The worn ropes broke, and suddenly he was free. In a moment he was through the door. She was there, held in the binding grip of a man about to die.

Travis slowed his pace, all attention focused on his prey, forgetting his own near nudity, not realizing the bulging, bandaged muscles displayed by his severed pants. But Katherine's captor was not so focused. His beady eyes shifted, and he stepped back a pace, dragging her along with an arm across her throat.

"Tired of living, partner?" Travis asked in low-voiced rage, his steps not faltering.

"I'm not looking for trouble," the man declared, keeping Katherine between them. "I just want the girl." He jerked on her sharply to indicate his meaning, and through the fine lace of the veil Travis could see her eyes—wide with terror.

He slowed now, steadying his breathing. She was alive,

unhurt. "How 'bout you let her go? There are other girls. More willing." Travis tried a smile, which barely moved his lips and failed to part his teeth.

The beady-eyed rat smiled grimly. "That seems fair. Only . . ." His stiletto appeared seemingly from nowhere and in a moment was pointed toward his adversary. "Only I want *her*."

Katherine watched in breathless terror. One moment Travis was there before her eyes, and the next he was not. She was twisted backward, then tossed away, and in an instant she lay half against the wall, staring at the scene before her.

As if by magic, the stiletto had changed hands. Travis held it low, cutting edge down as he gripped the man by his constricted throat. "Want her, you say?" Ryland growled, his face contorted with rage. "Want her?"

Only a strangled whine came from the other.

"Huh?" Travis shook him by the throat, lifting him from his feet to pin him like a squirming sausage against the wall. "Wanna see what it's like to never want a woman again?"

Travis's captive whimpered as the stiletto swept downward. It missed his nether parts by a hair's breadth, skimmed the inside of his thigh to cut lower, slicing through his pant leg.

Travis's hand poised again, but the man's head drooped in a dead swoon. Travis shook him once, but when there was no response, he loosened his grip, letting the body drop lifelessly to the floor.

It took Travis only a moment to cut the remainder of the ropes from his wrists. He reached for the man then, pulling a knife sheath from him. In an instant the knife was stuck securely into his waistband. "Lady." He turned quickly and knelt, gathering her into his arms. "Are you hurt?"

Katherine buried her face against the strength of his chest, feeling cold trembles shake her. It had been so close. And if Ryland hadn't come . . . She shuddered again, too terrified to cry.

"Did he hurt you?" Travis asked, touching her hair beneath the starched whiteness of the veil.

Katherine shook her head, not able to speak. Travis relaxed slightly, willing the tension to leave him.

"It's all right, lady." He stroked her like he might a fine thoroughbred. "You did good."

Somehow she found the strength to put her wooden arms around the width of his chest. Travis closed his eyes, gritting his teeth and swearing in silence. He knew better than to hold her, but found he could not let her go, for her scream still echoed in his mind.

Seconds ticked by. He soothed her gently, failing to notice the tenderness of his touch, the quietness of his voice as he felt her relax slightly.

"Katherine," he said finally, shifting her away slightly. "We have to go."

She stiffened again. "But—your leg."

"My leg's fine," he lied, for the entirety of his right side burned with pain. "We can't stay now." He nodded toward the unconscious form. "He'll tell what happened. Lacy'll have a lynch mob planted on her doorstep by morning, if not before." He pushed her to arm's length now, watching her carefully. "Unless I kill him."

"No!" She gripped his arms frantically, and he nodded finally, rising to his feet and drawing her up with him.

"All right. Then we'll leave. I'll need a shirt. Boots. And"—he glanced at his abused denims—"new pants."

"All right," she agreed, but still clung to his arms, too frightened to leave his strength.

"Go on now. And hurry. I'll see what I can find in the way of weapons."

She drew from his embrace finally, her body stiff as she skirted the downed fellow by a wide margin.

Travis remained still only until she'd rounded the corner. There was a moan from the floor, and Travis gripped the man by the front of the shirt.

"It's better than you deserve," he murmured, and, pulling back his fist, sent Katherine's attacker back into oblivion with a twitch. "Bastard," Travis finished, and hurried off in search of a more refined weapon.

Chapter 12

"You painted my horse!"

Katherine and Travis stood inches apart. A tiny flame flickered over a low wick inside the globe of a hurricane lamp, throwing shadows and light against the huge horse in the enclosed stall.

"Lacy was sure he'd be recognized," she said in a quick, apologetic tone.

"You painted my horse," he repeated.

"I saved your life," she reminded him, wondering suddenly if he might, indeed, be as dangerous as Daisy had always thought.

"You painted my goddamn horse! How could you pull such a damned fool stunt on an innocent animal?" He threw up his hands, pacing abruptly, his strides short and quick in the narrow space.

"Fool stunt!" Katherine's fists were planted on her hips as her own temper began to rise. "How dare you!"

"How dare you paint my horse?"

"Well, he's big as a barn. How were we supposed to keep him hidden?" She hissed the words at him as she leaned forward from the waist.

"Hell . . ." Travis lifted his arms in wide irritation. "Not by painting him like some goddamn lamp shade."

"Well, I beg your pardon. Perhaps I should have left him waiting on the boardwalk until you were well enough to make the decision yourself. But as it was, you weren't even coherent."

Travis leaned closer, glowering at her. "Co— what?"

97

"You weren't even—" Katherine began again, but Soldier had stuck his nose between them for the third time and doggedly refused to be pushed aside. "I thought you were in a hurry," she finished, pulling a hair of the stallion's stray forelock from her mouth.

"Damn!" Travis swore aloud, then continued to grumble as he slung blanket and saddle aboard the animal's broad back. His saddlebags were still tied before the pommel, and he straightened them efficiently as they settled against the stallion's withers. "Leave it to a woman. . . ." His voice trailed off. "Poor damn horse gotta . . ." He cinched up quickly, then checked his saddlebags. "I can't believe they'd . . ." Slipping the bit between Soldier's gargantuan teeth, Travis shook his head and patted the horse's dark nose in solemn commiseration. "Paint."

"Good heavens! You whine like a baby. It's just a little black walnut dye." She turned away, fumbling in the darkness. "You'd think a big . . ." Her voice faded off as she retrieved a small white bundle from a dark corner.

"Let's go," she said abruptly, stuffing a small lump of cloth inside the large bundle. "I thought you wanted to go."

"Jesus!" He cut short his glare to grab her by the shoulder and press her toward the stallion. "I shoulda run like hell the first second I seen you."

"And I should have spit in your eye," she hissed as he tossed her effortlessly into the saddle.

"Slide back."

She did so, but her impractical gown had not been designed for riding astride. An eerie sound of ripping seams filled the stall. "Now look what you've done," Katherine scolded. "You've ruined my gown."

"That's not a gown," Travis argued, trying to ignore the shocking amount of skin exposed as he blew out the lamp and pushed open the door. "It's goddamn trouble on the hoof."

They kept to the darkest of shadows and the muffling grass whenever possible. It was Saturday night, and although the town was at its liveliest, luck was with them. They saw only two people, both of whom were hurrying toward some destination of their own and not interested in a dark horse carrying a double load.

At the edge of town Katherine breathed a sigh of relief, realizing the tenseness of her muscles and a cramped feeling in her chest. Travis urged Soldier into a canter, heading west. In less than ten minutes they intersected the river, where Soldier lowered his head to taste the cold, swift-running water, and then they were off again, but going northeast now, traveling slowly down the center of the river.

It seemed to Katherine like a page of history she'd already lived through. Water splashed up from Soldier's big hooves, wetting his riders' feet and legs.

A mile or so slipped beneath them. The moon painted wavering shadows and glistening pictures of light upon the melodious waves, and Katherine found herself being soothed by the quiet. It was the kind of night one dreams about in the dead of winter, when harsh cold grips the earth and all the world waits for the warmth of spring.

For a time she tried to maintain some distance between herself and Ryland, but there was nowhere to put her hands without touching him, and so, with a mental sigh, she slipped her arms about his sturdy waist and rode along in continued silence.

In less than an hour they left the river. Soldier lurched out of the water, seeming glad to have solid rock beneath him again.

"Where are we going?" Katherine asked, gripping Travis more tightly to maintain her seat.

"The ranch," Travis said laconically.

"Where's that?"

"Somewhere safe."

"Can you be more specific?"

"No!" he snapped irritably.

Katherine tried to ignore him, but there was no escape from his closeness. She was offended by his words and his foul mood, and wondered grimly what would happen if she accidently hit him on the thigh she'd so carefully bandaged. She'd found pants for him, but they were considerably too small, stretching tightly over his bandaged thigh. It must burn like fire with that fabric pressing hard against the bullet wound, she reasoned, and was honest enough to admit she hoped so. He was, after all, an ungrateful lout.

It seemed an eternity had passed when Katherine's nose bumped Travis's back for the umpteen time. She woke with a start, her stiff fingers fumbling for a hold on his shirt as she realized the situation through her numbing fatigue.

They were still moving. There was a hint of light above the farthest mountains, and Soldier's steps were slow.

Glancing down, Katherine realized they had left the faint trail they'd been following and were now winding their way through the trees. The going was much harder here, slowing their progress, but she saw the wisdom of keeping under cover with the coming of day.

Hours passed. They climbed and descended, only to climb again. Sometime after noon on Sunday Katherine informed Travis she'd brought the food she'd not eaten for supper. They stopped not far from the river, where she untied her bundle. No words were spoken as they ate the Red Garter's sumptuous fare. The water from the river was icy cold as they splashed it on their faces and filled the canteen.

They continued to ride all day, eating nothing, speaking little. Katherine ached with fatigue. How long had it been since she'd had a full night's sleep? How long since she'd been able to lie her head on the pillow and know all would be well in the morning?

Her hair had been brushed and left unbound for what had turned out to be her final performance at the Red Garter. It strayed over her shoulders now, blowing into her face or feeling heavy and hot against her back, which ached from the endless hours on horseback.

Her head hurt. Her bottom was raw. And there was a crescent line of dirt beneath each fingernail.

"We're going to have to stop." Ryland's voice was low and blunt. "Horse is tired."

Thank the Lord, Katherine thought, and taking the arm Travis offered slid stiffly to the ground. He dismounted after, his movements no more graceful.

There was a large red circle in the center of his right

thigh, and Katherine grimaced, gazing at it, and bent to tend his wound.

"It's fine," he said, and turned away from her. "I'm gonna scout around, try to hunt up something to eat." He walked to his horse. "Sorry, old man," he crooned, patting the horse's heavy neck. "Gotta leave the saddle on." The horse was already grazing on the spiky grasses that grew in dense bunches beneath his feet, and didn't seem bothered by his master's words.

To Katherine, Ryland said, "Get some rest," in a tone much less gentle, and walked away.

Katherine pushed a wild strand of hair behind her ear. "What about you?" she asked, feeling fidgety and uncertain.

"Told you, I'm gonna try to find something to eat."

She took a quick step after him, realizing suddenly that her high-heeled slippers were not well suited for this rocky terrain and finding the thought of being left alone there made her nervous. He did not, however, seem to appreciate her reminder that he was in a weakened state, so she gripped her hands together and asked, "Should I build a fire?"

"Fire?" He turned slowly. His head was bare. His pants were two inches too short. There were no guns at his hips, and his hands, which he lifted now, palms upward, were empty. "Lady," he said with a stilted shake of his head. "You must think I'm one helluva hunter. Cuz I ain't got no gun." His scowl deepened. "And I ain't got no rifle. Hell! After you *ladies* at the dance hall got through with me, I'm lucky to be left with my hide in tact. Fire," he snorted, turning away. "What does she expect me to do, run down a buck or something?"

Katherine sat beside the small flame. Despite her fears, she had fallen asleep in Ryland's absence, and watched now as he turned the rabbit on a long spit over the fire.

It would be dusk in less than an hour, and Travis had insisted that they roast their meal now, before darkness, for they could not chance a fire at night, even though they were high up and surrounded by gray, jagged boulders on all sides.

He was a cautious man. Katherine watched him now. His

features were sculpted and lean. His hair was fair and swept back from his brow and ears, with streaks of dampness that attested to the fact that he had found water somewhere, perhaps even bathed. The thought made her jealous, for she felt grimy and itchy.

Curiosity, however, was her major foe. But despite that fact, she was *not* about to ask how he'd gotten the rabbit, though the question nagged at her. While it was fairly simple to deduce that he'd used the knife taken from Lacy's, and now stuck in his boot, to skin the hare, she had a bit of difficulty imagining him running the bunny down. So how had he procured their supper? She had no idea, but neither would she give him the satisfaction of asking. No. Not after his earlier boorish attitude.

"Did you find some water?" She had promised herself she would not speak to him. But that vow seemed childish now, for if she didn't talk to *him*, her options were sadly limited—Soldier being a fair listener, but not much of a conversationalist.

"Yep." Ryland nodded once, not taking his eyes from the fire.

"I'd like to wash up," she said, watching him. Every move he made seemed to have a purpose. Nothing was wasted.

"We ain't going to no Sunday social, lady."

She frowned, reminiscing about the days when he'd been comatose. "*You* washed," she reminded primly, to which he raised his eyes to hers, leveling a bland expression on her grubby face.

"It's good of you to notice."

She blushed, because she couldn't help it, although she would have given the night's meal to stop the color and deprive him of the satisfaction. She lowered her eyes, feeling suddenly hot in the stained satin gown, and pushed back a few stray hairs. "I *didn't* notice," she grumbled, feeling her nerves fray with his direct stare on her face. "I just thought something smelled better."

There was silence for several seconds, during which time she dared not look at him. And then the laughter started, low at first, and then louder.

It rumbled out from Ryland's chest until his head was thrown back and his shoulders heaved. "Lady . . ." he said finally, his voice low again between chuckles. "You been a peck a trouble." He shook his head slowly, his grin showing a partial row of straight white teeth. "But damned if you ain't full of surprises."

"And you're full of insults." She'd meant to snap the words at him, but instead the denunciation sounded frail and near tears, and she blinked once, wishing she were a man. A big man, with hard fists, and quick right jab so that she might punch Ryland right in his straight, sun-browned nose.

Silence settled between them, broken only by the stomp of one of Soldier's big hoofs and the sound of a distant woodpecker.

Katherine sat like a small child, hands curled softly in her lap. She felt foolish about her weak tone and hoped against hope that she would not cry, for surely she could not bear the humiliation of weeping in front of this insensitive clod.

"I didn't mean to be insulting." His voice was quiet.

She refused to look at him.

"I just don't know how to act around a lady."

She swallowed hard, still angry at him. "I'm not a lady." Even to her own ears the words sounded prim and perfectly modulated.

"Yeah."

She heard him turn the rabbit.

"I forget," he added, and let the silence fall again.

It was almost dark. Supper had been eaten, and Travis rummaged around in his saddlebags now, momentarily forgetting what he was looking for as he stared at Katherine's back.

It was nearly bare and looked smooth and soft, gently curved as she hunched before the flame, and slightly pinkened by the sun.

This was not good. His leg hurt like hell, he was exhausted, and his stomach still rumbled with hunger. Yet Katherine Amelia Simmons was all he could think about.

Damn it all, he should have taken advantage of all the nights on that comfortable bed he'd occupied at the Garter.

He should have slept day and night. But the truth was, she'd distracted him then, too.

Before the fire she shifted her weight slightly, momentarily showing her profile.

Damn, she was beautiful. But too good for him.

His loins ached.

Or *was* she too good? She swore she was not. In fact, she proclaimed herself to be a dove. Would a woman do that if she was not one? In his fairly limited knowledge of women he had found whores more likely to proclaim themselves to be ladies than ladies to say they were whores.

Travis took a deep breath, drawing his extra shirt from his saddlebag before untying his bedroll and straightening.

Who was this woman?

There was only one way to find out.

Striding around the fire, he stood before her, shirt in one hand, rolled blankets in the other.

Katherine lifted her face to his, seeing his serious expression, and found she was holding her breath.

Their eyes met and caught.

"It's gonna be a cold night." He said the words stiffly.

She pushed some imaginary hairs from her face and blinked, thinking of nothing to say.

"Clouds coming in. Might see some rain." His face was tense. "Here." He extended his arm, holding out the shirt. "Cover your . . ." He stopped, cleared his throat, and scowled as he realized what he'd nearly said. "It'll keep you warmer."

She was blushing again, but reached out, determined not to drop her eyes.

"Thank you," she managed, though she was certain her flesh burned red all the way to the top of those very same body parts he had managed not to mention. Their fingers brushed, with his garment held immobile between them.

"Katherine Amelia Simmons," he murmured, his tone low and strained. "Who are you?"

Though a moment ago she had fought to keep her gaze from the ground, now she could not lower it, could not break contact with his sky-blue eyes. She struggled for an answer, but could find none, not sure any longer exactly who she was.

Quiet lay between them, settled snugly against his shirt, which they both still grasped.

Ryland watched her, trying to read her soul, to understand, for he wanted her like he'd never wanted another and longed to hear from her own lips that she was not so far above him that he could not even dream.

And yet . . . Did he truly want to hear she was soiled?

No! Better to know the truth. That she was a lady—untouchable.

"You weren't with Patterson." He said the words as a statement, though he had not meant to.

It took Katherine a moment to understand his words, to realize the implication, to remember Daisy's predicament.

She nodded. "Yes, I was."

His jaw tensed and his fingers tightened on the faded red shirt as he drew a deep breath and let the silence lie.

"Then what's your price?" he asked finally, his tone so low she could barely hear him.

Price? She blinked again, finding he had abandoned the shirt and drawing it slowly to her nearly bare bosom. "Price?"

"For a night," he explained, his eyebrows low over his intense eyes. "What's your price?"

Her pink, little mouth, Travis noticed, formed a perfect circle as she said the word "oh" silently. He waited. The fire crackled behind him, warming the back of his legs. The sun sank lower, and still he waited. They stared at each other. Ryland's heart thumped in his chest. An owl called from downhill somewhere.

"Jesus, woman!" he stormed suddenly. "We could be done with the whole damn thing before you decide on a price."

"Two . . . two hundred!" she called, like a frenzied bid to a money-happy auctioneer.

Travis's jaw dropped. "Two hundred?" he asked in disbelief. "Dollars?"

Katherine swept back a dark tress and stood quickly, feeling stiff and breathless. "That's right." She raised her chin with defiance and forced pride. "Two hundred dollars a night."

"Two hundred damned dollars a night!" Travis still gaped in disbelief.

Katherine wrung the shirt in her hands, feeling her breath catch in her throat and taking a stilted step in reverse. "Too high?"

He snorted out loud, then shook his head. "Lady, at your prices I can't afford to shake your damned hand."

"Oh." Her mouth formed a circle again, as did her eyes. "Sorry," she chirruped with a shrug, but suddenly realized that she truly was, for there was something about him that made her heart thump and her skin goose-bump.

She hugged his shirt to her chest now, smoothing out the wrinkles she'd wrung into it and feeling the softness of the well-worn garment. "Well . . . good night then."

He snorted again, passing his bedroll to his other hand as he turned, muttering, "Hell! Can't afford to say good night! Can't afford to lace her shoe. I probably already owe my soul for them damned kisses."

Katherine watched him disappear into the trees. She was exhausted, and certainly wouldn't mind being left alone. She crossed her arms over her bosom now. The temperature was beginning to drop.

Rubbing her hands briskly, Katherine glanced about and realized that she would not have a blissful sleep. In fact, she wouldn't sleep at all.

For Travis Ryland had all the blankets.

Chapter 13

"Ryland," Katherine whispered, not touching him as she knelt down to call his name. "Ryland." His back was to her, and he had three beautiful blankets wrapped snugly around him.

She coveted them. She needed blankets to sleep. It had been true ever since she was a child. Even during the dog days of summer she needed at least a sheet to snuggle under. It was a type of security. Perhaps she should have outgrown the need, but she had not. And so she knelt now, teeth chattering as she dared to touch his arm.

"Mr. Ryland."

He turned over finally.

The moon was hidden behind a fat layer of clouds, but she could see his eyes were open. He had been awake long before she called to him.

"Is there something I can do for you, Miss Katherine?" he asked now, smiling as he bent his arms to place his palms casually beneath his head and watch her from the lovely comfort of his blankets.

She had braided her hair and tied it with a small strip of fabric torn from the bundle she had carried food in. Grasping the chunky braid now, she squeezed it in stiff fingers.

"I'm cold."

"Really?" His tone sounded no more than mildly interested. "It hasn't even started raining yet."

"And I can't sleep without a blanket."

"Is that so?" He gazed at the inky sky overhead. "Well,

hell, lady, I'd give you one of mine, but . . . I can't afford the privilege."

"I'll pay." She had known he'd be difficult. He was a difficult man. A difficult man that she'd like to punch in the nose. But exhaustion had taken its toll, and though she'd fought her weakness for several hours, she had now determined that one single blanket was worth all of the few hard-earned coins she now clutched in the cloth in her frigid left hand. "How much do you want?"

He drew a loud, noisy, martyred breath, and paused. "How much have you got?"

"Two and a half dollars."

Travis raised his brows and shook his head. "Ain't much for a woman who demanded two hundred dollars a night. Guess business ain't been so good, huh?"

"Listen, Ryland . . ." She didn't know exactly what she was about to say, but decided to tell the truth. "I'm very cold, and I need one of your blankets."

"I'm willing to barter."

"What?"

"I said"—he raised himself up on his elbows to stare at her from closer range—"I'm willing to barter."

"Barter what?" She leaned away from him, feeling the breath leave her body.

"What have you got?"

"I told you." She scowled. "I've got two dollars and fifty cents."

Ryland remained still for just a moment, then shook his head slowly, as if he almost regretted his refusal. "Won't do."

"Please, Ryland." She knew she was practically begging, but the difficulty of simple survival was beginning to wear on her nerves.

"You don't need to sound so desperate, lady," he said in an even tone. "Way I see it, a woman like you is worth a small fortune."

"What do you mean?" She knew what he meant, of course, but it seemed a likely question, something to buy her some time.

"Well now, lady—two hundred a night. And here my blankets are only worth, well—maybe fifty."

"Fifty! Dollars!" Katherine spat, outraged.

"Too high?" he asked, mimicking her earlier tone.

"They couldn't be worth more than a dollar," she said, ignoring his budding smile and trying to act businesslike.

"Well now," said Travis, obviously warming to the game. "That's not true. They're wool. Wool comes from sheep. And when was the last time you seen sheep in these parts. Nope." He shook his head. "These here blankets are mighty precious. Specially . . ." A quartet of cold raindrops slapped Katherine on her face. "Specially tonight."

Katherine tried to think of a way out of this mess as another drop splattered against her bare skin, pinging hard off her sunburned back. "I'll get more money eventually, and when I do, I'll pay you back."

"Lady." He leaned forward suddenly, his brows lowered now, his form tense. "You ain't listening. I don't want your money," he said, forcing a tight smile. "But like I said—I'm willing to barter."

"What do you want?" The words were whispered.

Silence.

"I don't mean to find fault, lady," Ryland said finally, "but maybe you're in the wrong business if you ain't figured out what I want yet."

She swallowed, realizing she had gotten herself in too deep this time. "I can't," she whispered weakly.

He stared at her. "Beg your pardon."

"I said," she cleared her throat, praying for strength. "I just can't."

"Can't what?"

"Can't . . . You know!"

He shook his head as if puzzled, but finally he said, "Oh," and nodded. "That. No, of course you couldn't. Too expensive. But then my blankets are quite precious, too. Notice the texture." He actually lifted the upper edge to smooth it over his whisker-roughened cheek. "Soft. Warm. And look at this here stripe. It don't look like much in the dark. But you should see it in the daytime. It's right pretty. Bright red.

Like a shining apple. I've often said to myself, Travis, that's the prettiest damn stripe I've ever—"

"Ryland!" Katherine grasped him by the shirtfront. Her knuckles were pressed up against his chest, and her face was mere inches from his. "I don't give a spit about that stinking stripe. I'm hungry. I'm exhausted. I'm scared. And I'm cold. So give me that stupid blanket or . . ."

His head was slightly tilted. His brows were raised. "Or what?"

She searched for a likely threat, but the truth was, she'd flat run out of spunk. "Just give me the blanket," she pleaded.

"Now, lady," he chided gently. "You was doing so good there for a spell. All fired up like."

"I think I'm freezing to death." She nodded numbly, quite sure it was true, and fully able to imagine her blue body being delivered to her mother without so much as Ryland's cherished striped blanket to cover her deadness.

He chuckled, because he couldn't help it and because she looked so damned pathetic. "You ain't going to freeze to death, Katherine Amelia Simmons," he assured her.

"I'm not?" she whispered.

"No. I think you're going to survive everything. You got yourself quite a grip there."

She let her hand fall away from his shirt, suddenly self-conscious about how she had gripped it. "I'm sorry."

He chuckled again. "Truth is, lady, if you're gonna threaten someone, it's generally more effective if you don't go around apologizing all the time."

"I'm sorry," she repeated dejectedly.

He shook his head. "Damn. I ain't never seen a woman like you. You really a dove?"

Katherine managed a nod.

"But you ain't going to . . ." He stared at her face. It was awful pale, so he narrowed his eyes and softened his language. "You ain't going to . . . lay with me?"

He waited for an answer, but she merely stared at him, eyes wide, and he relented finally.

"Listen, lady. Don't bother saying anything. By the time

you spoke up, there wouldn't be no time left anyhow. So how 'bout a kiss and I'll share my blankets."

"One kiss?" she questioned, her eyes shining like wide pools in the darkness.

"Are you willing to do more?"

"More?"

"Never mind. Yeah. One kiss. But not no stingy bird peck. A real kiss. Are you game?"

The silence was heavy and long before she finally answered.

"Yes."

They stared at each other, eyeball-to-eyeball, before he lifted the blankets from his body in an open invitation. "Come on in."

"But we agreed to just a kiss."

"One kiss, lady," he said huskily. "And since I have the pretty striped blanket, I choose the place. You're cold. I'm comfortable. Come here."

She did, shifting closer until he had scooped the blankets around her sun-pinkened back.

They remained immobile, staring into each other's eyes, Ryland's cool and blue, Katherine's wide and nervous.

"Now what? she asked.

"Lay down."

She licked her lips. "Lie down?"

"I ain't gonna eat you up," he said gently. "Lay down."

He must have found the only soft place in the whole of the Rocky Mountains to sleep, Katherine thought, for as her back touched the bottom blanket she could not help but notice the cushiony feel of leaves beneath her.

Travis eased down beside her, pulling the blankets up over her bare arms and shifting on his side to watch her.

"Nervous?" he asked quietly.

"No," she lied, then realized her usually husky voice had squeaked. So she cleared her throat and tried again. "No," she said more evenly. "I do this sort of thing all the time."

He propped himself up on his left elbow and grinned into her face.

He had a good face Katherine admitted in silence. Deep-set eyes, blue as a mountain lake in the daylight. His mouth was generous and tilted upward at the corners now. His bone structure was broad, across his brow, his cheeks, his jaw. Broad and lean, with the whisker-stubbled skin stretched tight over his square chin.

"So . . ." He raised his brows at her. "How do you usually begin?"

"Begin?" She winced as her voice cracked again. "Begin?"

"Kissing."

"Oh. Yes." Dear Lord. She was going to die. "Of course. Kiss . . . Kissing."

"Do you prefer the bottom or top?"

"Bottom of what?"

He shook his head. "It ain't no mystery why you ain't got a lot of ready cash, lady. How long you been in this line of work?"

"Oh . . ." She found her braid and gripped it now with frantic fingers. "About three days."

Ryland raised his brows again. It was the first answer with a shred of credibility to it. "Then maybe I'd best get things rolling."

She opened her mouth to disagree, but before a sound emerged, his lips touched hers.

They were firm lips, and warm. They slanted across hers like living flame, moving, caressing, urging.

His hand had settled on her waist. His chest pressed against hers, and his right thigh, heavy with taut muscle, lay with solid familiarity across her knees.

But it was his lips and tongue that took her breath away. They skimmed and tantalized and teased, or pressed and nibbled and urged, until Katherine found her arms clasped about his broad body, with her heart thundering against his and her lips answering each parry of their own accord.

Who would have thought a kiss could feel like this— could make her forget her fatigue, her discomfort, even her hunger. Or was her ravenous appetite simply replaced by a different hunger?

He had promised not to consume her, but in truth she felt as if she might be the one to devour him, for every nerve ending in her trembling body was screaming for release. What kind of release, she didn't know, but she'd best listen or explode.

His kiss slipped away as he lightly touched her cheek with his lips, and moved down her neck! She arched against him, aching. He took a detour, lifting his hand from her waist to stroke the hair from her throat and follow his fingertips with his kisses, up her tingling flesh to her ear.

"Oh!" She said the word on a gasp, feeling she would surely explode if he did not stop and refusing to consider what she would do if he did.

He kissed her again—just behind her ear—and she shivered, squeezing her eyes shut and trying to calm her breathing. But it was no use for already he had returned to her lips.

She kissed back, forgetting about the cold, poor dead Patterson, and the damned pretty striped blanket. Katherine was simply feeling.

It was Ryland who finally pulled away.

Her arms were clasped about his back, and her breath was sounding like a freight train going uphill.

Their gazes caught, hard and bright.

"So . . . " she rasped without thought. "How long have *you* been doing this sort of thing?"

He grinned, white teeth showing in the darkness. "What'll you give me for more?"

"I've got a little establishment in Silver Ridge," she said.

He touched her cheek with gentle, callused fingertips. "Not interested."

"A new satin gown?" she bartered breathlessly. "Only worn twice."

"Now you're talking."

"But . . ." She licked her lips, knowing she'd fallen over the edge and finding she did not care. "What would I wear?" she whispered.

Travis felt as if someone had hit him in the chest with something hard and broad, for just the sight of her teasing him was enough to make his heart ache. "I can only imagine," he murmured.

"I can't," she whispered in return.

He raised his brows.

"I can't imagine what it would be like."

Stark honesty shone in her silver-blue eyes, and the ache in Ryland's chest turned to a burn. He was falling under the spell of her eyes, going beyond the understandable and acceptable lust to a deeper more dangerous level.

But he could not afford that price. He pressed back a fraction of an inch more, employing all his strength. "I guess the debt's been paid."

His tone had changed, but she didn't notice, for the thrill of his nearness was having adverse effects on her ability to think.

She licked her lips, staring into his face. "Now I'm . . . curious," she whispered. "It's been a fault of mine." Her breathing was shallow and quick. "Ever since I was a little girl. Always wondering why or how or what if."

He could imagine her as a little girl. Long, dark hair. Bubbling laughter. A book perched on her knees, reading to her little brother. But she had no little brother, and the boy he saw in his imagination was himself, curled against his sister's side like an trusting puppy.

"Here." He peeled the blankets quickly away, his movements suddenly stiff. "Take the blankets."

She blinked at his abrupt change, confused and suddenly lonely. "Did I do something wrong?"

Travis held his breath, staring at her. "You shouldn't be here."

"Why?"

"Because I can't afford the price," he said, and knew it was true. He couldn't afford the heartache, the nightmares. "Gonna be a hard day tomorrow. Go get some sleep."

She grimaced, still holding him to her. "But the blanket's so pretty. I feel I owe you . . . more." She leaned closer, touching her lips to his again.

Ryland fought the desire—and lost.

She was kissing him, her body so near, her arms tight

about him. There was nothing he could do but growl low in
his throat and press her back into his blankets.

"We hate to disturb you folks."

A voice spoke from less than twelve feet away. A rifle
cocked, the sound cold and deadly in the darkness.

"But we been looking for you half the night."

Chapter 14

It was his ribs that ached, Travis realized abruptly. It was his ribs. Not his chest.

Goddamn it! He'd been careless. He'd let Katherine's seductive beauty distract him. The fire had been left burning too long, and these men had found them. And now he would pay. Or more accurately—*they* would pay.

Moving slowly, he pushed himself to a sitting position. Beside him Katherine pressed the collar of his worn shirt close to her throat, as if the strangers could see her low neckline even through the borrowed garment.

Travis could hear her breathing, could feel her fear.

And it was his fault. His fault for allowing himself to fall under her spell, to be lulled out of his usual cautiousness.

"What do you want?" he asked now, his voice low as his mind rushed to accumulate answers. How many were there? How well armed? How dangerous?

"Well now . . ." The closest man was little more than a gangly, just grown boy, and spoke in a thoughtful tone. "I guess that depends on what you got, mister. Huh, Luke?"

From behind Travis, Luke shuffled his feet and proclaimed, "Yeah," in a voice too high pitched to deny his nervousness.

"And seeing how much time we spent a trackin' you, we'd best get somethin' pretty good outta it. Huh, Luke?"

"Yeah." Feet shuffled again.

"We didn't do it!" Katherine said abruptly, her face pale in the darkness. "We didn't."

"You didn't?" Travis could sense the man's surprise at her

117

statement. But their assailant rallied quickly enough. "Well, now, that's nice to know." He tilted his head a bit, his face well shadowed by his hat as he seemed to think for a moment. "But why should we believe you when you two are hid up here like a couple of rats?"

"Because we—"

"Lady!" Travis's voice was low but unmistakably sharp. "Shut your mouth."

She did so with a snap, not because he'd told her to, but because she knew that she was out of her element, drowning in confusion and fear, while Ryland seemed perfectly suited for the situation, calm even.

"Yeah?" the man with the rifle urged, stepping closer. "What was you saying, ma'am?"

But Katherine had now clapped her bottom lip between her teeth and refused to speak.

"I asked what you boys want?" reminded Ryland with quiet coolness.

"And I'll tell ya, since it ain't no big surprise," said the man, then laughed at his own wit. "We're outlaws." He said the words with a certain amount of unmistakable pride. "I'm Jacob. That there's Luke," he introduced, with surprising courtesy for an outlaw. "And we want money."

"I'm afraid you came to the wrong place," said Travis.

"Yeah?" Luke shuffled his feet, issuing the only word he seemed to to recall.

"Well, we'll be the judge of that," proclaimed the other. "Hand it over."

"I'm telling you, friend," said Travis in a fatherly voice, "it ain't worth your trouble. You'd be wise to head on down the mountain. Find yourself better pickings."

"I ain't your friend," Jacob said, taking another step closer. "And I'll do the deciding 'bout what's wise and what ain't. Now hand over your money!"

Tension filled the campsite, but Travis shrugged finally, seeming resigned. "Go ahead, lady, give him the coins."

"No." There was not a moment's delay before Katherine's refusal. "I won't."

Travis narrowed his eyes at her. But she missed his

threatening expression as she stared imperiously at the man with the rifle.

"It's my money. I earned it by the sweat of my brow."

"Sweat of your . . ." Travis repeated in muttered disbelief, remembering her husky, seductive voice as she sang to a horde of randy men while he sawed at the bonds she had placed on his arms. "Huh!"

"I did," she said defensively. "I earned it. It's all I've got. And I'm *not* going to give it up to"—she nodded abruptly toward the rifleman, though her gaze remained on Ryland—"a couple of underaged brigands!"

"You are the most goddamn stubborn woman I have ever met," declared Travis. "Give them the money."

"No." It was a matter of pride now. "I won't."

"Hey!" interrupted the brigand nervously. "You two quit yer squabbling or I'll . . . I'll shoot y'."

Katherine's mouth fell open. "I beg your pardon."

"You beg my . . . Hear that Luke? She begs my pardon. Don't that beat all? Just hand over the money, lady, and no one'll get hurt."

"You wouldn't shoot me." Katherine wasn't sure how she knew, but she knew. Or thought she knew. The man with the rifle seemed hardly to be any older than some of the boys she'd taught in school. While Luke, whom she had caught only a glimpse of, acted nervous enough to die on the spot.

"What'd you say?"

"I said, you wouldn't shoot me," repeated Katherine, though she was a little less certain now, since the man's tone was sounding increasingly unfriendly.

"You don't think so?" he asked.

"No." She kept her tone firm. "I don't."

He shrugged jerkily. "Maybe you're right, ma'am." He took a step nearer yet, shifting the rifle slowly so that it pointed very directly at Travis's head. "But I sure as nuts would shoot *him*."

"Good work, lady," said Travis. "I think you'll get me killed yet. It's taking you a while. But I got faith."

"You wouldn't," Katherine said to the rifleman, but her tone had become shaky.

"Wanna test me?" asked the outlaw, shuffling his feet and trying a glare.

"No!" Her answer was quick, as were her hands. She shifted around in the blankets for the little cloth pouch she had carried to Ryland in an effort to buy the very things she dug about in now. In a moment her fingers touched a metallic lump, and she drew it quickly up to show to all. "Here it is. Go ahead. It's yours."

"Bring it here."

Katherine swallowed hard. Ryland's muscles tensed against her.

"Take it to you?" she asked dubiously.

"That's right. Bring it over."

Her legs shook when she stood. She had felt secure while sitting next to Ryland's solid form, but walking through the darkness toward the shadowed gunman was entirely different.

Only a stride separated them when she reached out. Her arm trembled, rattling the coins slightly.

"Thank ye kindly, ma'am." The outlaw accepted the proffered bundle, but when she took a tentative step backward, he stopped her. "Don't you be rushin' off now. Just stay put."

Katherine froze, her heart thumping against her ribs.

The little pouch was untied with some difficulty, and he poured the coins into his hand. "Where's the rest?"

Katherine locked her trembling knees and scowled. "I had to pay for our room."

"Where's the rest?"

"I told you—" Katherine began, but Travis interrupted now.

"I've been wounded and out of work. She's had to support both of us."

"She your wife?"

"Yes," said Travis.

"No," said Katherine simultaneously.

Travis tightened his fists and swore in silence.

"So what you been doing to earn yer keep?" asked the gunman, balancing the rifle on one hip as he tried to peruse Katherine through the dimness.

"I . . ." Katherine wet her lips and contemplated a likely lie, but truths came so much easier. "I sang at a . . . at a . . ." She cleared her throat, feeling the red heat diffuse her face. "A dance hall."

"You're a saloon girl?" asked Jacob, shocked. "A soiled dove?"

Katherine stepped back as if she'd been slapped. "I am most certainly not a . . ."

"Hey, Luke, looks like we ain't out of luck after all. We got us a soiled dove. And a good-looking one, too, if my eyes ain't foolin' me."

"Come on, ma'am. Grab your belongin's. You'll be ridin' with us."

"No." She whispered the word, stepping quickly back. "No. I . . ."

Travis shifted slightly.

"And you. Stay put," ordered Jacob.

"Sure." Ryland's tone was casual. "Been a hard day. I ain't going nowhere."

"You don't care if we take her?"

Ryland shrugged. "I don't deny she's one helluva kisser. But she talks too much for my taste."

"Well . . ." Jacob laughed. "We don't mind a little talk, huh, Luke? Let's go, lady."

"No. No. I . . . Mr. Ryland." Katherine turned slightly, finding Travis's face in the darkness. "Don't let them. I . . ."

"Did I mention she's got the pox?" Travis asked conversationally.

"The pox!" cried Jacob. "She's got the pox!"

"Yeah. 'Fraid so," said Travis. "But she's still a helluva kisser, and if you don't mind her babbling, she ain't half bad—"

"She's got the damn pox?" barked the gunman.

"Yeah," said Travis again.

"Gawd. Luke. Grab his horse. Let's get out of here."

"Horse?" Travis's voice had dropped a notch.

Jacob backed away another step, waving his rifle slightly. "We ain't leavin' here empty-handed. So you stay put, or I'll . . ."

Ryland charged like a trained cowhorse to thud his solid weight against Jacob. The rifle fell from his fingers. Luke's hands shot into the air as he surrendered.

Travis stood over Jacob's body, and picked up the rifle.

"Take my damn horse, will you?" he asked.

The gunman whimpered, and looked even more like a young boy.

"Damn sniveling pups," muttered Ryland, and leaning forward grasped the man by the shirtfront and dragged him effortlessly over to Luke.

Katherine hurried stiffly behind. "What are you going to do to them?"

"Drown 'em," Ryland said evenly, and reached for them.

Jacob and Luke went pale and cowered away.

"You can't drown them!" gasped Katherine, grabbing his arm. "We'll have to turn them into the authorities."

Travis waited a fraction of a second before snorting. "Now, there's a good plan, lady. First-rate."

She licked her lips, seeing the problem with that decision. "All right. We won't. But you can't drown them."

"Listen," Travis whispered in her ear. "I been shot. I been hunted. I been threatened. I'm hungry. I'm sore. And I'm tired." He glanced at the would-be outlaws, then turned back to Katherine. "Let me have my fun without making such a fuss."

Katherine barely nodded, and Travis walked back to Jacob and Luke.

"Please," Jacob said. "Don't drown us."

Travis's glare darkened. "Why not?"

"Cause we . . . we ain't ready to die. Please." Jacob said again, apparently unable to help himself. "We won't do it again."

"Won't do what again?"

"Steal. We won't steal."

"Who sent you?" Travis asked gruffly, leaning closer.

"Sent us?" There was honest surprise in Jacob's tone. "No one sent us. We was just hungry. And——"

"How do I know you're telling the truth?"

Jacob came woodenly to a sitting position. "We didn't

even have no bullets in the rifle. Take a look. I swear it's true."

"No bullets?" Travis said, thinking the statement too pathetic to be a lie. "You ain't got no damn bullets?"

"No. We didn't want to hurt no one."

Travis leaned closer, arms crossed, waiting for the real reason why they had no bullets.

"And . . . And . . . this don't seem t' be our line of work. There was an Injun fella few weeks back. We pissed him off pretty good." He swallowed hard. "Thought he was gonna take our scalps."

Travis narrowed his eyes, shifting his gaze to Luke, who failed to do so much as nod.

"Indian?" Ryland asked quietly.

"Yeah. Drivin' a herd of fat cattle. We was hungry then, too. Thought we'd help ourselves to a little beef." Jacob's eyes were huge in his pale face. "Won't do that again."

"This Indian. How'd he look?"

"Big and mean! Like he'd just as soon eat us alive. Kinda like . . ." He swallowed again. "Kinda like you . . . only darker."

"Where'd you see him?"

"Ten, maybe twelve days north of here."

Travis remained still, glaring at them and thinking.

"Please don't kill us, mister."

Drawing himself from his thoughts, Travis bent down, now eye-to-eye with Jacob. "Where're your horses?"

"We only got one."

"Jesus!" exclaimed Travis, nearing the end of his patience. "Then, goddamn it, where's your *horse*?"

"Back there—in the trees. But you ain't gonna take old Buck, are y'? He was our pappy's."

"Damn it all," swore Ryland. "Lady. Get their horse."

Katherine did so, feeling her way through the darkness to find an ancient white gelding tied to a tree.

Travis snorted derisively when she led the mount up to him and eyed the poor old animal with a shake of his head. "Get on the horse."

"You're letting us go?" Jacob whispered, seemingly unable to believe their good fortune.

"Just get on the damned horse," Travis snapped irritably at the two men, and they did so with surprising haste.

"Could we have the rifle back?" ventured Jacob. "It was Pap's, too."

"Get the hell out of here!" yelled Ryland. "And if I ever hear of you two causing trouble again, I'll drown you no matter what the woman says. You hear?"

"Yeah."

"Yeah," piped Luke.

"And find yourselves another profession," ordered Ryland. "Cause you're sad excuses for outlaws."

"Yes, sir."

"Y-yeah," managed Luke, his voice bobbling with gratitude.

"Jesus!" Travis snorted, then, "Go on! Goddamn it! Get the hell out of here."

It was truly amazing how fast that white gelding could retreat with a double load.

Silence took the campsite, and Travis turned, finding Katherine in the darkness.

"You were going to let them take me," she said in disbelief.

"But look at it this way," he replied. "They ain't so dim as they seemed. Cause they left you here with me."

Chapter 15

"You would have let them take me," Katherine repeated blankly. "You wouldn't have raised a hand—not a hand—if they hadn't threatened to take your horse."

Travis shrugged, watching her closely in the darkness. "Old Soldier and me, we go way back."

"B-but . . ."

She was beginning to sputter, he noticed—a sure sign of upcoming hysterics.

"But they could have . . . They might have . . ." Katherine clutched the front of her borrowed shirt in a shaky hand, feeling sick. "They thought I was a soiled dove," she whispered.

"Lady," he said evenly, "you *said* you was a soiled dove."

"They might have . . ." she tried again, but still the words wouldn't come. "Might have—"

"Damn it, woman!" He was across the distance in an instant, suddenly grabbing her arms in his large, hard hands. "And what about me?" He shook her now, all the fear he'd felt for her swamping his system. "What about me? What do you think I would do to ya? What makes you think you're safer with me? What makes you such a fool? Jesus, woman!" He drew a deep breath, calming his nerves though his grip was still hard. "If you had a hair of sense, you'd of rode off with them. Cause I'm telling you now, them two would have been a long shot safer than me."

He stared at her, trying to read her emotions, to shake some sense into her, to rid himself from the dull pain in his heart. What if *real* outlaws had found them. *Real* men with

125

real weapons! God knew the mountains were full of them. Desperate men with nothing to lose. What if she'd been hurt? What if . . .

"I think I'm safe with you," she said, her eyes luminous in the still night.

Travis remained silent, absorbing her words before he tightened his grip just fractionally. "Well don't."

"But I do."

"Don't!" he rasped. "Do you hear me? I ain't to be trusted. I ain't what you think." He dropped his hands away suddenly, holding them in tight fists at his side. "Some damn puppy to trot along by your side on a string. Jesus, lady! I've killed more men than you've seen. I've killed more men than you can name! You hear me? Do you?"

The night seemed to reverberate with his words.

"Yes." Her answer was no more than a whisper.

"Then why the hell are you still here?" he asked, leaning forward from the waist.

"Where else could I go?" she asked softly.

"Back east."

"I'm innocent, but there are men out there who are trying to kill me. You think I can just ignore that fact? That I can disappear back to my old life and pretend nothing happened?"

"Lady," he said softly, "I think you'll be lucky to have any kind of life at all when this is over. So you better take your best chance, and that means leaving here."

"Well, I won't." Her voice was surprisingly firm. "I'll see my name cleared, with your help or without it."

He glared at her in silence before swearing with verve and turning on his heel.

How had this all come about? he wondered. Why was he saddled with this damnable woman who lacked the wits to fear him?

Because she'd hung on to his stirrup like a tick to a hound's neck, that's why. Because she was the most stubborn piece of human flesh to ever walk the earth. Because she was determined to drive him insane.

"Ryland?" she called softly.

He didn't answer.

"Mr. Ryland? What's the pox?"

He groaned and looked to heaven, hoping for an answer.

"I was just curious," explained Katherine. "It surely seemed to put the fear of God into those two . . . outlaws. It was quite a clever ploy of yours I see now. And I was thinking. Do you suppose it would be so effective every time? That is to say, this might be the answer to all our problems. Is it a highly contagious disease? I mean, if I wore a sign, or something, proclaiming myself to be a carrier of the pox, perhaps everyone would give us a wide berth. Maybe . . . Maybe," she said, her perfectly modulated voice filled with excited hopefulness, "maybe the people of Silver Ridge would eventually hear of my horrid disease. Naturally they would assume you had contracted it from me. And that we would both die soon. So they'd leave us in peace. Forget the entire incident with Mr. Patterson." She paused, sounding breathless. "What do you think?"

Ryland closed his eyes. "I don't deserve this," he said flatly, turning away with a shake of his head. "No matter what I've done—I don't deserve *this*."

Katherine watched him roll himself in his blankets. "Aren't you going to tell me what it is?"

There was a pause before, "No."

"Why not?" she asked persistently.

"Because I don't want to."

Katherine scowled, licked her wind-dried lips, and wrung her braid. "Have I told you yet that I'm a very curious person?"

"Have I told you yet to shut up?"

"I need to know what it is Ryland," she said, her tone becoming snooty with his offensive attitude. "I'm concerned now that I might truly have the disease. What are the symptoms?"

Travis turned slowly, his face barely visible in the darkness. "Lady," he said gently, "shut the hell up."

She didn't know why she started crying. But the fear the outlaws had caused suddenly seemed to bubble to the surface.

The forest was silent except for Katherine's sniffles. Travis lay stiffly in his blankets, trying not to listen to the soft sounds that came from Katherine's direction. Not far away an owl called, and another answered back. Travis tried to concentrate on the sounds of the midnight woods, but found he could not. He waited, nevertheless, remaining still and cursing himself for his weakness.

"Don't cry," he finally said, his tone harsher than he'd intended.

She sniffled softly, then straightened her back. "I'm not."

Travis closed his eyes and tried not to smile, but he could not resist. Despite everything, she had backbone. "What are you doing then?"

"I'm cursing you under my breath."

"Really?"

"Yes. Goddamn it!" she railed, and then hiccuped.

He knew he should ignore her. But he couldn't, and suddenly he was behind her, pulling her wooden body against his. "Everything's all right. They're gone. You're safe."

"Through no fault of mine," she sniffled.

He smiled over the top of her head and, to his own utter amazement, felt himself begin to relax. "True," he said. "But I'm a hell of a man, huh?"

She didn't respond for a while, but spoke finally, her voice soft. "What would I have done if you hadn't been here?"

"Then you wouldn't have been here either, would you, lady?"

"But if I had been . . ." Her words trailed off.

"But I was. I was here. I'm still here." His smile turned to a scowl. She was soft as a globe of downy seeds under his hands. "Still here, lady."

Katherine relaxed a bit against his hard chest, drawing upon his strength, marveling at his composure, and wondering with sudden doubtfulness if he really would have let the outlaws take her—even if they hadn't mentioned the horse.

"Ryland." Her voice was soft and low-pitched. "I'm cold."

He remained still, waiting until the hammering passed from his heart. The pain that her softness caused. And then he shifted slightly, still keeping his arm around her as he urged her toward his bedroll.

They lay down together, neither mentioning propriety, and then he kissed her. Not passionately now, but gently, touching her cheek as he did so and drawing away soon after.

"You're a very beautiful lady," he said softly.

Katherine remained very still, feeling breathless. "I'm no lady," she reminded him, thinking of nothing better to say.

He shook his head. "You're the poorest liar I've ever met in my life."

Katherine considered apologizing, then tried to be offended, and finally settled on a grin.

"Ryland?" She had let her hand slip to his back so that she could feel every shift and bulge of that muscular expanse.

"Why not call me Travis?" he asked evenly.

"All right." She touched her tongue to her upper lip, feeling self-conscious. "I'll call you Travis. Trav, for short."

Trav! Not since Rachel—not since innocence—had he been called Trav.

Ryland let the pain and worry rip through him before trying to free himself of it. "It'll be a helluva day tomorrow." He closed his eyes, and Katherine felt him draw away.

"Travis?"

"What?"

"Did I say something wrong?"

"Jesus," he responded, his eyes still closed, trying not to see the little girl in the sunflower yellow dress. "Go to sleep."

"Who used to call you Trav?" she asked softly.

God! The pain was right there! Undiminished after all these years. All the pain. All the bewilderment. All the fear! Right there for her to see.

"Don't go looking for good in me, lady. It ain't to be found."

Katherine waited, watching him, and then, because she couldn't help it, she touched his face, ever so gently, like the taste of a forbidden fruit. Her fingers shimmied over the stubble on his jaw, feeling the roughness that had scraped her face earlier. "They said there was no good in Prince either," she informed softly.

Travis knew that if he had a lick of sense he wouldn't ask. "Prince?" he intoned dryly.

"Stray dog." Katherine nodded. "He limped up to our house one summer night. He was supposed to be a tawny-gold color." Travis's hair was long, well past his collar, and could definitely be described as tawny-gold. She pushed a lock of it back now. "His fur was rather a sooty tan when I first saw him," she continued. "He was missing one eye. And he'd snarl if anyone came near."

"Prince," Travis repeated dully and opened his eyes.

"Yes." Katherine caught his gaze with her own and smiled directly into their brilliant turquoise depths. "Maybe I'll call you Prince."

"Jesus!" Travis said with an outraged snort, and turned away.

"Ryland," Katherine whispered, her throat constricted, her heart thumping wildly in her chest. "Ryland, I think I heard a sound."

The knife was in Travis's hand before she finished speaking, and though he remained lying down, she could feel that every muscle was tensed, every sense alert.

"Where?" He asked the question in a voice so deep and low she could barely hear him. Her own answer, however, was not even spoken. Raising a shaky hand she pointed toward her left. Ryland's right fist tightened around the knife handle as he raised his left index finger to his lips in a signal for silence.

Travis rose, stealthy as a cat, knife poised, silent on stockinged feet.

Katherine's breath had stopped. Fear made her want to reach out to snare Ryland back to her side. But she did not dare. And yet she refused to remain alone, and so she rose after him, her legs stiff, her stomach churning.

He turned at the sound of her rising, then motioned subtly for her to stay. Katherine shook her head. The movement was just barely visible in the darkness. Ryland scowled, motioned again.

She shook her head.

He gritted his teeth, swore in silence, and reaching out, he pulled her close behind him.

Katherine scrunched up to his rear, feeling the heat of his body, the tension of his form. And so they sidled forward, slipping to the nearest boulder to flatten there, listening. She shadowed his every action. Moving only when he moved, breathing when he breathed.

No unusual sound met their ears. They waited a moment longer, then slid a silent step forward. Nothing. Another step. The curved edge of the boulder neared. One more step and . . .

Katherine's scream pierced the night.

Ryland's knife hand flashed upward.

And Soldier, scared witless, tossed his big head above the boulder's top and reared.

"Damn!" Travis swore, lowering the knife and leaning heavily against the rock. "Damn it, lady. You nearly made me stab my own horse!"

She was crouched behind him, but managed now to peek over one bulky shoulder. "Your horse?" she squeaked.

Ryland did not answer her, but reached up to soothe the stallion.

Katherine, however, was still in no mood to be left behind, and clung to his arm like a blood-sucking leach.

Soldier backed away, looking offended.

"Damn it, woman, let go," Ryland ordered.

Katherine shook her head spasmodically, causing Travis to turn slightly, looking down at her as she clung to his sleeve.

"There ain't nothing out there."

"How do you know?" Katherine whispered, her eyes not leaving the shadows beyond the boulders.

"I know," he assured.

"How?" she questioned.

"I just do."

"How?" she asked again, louder now, and straightening as curiosity about his certainty overcame her fear.

"Just do."

"But—"

"My ribs don't hurt! All right?" Travis stormed. "They don't hurt."

Yanking his arm from her grip, he stepped toward the horse.

"Your ribs?" Katherine remained where she was, watching as Soldier finally came forward to accept Ryland's rough pats and rumbled assurances.

"What have your ribs got to do with anything?"

"Forget it, lady," Travis ordered.

"Is it a kind of premonition?"

"No!" Travis spat, to which Soldier tossed his head, making his master lower his voice again. "No. It's not some damned premonition. It's a couple of pellets scraping against my bones."

"But I should think——"

Travis turned suddenly, his entire being tense, his brows lowered in fatigued anger. "I don't give a good goddamn what you think, lady. Just believe me when I say I ain't the kind to die in my sleep." With that he strode back to his bedroll.

Katherine remained as she was, Ryland lied down, and Soldier shuffled a few steps closer to reach his nose tentatively toward Katherine.

She wet her lips, still made nervous by the large horse, but she managed to reach out to fondle one long ear. He tilted his head, enjoying the caress.

Standing there in the darkness, scratching the stallion's drooping ear, Katherine realized her foolishness. He was not a frightening animal. And yet she'd been scared nearly out of her wits. She straightened her back slightly, thinking. She'd made a spectacle of herself—wakening Ryland, clinging to his arm, screaming in poor Soldier's face.

But she wasn't used to this kind of life. She wasn't accustomed to being scared, cold, hungry, and dead tired—and she didn't particularly care for it. And if she wanted to live through the experience, something was going to have to change.

Patting Soldier's neck with finality, Katherine found her braid with both hands and marched off to Travis's bedroll.

"Mr. Ryland."

He didn't answer.

"Mr. Ryland." She knelt now, causing the large shirt to droop over the pale satin gown as she touched his arm. "I need to talk."

He didn't moan or speak. He only covered his eyes with one hand, hoping she was yet another nightmare.

"Travis . . ." Katherine sat back on her heels, knowing she had gotten his attention. "You must teach me how to throw a knife."

Try as he might, Travis couldn't ignore her. He couldn't ignore her and he couldn't drown her.

"What?" he asked dubiously, rolling to his back slowly.

Katherine wet her lips, feeling a bit more self-conscious now that he was looking at her. "I need to learn how to handle a knife—like you do."

He didn't speak—just stared at her.

"Well, I mean. Look at the situation. I'm a wanted woman. But I'm . . ." She waved a wild hand. "I'm innocent. And yet I must fear for my life every moment. And you . . ." She leaned forward suddenly, so that her face was less than a full twelve inches from his. "You are so . . . capable." She nearly whispered the word, then shivered, remembering. "I need to learn to protect myself."

From behind her Soldier snorted. Travis's eyes did not shift from Katherine's face. His body did not move. "I'm only going to say this once, lady, so listen good," he said with finality. "I'll be dead and damned before I ever— *ever*—put a knife into the hands of a woman!"

Chapter 16

"It ain't gonna bite you, lady." Striding up behind Katherine, Travis gripped her hand that held his knife. "You're holding it like its a coiled rattler. You gotta tighten your fist and jab."

He did so now, bearing her hand along as they stabbed the smooth bark of an innocent aspen. "You stab. Yank. Then stab again. Before he's got a chance to get you."

Katherine was trying hard to concentrate, but Travis was standing too close, making it hard to remember everything he said. She chanced a glance over her shoulder at him. "I was thinking more of learning how to *throw* the weapon."

Damn, her eyes were big. Cool, entrancing blue, and fathomless as the very heavens. He'd been a fool to agree to try to teach her to use a knife, of course. She was a woman, after all, and women couldn't fight. And yet, it was that very fact that had made him choose his present course.

It had been one hell of a night. Tired as he was, he'd not slept after the Soldier scare. Instead, he'd lain awake, staring into the darkness, listening until he knew she was asleep. Then he'd turned to watch her.

Innocence was written all over her face, and it had made him ache to touch her. But he had not. Instead, he had struggled with what to do. Teach me to throw a knife, she had said. Ridiculous. She was too soft, too young, too lovely.

But were they not the perfect reasons to teach her some kind of self-defense?

135

"You can't learn to throw it till you learn to jab," he said, trying to draw himself from her eyes.

She blinked, feeling her heart beat hard against her ribs. "But I couldn't *stab* someone."

He raised a brow at her. "But you *could* throw a knife at him?"

"Well, it would seem less—personal," she explained.

He watched her for a second longer, then shook his head slowly and murmured, "Damnedest whore I've ever met."

They were so near. Katherine could feel his hard shoulder pressed against her back. She licked her lips, knowing her face was pink, if not from the sun, surely from his proximity. "I wish you wouldn't call me that."

"What?" His hand still held hers.

"A . . ." She paused, trying to catch her breath. "A . . ."

"Whore?" he supplied softly.

"Yes."

"Why?"

She blinked, wondering if she was forgetting to breathe again. "Because it makes me feel rather . . ."

He waited.

She failed to finish.

"Like a whore?" he supplied.

She nodded.

He grinned slowly, as if he'd made a point. "You said you was one. Remember?"

Katherine scowled slightly, thinking hard. "Well, yes. But that doesn't mean I like to be called that."

"Why don't you tell me the truth?"

She stared at him, her body stiffening. "Truth?"

"You ain't no dove."

Katherine remained silent, watching him. This had been the longest month of her life, and she found now that she ached to tell him the truth. To lay her problems on his shoulders, to lay her head against his hard chest and cry. "I *was* the one with Patterson," she whispered, remembering Daisy's predicament and her own vow to protect her.

Travis gritted his teeth. She was the most damnably stubborn woman he had ever met. "You don't know what you're in for, lady. You think this is some kind of storybook adventure. But it ain't. This is real life. This involves money. Missing money. And lots of it. The people of Silver Ridge paid out their hard-earned cash to get themselves rid of Dellas and his boys. But the money turned up gone. And Dellas didn't. They need someone to blame." He pulled on her hand lightly, turning her toward him. "They're blaming me." His gaze still held hers as they stood face-to-face now. "I'm gonna get you to Latigo's. And you're gonna stay there. Hear me? You're gonna stay there safe until there ain't no Dellas no more. Then you're gonna head east."

Somehow just hearing the words made Katherine breathe more easily. Home. She could see it in her mind's eye. Could imagine her mother's embrace. The white, frilly coverlet that adorned her bed. But somehow it was no longer where she belonged.

"No." That single word came hard, but all her life she'd done what she'd been told to do, and where had it gotten her? "You're planning on going after Dellas, aren't you?"

"That ain't your concern."

"It's my life, too. You can't protect me forever."

"Protect you!" His laugh was harsh, and he gripped her arms in callused hands. "I can't protect you for one day, lady. That's what I'm trying to tell you. Not her. Not you. Never!"

She tried to speak, but his face was so near hers, so filled with rage and frustration, and something more. Fear. But fear of what? "Who was Rachel?" She whispered the question, unable to stop it.

He didn't speak, but his grip loosened and he seemed to pull inside himself. "I can't protect you, lady."

"Who was Rachel?" she murmured again.

His eyes bore into hers. "She was an innocent." His hands slid down her arms, taking the knife from her. "Like you."

Katherine could not pull her gaze from him. So much sadness there. So much pain.

She reached out, touching his face. It was rough with stubble, lined with wear and fatigue. "We're innocent, Travis. There must be a way to prove it if we work together."

He wanted to hit something, to feel something crumble

beneath his fist. Every muscle tightened. Every tendon stood taut as memories assailed him. Death! So much of it. But he would not allow her to die, even if he had to lock her away for an eternity.

"All right." He nodded once. "We'll stay together. But you'll do exactly what I say. Hear me? Exactly."

She remained silent, watching him.

"We gotta change the way you look. First we cut your hair."

Katherine grasped her heavy braid in sun-pinkened hands. "My hair?"

"Changing your mind already, lady?"

Katherine swallowed hard and raised her chin. In twenty-one years she'd never cut her hair. But neither had she been accused of murder. "Cut away," she said stiffly.

Travis scowled. She was crazier than he was. A woman's hair was her glory—a symbol of her femininity. Hell, there were folks who considered cutting a woman's hair to be a sin. "You don't care?"

"No."

She was a terrible liar. He lifted the knife, judging the edge with his thumb. "All right." He stepped behind, pulling her braid with him.

Katherine closed her eyes.

He stood, blade hefted.

Time slipped past.

"What are you waiting for?" She was tense as a tree now, her mouth pursed.

"I'm waiting for you to come to your damn senses and tell me you'll go back home to your mama, where you belong," Travis rasped.

"Well, I won't." Katherine remained as she was, her head tilted slightly back. "Cut."

Travis put the blade to the top of her braid, made several quick strokes, and the dark, silken rope of hair came away in his hand.

"Well . . ." Katherine nodded stiffly. "Good. Now what?"

"Get ready to ride." He turned woodenly, feeling more the murderer than he ever had.

It took only a moment for him to bridle Soldier. A bit longer to roll the blankets and tie them behind his saddle.

"You ready?" He turned toward her slowly, still frowning.

Katherine stood like a pillar of salt, one hand lifted to her bare neck, her silvery eyes wide.

"Lady?" he questioned gruffly.

"Papa liked my hair." Her words sounded hollow. "Sometimes I thought it was the *only* thing he liked about me."

Travis remained as he was, stricken with the sudden knowledge that she was no less beautiful without her long hair, no less desirable.

"Lady." Travis said the word softly, knowing better than to get caught in her eyes. "Get on my horse."

"He said I looked just like Mother when she was a girl."

Travis tightened his fists. "We gotta get riding."

"She was only twelve when they met." Katherine smiled wistfully. "Her hair was loose and she'd put daisies in it. Papa said she was pretty, even though vanity was a sin." Her smile dropped away, and she looked lost. "He was a very practical man."

Travis knew he should stop her, should drag her to the horse and insist they ride. But he, too, could imagine a young beauty with raven hair. Rachel had been twelve when she'd died. "Listen, lady," he said softly.

"It's nothing." Her fingers slid down her pale neck. Her gaze dropped to the ground. "Just a little hair."

"Don't—"

"Not important," she said, turning quickly as if to search the site for any forgotten items.

Travis watched her. Her shoulders jerked, but stiffened quickly. He scowled and closed his eyes. But he felt her sadness, nevertheless. He was behind her in a moment.

"Katherine."

It was one of the few times she'd heard him use her Christian name. She turned stiffly, like a child needing a hug. "It's all right. Really," she said, swiping her eyes with the back of her hand.

He shifted uneasily. "I thought you didn't care."

"I don't," she sniffed, feeling maverick tears slip to his shirt and spread between them. "It's nothing."

He found the nerve to touch the ragged ends of the ebony locks, knowing he was testing his own control by doing so. "Then why are you crying?"

She sniffed and straightened her shoulders like a small soldier. "Because I'm hungry."

"You always cry when you're hungry?"

"Yes." She sighed, drew a shuddering breath, and, momentarily giving up the battle for strength, laid her cheek against his chest, much as she had imagined doing.

They stood together, saying nothing for a moment. His fingers brushed upward, pressing a strand of uneven hair behind her ear. Her eyes were closed, he noticed, her head tilted back slightly, and he studied her as she drew in jagged trembling breaths.

Travis whispered her name, bending his neck to kiss the corner of her mouth. "You're so very beautiful."

Her eyes flew open, luminous and moist and wide. Her lips parted, and then, "No, I'm not," she rasped, and, turning her face into his chest, let the tears flow unchecked.

Travis stood in dumbfounded amazement. Though he hadn't told her of her beauty solely to make her feel better, neither had he expected her to burst into fresh tears.

"Please don't cry, lady," he said softly.

But she did so, nevertheless, gripping his shirtfront in both hands as she wept quietly against his chest.

"Please." He looked toward heaven, feeling his nerves fray. "I'll . . ." He thought hard. "I'll buy you chocolates."

Katherine sniffled, feeling the deluge finally ebb and smiling with grim amusement at his attempt to soothe her. "Ryland," she said in a hoarse tone, "in the past month I've been shot at, hunted down, cursed at, and attacked. I hardly think the promise of chocolates is going to mend all my problems." She sniffled again, looking affronted. "I'm not a child you know."

He was silent for a moment. "You're right . . . I'm sorry."

Katherine remained quiet in his arms, thinking. A sparrow sang glibly from the nearby woods.

"Ryland?"

He shuffled her a bit in his arms, looking over her head to

the rising sun. "Call me that once more and I'm taking my shirt back," he warned dryly.

"Oh." She licked her lips. "Travis?"

"Yeah?"

"Could you really obtain those chocolates?"

Chapter 17

Travis tossed a package at Katherine's feet. She had sat alone in the woods for nearly an hour, waiting, tamping down her fear, and pacing until her nerves were frayed and her feet ached. She sat on his bedroll now, her high-heeled slippers empty beside her as she retrieved the parcel he'd brought.

"What did you buy?" she asked, looking into Ryland's freshly shaved face. Was he as handsome as he seemed or was it simply that she'd been removed from other human companionship for so long? In another week *Soldier* might seem irresistible.

"Supplies," Ryland said gruffly, "and that." He turned his back, leading his stallion away, but in a moment he stopped to loosen the ties that held his saddlebags and watch her.

Katherine pulled the package open, drawing out the masculine garments piece by piece. She swallowed once, looking up. "For me?"

Travis wasn't certain how to read her tone. They'd ridden for two days to reach Edgewood. But he'd left her in the woods and went into town alone. "Told you we'd be changing your looks," he said, but in truth she'd already changed a great deal. Her hair was short and uneven, and her skin, already a golden tan.

She licked her dry lips and nodded. "Thank you," she said, then, "how did you manage it on two dollars and fifty cents?"

Travis watched her closely as she drew the bundle to her chest. "I had a little extra."

"You mean you had money all along?" She scowled slightly, seeing him bend down to retrieve small packages from inside his leather bags.

"A little." He nodded.

"And you would have allowed those . . . renegades to believe you didn't." She stood, looking indignant. "So making them want to take me instead?"

Travis slowed his motions to look at her again. She was, despite it all, very beautiful, breathtakingly so, he thought, even when her temper was rising, or perhaps especially then.

"You would have allowed them to take me," she said, remembering that nightmare with growing anger.

"Did you look in the boot?" he asked, turning back toward his own packages as Soldier sampled cottonwood leaves.

"You *would* have let them take me, wouldn't you?" she asked, aggravated.

"Look in the boot."

Katherine lowered her brows angrily, knowing he had no intention of answering. "Fine." She dropped her hand into one boot, then the next. "I'll look in the silly . . ." Her hand came out with a small rectangular box. Her mouth went round, her eyes wide. "Chocolates," she breathed, and Travis turned away, hiding his smile in the woods.

"Try on the clothes, lady. I'll be back soon."

"Chocolates," she said again, opening the scroll-covered box to peek inside and assure herself that it was really true. "Sweet, rich, and dark." She licked her lips, then gingerly touched one, but immediately drew her grubby hand back, not wanting to defile such a treasure.

She needed a bath. No one should eat chocolates when they were dirty. It was a crime, possibly punishable by future chocolate deprivation. She giggled, feeling giddy.

Carefully closing the box, she hurried to the saddlebags to strap her delicious treasures quickly inside.

She'd found a stream not far from this spot. She'd go there now, bathe, change clothes, and hurry back here before Ryland returned. Gathering the newly purchased bundle, she headed downhill.

Once beside the stream, Katherine glanced quickly around, feeling exposed and uncertain as she began peeling off clothing. Ryland's shirt went first, then the soiled gown, though it was difficult reaching the buttons that ran down her back. Finally she squatted by the rushing stream, feeling wickedly exhilarated and breathless.

The water was icy cold as she scrubbed her hands and splashed it on her arms. It felt refreshing on her face, breathtaking on her throat and chest, and heart-stopping as she finally gathered all her nerve and waded in to the three-foot depths.

She remained frozen in place for a moment, then leaning back, doused her hair to come up sputtering and scrubbing. With no soap it seemed a bit ineffectual, but better than nothing—perhaps—if her feet weren't embedded in the mud.

Then she noticed the bear. It was big and black, and stood not twenty feet from her, snuffling at her clothes as if debating whether it was hungry enough to give them a taste test.

"Dear God!" Katherine whispered the prayer. "Don't let me die before I eat my chocolates."

The bear lifted her head, sampling the strange human scent on the breeze, then rose on her hind legs to take a better look.

"Don't panic," Katherine whispered to herself.

The bear swung its broad head, then quick as a huge cat, she dropped to her forepaws to scramble into the stream.

The scream seemed to rip up from the pit of Katherine's cramped stomach. Her legs unbent with a jolt. Her arms pumped as she scrambled for the opposite shore. But the mud still held her feet, and she fell, hitting the icy water with her chest and bolting upright, gasping for breath. Saturated hair streamed across her eyes, blurring her vision, but she struggled forward, on hands and knees now, panic and cold stiffening her limbs.

There was a splash behind her. She screamed again, feeling something paw her back.

"Lady." Travis breathed her name, catching her in his arms and pulling her to his chest.

She flailed against him, terror surging through her panicked system.

"Lady." He caught her flying hands to pull them gently between their bodies. "It's all right," he soothed. "Just a black bear."

Relative calm soaked slowly into Katherine's being, and she drew a deep breath, turning her head slowly to find the black creature that would surely cause her death. "Just a black bear?" she whispered.

"Yeah." Travis stood knee-deep in the water, she realized, holding her to his chest as if she were a frightened child.

"Black bear?" she questioned, glancing about feverishly but finding no evidence of the huge threatening animal. "Is that good?"

He chuckled in her ear. "They're usually harmless, unless they have younguns." He didn't mention that this one did and that he'd seen a pair of them ambling downstream a bit. Apparently, Travis's approach had scared the mother off, for she'd left the trout she'd been coveting to gallop away toward her cubs.

Katherine drew a deep breath, feeling suddenly limp with relief. "I've made a fool of myself again." Her eyes dropped to his chest, where his damp shirt clung to the hard slopes beneath his shoulders. "Haven't I?"

She felt like heaven in his arms. All wet and soft and slippery, full of curves and life and husky apologies. "I don't think anyone could make a fool of you," he said softly.

Katherine raised her eyes slowly, wondering at the sincerity in his voice, thinking he must surely be mocking her. But his face was absolutely sober, his eyes intense, his nostrils slightly flared.

"Teach me to be tough," she murmured, so terribly impressed by his strength and courage that it took her breath away.

"Lady . . ." He shook his head slowly, unable to stop the hot sensations that coursed through his being with lightning speed. "I kind of like you soft."

They were so close she could see each individual line on his face, the slight creases that radiated from his eyes, the pleasant grooves that deepened when he spoke. He was a masterpiece, a hardened, sculptured work of art. "Teach me," she breathed.

Then he kissed her because he couldn't help himself and didn't want to. She was soft, and lovely, and kissing him in return. Her breasts were pressed against his chest, and her kisses were hot and torturous.

"Lady!" He pulled his mouth abruptly away, determined not to take advantage of her loneliness, of her fear, of her vulnerability. "We shouldn't do this."

Katherine didn't answer, but caught his gaze with her own. "Why?"

He remained silent for a moment, grappling for strength. But it had run dry. "Can't you think of a reason?" he rasped.

She shook her head numbly and Travis came undone. He bent, sweeping her into his arms. Water rushed past and through his saturated boots as he carried her to shore. He failed, however, to notice anything but his precious burden.

Katherine's eyes were closed, and her breasts were pressed tightly against his chest.

With trembling arms, he deposited her on his bedroll, and though he meant to straighten, the sight of her naked and willing kept him where he was. He drew back, breathing hard. "Lady, you don't want this."

"All my life people have been telling me what I should want," she whispered. "Would it be such a sin if I wanted you?"

He stared at her, his nostrils flared. "It would be a mistake."

"Why?"

"Because I ain't worth it."

She lifted one hand, grasping his shirt in her fist. "I think you are," she whispered. "And I *do* want it. Would you kiss me again?"

"Lady, I—"

"I rather liked it."

"Lady!" he warned, but her lips were parted and waiting, and he lacked the will to restrain himself.

He kissed her hard, and she moaned, pressing up against him. There was no longer any hope for self-control. She'd made the choice, and despite the fact that she would hate him later, he could no longer resist. His arms wound about her bare back, pulling her closer.

There was a sweet, delicate hollow below her collarbone, and he lingered there, nuzzling, kissing, then moved downward.

She was arched beneath him, breathless and waiting. Her breasts were high and proud, dark-nippled and taut. His kisses skimmed between them as his hands cupped the outsides of the soft mounds.

"Beautiful," he whispered to them, then moved on, worshipping her with his hands and mouth.

Every fiber of her was firm, yet soft. Her legs were long, slightly bent, and quivering. He kissed her thigh, her knee, the flat plain of her shin, and then up he moved again, finally cupping her buttocks to shimmy over top.

"God, you're beautiful," he breathed.

She tried to say the same, but found she had no words. Though her lips were parted, she could not speak. And so she pressed more firmly against him, her eyes on his face, her arms clutched beneath his shirt.

Is this love, then, or simple lust, the like of which my father warned against? Katherine wondered dizzily. But his lips were on hers again, teasing, tantalizing.

He was between her legs now, and she pressed up against him, trying to ease the ache.

Travis moaned against her lips, giving her courage to slide her hand lower onto the steep rise of his powerful buttocks, pulling him against her with surprising strength.

"Travis . . ." She found her voice at the edge of her painful desire. "I need . . ."

He kissed her cheek, her ear. "Yes, lady? What do you need?"

She wasn't certain. But she hoped to get it soon, for her entire being ached with desire. "Don't *you* know?" she asked, her voice hoarse and desperate.

He chuckled in her ear, thrilled by her half-admitted innocence, her fiery response.

"There ain't much more I can do for you with my pants on, lady," he said, and pulled away.

His boots were wet and stubborn, but he jerked them from

his feet. On his knees now, his hands actually trembled on the metal buttons of his jeans.

Finally he, too, was naked, and pressed her back, able to wait no longer, needing to feel her softness beneath him. Her breasts crushed against his chest. Her legs slipped easily against his, and the hard, buoyant length of his desire was caught between them, throbbing with impatience.

"Lady . . ." The feelings were so intense now that he could barely speak, and yet . . . He could not hurt her. Could not bear to shame her.

"Shhh." She touched a gentle finger to his lips. "You've opened a new world for me. Don't stop now."

Travis stared into Katherine's lovely face, feeling breathless.

The tip of his manhood moved against the bottom of her midnight curls, teasing her. "I want you," she whispered, and opened easily for him to enter. Moist heat enveloped him. Taut muscles surrounded him.

Katherine pressed upward, trying to pull him in, rocking against the granite-hard shield of his body.

He groaned in tortured pleasure. "Lady, please. I don't want to hurt you."

"Hurt me?" She all but laughed. "Hurt me? Ryland . . . I already ache. And I expect you to fix it." She bit her lip and urged him toward her again.

"You're a . . ." he began, but she rocked against him again, so that he ground his teeth and waited for the delicious agony to stop. "A virgin."

She squeezed her eyes shut. "That's the problem?"

He moaned. "Yes."

"I'm not," she rasped. "I'm not a virgin," she vowed, pressing toward ecstasy again. "Remember? Patterson?"

"Lady," he gritted, but the battle was lost, and he pushed inward with one swift stroke. "You lie."

She gasped at the full length of him. Perhaps there was some pain, but it was lost in the pleasure. They moved together now, hips rising and falling.

He found her lips with his own. The tempo increased. Small beads of sweat lubricated and joined.

Travis felt her fingernails scrape against his back, felt the sharp intake of her breath, and knew that she was near. He pushed in again and again.

She was panting now and rocking hard against him until finally, with one sharp breath, she went limp and soft in his arms. Her climax forced his own. He shuddered against her, drained and sated.

It took several minutes before Katherine could speak, for he still lay atop her, though he was propped on his elbows.

"Well," she whispered, feeling so weak and content that the word was little more than a rush of breath from her throat. "Are we done?"

He eased gently off her. "Did you expect more?"

"No," she murmured, feeling her face grow warm with embarrassment for her own brazenness. Never in all her life had she felt such undeniable ecstasy. "I think that was quite sufficient," she sighed.

"Sufficient." His chest rose and fell like a bellows, and he was certain that an entire army could not force him to stand upright. "Sufficient? You have the damnedest way of putting words together, lady." He turned his head slightly to gaze at her. "Who are you anyway?"

"Schoolteacher." She said the words without thinking, for in all truth, she was beyond clearheaded thought, even if she had wanted to hide the truth from him at that moment. "I was a schoolteacher."

"Teacher?" Travis said slowly. "You were a school-marm?"

She nodded weakly, wondering where she'd left her clothes.

"A schoolmarm?" He sat up weakly. "And you never told me?"

Katherine licked her lips and reached for his shirt, which she quickly draped over her nakedness. "Well, that was before . . . You know . . ." She shrugged, noticing the glorious curves of his bare chest again. "Before I became a—"

"Goddamn it!" he interrupted, pushing angrily to his feet. "Goddamn it, woman! Don't you say it," he warned, shaking a finger at her. "You hear me? I don't ever want to hear you say it again."

Katherine blinked at him. Had he lost his mind, or did men always become unusually irrational afterward. "Hear what again?"

"That you're a dove. I never want to hear that you're a dove! Jesus!" He turned away suddenly, hands on his hips. "I knew," he raved at the trees. "I knew better. I *knew*. But . . . a schoolmarm! Jesus!"

"What difference does my vocation make?" she asked, rising slowly to rest her weight on one palm while still holding his shirt up to her neck.

"What difference?" He shook his head as if stunned by her naïveté. "You said you was a saloon girl. A man don't have to worry about ruining no—" He turned suddenly, hand flailing.

She remained absolutely silent, staring at him.

"Jesus, woman!" he rasped, entirely forgetting his train of thought as his gaze fell to the bottom hem of his shirt, where her dark curls were exposed above her moist core. "Cover yourself before I . . ." He shook his head, backing away a step. "Before I do something . . . quite sufficient again," he growled, and stormed off into the woods.

Chapter 18

It was nearly dark when Travis returned to their campsite. Katherine sat on a log, her slim hands clasped together, her lengthy legs encased in durable denims, and the remainder of her body dressed in equally boyish garments. She stood when he approached.

For a moment they stared at each other like errant children, neither finding the nerve to speak, then, "I shot us a couple geese." He lifted the pair by the legs but refused to look at her.

"You bought a gun?" she asked, knowing the question was silly and that he wouldn't answer. He didn't, but dropped the fowl and turned.

"Travis?"

"Yeah?" His tone sounded grumpy.

"Thanks for the clothes."

"Yeah," he said with a notable lack of courtesy. "Sure."

She took a step forward, brushing back an imaginary strand of wayward hair. "I think they fit quite well, don't you?"

She was intentionally trying to torment him. He knew it. She was a demon, sent from the bowels of hell to make him pay for all his sins. No one but a demon could look like she looked, could attract him like she attracted him. Only a demon would be a schoolmarm and proclaim herself to be a soiled dove!

"The boots . . ." she said, twisting slightly in a attempt to see his face. "The boots are a little large. But the rest—"

"Listen, lady!" he spouted suddenly, feeling his nerves

153

were at their breaking point, and spun abruptly toward her. "This ain't no goddamn—"

His jaw dropped, his hands flexed.

"What'd you do to them clothes?"

"Nothing." Her face flushed a darker shade of red. "I just . . ." She shrugged self-consciously. "Nothing."

Nothing! He stared at her. They were simple garments that he had purchased. Serviceable cotton shirt, secondhand knee-high boots, riveted denims. But old Levi Straus had never intended his jeans to look like this.

Every curve seemed visible and molded. Her waist was strapped to nothingness by the leather belt, her breasts caressed by the soft, deep-blue cotton of the humble shirt.

She squirmed slightly under his stunned perusal, shifting a strand of dark hair beneath the felt hat and licking her lips. "No one will realize I'm a woman now." She shuffled her booted feet.

"No." Travis thought he said the singular word with amazing clarity. "No." He shook his head, knowing that anyone who failed to see she was a woman, failed to be a man. "No. It'll sure enough be our secret," he said with a glare.

She bit her lip, looking nervous. "I have a confession to make."

His glare deepened, but he said nothing.

"I lied to you." Katherine pulled her shoulders back slightly, looking him straight in the eye. "I never really worked in the saloon. My aunt owned it. Left it to me. Daisy was with Patterson when he died. So you're the only man I've ever . . . been with."

Silence fell dark and heavy between them.

"Are you angry with me?" she asked softly.

He shook his head, then drew a deep breath. "Lady, get ready to ride."

"What are we doing here?" Katherine whispered the question in Ryland's left ear. Now that the gown and slippers were replaced by more practical clothing, riding behind Travis was far more comfortable. He, however, felt stiff as a board before her.

"You're staying here." He held out one hand, nodding toward the ground.

"What?" Below them was a homestead, barely visible in the moonlit dimness.

"Get off," he ordered gruffly.

"Why?" She held the back of his saddle and scowled. All right, it was true, she shouldn't have lied to him, and she certainly should have stopped him before things had gotten out of hand. But he didn't have to detest her so for what they had done. He didn't have to refuse to speak to her.

"Just get down," he gritted grumpily.

Katherine's first reaction was to do just that, take his orders, obey his commands. But she stopped her movement in mid-shift. "Why?"

He twisted toward her slightly. "Cuz I ain't having you ride with me no more, that's why."

In the darkness Katherine could feel her face go pale. Did he hate her so for her weakness where he was concerned? Did he think her immoral? Perhaps, in a way, he was not so very different from how her father had been; for it was obvious he detested her for what they'd done in the woods, while she still felt the magic of it in her soul. Her heart beat a hurried pace. "You're leaving me here?"

Travis stared at her, his face only inches from hers, and again he groaned inwardly at her innocence. Katherine was a gentlewoman, and of course he'd known it all along. But it was her seductive voice that made him hope she was the soiled dove she claimed to be. He'd known better, but he'd bedded her anyway.

They ought to just shoot him.

"No!" he snapped. "I'm not leaving you here. I'm just going down to get you a horse," he admitted irritably. "Now get the hell off mine."

"My own horse?"

Her eyes were bright now, and she leaned slightly forward, seeming painfully relieved to know he did not plan to leave her to fend for herself, even though she looked stronger after a good meal and the one chocolate she had allowed herself. "But how can you buy a horse at night? Surely someone will be suspicious. Even if I didn't come

down with you. And even though your appearance has
changed a great deal without the beard, and . . . ah, but
you don't intend to *buy* it."

"You know . . ." He stared at her, then grinned slightly.
"For an easterner, you're pretty bright."

"I can't let you do it." Her decision was firm; her voice,
the same. "I can't let you steal for my sake."

Travis shifted slightly in his saddle, narrowing his eyes
and trying to remember what it was like to be calm, to take
care of his business without harassment or constant objections. It sounded heavenly. "You can't let me?" he questioned dubiously.

"No." She shook her head. "It'd be wrong."

He laughed outright, but the tone sounded grim. He
leaned forward, trying to ease the pain in his right thigh. "I
killed my first man was I was thirteen." He stared straight
ahead, seeing behind. "By the time I was fifteen, I could kill
without blinking." He twisted in his saddle to look directly
into her face. "I don't think a little theft's going to tarnish
my sterling reputation."

Katherine remained silent, watching him, feeling her
heart ache in her chest as she searched for the words she
needed.

"I'm sorry," she whispered.

For a moment he was silent, then, "Didn't you hear a
word I said? I said, I kill! That's what I do. Like you're a
teacher. I'm a killer!"

"No, you're not." She couldn't manage more than a
whisper when she said it. Her hands felt cold and stiff; her
face, taut and pale. "I won't let you steal for me."

"Goddamn it!" He swore with reverent disgust and
grabbed her left arm with his free hand. "My sins are so
deep, lady, I'll be lucky to spend no more than an eternity
in hell. But I'll tell you this and I'll tell you now—I ain't
gonna be responsible for the death of no woman. You hear
me? You ain't gonna die because of me. So I'm going down
there, and I'm gonna find you a horse that can get you back
to your mama in one piece."

The intensity in his expression stole her senses for a

moment. "But . . ." She found her breath and her thoughts. "I can't ride."

"You'll learn to ride!"

She felt small and helpless and frightened by his mood. "Why can't I ride with you?"

"You think I'm made of steel?"

The question rang in the darkness, open for interpretation, but Katherine was beyond guessing his meaning.

"Why do you hate me so?" She could feel the pain in her heart.

Hate her? He should be so lucky! He should be so fortunate as to not think of her every moment, to ache for her every second. "Just stay put. I'll be back." He reached to take her hand, expecting her to slide from behind the saddle.

But Katherine hadn't become mired in such a mess by following practical suggestions. Indeed, Katherine wouldn't be Katherine if she started now.

"I won't let you go alone."

"What the devil are you talking about now?"

"I see your point." She nodded, though it hurt to do so, for there was a lump the size of an October apple in her throat. "I see that we need another mount. But I won't let you take the blame alone. I'll help. And I'll make recompense to the owner as soon as I can."

They sat in the darkness, staring at each other.

"Why don't I just tie you to a tree and leave you?" Ryland's question was more for himself than for her.

She sat straight and still behind him. "You won't."

"Damn!" He swore just once before turning Soldier toward the downhill slide.

"You'll do exactly what I say. You hear me?" Ryland told her. "Exactly."

Katherine nodded absently as she stared over his shoulder at the corral. There were at least fifteen horses confined there, most of them standing in hip-cocked contentment, watching as they approached them in the moonlight.

"Get off," he ordered quietly, and she did so, sliding quickly to her feet. "Hold Soldier. Don't get in trouble." He shook his finger at her as if she were a belligerent child. "Just stay put and . . . Here." He dug quickly in his saddlebags, fishing out her box of candies. "Eat your chocolates."

She took the box and watched as he lifted a lariat from a nearby post.

"Stay put," he repeated, and strode away.

Katherine scowled. He was treating her like a child, which was quite irritating. She was capable of making her own decisions. Hadn't she decided on her own to come west. She grimaced. Look how that had turned out. Still, it had been *her* decision. Her mother had practically had apoplexy, and her father, rest his soul, was probably still turning in his grave. It had been his wish that she become a schoolteacher. But she'd done that. She'd done everything they'd wanted her to. And now she was ready to do what *she* wanted to do.

She gave that a moment's thought before creeping, quiet as a breeze, up behind Travis. "Which one do you think?" Katherine whispered, practically in Ryland's ear.

"Jesus!"

It was the first time she'd ever seen him jump, but it probably would not be wise to laugh.

"Which one?"

"I thought I told you to stay put. Where's Soldier?"

"Grazing. I like the dark one. With the white on its face."

"That one?" Ryland lifted a gloved hand toward the leggy beast that stood with its neck stretched high over the fence toward Soldier. It snorted once, shook its head, then trotted the length of the corral, past its sedate companions to return again, legs lifting high. "Lady, you're about one bean short."

"What's wrong with him?" Katherine asked, mesmerized by the way the dark body seemed to float in the moonlight, how the head never dropped and the legs lifted in graceful cadence.

"Out here, we call that a good, quick way to die," he rumbled.

"Why?" She shifted closer to the rail. From the pack of tired-looking mounts a pale gelding lunged forward to take a nip at the prancing black. "Ohhh. They're mean to him," Katherine complained. "I think we should take him."

Leaning against the rails again, Travis turned his head to scowl at her. "Lady, I been around horses all my life."

"So . . ." Katherine whispered, straightening, "what's wrong with him?"

"First of all, it ain't no him."

"How can you tell?"

His scowl deepened. "Short of giving you a detailed explanation regarding the differences between male and female, let's just say it acts too daft to be a male."

Katherine raised her nose a haughty quarter of an inch. "I refuse to let you insult me. This is my theft, too."

"Shhh," Travis hissed, glancing nervously toward the house. "You want to just go announce our intentions? That way there won't be no misunderstandings."

"Listen!" She was holding her chocolates with one hand as she scowled into his face. "If I'm about to be hanged for horse theft, I'm going to be hanged for a horse I like. And I like . . ." She pointed, rather obtusely. "Her."

Travis leaned forward from the waist. "Well, you ain't getting her. Because she'd kill you. And when you die, I fully intend to do the killing myself."

"And here I thought you didn't want to be responsible for a woman's death," she hissed.

He waved her away with a flick of his hand. "Get back to Soldier before you wake the whole country."

Bending, he stepped lithely between the rails.

Katherine watched in silence. He was a stubborn man. Stubborn and irritating. And she liked the black horse.

Travis skirted the herd, avoiding the black, but every animal there was trailwise and savvy. They ambled away as a unit, then scattered to the far rails. He watched them go, not wanting to cause a commotion, trying to keep them calm.

Near the corner a spotted gelding stood quietly, head drooping. He was a big animal with solid bone. A little past his prime, but that fact only made him more desirable for a novice rider. Shaking out a loop, Travis judged the distance in the darkness and swung.

The gelding, however, had lived nearly as long as the man and had dodged enough ropes to make him an expert.

Dragging the empty loop back to his hands, Travis walked through the shifting herd again. A mare, splayfooted but sturdy, bolted past. Travis halted, crooning softly, settling the herd, searching again.

Another gelding—too belligerent. A mare—lame.

Ahhh—there. A brown gelding—not large, with solid feet and legs. True, even in the darkness, Travis could see he was no beauty, but he would carry a woman well, and—

"Ryland," came a loud whisper. "Travis. I'm taking this one."

Travis shifted and turned, afraid of what he'd find.

"The hell you are. Close that gate."

"Come on, girl," Katherine coaxed, extending a hand toward the dark, flighty mare.

The black took a step toward the gate, then another step. Her shoulders were through, and from around her neck some kind of strap dangled.

"Close that gate!" Travis ordered again, louder now.

Katherine did so, but the horse was already through. A dog barked—yipping twice before howling. The black mare skittered sideways. Katherine soothed her, one palm held upward, a chocolate in its center. Another dog barked.

"Travis. We'd better go," Katherine called, pulling on the belt that held the mare. "Come on."

Travis gritted his teeth. How had he come to this? He'd been a good bad man—respected and feared! And now here he was—reduced to common horse theft, with a woman who told him what to do and was about to drive him insane. But damn her bossy ways, he was not going to be responsible for her death on that black devil—unless he orchestrated it more carefully and had time to enjoy it.

He shook out his loop again and swung for the squatty gelding.

"Travis," Katherine called, sounding more nervous.

"Quiet."

"Travis." Her voice was rising.

"Shut . . ."

A bullet whizzed over the corral. Horses bolted. Katherine

jumped, and Travis, being no stranger to the penetrating potential of firearms, swore a blue streak and zigzagged toward the gate.

"Get on Soldier," he yelled, diving between the rails.

"What?" Katherine gasped. The black was prancing circles around her, made nervous by the sound of bullets, Travis's unorthodox exit from the corral, and the sight of the two bristling hounds that charged them all.

"Get on my horse," yelled Travis, sprinting for his mount.

"But . . ." Katherine minced a half circle in front of the black, still holding the too short belt and trying to watch all the descending elements at once. "I . . . Oh . . ."

She was grabbed from behind suddenly and yanked upward. Her hand scraped along the leather belt, but it was ripped from her grasp as she was deposited, facedown, across Ryland's saddle horn.

She wriggled violently, trying to see past his huge body as he spurred for the trees. "But my horse," she complained.

Another shot rang out, closer now, and Katherine winced. But when she righted herself on the saddle, she turned to look and saw that the black mare charged along behind them.

Chapter 19

"So what do we do with her now?" Katherine asked, watching the black mare that grazed not far from Soldier in the early morning light. They'd ridden all night, heading north and putting as much distance as possible between themselves and the ranch the black had come from. The mare had followed, never far behind, keeping up easily.

Travis squinted against the sun, looking fatigued and irritable. "Ever eat horsemeat?" He fingered the gun he'd purchased just days before and stared thoughtfully at the mare. "It ain't half bad."

"You wouldn't dare." Katherine rose to the bait like a winter-starved trout.

He smiled, the expression grimly lifting the corners of his mouth. "You sure?" he asked, and lifted the revolver.

How she managed to get her hands on his gun, Ryland was never sure. Perhaps being near her was dulling his sense of survival, or perhaps he simply had never considered she might do something so foolhardy; but whatever the reason, she was suddenly gripping the muzzle of his firearm with pale-faced intensity.

They stood facing each other.

"Can I ask what you're doing, lady?" he asked, watching her with mild interest.

Katherine stared at him, feeling breathless and angry. "You will not shoot my horse."

"You ain't hungry?" he teased.

"I *am* hungry."

"Then let go of my damn gun, and we'll have us some

163

breakfast," promised Travis as he warmed to the confrontation. Goddamn if this woman wasn't driving him insane.

She scowled, not sure if he seriously intended to shoot the animal or not. "You said I needed my own mount."

"Let go of my gun."

"You said I couldn't ride with you anymore," she reminded, her voice rising.

"You ain't going to be riding at all. Never again if you keep hanging on to the ends of men's firearms. Now let go."

"She's my horse."

"She's a damn menace," growled Travis. "Believe me, I know."

"How do you know?"

"Cuz she acts like you," he stormed.

Katherine raised her chin. "I take that as an insult, and I will *not* let go of your gun. Not until you come to your senses. You said I needed a horse. So I've got a horse. Why are you being so obstinate?"

"Obsti— what?" Travis questioned, tilting his head.

"So . . . male," Katherine explained, her frown deepening.

"Listen, lady. You said yourself you can't ride. And I'm saying, you can't ride this horse."

From the tops of the surrounding forest a hawk swooped on outspread wings. The black mare's head lifted, and like a pouncing cat, she leaped sideways, as if frightened the bird might be eyeing *her* for its breakfast.

Ryland shook his head. "See what I mean? She's flighty as a damn sparrow. Got no sense." Gently now he eased the gun barrel from Katherine's hands. "She wouldn't be a pretty way to die."

"But you can't shoot her."

"And we can't have her following us around like a damn dog, either. You think we don't have enough trouble without that?"

Katherine bit her lower lip and shrugged. "But couldn't you train her?"

Travis blew out a breath and shook his head. "It ain't the training. It's the horse."

"But you're good with horses, Travis." She reached out to

touch the front of his shirt softly. "*You* could train her. I know you could."

Travis knew he'd been baited, but he was enjoying himself, and he liked the way Katherine looked trying to charm him. Her eyes were the size of silver dollars, and her lips were slightly parted, begging for a kiss. She leaned nearer. "We can't shoot her, Travis. It wouldn't be right."

He tried to resist her, but couldn't. "I suppose you do need a mount," he said gruffly, and turning on his heel, hurried toward the woods. "Catch the damn thing, and we'll give her a try."

It was amazing how much tossing about a body could do and still remain in one piece Katherine thought as she clasped her hands together.

The mare was like a black storm cloud, corkscrewing about the clearing with Ryland clinging to her back with stunning tenacity. But no one could last forever, and when he hit the dirt for the third time, he landed only inches from Katherine's scuffed boots. A grunt was wrenched from him as his body thudded with solid finality.

"Travis." She bent quickly, placing her hands to his arm as he lay still and silent on his back. "Travis, are you hurt?"

His eyes were closed, his breathing coming in sharp gasps.

"No." He answered finally in a hoarse tone. "No, I ain't hurt." He didn't open his eyes. "I feel great. Never better." The words rasped between his teeth. "Wish I could do this more often."

Katherine grimaced. Her hand slid over his chest, checking for injuries—perhaps. "She can really buck, can't she?"

Ryland's eyes opened slowly. "You noticed that, too?"

She bit her lip and nodded. "Are you hurt?"

"'Scuse me for mentioning it, but . . ." He winced. "Didn't we already discuss this?"

"Tell me the truth."

He hesitated only a moment. "Yeah, lady," he answered. "I think you might say I'm hurt."

Katherine winced as if she'd taken the falls herself. "Where?" she whispered.

He moved cautiously, groaned a complaint as his eyes widened. "Everywhere."

"Ohhh." Katherine's second hand reached his chest. "I'm so sorry."

"Really?"

"Yes." She nodded, and he noticed, without half trying, that there were tears in her eyes.

He shifted again, then drew a breath and let his body lie still. "How sorry might you be?"

She touched his face, feeling suddenly exhilarated. "Can I do anything to ease the pain?"

"That depends." He winced again, letting his eyes fall closed, then opened one to study her. "How sorry are you?"

She was leaning over him to look into his face. It was broad boned, and his beard was growing back. He looked devastatingly masculine. "*Very* sorry."

"Yeah?" He opened his other eye slowly. There was a darkening bruise across his temple. "Then I think there might be hope."

She bit her lip again, feeling breathless as his gaze fell on her face. "What can I do to help?" she asked again, her tone husky.

He raised his brows slightly. "Let me think."

They stared at each from inches apart, and she nodded. "I'll take a look while you think."

His brows rose another fraction of an inch. "Take a look?"

"Yes." Her fingers were already on the buttons to his shirt, drawing them open.

Travis expelled a slow breath, feeling his senses warm. "All right."

Gently Katherine tugged his shirt from his jeans, and the final two buttons fell open. She drew the edges apart, exposing the massive width of his chest and abdomen.

She studied him as she gently explored him with her fingertips. "Feels pretty good. Except here," she said, and leaning forward, she pressed her lips to that darkened area. "And . . ." She raised her eyes to the top of his shoulder where the muscle bunched in a hard cap and the skin was scraped raw. "Here." She kissed that, too, while sliding his sleeves lower. There was a still healing scar on his right arm where the bullet had pierced him. "And here." Her lips lingered there. Beneath her mouth his biceps tightened and relaxed.

Katherine raised her gaze to his face. "Perhaps you should move to your bedroll so that I could examine you."

Their gazes caught.

"Perhaps," he breathed.

Ryland grimaced with pain as he stood. His back ached as if a large man had been very busy with a sledgehammer, and everything below his waist was throbbing in agony.

Beneath the shade of a birch tree his blankets felt soft and yielding above the springy grasses. From a nearby bush a song sparrow serenaded them. And all around the purple heads of the Rocky Mountains shone with breathtaking grandeur.

Travis eased himself onto his back, almost suppressing the groan of pain caused by his movements.

Katherine sat back on her knees, watching him with an agonized expression.

Again their gazes caught.

The truth was that despite it all—the lynch mob, the saloons, the men who'd lusted after her, and even the one time they'd shared passion—Travis knew she was still an innocent.

"Have I mentioned how sorry I am?" she asked softly, the truth showing clearly in her luminous eyes.

He should draw back, of course, but didn't. "No, you haven't."

"Shall I show you?" she whispered.

He could not pull his gaze from her, for she was beautiful beyond description, with her cheeks slightly pinkened by her tentative brazenness. "You're looking for trouble, lady," he warned softly.

"I think I already found it." She shrugged, smiling a little. "On a dark street in Silver Ridge."

He remained silent, remembering his first sight of her, how her night rail had pressed intimately against her backside. "I'm not a good man to mess with. And I'm not strong where you're concerned. I can't resist you."

"Then don't."

"You're making a mistake."

Their gazes held.

"I don't want to be alone forever, Travis."

He tried to think rationally, to do what was right. "There are good men. Men who would treat you good."

Katherine bit her lip. "But I want you."

Her whispered words seemed to echo in the forest.

"Don't, lady," he pleaded.

"But I do."

He kissed her with trembling passion, unable to resist, and she answered back.

Her clothing came off slowly. First her shirt peeled away as he kissed every inch of smooth flesh revealed. She was soft and warm, and shuddered when he kissed her nipple. He slipped off her jeans, so that she lay naked in his arms finally. Then he drew away slightly to view her more fully. Katherine bit her lip, lowering her gaze and covering her breasts with an arm.

"Please." With utmost tenderness he lifted her arm so that all was bared to him once again. "I've never seen such beauty before, Katherine." She raised her eyes to meet his. "And I never will again."

She kissed him softly. Her lips were warm, playing gently across his, and finally slipping lower, daring to caress his chest. Travis gritted his teeth, feeling as if he would die of the raging sensations.

Her kisses slanted across his abdomen. He drew in a sharp breath as they brushed above his waistband.

"Lady, I can't take much more of this," he groaned, and she drew away, looking flushed and breathless before kissing his mouth again.

Finally his clothes joined hers.

They lay naked and impatient in each other's arms, feeling the soft caress of the sun, the gentle, skimming touch of fingers along shivering limbs.

Travis's hands lowered to her waist and, lifting her slightly, finally set her firmly atop him.

She moaned as he slid inside, tilting her head back, so that her slim graceful throat was revealed. He groaned, wanting to touch every part of her, but his need was too strong to be denied now, and he drove into her, drawing gasps of pleasure from them both.

Katherine was astride as they rode toward that elusive summit, giving and taking, her hands upon his chest, her eyes closed.

The tempo increased to a feverish rate, hot flesh against hot flesh, until she gasped for air as she rose to ecstasy. Her taut breasts thrust forward, and her strong lean legs gripped him with shocking strength as she reached the pinnacle of fulfillment.

She collapsed against him.

Travis gasped for breath, remembering he had heard of young stallions fainting dead away from the sheer exhilaration of a mating.

It was possible. And if ever there was a woman who might cause a man to lose consciousness, this was the one to do it.

Her breasts felt warm and soft against his chest as she shifted off him, easing to the left, avoiding his wounds. She lay beside him finally, cuddled against his side as one of his arms cradled her.

"Travis?" Her voice was very small when she spoke, sounding not at all like the seductress who had tantalized him moments before.

He stroked her hair absently from her face, waiting for her to go on.

"Do you hate me again now?"

He loved her. He knew it. He felt that nearly forgotten burn in his soul and closed his eyes. "No, lady," he answered softly. "I don't hate you."

They were silent for a moment.

"I know I've been difficult." She took a deep breath, still staring at his chest where her hand lay against his hard pectoral. "But do you think you might learn to like having me around?"

A dark-haired girl with sparkling eyes called from his memory, lifting a hand to urge him to take it. And he had, forgetting his worries to run beside her through the gleaming fields of cotton.

"Yeah." He knew he should deny his feeling, should rise now and leave her. "Yeah." He shifted his gaze. "I might someday."

Katherine told herself she should be angry, for in truth he'd insulted her again. And yet those words, spoken in husky tones, did nothing less than make her spirit soar.

She wriggled slightly closer, feeling foolishly happy and hiding her smile against his bare chest.

Damn me, Travis thought. Damn me for falling in love, for admitting a part of my weakness, for making her happy.

Only pain would come of it. And yet she felt like a sharp shard of heaven against him.

He cleared his throat, nervously looking for some harmless discussion to keep him safe from the tearing emotions caused by her nearness. "What are we going to do with that damn horse of yours?"

Katherine straightened her smile and snuggled closer still. "Maybe she simply doesn't like men."

"Yeah?" He snorted. "Well, I don't mind telling you, lady, my backside don't think so highly of her, either."

She laughed, the sound low and sexy as she eased up on one elbow. "Maybe I'll be able to ride her."

It was a ridiculous statement, of course. Laughable. And yet, as their eyes met, Ryland could not laugh. For it was true, he thought with breathless memory, she was one helluva rider.

Chapter 20

Katherine slept in his arms that morning. Her lashes were dark and full against her golden, heart-shaped face, her lips as bright as wild strawberries and slightly parted as she breathed softly in her sleep. Curled on her side with one arm beneath her cheek, the rest of her body was hidden from him by his own blankets. Still, he longed to take her again.

Travis rolled carefully onto his back to place a heavy wrist over his eyes. What had he done? How would he keep her safe? It had been difficult enough before, when she meant nothing to him. But now that he loved . . .

No. He would never admit it again. Not even to himself. Love was a weakness, and weaknesses made men die. And women, and young, innocent girls with laughing eyes and gentle souls.

Travis pressed his wrist more firmly against his eyes and considered his options. He could not let her be hurt. But what could he do?

Take her to the ranch and make Latigo promise to protect her. Then he would leave and find Dellas. He'd learn the truth and clear her name. When it was safe for her to travel east, Latigo would see that she did so. There would be a husband for her someday—and children.

The thought made his heart hurt. Still, it was what she needed, and that was all that mattered.

"Where are we going?" Katherine asked. They'd ridden all day, and when they'd stopped, he'd shot a deer. The venison roasted now over a low fire. Ryland had mixed up a batter of flour and water. A little sugar had been added, and biscuits baked now on a black pan over the blaze. She licked her lips and tightened her fist around the tin cup. It was the first coffee she'd had in several days, and the rich dark fluid made her feel better.

"I already told you, we're going to Latigo's ranch."

"But we can't simply ride off and pretend we're not wanted. We must go back to Silver Ridge. Clear up the misunderstandings before—"

"Didn't I tell you not to talk foolish?" Ryland snapped.

Katherine pursed her lips and kept silent.

He was quiet, too, for a moment, then, "The night Patterson died, was there anyone hanging around your place?"

"At The Watering Hole?"

"You have another place I should know about?"

Katherine bit her lip. "Not that I know of."

She watched his scowl deepen.

"Who could have taken that money?"

Katherine shook her head, wondering what Travis would do if she walked around the fire and sat next to him, snuggling against his side. "Why would anyone stab the mayor after he was already dead?"

"How the hell should I know?" Travis snapped irritably, then rose jerkily to his feet. "I gotta get you a horse."

It was Katherine's turn to scowl. "I've got a horse," she reminded him. Not for the first time, she wondered how he could be so tender at times, so gentle that the mere brush of his fingertips stopped her heart, and then act like this at others?

"Yeah? You got a horse?" Ryland's gaze met hers for a moment. "Well, you got some time before supper. Why don't you take that little mare of yours for a nice lope around the camp fire?"

His tone was gruff, his expression cold, causing Katherine's temper to rise slowly.

"Maybe I will."

He snorted. "And maybe there won't be enough left of you to stick in my saddlebags and take home to your mama."

Katherine lifted her chin. She'd been watching Travis with Soldier and decided riding didn't seem so difficult. If you wanted to go left, you pulled to the left. If you wanted to stop, you pulled back on the reins, and if you wanted to go faster, you squeezed your legs. At least that was how it was done on a horse that accepted a rider. On Moondancer, as she'd named the black mare, she wasn't sure what the proper procedure might be. Close your eyes and pray fervently perhaps.

"Well?" Travis said, sounding belligerent and looking the same.

"Well, what?"

"What're you waiting for?"

Katherine curled her toes in her oversized boots and frowned. "You think I can't do it?"

He snorted again. "Damn right."

"Fine." She thumped her cup on the ground. Coffee lapped over the rim and onto her fingers. "Then I guess I'll have to prove my mettle." She stood quickly and paused for a moment, calling up her courage. "May I use your lariat?"

Travis raised his brows, amused, and nodded.

Katherine's hands were shaking slightly when she unbuckled the saddlebags. Inside were the chocolates, carefully wrapped in Ryland's spare shirt. She drew out the box and bit her lip. Since Moondancer had shown a weakness for candy in the past, it seemed a good way to soften her now.

Katherine approached the mare, who grazed not far from Soldier, having found some security by the big stallion's side.

"Here, girl," Katherine crooned, reaching out a hand with a candy at its center. "I could most surely use your help."

The mare nickered low in her throat, seeming intrigued by the smell of the sweets, and stepped forward.

It was a simple enough task to get the lariat over the black's neck as she ate the chocolate. And when the rope was pulled, the mare followed, seeming unconcerned.

"Good girl," Katherine said, feeling braver with her budding success. "Smart girl. Now I'm going to tie you right here." She did so, looping the end of the lariat around a tree like Travis had shown her and tying it in a slip knot. "And now . . ." She bit her lip, backing away a step and wondering how such a lamb of a horse could turn into a deadly cyclone in a matter of a few breathtaking seconds. "Now I'm going to get the saddle. You stay put."

She knew Ryland was watching as she strode past him toward his gear.

The saddle was heavier than it looked, and though Katherine managed to lift it, the stirrups bumped her shins as she went along, causing her pain at every step. Nevertheless, she kept her eyes straight ahead, ignoring the snort that issued from the direction of the camp fire.

Dumping the saddle on the ground, Katherine returned for the woolen saddle blanket and bridle, and then she stood, her knees trembling a bit. She kept her hands clasped tightly together to keep them from doing the same.

"Now, girl." Katherine approached the mare empty-handed to discuss the situation in what she hoped were simple equine terms. "I'm going to take the blanket and put it on you. It won't hurt."

Moondancer turned her soft, dark muzzle to gently nudge Katherine's arm.

"All right." She stroked the horse between her ears, accepting the mare's action as agreement, and placed the blanket on her back.

The saddle was next. Katherine took a deep, steadying breath as she wrenched the thing from the ground and with one quick prayer hoisted it aboard the mare's back.

Moondancer jolted forward, and the saddle slid sideways, falling to the ground with a thud.

"Now, girl. Please." Katherine glanced at Travis by the fire. He was watching her with a smirk on his face. She took another deep breath and straightened her shoulders.

Rounding the mare's rear, Katherine hefted the saddle again. This time the mare lurched forward, but Katherine was ready, and caught hold of the saddle horn before it could fall.

"There now," Katherine crooned, and stroked the velvet neck with her trembling free hand. "See. It's not so bad. I won't hurt you."

The mare blew through her flared nostrils. They were wide, showing pink inside and making her look wild.

"Relax, sweetling," Katherine whispered shakily. "I'm just going to pull the girth up tight now." She smoothed her hand down Moondancer's shoulder and wondered for the hundredth time how she would manage this. "R-ready?" she stammered, then reached.

Katherine's buttocks hit the ground before she knew the horse had moved. The saddle was propped at an interesting angle beside her, and Moondancer waltzed a few steps to the side, her eyes outlined in white.

From the campsite Katherine could hear Ryland's chuckle.

She gritted her teeth and tightened her fists. If she had been a swearing type of woman, she would find some choice words for him now.

Drawing herself slowly to her feet, Katherine dusted off her pants and tried to think. But no new ideas came to her, and so she retrieved the saddle and tried again.

The scenario went the same as the first time—hefting the saddle, crooning, petting, that fateful reach for the girth, and then the mare reared again, knocking her would-be rider on her rump before dancing sideways.

Katherine remained as she was for a moment longer, trying to gain her confidence as she listened to the chuckles from the cookfire again.

With renewed determination Katherine rose and crooned to the mare. "All right, girl." She tried to recall how Travis had gotten the animal saddled. Had he done something with her ear? But even if she could get the beast geared up, then what?

The image of herself flying through the air was not a soothing one, although the memory of Ryland doing the same gave her peace of mind.

"Come and eat." Travis interrupted her thoughts. He had come up behind her, causing Katherine to jump.

She steadied her nerves and lifted her chin defiantly. "I'm busy."

Travis chuckled low in his throat. "Busy getting yourself killed. Now come and eat." He reached for her arm, but she jerked from his grasp.

"I am busy here," she said angrily.

"Well, I tell you what." He placed his fists on his hips and grinned at her. "You come and get something to eat. Build up your strength. Then tomorrow morning, first thing, you can try again. I'll even help."

Katherine realized she had been defeated, at least for the moment, and nodded once in silent agreement, both to her own thoughts and his offer of food.

They were silent through supper, but Ryland glanced at her now and then, his mood seeming irritatingly lighter, with his chuckles sounding at regular intervals.

Katherine had not laughed at him when he was thrown by the mare, and his laughter made her angry. Never again would she entertain him with her feeble attempts at saddling Moondancer.

No, sir! Katherine stared into the fire, munching silently on her biscuit and contemplating the night ahead. No, she would not humiliate herself by trying to saddle the mare again.

But she would ride Dancer just the same.

The night was blessedly bright, the moon nearly full, and the stars were like candles in the sky when Katherine left her blankets to find Moondancer. The mare was tied, and turned her head to watch her mistress's approach.

Katherine raised a finger to her lips for silence. The knot came loose easily enough, and they moved quietly away in the darkness.

Soldier lifted his big head and finally followed along.

Not far from camp, but well hidden by fir trees, Katherine stopped her little caravan. Once again her hands were shaking, but Ryland's obvious humor at her failure had built up her determination.

"Now, girl," began Katherine, taking a firm grip on the lariat. "I don't know who it was that started this whole trend of people riding horses. But it's a time-honored tradition, dating as far back as the Romans." This was what her school kids had referred to as her preachy tone—something to be dreaded and avoided at all costs. "So I'm telling you this once, and once only. I *am* going to ride you. Now . . . I've taken your . . . abhorrence for saddles into consideration and I'm willing to be flexible, since they are indeed quite cumbersome and ungainly." Katherine scowled nervously as she stroked the glossy neck. But—you must concede to the bridle."

Ten minutes later it was Katherine who conceded. She felt exhausted and foolish and near tears.

"All right." She placed her hands on her hips and glared at the mare, who stood looking sheepish at the end of her lariat. "You win. No bridle. But I'll be *darned* if you're going to win this entire war." Stepping closer, Katherine fashioned a loop around Moondancer's nose.

Finding a tree near a large smooth boulder, Katherine tied Dancer before drawing one precious chocolate from the box. She had brought them as treats for the mare, but since the black had done nothing right thus far, it hardly seemed proper to offer her the entire candy, and so Katherine bit off half herself.

It was wonderful, soothing and sweet. She closed her eyes, enjoying every moment until Moondancer nudged her arm, begging with her huge, luminous eyes.

"Not until you deserve it," Katherine said firmly, and setting the treat on a rock just out of reach, added, "This is it then. Don't panic."

Moondancer blinked at her, looking anything but panicked.

"All right. I'm going to climb onto this rock." Katherine patted the gray boulder. "Then I'm going to ease—very slowly and carefully—onto your back. Hear me?"

The mare tossed her head, trying to reach the candy.

"Well, here I go."

The boulder felt smooth and cool, and Katherine paused there, rethinking her entire idea.

So what if Ryland had laughed at her? So what if she couldn't ride a horse? So what if she'd chosen the wrong horse?

She wasn't an outlaw. She wasn't a cowboy. She wasn't even a *boy*. She was a woman, for heaven's sake. From Boston! Where she'd had a very . . . satisfying life.

Well, perhaps satisfying wasn't quite the word. Quiet, then. But "quiet" didn't sum it up, either. Staid? Tranquil?

Boring! She'd had a boring life! And by gosh, she *was* going to ride this horse.

Katherine was aboard before she knew it—clasping the long black mane with a death grip and squeezing her eyes shut.

Nothing happened. Moondancer shifted once, tossed her head, pawed.

Katherine eased one eye open and drew in a soft careful breath. "Aren't you going to buck?"

The dark head shook as the mare pawed again.

"No bucking?" Katherine whispered. "That's splendid. That's wonderful. Thank you." With aching trepidation, she eased her fingers from the mane they were wrapped in, to tentatively pat the glossy neck. "I did it. I did it." She was off the horse in record time, sliding to the ground in trembling euphoria. "All right. It wasn't for very long, and we're not ready for stunts yet." She retrieved the chocolate from the rock to offer it to Moondancer. "But for the two of us, it's nothing short of miraculous."

Chapter 21

Travis and Katherine rode hard every day, heading northeast toward the ranch, making their own trails and stopping only long enough to procure and eat their meals. Around them boulder-strewn mountainsides rose to enormous, glorious heights. Mule deer abounded here. Rabbits and squirrels frequently scurried across their path, while coyotes and bears were seldom seen, but often enough to lessen Katherine's fear of them.

Sometimes she sat behind Travis, but often he would order her to sit in front of him, teaching her the subtleties of controlling a horse.

She had learned her lessons well. Much better than he knew, she thought, feeling fatigue seep into her limbs again as she held onto the cantle of his saddle and tried to stay awake.

Katherine had taken to sleeping as far as possible from Travis at night. After all, she had her own blanket, and he seemed to have no desire to be near her, anyway.

Instead, she spent most of her nights with Moondancer, determined to master the horse. It had not taken her long, however, to realize that the mare did not need mastering. She needed mothering. It was true that she was flighty and silly at times, but besides her dislike for conventional tack, she was easy to ride, smooth gaited and gentle. A kind horse.

It had taken Katherine several hours to learn to mount without the aid of a rock or other object, but now she was quiet adept, being able to grab a hank of mane and swing aboard with a fair amount of grace and speed.

Moondancer didn't accept a bit either, but was quite manageable with the looped lariat. Quite manageable until she spooked, bolted, or skidded to a halt, tossing Katherine over her ears. Still, the horse always seemed sorry for her behavior, and would place her forehead against Katherine's chest as if asking for forgiveness.

Chocolate consolation for both generally followed. Though Katherine was careful with the allowances, her stock was getting rather low.

Her eyes fell closed, thinking of the time when she would prove her equestrian prowess to Ryland. Never again would he laugh at her, she thought with sleepy satisfaction. But suddenly she felt herself slipping.

"Damn it woman!" Ryland snapped, grabbing her arm and pulling her upright. "All you gotta do is sit back there. I'd think you could manage that much."

Katherine settled her hands on the cantle again, pursed her lips, and fell back to her imaginings.

Day rolled into darkness, finally causing Travis to pull Soldier to a halt.

"We'll spend the night here," he said, without so much as offering an arm to help her dismount.

Katherine, however, had grown accustomed to his grumpy silence and irritable distance, and, pushing off wearily from the saddle, slid easily over the stallion's rump to the ground.

Ryland scowled as he watched her dismount. She was becoming as competent as a man, he realized, watching as she wordlessly gathered wood for a fire.

Not that it diminished her feminine qualities. In fact, her boyish clothes and short hair made her even more appealing. Now he noticed how her hips swayed when she walked, how her jeans hugged her buttocks, and the incredible length of her legs.

He couldn't take much more. He couldn't bear to have her sit behind him—touching him or not touching him. He could not bear it! But he would *not* succumb to her charms again—no matter what! Never!

Travis was anxious to reach Latigo. Or possibly, if luck

was with him, he would catch up with Cody Blackfeather in a few days. Jacob, the poor novice outlaw, had told of seeing an Indian driving a herd north, and his description of the man left no doubt as to his identity. Blackfeather and the boys from the ranch must be finally moving Latigo's new herd home. And Blackfeather meant safety for Katherine. At least as much safety as could be found before they arrived at the ranch itself.

Once there, he would leave her with Latigo until Dellas was gone and her name was cleared. Then he'd send her back east.

Just like that. Simple. All planned out. And he was not included in those plans, for she would marry someday—a man with a steady job and probably a paunch. Yes. Her husband would have a paunch, and somehow that knowledge made him feel better. The man would be rather short and would probably be balding, but he would be good to her—keep her safe and out of trouble.

But what man would accept her as a wife if he knew of her dalliances with Travis Ryland? No decent man. And so Travis was determined to not touch her again.

Not that he'd have the opportunity. For it was obvious she'd realized her mistakes and was keeping as much distance as possible between them. But not nearly enough, Travis thought as he watched her bend to deposit her bundle of wood. Even now he could imagine how she had felt beneath his hands. How she had arched and moaned.

"Damn!"

To his surprise he'd said the word aloud, causing Katherine to jump at the anger in his tone.

"What?"

She looked defenseless as she stared at him, eyes wide and startled, slim body looking delicate and feminine despite her garb.

He stared back, wondering what to say now. "What the hell are you doing?" he snapped.

She straightened and placed her hands on her hips, looking not angry but hurt. "Gathering wood," she said shortly.

"Well . . ." He scowled, trying to look meaner yet, and

wishing he still had his beard to help on that front. "Well . . ." he repeated, waving slightly. "Do you have to do all that bending?"

Katherine continued staring at him, her eyebrows raised in stark amazement.

"Aww. The hell with it!" Ryland said, embarrassed, and, turning Soldier with a jerk, headed into the woods.

They roasted the remainder of the venison in absolute silence as Katherine practiced throwing Ryland's knife into a nearby tree.

Travis, Katherine realized, was even more sullen than usual. She wondered at his mood, but was not about to ask for an explanation. Conversation between the two of them seemed impossible lately. He refused to answer her questions directly, and although he'd said they were heading toward Latigo's ranch, that information told her very little.

Perhaps it was time she rode Moondancer, for Soldier must be tiring, but she was loath to do so until she was certain she could carry it off without making a fool of herself. And she wasn't absolutely certain yet, Katherine thought as she unconsciously rubbed the hip that had been bruised during her last fall. As long as the mare continued to follow Soldier without restraint, she would wait a bit longer.

Her hand was slow as she retrieved the knife from the tree and chanced a quick glimpse toward Travis.

Their eyes caught, sparking fire-hot emotions.

"I'm tired," she said, holding the knife in one hand as she walked away to lift her blanket from the ground. But as she drew it from the others his voice stopped her.

"Take another."

She turned abruptly, finding his well-chiseled face, by the irregular flicker of the firelight. "I beg your pardon."

She still talked like a lady—and after all they'd been through. "Take another blanket, too."

She straightened, drawing the pretty striped one to her chest. "I'm not cold."

His scowl deepened. "You're not getting enough sleep. I don't need you falling off and breaking your neck."

She waited to hear him say it would slow them down, but

apparently he didn't feel that reminder was necessary, and since she didn't want him questioning her about her obvious fatigue, she simply agreed.

"All right." She bit her lip. "Thank you."

He nodded, and then turned back to the fire in silence.

The night was like magic, filled with the iridescent glow of the moon and the twilight music of mountain life in the wild. No longer did the sounds frighten Katherine. Instead, she felt content and exhilarated.

Moondancer was hers—properly stolen and trained and ridden.

She leaned forward, lying across the mare's heavy mane to wrap her arms about the glossy neck. She'd never had a pet—except for Prince, of course, who hadn't trusted her enough to let her near, rather like a man she knew. But she wouldn't think of Travis now.

No, tonight was hers—a few moments of pure delight to escape the horrors she had faced in the past month.

Travis came abruptly awake, the pain in his ribs sharp and piercing.

His hand went immediately to his side, feeling for the revolver. He drew it slowly from under his blanket, but did not sit up.

The night was silent. Soldier had made no sound of warning. He was certain of that. What *had* awakened him he couldn't say exactly, but he knew trouble when it was near.

And it was near now. He lay still, listening. Off to his right, far into the brush a twig snapped. Someone was coming. Slipping from his cocoon, Travis hurried stealthily to where he'd seen Katherine bed down.

He touched her blanket while scanning the woods. Nothing yet. He shifted his gaze, ready to urge the woman to silence.

But the blankets were empty, and for a moment raw panic gripped his gut, thinking Katherine had been taken. But he took hold of himself and knew Soldier would have wakened him if someone tried to hurt her. Pain would have alerted him. Besides, Katherine was not one to go quietly.

Where was she then? And where was Soldier? Travis
turned his head quickly, still crouching. The stallion usually
stayed close to camp.

But then he spotted Katherine, winding her way through
the trees toward him. Another horse whinnied from the
woods, and he swung about.

"Red!" a man yelled.

Moonlight shimmered off a rifle barrel, and Travis heard
another noise off to the left. And another. A bullet screamed
from the darkness, snapped off too quickly.

"Run, lady!" Travis yelled, diving for cover. "Take
Soldier!" His shoulder hit the earth, and he rolled, revolver
still in hand. "Run!" he ordered, but Katherine was frozen in
her tracks.

The nightmare had returned. Men were there in the
darkness again. Bullets whined. Death stalked her. She
swallowed a scream. Ryland's voice sounded, but it was
garbled, lost in the frenzy. But she heard "Soldier" and
knew he wanted her to flee, to run for her life, but she could
not.

"Where is he?" a man yelled.

"I got him. I think I got 'im!"

She was running before she knew it. Bolting back down
the trail toward the horses. They came to her at a trot,
skittering nervously as more yells erupted from camp.

"Dear God!" Her hands shook, but she managed to bridle
Soldier and tighten his girth. Then she was on Moondancer's back, gripping the rope and reins in stiff fingers as she
pushed the horses toward camp.

Another bullet, so close she could hear it pass, but she
held Moondancer steady and screamed Travis's name.

He heard her voice through the nightmarish din. And then
out of the darkness she came, like a moonlit wraith, riding
low, running flat out.

"Where are you?" she yelled, and he stood.

"Lady!" Travis called out, but just then a man lunged up
from the shadows and fire spat from his gun. Pain exploded
in Ryland's head.

"Travis!" Katherine screamed again, seeing him falter.

Ryland clawed for consciousness and pulled the trigger. The man groaned and fell.

Katherine wheeled the horses, charging toward Travis, allowing him only a moment to holster his gun and swing.

He caught Soldier's saddle horn but lost his footing. The stallion lurched, nearly dragged down by Ryland's weight.

Travis scrambled, running along, grappling for a better grip, and then with one desperate lunge he was up, draped against his horse's side.

A bullet sang off a nearby tree. Soldier reared, jerking a rein free and nearly losing his rider.

In the darkness Katherine saw Travis's body jerk, and for a moment she thought he would fall, but he gained control and urged the stallion into a gallop.

"Come on!" he yelled, and she did so, allowing Dancer free rein.

More bullets winged after them, but they were running now, wild as the night.

Boulders flew past. A broken tree lay on crushed branches across their path. A scream rose in Katherine's throat, but before the sound was freed, they were over.

Moondancer jolted back to the earth. Katherine was pitched downward, and, feeling terror grip her, scrambled wildly to right herself, her fingers tangled in the midnight mane as she hooked her knee over the mare's back, clawing frantically to stay aboard. A skittering turn to the left and Katherine was astride again, terror strangling her, the night blinding.

Horses crashed along behind her amid terrifying yells and spattering gunshots.

Travis was ahead, leading the way. All she could see was his pale shirt, but Moondancer followed the stallion's every move, weaving and dodging, allowing Katherine nothing to do but hang on and pray.

The trees thinned, showing the glossy, silvery bark of aspen. The horses spurted forward, allowed some room to run now, their nostrils distended, their legs pumping.

Just ahead dark shapes loomed up from the ground.

Fresh terror seized Katherine, but already the elk were gone, crashing through the brush to their left.

Travis glanced quickly behind, and then, with the suddenness of thought, he was out of the saddle and running, motioning for her to follow. In a heartbeat they were beneath the total blackness of a stand of fir. The horses stood side by side, breathing hard, ears pitched up as their pursuers thundered past.

"Damn it! Where'd they go?" a man yelled.

"Over there! I here 'em running."

And then they were gone, following the elk at breakneck speed. Hoofbeats pounded into the darkness, allowing silence to descend in muffled waves. From somewhere in the night an owl called.

Katherine closed her eyes. Her hands shook, and when she tried to take a step, her knees buckled, spilling her to the hard earth where she stayed, crumpled and shaken.

Dear God, they'd almost been caught. No. Not caught. Killed! For those men had no intention of taking them to the law, but to shoot first and check their identity later.

But they had escaped. She had done well, had saved Ryland. Had ridden that wild ride without failing. Pride filled her, giving her strength.

"Jesus!" Travis was before her, pulling her to her feet with his hands hard on her arms. "What the hell were you thinking?"

She stared at him dazedly. Why wasn't he thanking her for saving his life?

"How the hell could you pull such a damn fool stunt?" he asked, shaking her. "You could have been killed! You could have . . ." he began, but suddenly his glazed eyes closed and he collapsed, striking his head on the rocky ground.

Chapter 22

"Travis," Katherine whispered, slipping to the earth beside him. She reached to touch his shoulder. It was wet with something warm and sticky. "Dear God." She closed her eyes, refusing to look for a moment, knowing he'd been shot again.

Somewhere in the night men hunted them, and it would be deadly to stay there and wait for their return. She had to get Travis to safety.

"Please, Travis. You must get on Soldier."

His lips moved, issuing a faint sound, and she leaned closer trying to hear.

"What?"

"Leave me." The words were weak but discernible.

"No." She stiffened, holding her breath for a moment. "Don't be ridiculous."

"Leave me!" His voice sounded very loud in the stillness as he sat up to grip her arm in a hard clasp. "Do you hear? They'll come back. I'll hold them off for a time. Ride north and east until—"

"No!" Her hands shook as she jerked her arm from his grip. "I won't. You're getting on that horse."

Silence lay between them.

"Katherine," he said softly. "You don't know what we're up against. That was Dellas. I seen the silver conches on his hat." He was still, breathing hard. "Just like before. And I remembered. Latigo was right. It was him," he whispered.

"What are you talking about?"

"Go!" His left hand grabbed her arm again. "Hear me?"

His right hand lifted, but his fingers merely bumped numbly against her other arm.

"Listen. Listen to me. Dellas is on our trail. He killed her. He'll kill you, too, if you don't leave now."

"Killed who?" She shook her head.

"Go!"

"No." Her voice trembled. "I won't leave you."

"Goddamn it, woman!" he swore, and with the little strength he had left pushed her suddenly away. He yanked the revolver from its holster. "Leave me now," he ordered through his teeth, and lifting the muzzle, he pressed it against his ear. "Or I'll shoot myself, and there won't be no point dragging my corpse along."

Katherine's breath came in short, ragged gasps. "Please!" She stumbled back a step. "Ryland!" Her voice broke. "What are you doing?"

"Go," he rasped.

"No."

"Goddamn it!" he swore, and cocked his gun.

A noise issued from the woods behind.

Katherine gasped and Travis twisted about, jerking the muzzle of his weapon in the direction of the sound.

Soldier stood, ears pitched forward, watching as his master's aim leveled on him.

Travis swore, releasing the hammer, and Katherine bent. Grasping a stout branch in both hands, she stepped up beside Ryland to swing with all her might.

The thick bough hit his wrist with numbing force, almost knocking the gun from his hand. He jerked about, grappling for control of the firearm, but the rapid movement seemed to disorient him. His head bobbled for a moment, and then, with painful slowness, his shoulders slumped to the earth.

"God!" Katherine covered her mouth with a trembling hand. "What have I done?" she asked, but before an answer could form in her mind, he moaned.

She scrambled toward him, easing the revolver from his limp hand and stepping quickly back. The moon was slipping toward the horizon, drawing away the last vestige of light.

"Don't panic," she whispered as Soldier shuffled closer.

Setting the gun quickly on the ground, Katherine hurried to Ryland's side. A pulse still beat at the base of his throat.

Scrambling through the underbrush, she grasped Soldier's reins to lead him quickly forward.

"Wake up, Travis. Travis!" She slapped his cheek, noticing blood in his hair and trying not to think of the extent of his wounds. "Travis!" Her voice shook, and she wanted to cry, for surely she could not get him onto his horse if he didn't awaken. "Please," she whispered, but now Soldier had drawn close and nudged her arm with his nose. Behind him Moondancer emerged from the woods, drawing Katherine's attention.

"That's it," she breathed.

Positioning Soldier just so, she begged him not to move as she untied his reins. Her fingers felt stiff and her heart hammered in her chest, but she finally got the knots loosened. Soldier stood quietly as Katherine tied a rein about Ryland's chest. She felt as if she had done this all before, in a past nightmare that still haunted her memories. Hurrying to Dancer, Katherine led the mare forward before tying the second rein about the mare's neck and removing the lariat. In a moment the lengthy leather rope was looped about the base of Dancer's neck and slipped over Soldier's saddle to be tied to the rein that bound Ryland.

A noise issued from the woods. Katherine held her breath.

A fox stepped into view, then stopped, poised, before dashing away.

Katherine closed her eyes, feeling her knees tremble. But there was no time for fear.

"Please, God," she prayed, and then, hurrying around Dancer, she took the mare by the dangling rein and led her slowly forward.

The lariat was taut in a moment, and Dancer stopped, shifting her weight backward.

"Come on, girl," Katherine pleaded, and pulled again.

Ryland's body was lifted from the ground slowly, but finally he was draped, unconscious, atop his saddle.

Soldier took a tentative step forward. Katherine dashed to his side to stop him, but now Dancer was left untended and shuffled back a step.

"No!" Katherine gasped, and scrambling to Soldier's far side, she heaved Ryland astride. "Thatta girl. Hold still now. Hold still," she pleaded, and, fumbling with the knot, set Ryland free.

With strips of cloth torn from a shirt found in the saddlebag, Katherine tied his feet to the stirrups and his hands to the horn. He slumped groggily over his stallion's neck, and with trembling haste, she secured additional ties to bind him more securely. Finally the one remaining rein was returned to Soldier's bit and the lariat to Dancer's head.

She remembered the gun at the last moment and unbuckled Ryland's belt, settled it around her own hips, and slipped the revolver into its holster. It lay heavy and solid against her thigh, and with another whispered prayer, Katherine leaped to her mare's back before urging both horses into the secretive darkness of the woods.

The night got blacker as the hours passed, but Katherine kept the horses moving, hoping she was heading north and listening to every noise that issued from the woods about her.

It was almost impossible to make any headway, for there was no trail and the terrain was rocky and steep, with no water to ease the horses' thirst. Nevertheless, she refused to stop, sure that she must put as much distance as possible between themselves and the outlaws that searched for them.

From a branch overhead an unseen bird chirped, causing Katherine to jump nervously. Another bird answered, and she realized dawn was approaching. She would have to find a place to hide, she knew, but closed her mind to that thought for a moment, for Ryland had not made a sound in many hours, and she feared she lacked the courage to look into his face. Nevertheless, she had no choice but to stop soon.

Dancer stumbled into a walk, and Katherine murmured an apology, knowing the horses were exhausted.

Morning seeped slowly over the rim of the eastern mountains, casting a grim light on Katherine's world. She could see nothing but trees and rocks, and she closed her eyes, wondering for a dismal moment if Travis had been right. Perhaps he would have been better off left to die where he was than to be dragged on this torturous trip through the Rockies with very little water, food, or hope of survival.

Dancer stumbled again as she reached the top of a rise where she shuffled to a halt.

Katherine's gaze skimmed the view ahead. More trees. Endless rocks. She felt a sob rise in her throat, but just then she saw the stream. It burbled along down the mountain at a rapid rate and seemed to Katherine to be a sign from God.

Dancer's ears pitched forward at the smell of water, and from behind, Soldier nickered.

Their descent was quick as the horses slid and scrambled toward the stream, but finally they reached their destination, allowing them to quench their thirst.

Ryland was still slumped over Soldier's neck, showing no signs of life.

Overhead a red-tailed hawk screamed as it took to flight. Katherine raised her face to watch, hopelessly following the bird's gliding motion with her eyes, watching until it disappeared beyond the yellow face of jagged rock.

Her gaze skimmed downward, half-noticing the bright color of the bluff and how the fir trees created black shadows against its surface.

Her attention wandered, but suddenly the shadows seemed strange, drawing her gaze rapidly back.

Beneath her, Dancer lifted her muzzle from the water, letting droplets fall back to the rushing stream, but Katherine was only vaguely aware, for already she was pressing the horses through the water toward the bluffs.

Ahead the shadow did not shift or lighten, but remained black and mysterious until they stood only a few yards away and Katherine could be certain it was not a shadow at all, but a cave.

"Damned if you ain't the luckiest woman on earth."

"Travis." She breathed his name, sliding from Dancer's back to hurry to his side.

His face was pale, but he was awake and alert enough to speak in a faint voice.

"Are you all right?" she asked, touching his leg.

He made a poor attempt at a smile. "I felt better, lady."

"I'll get you down," she said, seeing his shoulders sag toward Soldier's neck again.

The cave proved to be empty, perhaps five feet high and twenty deep. The floor was damp and mossy and smelled like a fruit cellar.

Soldier stood patiently by the mouth of the cavern while Katherine struggled with the knots and finally did her best to ease Travis from the saddle. In the end, however, his descent was rapid and painful, and he moaned as he landed half atop Katherine, at the buckskin's feet.

"Sorry," she panted, feeling crushed and bruised herself, but he shook his head.

"Swear."

"I beg your pardon," she said, struggling to bring them both to their feet.

"Gotta learn to"—he grimaced, but finally balanced unsteadily on his feet—"swear."

She moved him carefully toward the cave, staggering under his weight. "Why?"

"Helps." He tried to nod, but the movement was jerky.

"Really?" It seemed wise to keep him talking, for she felt safer with him conscious, less alone.

They fell together just inside the cavern's mouth, with Travis's buttocks hitting the rock first and Katherine trying unsuccessfully to slow his fall, so that she finally toppled down beside him.

"Sorry," she gasped again, but one look at his expression changed her mind. "I mean . . ." She bit her lip. "Damn!"

Travis lay back against the mossy floor and smiled wearily. "Sounds good."

She bit her lip again, watching his face and wondering dismally if she would give her own life to save his, as he certainly would do for her. "You like that?" she asked, not listening to her own words.

"Yeah." His voice was weak, but his chest rose and fell steadily, and the fingers on his right hand were moving again. "You got a knack."

There was silence for a moment, then, "Travis," she said softly.

"Umm."

"Please don't die." Her words were no more than a whisper as her fingertips touched his cheek.

"I'm sorry, lady," he murmured, and his eyes fell closed.

"No!" She leaned closer, frantically clutching his sleeve. "Remember? No apologies. Travis?" she breathed, but he didn't answer. With a sob she pressed her ear to his chest.

His heartbeat was steady and rhythmic, and Katherine remained as she was, eyes closed, listening to that comforting beat until sleep took her.

Chapter 23

Katherine woke groggily, her head resting on Travis Ryland's chest. Bracing a hand on the floor, she pushed away to look at his face.

His eyes were open, but his expression was puzzled. "Who are you?" he murmured.

Katherine swallowed hard, feeling eerie sensations creep up her spine. "I'm Katherine."

He scowled, then shifted his eyes. "Head hurts. Where am I?"

"You were shot." She shifted back a few inches. Panic would not help she reminded herself. "We were attacked by Dellas's men. Remember?"

"Dellas?" The word came out in a gasp, and he shrank back as if he were a mere child trying to hide from some threatening evil. "Rachel?"

She drew a deep breath and took his hand. "It's all right now, Trav. We're safe," she soothed. Dear God, what was she to do? She'd planned to remain hidden during the hours of daylight, but what would it help to keep him safe from Dellas if he died of the wound he'd already sustained? Or if he lost his mind forever?

That thought made her stomach lurch, but his fingers had tightened about hers, drawing her mind back to the present.

"It's all right," she said again. "But we have to get to Latigo's ranch. You remember that, don't you?"

Travis blinked and scowled, but shook his head finally. "Latigo?"

"Yes. He's a friend. Don't you recall?"

"No." His scowl deepened. "Why does my head hurt?"

"Here." She helped him to sit. "Let me have a look." She tried to sound cheerful and casual, and steadied him as she moved around to examine the side of his skull.

Blood was still caked to his hair. Katherine swallowed hard and closed her eyes, not touching him lest he feel her hand shake.

"Am I going to be all right, Rachel?"

"Yes." She opened her eyes and forced herself to lift her fingers to his head. "Of course you are." She swallowed again and pulled her hand abruptly away. "It should be washed. I'll be back soon," she vowed, and pushing herself to her feet, left the cave.

She'd neglected to hide the horses, but they had remained close, and grazed in a copse of aspen where they were probably as well hidden as was possible. Hurrying to Soldier, she took the remainder of Travis's torn shirt from the saddlebags and untied the canteen from the horn before going to the stream.

Though she dreaded the task ahead, Katherine could not long delay her return, and soon found herself in the cavern again, propped on her knees beside Travis, carefully bathing his wound.

It took a good deal of time to wash away enough blood to determine the extent of his injuries, but finally when the area was clean, she settled back on her feet and pressed her knuckles to her mouth, to stifle her sob.

He heard her nevertheless.

"Rachel? Are you all right?" he asked, trying to twist about to look at her.

Katherine swiped her nose with the back of her hand and nodded. "Yes. I'm fine." She drew in a shuddering breath. "The bullet just took out a furrow of flesh." She pressed her knuckles to her lips again and prayed a silent thank-you. "You're going to heal."

"But I can't remember . . ." He frowned. "What's his name?"

Katherine forced a smile. Blessedly the bullet hadn't entered his skull, but something had addled his wits, either the bullet or his subsequent fall. "Latigo." She nodded.

"That's all right. You will. But meanwhile, we'll have to start riding again."

He mounted with Katherine's help, but she tied him in place despite his consciousness.

It was difficult to tell which way was north, for it was impossible to be certain what time of day it was. But she couldn't bear to remain in the cave doing nothing, and so she made her best guess, put the sun on her left side, and urged the horses out of the valley.

They traveled for the remainder of the day and the next night, with Katherine setting her sights on what she hoped was the North Star. For the most part Travis was silent. Whether or not that meant he was unconscious, she wasn't certain, but she kept them moving, pushing them on until she felt herself slipping from Dancer's back. She awoke with a jolt, grabbing the mare's mane and breathing hard. She needed sleep.

Despite her fears of being unable to get Travis mounted again, Katherine finally found a quiet, sheltered meadow and helped him from the saddle. They fell exhausted onto the grass, not tying the horses or trying to hide, but merely tumbling mindlessly into sleep.

Hunger woke her sometime around midday. Ryland still slept, so she slipped quietly away, first checking on the horses, and then gathering dry, clean wood for a fire. She made biscuits and coffee, and did not tell Travis this would be their last meal, for he looked weaker and more disoriented.

Worry finally drove Katherine on, for even mindless travel seemed better than doing nothing.

Darkness came again. From behind, Katherine heard Ryland moan and pulled Moondancer to a halt.

"Travis?" She touched his arm gently, noticing how he braced his bound hands against the pommel of the saddle. "Are you all right?"

He didn't answer at first, but spoke finally. "My head."

She found a sheltered spot and removed Soldier's tack, for there would be no hope of making a speedy getaway regardless of whether the horse was saddled or not.

From his place atop his bedroll, Travis moaned again, pressing the heels of his hands to his forehead.

Katherine knelt by his side. He lowered his arms, looking lost and dreadfully pained. "I hurt."

He still thought he was a child, and Katherine felt a sob rise in her throat. Dealing with the pain of the grown man was difficult, but coping with the agony of the child seemed beyond her endurance. And yet she knew the boy would allow her to help, to touch him, to soothe, unlike the man.

"What can I do?" she asked, moving closer.

He took her hand in his and placed it carefully to his brow. "Tell me a story, Rachel," he pleaded.

Sometime later he lay with his head upon her lap, his eyes closed and his expression peaceful. From somewhere in her imagination Katherine had conjured a story of a handsome knight and a maiden in distress, weaving a lively tale until she knew he slept.

The following days were filled with gnawing hunger and torturous worry. They rode endlessly, stopping only when Travis could no longer bear the ache in his head. Then Katherine would find a hidden spot. The stories she told Ryland to ease his pain became as important to her as to him, for they were a way to escape the terror of their hopeless future. For a short time she could forget her problems and be in a world where she would live happily ever after. Where the tall, handsome knight would love her in return. And during that time, in the hushed darkness, she could touch her knight, could smooth the hair back from his forehead, and know he would not draw away.

It was nearly dawn when Travis's scream woke Katherine.

"Leave her!" He was kneeling, his fists flailing the earth and tears streaming unchecked down his face. "Leave her be!"

"Travis!" She scrambled to his side, catching his hands in her own. "It's all right! They're gone."

"Katherine." He breathed her name like a prayer. His fingers trembled as they touched her cheek, and his expression was hopelessly confused. "I thought they took you."

"No." She shook her head, feeling her throat constrict

with the force of her emotions. He knew who she was now. "I'm safe."

"And . . ." He wrinkled his brow and touched his fingers to the place where the bullet had dug a furrow across his skull. "Rachel?"

Katherine bit her lip. "You've been sick, Travis. We have to get you to Latigo's ranch. Do you remember where it is?"

For a moment she thought he would answer, but finally he shook his head. "I don't remember no Latigo, Rachel."

All Katherine's hope crumbled, and she closed her eyes in defeat.

"I'm sorry, Rach," Travis whispered.

Katherine opened her eyes with a sob. "Don't be sorry." She pulled him gently into her arms, feeling the tears slip down her cheeks and letting them fall onto his neck. "I love you, Travis," she murmured hoarsely.

His arms tightened slowly around her, cradling her with careful strength against his chest. "I love you, too, Katherine," he whispered.

She saw a doe and fawn the next day, but dared not chance a shot at them, for she would surely miss and only succeed in alerting any pursuers to their whereabouts.

They rode on. Travis was unconscious most of the time, but Katherine was sure he was starving, as was she. Another day and night passed. They rarely stopped now, for hunger kept her awake despite her fatigue.

Cresting a ridge, Katherine stopped Moondancer to look about. There was nothing to encourage her. Not a building. Not a fence. Only mile after mile of rugged tree-covered mountains.

Travis moaned, and Katherine tightened her grip on Dancer's rope. She would not give up, for she loved him, and in his foggy state he had said he loved her in return.

Her hand dropped slowly to the revolver she still wore on her hip. She had no choice. If she wanted to survive, if she wanted Travis to survive, they needed to eat.

Pressing Moondancer down the slope, Katherine refused to think of what she would do next. She would just do it! Because she must.

Finding a quiet place where aspen grew and a sparkling stream tumbled along, Katherine slipped from the mare's back, allowing her to drink and graze.

"I'm sorry, Dancer," she whispered, and slowly pulling the revolver from its holster, she aimed at the mare's head.

For just a moment Katherine closed her eyes, trying to steady her hands and quiet the ache in her heart. The mare had done nothing to deserve death. Indeed, she had done much to earn her a long life on green pastures, but Soldier could carry two riders, and Travis would not live much longer without nourishment.

Carefully, and with shaking hands, Katherine eased back the hammer. But before she could shoot, a strange noise drifted up to her. Katherine opened her eyes, canting her head slightly and listening. It came again.

"Dear God!" She said the words in a whisper, then held her breath and listened again.

Nothing. She waited, closing her eyes to concentrate on the noises around her.

It seemed like hours before she heard the sound again, but she was certain now. It was the deep-throated bellow of cattle.

Katherine hurried through the mountains, pressing the horses hard toward the east. She'd set a landmark for herself, but it was dark now, and she could see little, so she listened, straining to hear every sound.

But the bellowing didn't come again. Was she still traveling east? Katherine was no longer certain. Perhaps it had not been a cow at all. Perhaps it was a creature of the wild calling for its mate. Perhaps she had imagined the sound. And perhaps, even if there were cattle nearby, she would miss them in the darkness.

A sob sounded from her own throat, and she realized with some surprise that she was crying.

She swiped at the tears. Had she put them both through endless torture only for them to die now?

What was that? Katherine's thoughts bumbled to a halt. It sounded like a horse. She'd found them.

But who had she found?

Dellas! The name slammed into her consciousness. Maybe the outlaws were very near, near enough to hear their horses. Katherine licked her lips, feeling her heart pound in her chest.

A whinny sounded from somewhere up ahead. She held her breath and waited.

Nothing happened but the passing of time.

Drawing a deep breath, she pressed her mare forward again, up a rocky incline and then down, only to climb again.

For a while she thought the fire was a star, misplaced in the endless wilderness about her. But her mind cleared finally, and she realized with numbing suddenness that she was looking down at a campground.

Murmuring a few words to Travis, Katherine left him atop Soldier, bound in the saddle, as she quickly tied the stallion to a stout pine.

Her hands shook as she pulled herself onto Moondancer's back. The descent was sharp and rocky, but hunger and desperation made her choose the most direct course possible, so that they slid and bounced down the mountainside, coming to a halt where the trees thinned at the edge of the valley.

Slipping from the mare's back, she peered through the branches toward the camp. The fire there made the night seem blacker and more desolate. Three men lounged around the lively flame, and the smell of coffee and bacon wafted toward her.

Katherine swallowed hard, feeling a sharp ache in her throat and mouth as the aromas tortured her. But she would not think of that yet.

Could one of these men be Dellas? she wondered, straining her eyes to see better. One man was old, with white hair and a lengthy beard. She could see little of the other two, for they sat with their backs to her. But on the far side of the old men was a wagon of some kind.

She bit her bottom lip, swallowing again and trying not to think of the food that wagon might hold. Surely this couldn't be Dellas's gang, she decided, for a wagon would slow them down. Wouldn't it?

But what if it were Dellas? What would she do then? March back up the hill to inform Travis they wouldn't be eating for a few more days. It was very likely he didn't have that much time left unless he had some nourishment.

Though her fingers felt stiff, Katherine's body shook as she tied Dancer to a tree. There was nothing she could do now but obtain food in whatever way possible. And since she had no way of knowing who these men were, she would have to assume they were unfriendly and take every precaution.

The revolver seemed heavy as she pulled it from its holster. The pines through which she stole were huge, allowing little undergrowth, leaving her to feel exposed even in the moonless night.

Voices drifted from the camp now. The old man brayed a sharp cord of laughter, startling Katherine with the sound. She stopped abruptly, breathing hard and trying to conjure up some shred of courage.

But in the end it was the smell of bacon that drew her irresistibly toward the fire. She clung to the last tree for sometime, until she could wait no longer, and then, cocking the revolver, she walked into camp.

"Put down your guns." Her voice sounded strange, as if coming from another source, but the three men by the fire turned immediately toward her, proof that the words had indeed come from her mouth. They stared, not moving, hands held stiffly away from their hips.

"I said put them aside."

She watched them do so, but was surprised that they obeyed. "Good. Now I want to know two things. Who are you? Where're you headed? And is there anyone here with some medical knowledge?"

For just a moment there was silence.

"I ain't no scholar, mister. But it seems to me that's three things," said a small man to the left of the fire.

"I don't give a damn!" Katherine spat, and feeling the revolver shake, she grasped it with both hands.

"Listen. We're peaceable folks," said the old man. "Why don't you just sit a spell, and we'll dish you up some vittles."

At the thought of food Katherine's throat ached again, almost choking her with her painful need. "Who are you?" she rasped, moving the revolver from one man to the next in a nervous motion.

"Take it easy now, boy," soothed the old man.

"We ride with Cody Blackfeather," said one of the others. "No need to—"

"Who's that?" she asked, pointing the gun at the man who spoke.

"Who? Blackfeather?"

"Yes."

"It's me."

He came from out of nowhere, and suddenly the gun was grabbed with ease from Katherine's hands by a dark man named Blackfeather.

Katherine stumbled backward a step.

"Who are *you*?" He asked the question quietly. His face was impassive, his hair long and black as a raven's wing, with sharp, strong features that could only be Indian.

"Me?" She backed away again, feeling sick for having failed Travis.

"It seems that's who we were talking about."

"I'm Kath . . ." She stumbled on her answer for a moment, realizing with abrupt panic that she would be a fool to give her real name. "Kat! I'm Kat . . . Gilbert."

He gave not the least impression that he might believe her, but remained silent, watching.

"He was sayin' something about a medic," said one of the men, approaching rapidly. "You hurt, boy?"

She shook her head, not daring to mention Travis until she knew more about them.

"Then he must have him a friend who is," reasoned the old man, hurrying up at a stiff gait. "Dellas is—"

"Hey! Horse coming!" warned someone.

But Katherine could make little sense of the words, for she thought with sudden panic that they *were* Dallas's men! Dear God! She backed away, hoping they wouldn't notice. Hoping she could slip away while they went to meet the newcomer.

"Blackfeather, look at this. It's some poor bugger tied to a horse."

"Is he dead?"

"Can't tell."

"No." Katherine only breathed the word, finding she had no strength to move. How had Soldier broken free? But there was no time to wonder, for already they were reaching for Travis.

"No!" she screamed, and throwing herself at the nearest gun, grabbed it and pointed. "Back away! All of you!"

Every man remained immobile.

"We ain't planning to slow-roast him over the fire, mister."

"Back away, I say!" she threatened, trying to cover them all with her shaking weapon.

"Let us get him down. Take a look. Maybe we can help."

"No!" Even to her own ears she sounded hysterical. "I know you're Dellas's men. I know what you're like."

"Calm down now," ordered the Indian softly.

"I'll shoot!" She swung the gun toward him. "I swear I will!"

"Let's just . . ." His hand whipped out a second time. And again, with the speed of summer lightning, the revolver disappeared from her hand. "Talk!" he said, and thumping her hard against the chest, he pushed her to the ground.

She hit the earth with a jolt, and before she could recover, two men were holding her down. "No!" she screamed. "Don't hurt him! It was my fault! All mine! I stole the money and wanted Dellas dead. He had nothing to do with it."

"What the devil's he talking about?" asked someone.

"How the hell would I know?" muttered another.

"Damn! Blackfeather. Come quick!" called the old man.

He did so, leaving Katherine and hurrying up to Soldier. "Get him down." His voice was hard as flint. "Here. Use my knife."

"Please." She quit struggling and remained as she was, half-reclining against someone's chest. "Please don't hurt him," she begged. "He's a good man." She thought fast. Perhaps these weren't Dellas's men after all, and maybe, if they did not know what could be gained by turning Travis in, they could be persuaded to help. "He's a man of God, traveling from town to town, ministering to the poor miserable sinners of the West."

The men suddenly stared at her in blank, utter silence.

"He is," she whispered, then swallowed hard and dredged up her courage. "We were attacked by outlaws, heathens. They shot poor . . ." She shifted her gaze nervously and remained still, leaning back against a strange man's chest, and praying for an improvement in her lying ability. "Reverend Swenson. Shot him in the head, and he fell. They stole what little money we had . . . and his bible."

The old man's mouth had fallen slightly open Katherine noticed, and she blinked, wondering what to make of that fact.

"It's all true."

"Why didn't they shoot *you*?" asked the Indian evenly.

"I got away." She nodded woodenly. "Fast horse. I tied her near the bottom of the hill."

"And your . . . partner. He's a preacher, you say?" questioned one of the men that held her.

If she hadn't known better, she would have sworn there was amusement in his tone. She thought fast, planning to assure him again that it was the truth, but the man called Blackfeather spoke first.

"Shut up, Finch, and keep the kid out of trouble. Saws, clear a spot in the wagon. Jimmy, spread a bedroll by the fire for the reverend here, then fetch Kat's horse." Men scurried to obey orders as Blackfeather eased Ryland from the saddle.

"How do I keep him out of trouble?" asked the one man who still held Katherine.

"Feed him," said Blackfeather, and taking Travis in his arms, he hurried him toward the blaze.

"*Him*?" murmured Finch, raising his brows and smiling directly into Katherine's face. "All right. I'll feed 'im."

Sometime later Katherine sat with her knees pulled to her chest and her head spinning. She'd eaten something warm and filling without taking time to identify it. "Is he going to live?" Her voice cracked with the question.

"I'm no physician. How long ago did it happen?" asked Blackfeather.

Katherine shook her head. Fatigue lay on her like a smothering blanket. "Maybe five days. Six." A lifetime ago. "Is he going to live?"

"How long has he been unconscious?"

She shrugged weakly and, shivering, reached out to touch Ryland's hand. Something wet dripped from her cheek onto the blanket that covered him. "He's been in and out," she whispered. She sniffed, not wiping away her tears, and tightening her jaw to draw her shoulders slightly straighter. "But even then he was out of his head."

"It's a marvel you got him here," said the young man they called Finch.

"Marvel! Hell, it's a goddamn miracle," countered Saws in his lispy voice, but Blackfeather merely lifted his gaze to stare at Katherine as if examining something about her that others couldn't see.

"You'll stay with him tonight," he ordered, finally lowering his eyes. "There's room for you both in the chuck wagon."

Chapter 24

The wind rose with the coming of the day, shaking the wagon and urging forth ghostly creaking noises. Katherine lay in silence, watching the heaving movement of the canvas overhead. It was gray and weathered, and stretched over its arched wooden frame like hide over the ribs of a gaunt steer.

Perhaps she should have tried to escape from the camp during the night she thought foggily. If she were heroic, she supposed she would have somehow managed to get Travis safely to Latigo's ranch by now. But she was not heroic. She was tired and scared, and although there was no way of knowing if Blackfeather was friendly or deadly, she found she had no more strength to try to survive alone.

"Where are we?"

Travis's voice was low, and his face very pale when Katherine rolled to her side to stare at him.

"You're awake." They lay very close together, and seeing him conscious reminded her how empty her life would be without him.

Their eyes met in the dim light of dawn, but Katherine could not tell which Travis Ryland he thought he was—the small boy who displayed his gentle soul in his eyes or the man who denied having a soul at all.

"How is he?" asked Blackfeather from the end of the wagon.

Sleep deprivation and uncertainty made Katherine jerk nervously at the sound of the man's voice. "He's awake."

The tall Indian pulled himself lithely onto the metal-bound wooden tailgate, carrying a bowl and easing himself carefully up to Travis's head. "Are you planning to survive?" he asked quietly. "Or should we arrange funeral proceedings?"

Travis lifted his gaze, scowling into Blackfeather's face. "Would it matter to you one way or the other?"

For just a moment Katherine thought she saw the glimmer of a smile reflected in Cody's black eyes, but it disappeared like the fleeting shadow of a hawk in flight. "Kat would be distraught," he said.

Katherine bit her lip and winced, but Travis only shook his head very slowly, as if it would be too painful to show his bewilderment in any other way.

"Your partner here. Kat . . . Gilbert, wasn't it?"

She nodded, her eyes not leaving Cody's, but he did not seem to notice her nervousness as he continued to study Travis's face.

"How does your head feel?"

"It hurts."

"Anything else hurt?"

"*Everything* else hurts," Travis said quietly.

"Good." Cody nodded, not explaining his reaction, and handed Katherine the bowl he still held. "Make him eat this slowly. Keep him quiet. Keep him still." Straightening as much as the wagon's low roof would allow, he turned to leave.

"Mr. Blackfeather," Katherine called before she could guess what she intended to say.

He turned back, his expression unreadable beneath the canvas.

"Why are you doing this?" she murmured.

His gaze flitted to Travis for a moment. "The truth is, Kat,"—he turned his attention back to her—"I've never seen anyone tie a man to a horse and take him through the Rocky Mountain Range before." His eyes showed that unreadable, almost amused, expression again, though it did not touch his lips. "I'm wondering if he was worth the trouble."

He was gone in a moment, leaving Katherine to stare at the wooden box that held salted jerky.

Travis ate the broth without complaint or commotion, not seeming to feel the ravenous hunger that had plagued her. His eyes rarely left hers, as if he could not recall her name, but remembered something of her face.

"Tell me a story," he said finally, his tone very soft.

Katherine settled him gently back against a rolled blanket and smiled, not allowing herself to consider the fact that his mind might never heal. Only thinking what a beautiful child he must have been, beautiful and brave and very charming.

Rain pattered against the canvas top, but inside their little haven the two were warm and dry, for the wind came from the east and did not blow through the circular openings at the front or back of the wagon.

Katherine's bold knight, Sir Valemeer, came again, wielding his sword for right and justice, and his beloved Lady Catrina.

Travis fell asleep as Kat wove her tale, but long after his eyes closed and his breath became shallow, she watched him.

The wagon was pulled by two mules, Stupid and Dunce, if Katherine understood the cook's ravings correctly. Old Sawdust drove the conveyance they rode in, even though most of his huge supply of sundry culinary necessities were now packed, rather precariously, on a trio of horses tied to the end of the tailgate.

They moved just slightly faster than a slug over a sunny rock. But Katherine found no need to complain, since the men headed north as directly as possible, and kept the two of them fed and well hidden.

At noon she took her meal with the crew. There were five men in all, the small, blond-haired Finch, being the youngest, and weathered Saws, the oldest.

In between there was Jimmy, who rarely spoke but played a harmonica in a way that made Kat want to cry; Elky, whose legs were comically bowed; and, of course, Cody Blackfeather.

Following supper, Travis fell asleep only minutes after Kat began her continuing story, and so she crept silently from the wagon. The night was very dark, for clouds still covered the moon. Jimmy sat with his back to a fat log and his face to the fire, while Cody cleaned his saddle not far away.

Filling a bowl, Saws handed it to Kat in silence. She murmured her thanks and moved to the fire, where she tasted a few bites and cleared her throat. "I was wondering if, by chance, any of you might have heard of a man named Latigo."

For three heartbeats no one answered.

"Yeah." It was the venerable old cook who finally spoke. "Yeah, I heard of him."

That news seemed almost too good to be true, but Kat knew she must be careful, for perhaps there was a price on Travis's head. She could not afford to give these men a clue to his identity by allowing them to somehow connect Latigo's name to Travis Ryland.

"Was Latigo's soul in particular need of saving?" ventured Saws in his lispy tone.

Katherine scowled. "I beg your pardon?"

"The good reverend. I was wonderin' if he'd heard Latigo's soul needed saving."

"Oh!" Katherine remembered her lies with a start and silently reprimanded herself for not keeping her fabrications more firmly planted in her head. "No." She took several bites to allay their suspicions. "I just heard he had a ranch somewhere in this vicinity."

"What does vicin'ty mean?" questioned Saws, tipping his battered bowler hat back to scratch his head.

"His property is not far from the ranch we work for." Cody lifted his attention from his saddle. "We'll be passing near there."

"Yeah. Real close," Saws agreed, "if we can push these fat old hogs that far."

Katherine could only assume he referred to the cattle they were driving. She'd seen the animals earlier in the day, and noticed even with her unexperienced eye, that they did not look like the scrawny long-horned type of bovine she had seen driven through Silver Ridge.

"Herefords! Bah!" Saws spat disgustedly. "Don't see what L—"

"We should reach Latigo's ranch in less than two weeks' time," interrupted Cody smoothly. "Do you know him?"

"No!" Katherine flushed now, realizing she had used a bit too much emphasis on her denial. "No." She ducked her head to eat again. "I was simply curious."

Katherine figured there were perhaps fifty horses in the herd that followed the white-faced red cattle. From her place in the wagon near Travis she recognized Moondancer and Soldier. They stayed apart from the rest of the herd. The stallion's artificial color had been mostly washed off by the rain, but he and Dancer had seemingly found a soft place to roll, for they were covered with a reddish mud that made it difficult to distinguish them. Or was it possible one of the men had intentionally disguised the horses?

"What are you looking at?" Travis asked.

She smiled down at him, grateful that he spent more and more time conscious now, and intentionally smoothing the worry from her expression. "The horses."

"Do I have a horse, Kat?"

He had taken to calling her Kat, and rarely referred to her as Rachel now, except at times when the dreams would haunt him. Still, he did not know who she was, and seemed to be building his life solely from the things she told him.

"Yes." She smoothed the hair back from his forehead, taking some comfort in the fact that this new Travis would not disallow her touch. "You have a horse. An enormous, beautiful stallion."

"Like Sir Valemeer's?"

"Yes, rather like that, but not black." For a moment the realization that Travis could not sort fantasy from reality plagued her, but she pushed the worry aside, forcing herself to believe he would someday be well. "He's what they call a buckskin, I believe. Tan, with black legs and . . ."

Travis reached out, taking her hand in his callused palm to pull it gently to his chest and distract her attention.

Katherine could not help but remember the times they had shared themselves completely, the times when she had felt his sensual power swell and overcome her senses. She swallowed hard, lifting her gaze to his innocent expression.

"And what, Kat?"

"And . . ." She pulled her thoughts from the past. "Black points on his ears."

"Did you get him for me?"

Dear God! Did he think she was his mother? The thought made her blush, for her recollections of him were far from maternal. "No. You had him when I met you. You were riding him."

"Really?" He lifted his brows at her.

She nodded and looked through the back opening in the canvas again, feeling as if she were merely weaving another tale for his amusement. "You were sitting so straight and tall, and I thought you very handsome."

She hadn't meant to say that exactly, but the idea of him thinking of her as his mother disturbed her.

"Where was I going?"

Katherine licked her lips. What could she tell Travis Ryland of himself? That he was a bounty hunter? That there was a band of ruthless outlaws out to kill him? That there was very possibly a price on his head because he had, by his own admission, killed more men than she could name. What could she say?

"Where was I going, Kat?" he repeated softly.

"To church," she answered.

"What?"

"Yes." She nodded, building on the lie she had told the other men. "You're a minister who travels from town to town."

"A minister?" He scowled.

She nodded vigorously.

"I thought maybe I'd be a cowboy, like Cody. Or a . . . an outlaw."

"Outlaw?" She breathed the word, then shook her head again. "What would make you think that?"

"Nothing. Just thought maybe—"

"Well, you're not. You're a very good man. Winning the West with the . . . the reins in your left hand and the Good Book in your right." She raised her own hand, then cleared her throat and let it drop slowly to her lap.

"The Good Book?" he questioned.

"The Bible."

He nodded silently. "Where is my bible?"

"They took it," she said quickly.

"They?"

"The . . . bad guys."

"Why?"

"I don't know." She shrugged, feeling very foolish suddenly and fiddling with his blanket with her free hand. "How would I know?"

"And they shot me?"

"Yes." She bit her lip.

"Did they . . ." He drew her hand to his mouth to gently kiss her fingers. "Did they try to harm you?"

She felt her cheeks heat as a flame scorched a trail through her fingers to her body. "Yes. But I escaped."

For a moment his jaw hardened, making him look very much like the man she had first met on a dark street in Silver Ridge.

"That makes me mad." He said the words in a flat monotone. "Not like a preacher should feel."

Katherine blinked, realizing she was breathing hard. "It's not surprising that sin makes you angry. After all, you try to do God's will and think others should also."

She lifted her gaze nervously to his and found with consternation that she could not pull it away. His eyes were very blue and deep and warm.

"Are you sure I'm a preacher?" he murmured.

The tension made it hard for her to breathe. In all her life she had never wanted anything more than she wanted to kiss him now.

"Are you sure?" he asked, touching a hand to her side to draw her gently closer.

"Yes." The word squeaked from her mouth as she jerked quickly back. "Absolutely."

"Why are you traveling with me, then? Are you my wife?"

Her jaw dropped. "Wife?" For just a moment the temptation to say yes was overpowering. But the discussion of preachers and God made her shake her head. "No. No, I'm not."

"My sister?"

"No!" That answer came easier.

"Then what?" He shook his head as if unable to find a place for her in the life she described.

"I just help you. Assist you. Yes." She nodded. "I, too, was called to do the Lord's work."

"Why do you dress like a boy?"

"Oh, that! It was your idea actually. You felt I would be safer if people didn't know I was a woman."

He stared at her. "Because you're too tempting?"

"Tempting?" she breathed.

"Every man would want you, of course. For his own."

For a moment Kat was certain she would melt from the intensity of his eyes, but found she could say or do nothing to break the spell.

"So we work together?" His voice was low now, and his hand pressed her gently toward him again. "Very close together?"

She was being drawn into the flame of his person, pulled irresistibly downward. "I have to go!" she sputtered, trying to yank away but finding her hand was still caught in his. "Talk to Mr. Blackfeather."

"Kat?"

She refused to look at him. "Yes?"

"Don't leave me."

"But Mr. Black—"

"Tell me about yourself. I can't remember, and there must be so much to know."

"About me?" She winced at the sound of her own voice. "There's not . . . not much to know."

"Where did you grow up?"

She swallowed, feeling painfully foolish with her hand held tightly in his and the lies building around her like smothering grains of sand. "Boston," she managed finally, feeling it would surely be safest to tell the truth whenever possible.

"And your family is still there?"

"Just my mother. My father died some years back."

He watched her closely, making her feel very nervous, so that she lowered her eyes and searched for something to say.

"He was a minister . . . too," she added quickly, lifting her gaze to his.

"He must have been very proud of you."

Her lips parted for a wordless moment. "No." The denial sounded hopelessly flat to her own ears. "He wasn't." Katherine bit her lip and wished suddenly that she had not spoken, for she knew immediately that he had heard the pain in her voice, pain that should not be there and certainly should not be acknowledged. "I must go," she said, lowering her gaze again.

"Why?"

"I beg your pardon?" Her fingers smoothed a wrinkle on his blanket as she scowled down at it's curved course beside Travis's arm.

"Why wasn't he proud?" he asked softly. "I would be if you were my . . . daughter."

Her breath caught abruptly in her throat. He had planned to say something other than "daughter," she knew, and yet it truly didn't matter what term he used, for never in her life had anyone suggested she was worthy of pride. "Why?" she whispered, not looking up, but feeling his gaze like a hot ray of sunshine on her face.

"Because you're an angel."

"I'm not." She jerked her hand from his and tried to move away, but his voice stopped her.

"I'm sorry. I didn't mean to say that, Kat. Don't go."

She settled back on her heels, feeling fear rise in her chest. After all she'd been through with this man, why was she afraid of him now?

"You should sleep," she said softly.

"No." He shook his head. "The dreams. Tell me a story about Catrina."

She bit her lip. "And Sir Valemeer?"

"No. Just her."

"But she's . . ." Katherine shrugged. "She's ever so dull without *him*."

His hand reached out very slowly, and, with ultimate gentleness, lifted hers from her lap. "I don't think so," he murmured.

Chapter 25

"What's that?" Katherine asked, lifting her gaze nervously from the camp fire, and letting her fork pause in midair as a furtive animal slunk past the chuck wagon.

For three days she and Travis had traveled with Blackfeather's crew. Each evening was similar to the last, with one or two of the men watching the herd while the others ate or rested. Saws was just now cleaning his cooking utensils, and Elky was carefully carving something from a chunk of wood.

"It ain't nothin'," said Finch, but Saws snorted.

Elky laughed aloud. "It's Finch's cow dog."

Saws brayed his donkeylike snort again. "Cow dog my a . . ." he began, but one sheepish glance at Kat's face made him change his choice of words. "Cow dog, my beard! The mutt wouldn't know a cow from a cottonwood if you stood 'em end t' end. Yep, was a shrewd deal the boy pulled off that time."

From her right, Katherine thought she detected a muttered curse as Finch cleaned his teeth with his bowie knife.

"We was waitin' in Little Big Rock for the herd t' be delivered, and Finch got himself in a card game. When it turns out the other fella was short on cash, he up and bets his dog. Scraggly lookin' red hound with droopy ears and eyes sad enough t' make y' weep just t' look at him. He had him tied up, he did, and when he learns Finch was gonna be drivin' cattle, he says that sorry lookin' mutt was the best thing on four legs for herding beeves. Anyhow, Finch won, only the dog don't know spit."

Elky laughed again. "He can trail a scent like a lobo wolf, though," he said. "Cuz we can't lose him, no matter how hard we try."

"I ain't tryin' to lose him," disagreed Finch without much force. "He's a right marvel at trackin'. He could trail a bird in flight if you'd give him a whiff of a feather. Remember the time we found them droppings? You should of saw it," bragged Finch. "I just pointed to the sh— stuff and said, 'scent,' just like I was told. And sure enough, the dog tracked that ol' bighorn just like magic."

"Only the sheep got away," added Saws. "And so did the mutt. And Finch hasn't been able to get close to him ever since."

"Well, he's a better dog than any of you boys has ever had. Best tracker in the state, I bet. Probably in the country. Hell, in the—"

"Shut up, Finch," said Saws and Elky at once.

"Anyhow, he slinks around camp sometimes," said Saws. "Don't know how he stays alive, skinny as he is."

Katherine sighed, staring into the darkness. "It sounds like Prince."

"Prince?" There were grins from several directions as the men sat quietly, awaiting an amusing explanation. Cattle drives weren't generally known for their excitement.

"When I was a girl, I . . ." Kat realized her mistake immediately and stopped, her mouth slightly ajar and her eyes wide. "I mean a boy! When I was a boy!"

From beside her Elky cleared his throat. But Finch was not so tactful, and giggled in glee.

"I told y'! I told y', didn't I?"

"I meant boy!" she gasped, jerking to her feet, but Saws shook his head and tried to subdue his grin.

"Don't fret on it, kid. We been on the trail a good while. But it ain't been so long we cain't tell the difference."

"I meant—" she sputtered.

"I knew it!" yipped Finch with a solid slap to his knee.

"You and every man with . . ." Elky's gaze slipped to Katherine's face before he cleared his throat again and finished, "You and everyone else."

"Well . . . I'm going to see if the dog is hungry."

Katherine rose abruptly, blushing to her toes, and quickly leaving the campsite.

Outside the circle of firelight, Katherine drew a deep breath and frowned. So they knew she was a woman. Apparently they'd known all along. Did that mean they also knew Travis wasn't a minister? Did they know his true identity? Were they even now planning on delivering them to Dellas? Or to Red?

Her hand shook as she lifted a morsel of pork from her plate. She'd caught sight of the dog's slinking form again and hoped to coax him into trusting her, although she didn't know why. Perhaps it was just her nature. She simply wanted to be loved.

But maybe not. She stood very still, thinking.

In the past Travis had avoided her. He'd let down his guard at times, but only for fleeting moments—tiny fragments of time that left her grasping for more. It was a familiar pattern, for her father had been much the same. Almost loving her, almost accepting her at times, but finally drawing away in disapproval.

Perhaps she hadn't realized it before she'd begun telling Travis about the fictional Catrina. But Catrina had become unexpectedly like herself, and against her will, she'd told him more about her own character than she'd planned. And perhaps more than she had known herself.

It made her feel exposed and strangely suspicious of her own weaknesses.

For the first time in her life a man she loved was not running away, and it scared her.

The days passed quickly.

Though Travis's wound was healing well, his memory had not returned, and it had come to the point where Katherine couldn't tell if she should be worried or glad.

What would she do when he found out who he truly was? When he realized she had lied to him, had fictionalized his entire past?

She stood in the darkness again, listening to the silence and waiting for the dog to approach. He'd become a bit bolder and would sometimes snatch up bits of food if she threw them to him.

Thoughts of Travis made her restless, and she finally scraped the remains of her supper onto the ground and strolled thoughtfully back to the wagon.

Thunder rumbled up from the south, and a gust of wind carried voices from the camp fire in a crescendo that quickly dropped away.

She sighed, moving closer to the campsite until she rested her palm upon the hard metal rim of the wagon wheel. It felt cool and pitted beneath her hand.

"When are you going to tell her?"

"Save your disapproval for someone else, Blackfeather," came Travis's quiet response. "It's none of your concern."

Beside the wagon, Katherine leaned a bit closer to listen.

"So you're planning to leave her with Latigo?"

"You got a problem with that, too?"

"Me?" Cody sounded mildly surprised. "No. She's Lat's type. Pretty and smart. He'll like her."

There was a momentary pause.

"Shut up, Blackfeather."

"Well, you want him to like her, don't you? Since he'll have to see to her well-being after you get yourself killed."

"I should have expected such a show of confidence from a man brought up at Latigo's knee."

"I have every confidence you'll achieve what you hope to."

"What the hell's that supposed to mean?"

"It's lucky you're smart enough to realize you're not good enough for her."

"You've been around Lat too long," Travis said. "It's getting so I can see right through you."

"And you've tried to be your father's son ever since Rachel. Worthless. Wasn't that the term he most often used?"

"Damn you, Blackfeather. That's got nothing to do with this."

"Then why not admit the truth?"

"The truth!" Travis snorted a burst of harsh laughter.

"Hell, that's all we need. Me admitting the truth. Condemning her to . . ."

"To what? Life with you? Lat might say it's not your place to make choices for her."

"Stay the hell out of it! You hear me? You don't know nothing about her."

"I'm thinking it's strange she'd waste her time saving your life. When the truth is, you didn't want it saved. You'd just as soon give it up. Especially if you might have to disprove your old man's opinion of you."

"Goddamn it! I was just a kid. I couldn't keep Rachel alive. But this is gonna be different."

"She's carried you a long time to give up now."

"You and Lat, you know how to twist the knife, don't you? You think I don't know I failed her? But I'll tell you why she's been killing herself for me, it's cuz she thinks I'm some kind of prince. Some kind of brave knight, all full of wondrous deeds and gentle thoughts, who—"

"No." Katherine stepped suddenly to the opening of the wagon. "Hardly do I think you're a prince."

"Katherine." Travis could manage no more than a whisper.

"You've been deceiving me. Playing me for a fool. Pretending you can't remember your own name." Her voice cracked, and in that moment Travis almost reached for her, but held himself back. "You must have thought this all very funny."

Ryland clenched his fists at his sides and wished he could hit something. All he'd wanted was to protect her. "I ain't laughing, lady."

"Then I commend your self-discipline," she said coldly. "But I would like to know—what was the purpose of this little charade?"

"It kept you out of trouble, didn't it?" he asked, trying to loosen the tightness in his chest and look casual as he leaned against the bowed frame behind him. "You liked the little boy, didn't you? You were safe with him. Could stay close and pretend I was some . . ." He snorted, feeling sick as he watched her face. "Some pure preacher man. Or some poor wounded kid. Or some knight on his black charger." He was on his feet, without meaning to rise, standing before her with his heart beating hard and fast in his constricted chest. "Reins in my left hand and the Good Book in my right." He laughed grimly. "Anything was better than who I am, wasn't it?"

She stepped back a pace, looking pale and frightened in the darkness, but her fear only added to his fury, and he grabbed her arms.

"Wasn't it?" he asked again.

He felt her shiver beneath his hands, but in a moment her chin rose, and her gaze lifted to his.

"I won't be bothering you again with my presence or my fantasizing, Travis Ryland," she said quietly. "I'll stay with Latigo just as you wish. And if you want to get yourself killed—well, that's your choice." She backed away, pulling her arms from his grasp before turning. "I'll need someone to teach me to defend myself," she said to no one in particular. "Since Mr. Ryland is giving up the job."

Jimmy shuffled his feet nervously, but said nothing. All eyes watched her.

"I'm a hell of a quick draw," said Finch, taking a step forward.

Travis tried to glare the boy down, but the other's gaze was caught on Katherine's prim expression.

"Very good," she said stiffly. "Then I would dearly appreciate it if you would teach me to be the same."

"Sure." Finch grinned, pulling out one revolver and motioning her forward, but before she'd taken a step, Travis was between them.

"What the devil do you think she is?" he shouted. "Some kind of stray kid you can teach to be a man?"

"No." Finch shook his head, still grinning. "Nope. I sure don't think that, Rye."

"Then back off," ordered Travis, his voice so low it barely reached his own ears.

"Excuse me, Ryland," said Katherine as she gave him a wide berth to stand beside Finch. "But I believe you wished to be done with me. So I'm offering you that opportunity, but I fear I am not inclined to trust my life to Latigo, whom I've not even met. I find it's unwise for a woman to depend on a man." She took the revolver slowly from Finch's hand, pointing it very directly at Travis's chest. "So I plan to learn to take care of myself."

Travis remained absolutely still. With the light of the fire glowing behind her she looked very slim and straight. "You shouldn't aim at something you ain't prepared to shoot," he said dryly.

"And what makes you think I'm not prepared to shoot?"

"Because I know you clean down to your bones, lady. I know you better than you know yourself."

"You think so?" With slow precision she cocked the revolver. "If I'm not mistaken, I just tug on this little lever right here. Is that correct, Mr. Finch?" asked Kat, her index finger steady on the trigger.

"Listen, Kat. Ryland here didn't mean to make you mad. He was just tryin' t' keep you out of trouble."

"And you knew him immediately, when we first arrived," she said. "You must have thought it quite amusing that I would proclaim him to be a minister of God." She laughed, but the sound was harsh and clipped. "Remind me to shoot you after I shoot him."

"This talk of shootin' . . ." Finch shook his head. "It's bad for digestion, and after one of Saws's meals, it could be fatal. Give my gun back, Miss Kat. We didn't mean t' hurt yer feelings. In fact, that's why we didn't tell y' right off that we knowed him. You seemed so set in convincing us that we didn't. And then when you figured out we knew all along that you was a woman, well, we couldn't hardly bear to disprove yer stories no more."

"How long have you known Travis, Finch?" she asked, not lowering the gun.

"Hell, I don't know. Ten years or near about."

"Ten years?" She did not quite manage to keep the surprise from her tone.

"We all worked fer Latigo together," said Sawdust in his lispy voice. "He's got him a tendency to collect stray boys. Teach them living skills. That sort of thing."

"And that's all I'm asking," said Katherine calmly. "To learn living skills. A girl's got a right."

"Sure she does," soothed Finch. "Now give my gun back, and we'll get started."

"When I'm dead and damned," said Travis in a low voice.

"Well." Katherine smiled grimly. "From what I hear, that shouldn't give me too long to wait. Mr. Finch, shall we begin?"

"No!" Travis said and, grabbing the Colt's barrel, yanked it to him.

Katherine, however, was not ready to relinquish her hold, and was snatched to his chest like an apple from a tree.

"You go learning to shoot, lady, and pretty soon every two-bit kid with a gun thinks he can prove something if he kills you." He shook his head slowly, his face very close to hers. "You ain't learning."

"Yes." Her gaze was as steady as the earth and as cool as the evening air. "I am. Mr. Finch has agreed to give me lessons. Did you fail to hear him?"

"Mr. Finch is an idiot," proclaimed Travis, knowing his teeth were clenched and that his breath came like the puffs of smoke from a steam engine on an uphill climb. "And he won't be touching you."

Her brows rose above her unusual silver-blue eyes, alerting Travis to the fact that he had spoken rather out of turn. He hadn't meant to say Finch wouldn't touch her, but that Finch wouldn't be teaching her to shoot.

"I realize now that you do not care if your life is shortened," remarked Katherine, "but I, for one, hope to live to a ripe old age. Maybe even have children. So I *will* endeavor to learn to defend myself, with your blessing or without. And if I blow my head off in the meantime . . ." She smiled up at him, looking irritatingly cool beneath his best glare. "My death will be on your conscience." Her lids fluttered for a moment, while her sticky smile remained adhered. "If you have one. Now, if you will let go of the gun, I will proceed to—"

"I'll teach you, goddamn it!"

"Really? The great Travis Ryland himself? The killer extraordinary. The Ghost."

"Shut the hell up!" he growled into her face. "And get to sleep, cuz you're going to have a long day tomorrow."

Turning, he glared at each man in turn. "What the devil are you staring at?"

Sawdust and Jimmy shook their heads in unison, Finch mumbled something under his breath, and Cody, damn his soul, laughed with his eyes in that way that drove Travis insane.

"Sleep in the wagon," he ordered Kat brusquely. "And stay out of trouble."

Chapter 26

"Who taught *you* to shoot?"

"It's none of your damn business."

Katherine watched as Travis answered, his glare unaffected by the beauty of the morning. The storm had blown itself out sometime before dawn, leaving the sky a robin's-egg blue.

"Was it your father?" Kat asked. She'd spent most of the night in thought and tears, and had finally made a new resolution. Travis Ryland would no longer frighten her with his blustery ways and aggressive demeanor. The truth was, there were more than enough *real* outlaws to worry about. It was time she established her innocence and went on her way. And though the route to achieving that goal would not be simple, she had come up with a plan.

Just now, however, Travis was still scowling at her, and snapped, "Didn't I just say it's none of your damn—"

"Yes." Katherine interrupted abruptly, and stepped forward so that she was only a few yards in front of him, with her fists on her hips and an experimental glare of her own. "You did say its none of my damn business, but I disagree. It just so happens my life is in danger, and I would feel a bit more secure if I believed you had learned to shoot from someone with skill."

His scowl lessened and he looked a bit taken aback. "I've never before knowed anyone who could take half a day to say what shouldn't be said at all."

With that statement Katherine found it difficult to hold

her own glare. "When I figure out what that means, I'm going to come up with a scathing remark," she assured him.

"It was an insult."

"I know it was an insult, Ryland. What else would you say to me?"

She watched his right eyebrow quirk into a little peak and wondered, with mild interest, if he was as angry as he looked.

"Let's get to work," he said brusquely.

"I asked you a question."

"Goddamn—"

"There's no point in swearing, Ryland. I've heard it all, and you know what, it's quite unimpressive. So you might as well just answer my questions and get it over with."

"You're the most ornery woman I've ever met in my life."

She smiled, feeling a wonderful exhilaration with the knowledge that she could not only hold her own, but could challenge him. "Lucky for you, we're almost to Latigo's and you'll never have to see me again. Now, did your father teach you to shoot?"

He paused for only a moment. "My father didn't teach me anything, lady. Except how to duck a fist."

All Katherine's self-satisfaction vanished. "Oh." She said the word very softly. "I'm sorry."

"Yeah?" He watched her, the color of his eyes identical to the sky. "So was Rachel. And look what happened to her."

"What did happen?" she breathed.

"Leave it alone, lady." His tone was deep and his fists clenched. "It's done and over with. I'm not a kid no more."

"She was your sister, wasn't she?"

Travis drew a breath deep. "Pa said she resembled Ma. Dark hair and eyes as bright as the morning. Maybe that was why he loved her. She was pretty." He shook his head. "And smart. Just like . . ."

Their gazes caught and fused. The surrounding forest seemed to be still and waiting.

"Let's get this lesson started."

"I'm sorry, Travis," she said softly.

He swallowed, easing his fists open and turning his gaze away. "You already said that."

"I'm saying it again."

"Well don't." He turned his gaze back to her and lifted the revolver Finch had loaned him. "Come here."

She did so, taking a few stiff strides so that she stood directly before him, her gaze steady on the gun in his hand.

"See this?" he said, looking at the gun. "This is a six-shooter. A Colt Walker." With a single movement of his hand a bullet slid out of the cylinder where an indian and soldier were etched in fine detail. Five other bullets dropped into his palm. "You take these and push them into their holes like this." He demonstrated twice, sliding them along the smooth notch and into their chambers before handing her the revolver. "Try it."

The gun felt cool and heavy in Kat's hand. Its deadly potential made her movements slow and stiff, but she finally filled the remaining chambers and looked at Ryland for the next step.

"After all the shots are fired, the shells will still be there. You'll dump them out and refill."

She nodded her understanding.

"Do it again."

The first five bullets slid in smoothly, but his stare made her nervous, and she dropped the last one. Squatting down, she searched through the spikey grasses, feeling foolish.

"That's your lesson."

"What?" She glanced up at him, squinting in the bright sunlight.

"When you can fill them chambers faster than you can count to ten, come and get me. I'll be under that tree."

She watched him walk away, and was amazed to learn how many curse words she could mentally rattle off before he eased himself down against the trunk of a white birch.

By noon Kat's fingers were raw, and she had remembered half a dozen more swear words to add to her growing list.

"I'm ready." She gazed down into Travis's face. He had sat unmoving for so long that for a time she had wondered if he had fallen asleep, but each time she'd glanced his way, he had been watching her.

"You sure?" He smiled, looking superior.

"Yes."

"All right." He pushed his hat back on his brow a fraction of an inch. "Let's see."

Katherine licked her lips. He would *not* intimidate her she reminded herself. But he'd spent a lifetime learning to do just that, and had become very good at it.

Nevertheless, she shoved the first bullet quickly into the chamber.

"Count."

"I beg your pardon?"

"Gotta do it as fast as you can count. Remember?"

Another curse word popped into her head. She smiled despite herself and counted as she dropped bullets into chambers. The sixth one slipped in on the word "ten."

Kat lifted her eyes to Ryland's. "Well?"

"You count mighty slow for a schoolmarm."

"Damn you." She said the words very clearly and with a good deal of satisfaction.

He lifted his brows as he watched her. "But your swearing's coming along real good."

"Thank you."

"You bet. Now . . ." He rose a bit stiffly to his feet, taking Finch's empty holster with him. "Wear this low on your right side." He reached about her, passing the leather belt to his left hand and drawing it up snugly against her hips. His fingertips brushed the metal buttons on her jeans, and she bit her lip and refused to look at him.

For just a moment his movements bumbled, but he managed the buckle and pulled away.

"Wear it too high and you'll have to cramp your arm to get at it."

His voice sounded strange, but Katherine dared not analyze his stilted tone.

"Like this?" she asked, knowing her face was hot and pushing the revolver deep into its leather pocket.

"Yeah. But tie it down."

"What?" She chanced a glimpse at his face. "Tie what down?" she asked, lowering her gaze quickly and fumbling with the buckle.

"I'll do it." He dropped to his knees and slipped one hand between her legs.

Katherine gasped, and Travis raised his eyes, examining her face. "First rule is to stay calm, lady."

She took a steadying breath and tried a false smile. "Have I said 'damn you' yet?"

"Yes. You used that one," he reminded her, his right hand resting on the inside of her knee and his face lifted to hers.

"I have more curses," she assured him, standing very still, lest his hand slip one way or the other and cause that shameful gasp to escape her again. "Better ones."

"Really?" Very slowly he slid his hand around the back of her leg in search of the narrow leather thong that hung from the holster's bottom. "Let's hear them."

He was a deceitful, no-account bounty hunter she reminded herself, but somewhere in her mind she remembered the gentleness of his touch, the surprising ferocity with which he had protected her on more than one occasion.

"Katherine?" he said, calling her back to the present. "You were going to try out some of them new curse words."

"Oh, yes. Well . . ." She licked her lips. "I'm saving them for the perfect moment."

His gaze lowered again, and he brought the ends of the thong together, though a bit shakily. "Now's as good a time as any," he muttered.

"What's that?"

He hesitated for just a moment, with his hands poised at her lower thigh. "Now would be a damned good time," he said, rising slowly.

They stood mere inches apart.

"For what?" Katherine breathed.

They both knew they were falling back under the forbidden spell and felt themselves leaning together, as if a strong wind blew at their backs.

But Travis pulled away with a jolt and clenched his fists at his sides. "Damn good time for a lesson."

"Yes." Katherine backed away a cautious step, feeling as though the distance was necessary to clear her head and sweeping back a stray lock of hair from her face. "What now?"

Travis blew out a long breath and set his palm to his own revolver, as if the feel of the handle would remind him of his mission. "You grip it like this, see?"

Regardless of Kat's determination to keep her mind on track, his movements seemed sensual to her.

"Firm, but not hard."

She watched his hand curl around the smooth wood.

"You slip it in real easy."

His index finger did just that, nestling carefully against the trigger.

"And you pull straight up."

Their eyes met—Katherine's wide, and Travis's clefted by sun-bleached brows. The woods were utterly quiet, waiting for them to weaken.

"Damn," Travis breathed, but he fought against his desire and gripped the gun harder. "Don't yank at it," he instructed.

"No. I wouldn't," she vowed.

"Then you . . . hold it . . ." The gun was out, and his eyes dead level on hers. "Hold it like you would a . . ."

"How's it going?" Finch asked from the sheltering woods.

Katherine jumped, and Travis swung about, the revolver moving like part of his arm to point directly at the intruder's heart.

"Didn't mean t' startle y'." Finch grinned, sweeping his gaze from Travis to Kat and back. "I was just curious how someone with Ryland's reputation would learn a gal t' shoot."

Katherine wondered how much he had heard and seen and could feel the blush seep down toward her toes.

"It looked real interesting, Rye. But I was a wonderin', what do you hold that gun like? You hold it like you would a . . ." He paused with his grin broadening until it threatened to split his face.

"Rolling pin!" Katherine supplied suddenly. "Just like a rolling pin, firm, but not hard."

Finch laughed out loud, and Travis's brows lowered ominously.

"How'd you find us?"

"I followed the mutt." He cocked his head toward the left,

though the dog was not in sight. "He was sniffing round, looking all forlorn, like. Then he picks up a scent, right amidst all them cattle tracks and everything, and his head comes up. Off he goes." Finch lifted his hand to scoot it forward, as if sliding it uphill. "Led me right here."

Travis's revolver finally eased into his holster. "You going to tell me why?"

"Yeah." Finch laughed again, seeming to find something irresistibly funny about the entire situation. "Jimmy up and found him a couple of strays. Blackfeather thought you might be interested."

"Strays?"

"Yep. Matter of fact, we met up with these two fellas before. Couple of brothers riding a white nag. One's been shot, and both of them is looking half starved."

"Luke and Jacob," Katherine said.

Travis scowled. "What's it got to do with me?"

"They had them a little run-in with Dellas," Finch said with a nod. "Cody thought you'd maybe wanna know."

Chapter 27

Katherine noticed Jacob Jameson's pallor when he spoke to Travis.

"Dellas, he was having him a discussion with his boys. Talked about a horse, and somebody named Grey, and about . . . about a fella they called The Ghost," said Jacob, lifting a bony hand to rub his opposite arm. "One fella, he says they had t' head back t' town before you got there and riled up the folks. Then this other, he says nobody'd believe Ryland, cause all the folks thought you had killed the mare." For a moment Jacob looked completely baffled.

"They *mayor*," Travis supplied. "Mayor."

"Oh! A man. Yeah. That makes sense now. Anyhow, this redheaded fella, he says the people in town all thought you'd killed him. They didn't know this Grey had hired Dellas t' steal the payroll."

"Grey?" Katherine asked. "He hired Dellas to steal his own miners' wages."

Travis nodded. Everything had suddenly become very clear to him.

"Then he hired me to kill Dellas, and set me up as the thief. Only Grey had the money all along. The money the townspeople had thrown in the pot to put a stop to Dellas."

"We have to go back to Silver Ridge," Katherine said quietly. "We have to tell the people what Grey has done. Then our innocence will be established."

"Is my brother gonna live?" asked Jacob weakly.

"Which way did they go?" Travis asked, his tone deep.

"I don't know. Could be—"

"Which way?" Travis leaned closer to grab a handful of Jacob's shirt.

The young man pulled weakly back. "I couldn't say. But it looked t' me like Dellas had plans of heading back t' town."

There was a moment of silence, then, "If you're lying, I'll have your liver for supper," Travis vowed grimly.

Jacob paled another shade, and for a moment Katherine thought he might faint.

"I ain't lyin', mister. I swear it." Suddenly there were tears in his eyes. "They shot my brother. Woulda shot me too if'n they could."

Travis's fist loosened, allowing the boy to lie back against the log again. "Why didn't they?"

Jacob shifted his gaze nervously to Cody, not sure if he could trust him any more than he did Travis. "They was having them a disagreement. The fella named Red, he wanted t' shoot us straight off. But the old buzzard, Dellas, he had him a branch that was a burnin' on the end, and he lifted the thing and looks at us and says . . . He says they'd have them some fun with us first," he finished.

Katherine felt the small hairs rise on the back of her neck, realizing the extent of the evil the boy had encountered.

Travis stood very still, clenching his fist above his revolver. "What happened?"

"There was a fight broke out amongst the men. Me and Luke, we saw our chance and hightailed it."

"You sure they didn't follow you?"

"I'm sure. We wasn't nothin' t' them. Just . . ." He swallowed again. "Just sport. But . . ." His gaze caught on Travis's. "They wanted you something fierce."

Ryland stepped back a pace, visibly trying to relieve his tension.

"Listen, fellas, me and my brother, we seen the light. We ain't gonna be outlaws no more. And if'n you could fix him up . . ." He paused long enough to swipe the back of a hand beneath his nose. "We'd stay on the straight and narrow till hell freezes up solid."

The announcement was delivered with such honest desperation that Katherine felt like crying herself.

"He'll live." Cody's tone was flat. "We got the bullet out, but he's not likely to want to sit for a while."

With that news the tears actually exited Jacob's eyes. "Pretty damn low, ain't it? Shootin' a man in his backside."

"The two of you will sleep in the wagon until he's healed up," Cody ordered quietly.

Not needing to be told twice, Jacob hurried over the tailgate and out of view.

"Pick up any more damn strays and we won't have 'nough food t' last till morning," Saws grumbled.

"You brought enough supplies for a hundred foot soldiers, old man," Finch argued.

"And a good thing, too, the way we're packin' in extras. Hell, you'd think my wagon was a sickbed on wheels, makin' me stow my goods on them raw-boned broncs like . . ." His voice trailed off as he bent to stir the stew.

"This change your plans?" asked Blackfeather.

"Yes," said Kat. "We've got to get straight back to Silver Ridge to expose Grey's true nature."

"No!" Travis turned toward Cody. "She'll be safest here with the crew. We'll stick close until we reach the ranch."

"But Travis—"

"No!" The word was issued from his throat like a savage growl. "You'll go to Latigo, and you'll stay put like you said."

Katherine spent the remainder of the day doing nothing but drawing, cocking, and releasing the trigger of Finch's gun. It was tedious and tiring, and it made her wonder if Travis had any intention of teaching her to shoot at all, or rather planned to waste her time until they reached Latigo's ranch, where he would let her rot like an aged cut of beef.

But if such was his plan, he could think again.

Katherine pulled the revolver smoothly from the holster, staring over the barrel and into the distance. Travis Ryland would not be facing Dellas alone. Of that she was certain.

*   *   *

"Wake up, lady," Travis ordered brusquely.

Katherine rolled over, noticing the sky was only slightly lighter than pitch. Her right arm ached all the way to her shoulder. Her fingertips were chafed, and her thumb hurt from scraping against the fine metal ribbing on the hammer of Finch's Colt. "What do you want?" she asked, her voice still husky with sleep.

"You're the one wanted to learn to shoot, remember?"

With the Jameson boys in the wagon, she'd found a sheltered spot not far from camp and had make her bed there. Dimly she wondered if Travis had slept at all, or if he had climbed to some distant ridge to scout the country for any sign of trouble, as Finch said he had done on the previous night.

"You want to change your mind, it's fine with me. It ain't giving me no joy knowing you'll be wandering around thinking you can protect yourself."

Regardless of the kink in her back, Kat sat up now. "What have you got against teaching me to shoot, Ryland?" she asked, still groggy with sleep. "You afraid I'll become a faster draw than you?"

"Lady." She saw him shake his head in the dim beginnings of dawn. "You're probably faster than I am now."

"What?" Her mouth fell slightly ajar. "I thought you were a deadeye shot."

"I'm steady," he said with no show of pride. "I ain't fast."

"But Finch said—"

"Finch's been listening to Latigo too long."

She scowled, but he answered before she voiced a question.

"Like Saws said, Latigo collects stray boys like a crow collects shiny rocks. He takes them in, intending to give them a meal and send them on their way. Only they stick around, and pretty soon he thinks he's their pa."

"Is that what happened to you?" she asked softly, trying to remember not to care.

But Travis turned his face to the east and hardened his jaw. "If I'm going to teach you to shoot, I'm planning to do it right. We don't have no time to waste."

"I think I have a right to know, Travis."

His gaze was pulled slowly back to her face. Her hair was crumpled and her oversized shirt slightly askew, but despite it all, she looked beautiful.

"I was nine. Maybe ten. We lived down in Kentucky. Had us a couple of slaves. Pa was home, and he was drunk, but not drunk enough, so Rachel, she sent me off to pick apples." Strange how the memories still made his gut feel raw. "When I came back, the Negroes were gone . . . and Pa was dead."

Kat's inhalation seemed louder than her words, which were breathed out like a secret prayer, "I'm sorry."

Travis shook his head. "I never could care, lady. It used to make me feel bad that I didn't. Thought Rachel would be disappointed that I wasn't sorry for his death. She always said he wasn't a bad man, it was just missing Ma that made him mean. And the whiskey that made him blame me for her passing."

"That's ridiculous," Katherine murmured, her voice as pale as her face in the darkness.

"She died just after birthing me."

"Travis, I—"

"I never knew her, so I didn't miss her. And anyhow, Rachel was more a mother to me than I could of ever hoped to have." He turned his gaze away, somehow not able to look at Kat's perfect face when he said the next words. "Only she was shot, too. Found her when I come running back, spilling apples all the way. They'd . . ." He drew a deep breath. "God knows what they did to her before they shot her." His throat hurt as if it had been cut. "She was only fourteen." His hands were shaking, and he pressed them against his thighs to stop the trembling. "She was gut shot, but she lasted three days, and then she cried. Cried cuz she didn't want to leave me alone."

From the hill where the cattle had bedded down, a cow lowed and was answered.

"Was it Dellas?" Her voice was very soft, and painfully husky.

Travis turned his gaze back to Kat. Her eyes were wide,

and her body seemed no less tense than his. "How did you know?"

"You wouldn't agree to kill him otherwise. Not unless he was truly evil."

Ryland drew a deep breath, knowing he should turn away from her before weakness overcame him and he took her in his arms. "You don't know me, lady."

Her eyes did not falter from his. "The hell I don't!"

"I killed more men than—"

"When?" she interrupted.

"Latigo, he found me, took me west with him. But I thought the Yankees had killed Rachel." He shook his head, trying to clear it of the horrors that haunted him.

"You fought for the Confederacy?"

"I wore the gray colors, but I didn't fight for no one but me."

"And Rachel."

It was difficult to breath when she looked at him like she was now. "Don't make me out to be no hero. I'm a long shot from that."

"Not to me."

Suddenly he stood, his heart all bound up in his chest and his head aching. "I killed innocent men! Don't you see that? And for what? Nothing!"

She rose slowly, biting her lip and watching him. "That's what war is, Travis. You didn't invent it."

He took a deep breath, trying to steady his will. "Latigo, he never told me it was Dellas that killed her. But he knew all along. Then, a few months ago, when Dellas began causing trouble in Colorado and I started asking questions, he told me the truth." For a second Ryland squeezed his eyes shut and rubbed his fingers across his brow, which throbbed with a well-remembered pain. "I wanted to kill Lat when he first said it."

"He must have had his reason for waiting."

"Lat's always got his reasons." Travis nodded, but the movement felt stiff and unnatural. "Said he'd thought I'd get myself killed if I took on Dellas too soon. Said I had a better chance with the Confederacy. Only he'd never been to war. Didn't know what it does to a man."

Suddenly, she was holding his arms, her small heart-shaped face lifted toward his. "What did it do to you?" she whispered.

"You see so much death. So much dying." He could see it now. As if it had never ended. "Sometimes it seems like you're already dead. Like it don't matter. Nothing matters."

"You matter, Travis."

He was trapped in her eyes. He knew better than to let it happen, but he'd been caught off guard again. "I can't protect you, lady," he breathed. "Latigo padded my reputation, made me out to be a fast draw, a ruthless killer. Hell!" He snorted. "Some say I'm a ghost; that I couldn't have lived through what I did. So I must have died and come back. Lat, he liked that idea, thinking that would scare folks real good, that surely that would help me survive, but I'm telling you it's all a fairytale. I can't keep you safe."

"I'm not asking you to."

"Wearing a gun, it don't keep you alive, lady. There's always someone faster. Somebody with something to prove. You got to go back east. I won't watch you die."

"I'm not going to die."

Travis hugged her then, crushing her against his chest. Above her head his eyes fell closed, and against the softness of her breasts his heart ached with a longing he was powerless to ignore.

"Death surrounds me, lady."

"No." Her voice was almost silent against his chest. "I love you."

He grabbed her arms, pushing her away to glare into her face. "Don't say that again. You'll stay with Latigo until this is all past. Then you'll go home. Back to Boston."

Her mouth had fallen ajar, and her silver eyes were round. "Travis . . ."

"Don't say it! You'll stay with Lat! Promise me!"

She shook her head.

"Promise me!" he said, gripping harder.

"All right," she whispered. "I promise."

They remained immobile, staring at each other and breathing hard.

"Good." He nodded once, feeling his guts roil. "You'll be

safe with Lat. Three men can defend the house. He'll make certain nothing happens to you."

"Are you expecting me to trust him?"

Her tone was very cool now. Travis narrowed his eyes and studied her. "What are you asking?"

"You say I can't trust you, the man I . . ." She stopped the words before they were out. "You say I can't trust you to protect me. But you expect me to trust this Latigo?"

Travis still held her at arm's length, but didn't answer.

"You promised to teach me to defend myself. I'll not let you back out."

Travis drew a deep breath, letting his fingers tighten slightly on her arms. "I ain't made of steel, lady."

"Hardly that, Ryland."

"Being with you . . . alone. It's—"

"I don't give a damn what it is," she said, and, pulling her arms from his grasp, stepped quickly back, her strawberry lips pursed and her eyes hard. "You owe me that much."

The dog followed them out of camp that morning and cowered behind a log when Katherine tried her first shots. By nightfall she could hit a two-inch knot on a pine tree four times out of ten. Thirty-six hours later she had doubled her odds.

"So, Rye, can she shoot the stinger off a bee yet?" asked Finch. "Or you still workin' on the grip—firm, but not hard?"

Travis, as usual, sat with his back to the fire, for death would come from behind when it came, and the firelight was blinding. "Shut up, Finch."

"You ever know anyone as closed mouthed as Ryland? Won't tell y' nothin'," exclaimed Finch. "But I got me another source, Kat," he said, turning to her. "How's your fast . . . Damn." He interrupted himself as his gaze found her. "She's mighty purty when she sleeps, ain't she?"

Travis jerked about quickly. Kat lay propped with her head cocked back against a log. Her hat had fallen off, leaving her blue-black hair to shine in the glow of the firelight and her downy lashes to paint delicate shadows beneath her hidden eyes. Clothed in boys' garb, she looked like a lovely child who had fallen asleep playing dress up. The sight made Ryland's chest ache and his breath stop for an instant. "When have you been watching her sleep, Finch?" he asked. The words sounded hoarse and deadly to his own ears.

But Finch had known him a long time, and held up an unoffending hand, as if to ward off his anger. "I ain't, Rye. I was just checkin' t' see if you was awake."

Travis loosened his fist, forcing his muscles to relax, and turned back to the darkness again. "Shut up, Finch," he said dryly.

Saws chuckled behind him. "The wolf's still got a bite, don't he?"

"When the she-wolf's around," Elky said.

"I was hopin' she could tell us another one of them stories like the one last night," said Jacob, to which Luke nodded, and shifted uncomfortably on his blankets.

"Sorriest bunch of cowpokes I ever seen," grumbled Sawdust. "No better than Kat's Shadow there." His narrow eyes shifted to the dog that had slipped up behind Katherine and now lay snuggled up against her body. "Pretty soon you'll be rollin' over fer her t' scratch yer bellies, and sleepin' by her feet at night." He snorted at his own wit, then turned his gaze to Ryland. "Well, maybe not sleepin' at her feet. Hell! Ain't someone gonna carry her to her bedroll?"

Jacob, Luke, and Finch offered at the same time, although Luke was a little slow in rising to do the job.

Travis, however, reached her first, brushing their arms away with a sweep of his own.

"You wanna keep them hands, boys?"

There were mumbles, a grin from Finch, and three young men backed away as Travis bent and lifted her into his arms.

Every man watched him as he carried her from the circle of firelight, but it was Cody's laughing eyes that made him want to swear.

She felt like a memory in his arms, like a dream he had once had. Not real, and yet not quite fantasy, but something so poignant in his mind that it would never be forgotten.

She had already spread her blankets beneath the sweeping branches of a lodgepole pine, and he set her there, gently settling her weight upon them, only to find he lacked the strength to draw away.

The moon had lifted over the mountain peaks and shone its gilded light upon her face now, shadowing and illuminating each feature with mystery and beauty. Travis's breath was trapped, and against her side his heart beat like the thundering hooves of a running stallion.

Katherine Simmons was the very image of everything that was good and fine. She was strength, and sweetness. She was beauty, and practicality. She was smart, and she was ignorant.

He watched her in silence.

She was his. And yet she was not.

"I love you, too," he whispered, and, closing his eyes, pulled his arms away to retreat into the night.

Chapter 28

Katherine lay quietly in the darkness. She had awakened while Travis carried her, had felt his emotions, had heard his words.

He loved her. She held her breath, waiting for the euphoria to come. But it did not. Fear came instead, so strong it seemed to rip at her gut. But fear of what? Rejection? Loneliness? Her father had loved her, too.

Or was it the fact that love would not keep Travis safe that worried her? In fact, love was more likely to destroy him, for he was determined to kill the men that threatened her safety. Just as he was determined to clear her name.

She knew him. She knew his intent. And she knew she must do something about it before it was too late.

Kat tried to sleep, but the memory of Travis's voice haunted her. He loved her. She sat up, hugging her knees and gazing into the darkness. He saw himself as evil, and would not allow himself to touch her again. She knew that, too.

But she was not so strong. She was terrified—terrified of being rejected, but more frightened of being alone.

Katherine was on her feet before she had time to think rationally. He loved her. She loved him, and there was no way of knowing how long they would have together. Surely wasting an opportunity for happiness was a greater sin than any her father had warned her against.

The camp fire had burned down to glowing embers. From somewhere in the darkness harmonica music rose in a sorrowful tune.

Katherine moved on, her feet bare and silent, her heart hammering against her ribs. Never in all her life had she imagined she would find herself sneaking through the night to seduce a man who would surely ward off her advances.

Voices drifted to her finally. They were low and male, and rose and fell with the conversation.

"Damn it! You think I don't know what she is?" It was Travis's voice, harsh, but quiet.

"I think you have no idea what she is, Ryland. You keep selling her short."

"I won't let her die."

"Playing God again?"

"I've never hit you, Blackfeather, but it's not too late to start."

"She's not learning to shoot to defend *herself*. She's learning so she can defend *you*."

"She promised she'd stay at the ranch."

"It could be you're more important to her than a lie," Cody suggested.

Katherine could see them now. They stood watching each other in the moon-shadowed night, their faces almost invisible beneath their hat brims.

"I'll lock her up," said Travis flatly.

"At Latigo's?" Cody snorted, issuing a sound that was as close to a laugh as Kat had ever heard from him. "And we'll slip her meals under the door. Maybe Finch can stand guard. If she cries, we'll just shove a sock in her mouth."

"Shut the hell up!"

"It's a good plan, Rye. Make men out of all the lot of them. You know how soft they are. Then when you're killed, we'll just tell her it was for her own good. She's a smart girl. She'll understand."

"What do you want me to do?" Travis took two stiff steps forward, so that he stood only inches from Blackfeather, his hands closed to fists at his sides. "Send her back to Silver Ridge? Let her tell them she's innocent? Who could doubt such a pretty face? Maybe they won't kill her right off."

"She's not a child, Rye. Let her decide."

"No!" The single word was sharp, but still low. "She'll stay with Lat if I have to tie her to the bed."

"The bed?" Cody's tone was curious.

"Believe me, it works," said Travis dryly.

Katherine could feel herself blush.

"Can we turn her loose after you're dead?" Cody asked evenly. "Maybe she'll fall in love with one of the boys at the ranch. Give Lat those grandchildren he always wanted. Of course, it won't be the same as if they were yours. But just say the word now, and I'll make sure they inherit your share of the property. Wouldn't want there to be any misunderstandings," he continued, but Katherine was already slipping away.

All along she'd thought she was fooling them. Thought they believed she was only worried about her own safety. She'd even promised to stay safely at Latigo's. It was unkind of them to doubt her word. She should be offended.

She'd have to leave before they reached the ranch and find Dellas before Travis did. Jacob said the outlaw was headed back to town. But what town? Silver Ridge? New Prospect? And even if she could find her way there, how would she find Dellas? One didn't simply ask around regarding the whereabouts of known killers.

She needed time to think, to plan. How long until they reached Latigo's ranch. Two days? Three? There was no telling.

Hearing a slight rustle behind her, Katherine hurried back to her bedroll. Some yards off to her right Shadow followed on a parallel course, finally settling into a crouched position when Kat rolled into her blankets and feigned sleep.

Moments later Travis reached her, his movements making no more than a whisper of sound. Although she refused to open her eyes, Kat knew it was him. No one else made her heart palpitate and her breathing escalate. No one else made her hot and cold and angry and overjoyed. No one but Travis Ryland.

He remained as he was, motionless and silent. She wondered if he was looking at her, and what he was thinking. But she dared not open her eyes lest he somehow see the truth in them and realize she'd heard his conversation with Cody.

Finally, when Kat felt she could not bear his gaze any

longer, he moved away. She opened her eyes, knowing he would again leave camp to search for trouble and praying God would keep him safe until morning.

Travis was sitting before the fire when Kat made her way there shortly after dawn. She said little during breakfast. It had occurred to her during the night that every man present probably knew of Travis's plans to keep her, against her will if necessary, at Latigo's ranch. That thought, along with lack of sleep and the fact that she had only one remaining chocolate, made her feel grouchy and out of sorts. As she watched the men she reviewed her plans. She would not fail.

Shifting her gaze to the fire, Kat took a sip of coffee, barely tasting the bitter black liquid as her mind scurried over facts. She'd awakened to find Shadow's head resting on her feet, a new and encouraging sign of affection she thought. Affection she planned to use. Reaching down, Kat gently stroked the dog's nose, which was flat on the ground, just poking out from behind her right hip.

There were so many potential problems. So many elements that must fall into place in order for her plan to work. Kat lifted her gaze from the fire and found it nabbed, hard and fast, by Travis's solemn eyes.

"You all right?" His voice was low and somehow managed to send little motes of emotion fluttering in her belly.

"Yes." She mustn't let him guess her thoughts Kat realized, and held her gaze steady on his for what she hoped was the perfect amount of time before dropping it back to the entrancing flame. "I'm fine."

He still watched her. She could feel his gaze on her face and felt more warmed by it than by the nearby cookfire. "We should reach the ranch within three days' time."

"Good." She did not look at him when she said it or try to sound happy about the prospect of reaching their destination, for he knew her feelings.

Travis was silent for a moment, allowing Kat to hear the quiet, melodious voices of the cowboys who bantered not far away.

"You want to continue your lessons?"

"Yes." She lifted her gaze again, feeling suddenly like she might cry, and knowing she must get a firm grip on her emotions or have him suspect her plans. She drew a deep breath, settling her right hand back on the coffee mug and feeling Shadow wriggle a bit closer to her back, as if he might become invisible if he hugged her tightly enough. "I appreciate everything you've done for me."

She knew immediately it was the wrong thing to say.

"What's that?" His brows arched over his azure eyes.

Sweet heavens! She was no actress, she thought frantically, but kept her mouth shut against the sputtering explanations that tried to escape. She shrugged and lowered her eyes, though her heart was pattering a hard pace against her ribs. "I know you think it's ridiculous for me to try to learn to shoot." She sighed. "And perhaps you're right."

He watched her in silence, until she could not keep her eyes from his a moment longer.

"You're a hell of a woman, Katherine Simmons!"

Nothing he could have said would have surprised her more. His expression was very sober, and in his eyes was a mirror reflection of the love she held for him.

Let me go with you, she almost pleaded. *Let me fight at your side. And if we die, we die together.*

But in the flutter of a moment he had conquered his weakness. His expression went blank and hard, and he rose rapidly to his feet. "Let's go if you're determined."

It took Katherine longer to break the spell, and when she did, she felt as if her heart would shatter as well.

It was near dark when Travis suggested they catch up to the herd.

Katherine nodded, holstering her gun and refusing to look at him.

Instead of her usual target practice, he had found the hoofprints of deer and insisted they track the animal and that Kat shoot a buck.

She had wanted to object, but one look at his face had made her realize he expected nothing else.

In actuality, it had been Shadow that tracked the deer, following the animal's path like a scrawny red wolf on a scent. They had come upon their prey in a clearing, with the sun behind them and the breeze in their faces.

Three deer lifted their delicate muzzles to test the wind, and for an instant the beauty of the scene had held Kat transfixed.

"Shoot," Travis had ordered, placing the gun in her hand, and in that moment Shadow charged toward the deer.

"Shoot," Ryland ordered again. Without another thought, Katherine pulled the trigger and watched the buck fall.

The gun had simply appeared in her hand.

Taking a deep breath now, Katherine shifted her gaze to the buck that lay nearby. Never in her life had she killed anything larger than a beetle. It had been a beautiful beast, with velvety antlers and huge round eyes. Now it was dead, lying on its side in a valley, with the cloud-speckled sky reflected in the lake where it would have once drunk.

Katherine swallowed, wanting to cry and refusing to let herself. She would wait until nightfall, confiscate the wagon, and blubber her head off she decided.

"You didn't think I could do it, did you?" she asked, turning to him. The sun was falling toward darkness, and framed him in its fading light.

Travis kept his gaze on the north and scowled. "I told you never to face the sun. It'll blind you."

"Damn the sun!"

Travis turned, his brows raised, but he was no more surprised than Kat.

"We need to expand your vocabulary."

Katherine felt her face flush but refused to lower her eyes from his. "I've never seen anyone run as scared as you do."

He said nothing for a moment, but watched her until he finally bent to retrieve his saddlebags from the ground. "I never said I was a hero, lady."

Two long strides brought her up behind him. She gripped his arm suddenly, holding on tight and pulling him around to face her.

"I know you love me," she said evenly, feeling an aching desperation to hear the words again, to have them said to her face, to touch him. Katherine's stomach clenched into a hard knot.

"There's a hell of a difference between lust and love, lady. It's time you learned that."

She stepped back, feeling as if she'd been slapped. Her throat hurt, and her body felt stiff, but she managed to turn. Clenching her jaw, she breathed through her teeth, refusing to cry and hurrying away.

"Where are you going?"

Travis's voice was low but carried easily to her. She ignored it, lengthening her strides and setting her sight's on the lake.

"Where're you going?" he asked again.

She hurried on, but in a moment he was behind her, grasping her arm.

Katherine swung about of her own accord. "I'm going to bathe," she shouted. "Is that all right with you? And look . . ." She straightened and hurried her hands to her borrowed gun belt. "I'm leaving the revolver." She did just that, releasing it from her leg and her waist to let it bump harmlessly to the ground. "I'll be completely unarmed. Helpless." The smile that parted her lips was forced and stiff, she knew, and she took some satisfaction in the glare he directed at her. "So if I get killed, it'll be your fault. On your conscience." The smile smoothed, and her body relaxed a bit. "Forever." She turned easily and strode away.

"Goddamn it, woman!"

She smiled as she unbuttoned her shirt. The air felt warm and titillating against her bare shoulders. "Want to come . . . and lust?" she called out.

But her only answer was Travis's groan from behind.

Chapter 29

Picking up Kat's discarded gun belt, Travis swore and paced after her. But her back was now entirely bare, which could only mean her front was the same.

He gripped the leather in his hands and gritted his teeth. In three days' time he would be leaving her—forever. And he would *not* confuse her life further by touching her again.

He jerked his gaze abruptly toward the west, where the sun had just sunk below the uppermost peaks. The remaining light was no longer bright, but had faded to a rosy blush that painted the world for a few minutes of glory before nightfall.

Travis swore again, then swung his gaze back to Katherine's retreating back, which was smooth-skinned and curved down to her waist. Below that her jeans were still blessedly in place, but they swayed dramatically with her rapid hike through the coarse grass as she neared the lake.

His grip on the gun belt tightened even more. He would not be tempted by her this time. He would stay where he was, watch for trouble, and keep his eyes averted.

He resolve lasted for nearly five minutes, and then he was at the water's edge, still holding her weapon tight in his hands and trying to breathe with some semblance of normalcy.

But she was naked, and though her back was turned toward him, she stood only thigh-deep in the water.

Travis shifted his gaze to Soldier and did his best to forget the pale, curving slopes of her buttocks above the surface of the lake. "It's time to get back to camp," he said, his tone strained.

"What?"

He knew immediately that it had been a mistake to speak, for with some kind of sharpened sixth sense he realized she had turned to face him.

Soldier blurred in his vision, but Travis kept his eyes on the stallion. "Time to get back."

"I take this to mean you have no desire to bathe."

Her words shot fire through his system, causing his blood to boil through his veins like water into a thermal pond. Nevertheless, he took a deep breath and remained motionless. "Don't go looking for trouble, lady."

"Trouble?" Her laughter was like liquid silver. "Isn't it time to stop running, Ryland?"

"Get the hell outta there, and get your . . ." An image burned across Travis's mind. An image of her bare buttocks perched upon Moondancer's back, her mile-long legs gripping the mare's black hide. "Get on your horse," he rasped.

"But I'm not dressed."

"I know you're not—" He swung about. His gaze slammed into her. "Katherine." He could do not more than breathe her name, for her breasts were full and high, painted a rosy hue by the sinking sun.

Her waist was small, and accented by her tiny navel at its center. It was that indentation that held his vision, for he could not, for some reason, dispel the idea of slipping his tongue into that narrow hole, of feeling her body jump beneath him.

"I'm no good for you, Kat. I'm leaving soon. You'll be free. Go back to Boston. Marriage. Children." He was babbling incoherently, he realized, but feared if he stopped speaking, he would act. At this moment in time there was only one action worth doing. "Get dressed before—"

"If it were simple lust, Ryland," she interrupted softly, "you would have no reason to hold back. But if it was love . . ." She moved toward him as if the current carried her forward, like a fairytale mermaid Rachel had once told him about, with her skin slick and gleaming and her sable hair glossy with droplets of water. A thigh slipped above the surface, showing pale and smooth in the evening light. "If it was love, you'd run like hell."

He stepped back involuntarily. "I don't know nothing about love, lady. Don't you think I do."

"You lie, Travis. But not very well."

He tried to back farther away, but his legs refused to move, for his legs were attached to other parts of his anatomy that demanded satisfaction from their burning frustration.

"I can't give you what you deserve."

"Have I asked for anything?" She stopped. Water dripped from the dark triangle of hair between her legs, running in tiny rivulets down her thighs to merge into the lake below.

"You deserve—"

"I deserve to have the man I . . ." She stopped abruptly, not wanting to scare him away with her admission of love, and drew a heavy breath, her gaze not leaving his. "The man I want."

She was moving again, barely causing a ripple in the water as she glided toward him.

"You don't know what you're doing," he said hoarsely. Now would be a good time to saddle Soldier and head out, he thought, but his feet had become rooted to the ground.

"You don't give me much credit, Travis," Katherine murmured. She was close now, only a couple feet away. "I'd like to think I learn fairly quickly. I know what you are," she whispered. "I'm not asking for more than you can give. Just this one time." She shrugged, looking suddenly very innocent and small. "Life's too short, Travis. Too uncertain to waste the good that comes along." She reached slowly, touching his rough cheek with her fingertips.

Against his will, Travis's eyes fell closed. Raising one hand, he crushed her fingers to his face, feeling the aching burn of her tenderness against his flesh. "You'll regret this," he rasped.

"No," she said, and he opened his eyes to watch her shake her head and smile. "I won't."

Perhaps not, he thought. But he would, for he would compare every day of his life to the fleeting seconds he spent in her arms. And nothing would ever come close to that ecstasy.

Katherine saw him weaken, and could not contain a silent prayer of thanks. Maybe it was sin. But maybe it was the highest form of pleasure allowed a woman and a man in love.

Stepping forward, she raised herself on her tiptoes and kissed him very softly on the lips before drawing back to watch his face.

"If I was any good, I'd leave. Right now," he rasped. But he stayed as he was, and Kat smiled.

"You wouldn't want to disappoint a lady. It would be ungentlemanly."

"Kat, I—"

But she kissed him again, stopping his words with her lips. "You make a really bad, bad man," she whispered, drawing away.

"Kat."

She kissed him again, then pulled back only an inch or two so that she could feel the rush of his breath against her lips. "Don't you know you're supposed to ravage me?"

"Please."

"And begging . . ." She leaned forward, kissing the corner of his mouth this time. "Begging does not make you seem terribly dangerous." Kat waited for him to speak, but he did not, so she let her kisses slip down his jaw to his throat. It was broad and taut. Her nose brushed against his sun-bleached hair, causing her fingers to rise and push it back. "But maybe I am making it difficult for you," she murmured. "After all, I am wearing no clothes for you to rip off." Her hand slipped lower, touching the top button of his shirt. "Unlike you. But then . . . " Her fingers skimmed up to the hollow at the base of his throat. "I am a wanted outlaw, too." There was little point in waiting for him to answer. "Therefore there is no reason I can't ravage *you*."

A single groan escaped him.

Her hand continued downward, over the expanse of his abdomen.

"Lady," he gasped, but there was no need to say more, for Katherine, too, felt the hard shock of excitement that ripped

from his body to hers. She hugged him to her, feeling they
would surely fall if she let go.

But in a moment her impatience for more was too great.
Her fingers found his wooden buttons of their own accord.
The small spheres slipped easily through their designated
holes, baring his chest by slow inches until a narrow band of
his torso was exposed from throat to waist.

Katherine allowed her gaze to settle on his muscled chest
before placing her palm flat against its center. She felt his
shudder and closed her eyes momentarily, savoring the
emotions before pushing his shirt aside to kiss an indentation between his ribs.

There seemed nothing to do now but to explore the
expanse of him, to let her kisses fall where they would, until
she looked up, restless and tense, into his face.

"Are you quitting?" His voice was strained.

"No," she whispered. "I've only just begun."

"Then I give in," he rasped, wrapping her in his arms.

They pressed together, with their souls enmeshed and
their emotions flaring. His clothing slipped away, and they
were naked, flesh to flesh and heart to heart.

"Katherine." He whispered her name like a solemn chant,
and, bending, lifted her in his arms to carry her back into the
lake.

Water lapped at her buttocks in velvety waves, then slid
higher, until Travis released her legs. But her feet never
touched the ground, for his arms wrapped about her in a
steely grip, suspending her with the buoyancy of his touch.

Her legs wound about him with natural ease, and he
groaned, pressing hard against her, making her eyes fall
closed as he kissed her ear, her throat, the delicate hollow
above her collarbone. Within a moment he had slipped into
the core of her being. Katherine gasped, arching against his
strength as she reached for more.

Water sloshed against their rocking bodies, washing them
rapidly up a steep incline toward utopia.

For a moment they were perched on the edge of satisfaction with Travis's legs braced far apart, every muscle
straining to reach the summit just before them.

"Travis," Kat gasped, and pressing into his desire pushed them over the top and into the swirling world beyond.

They remained bound together, breathing in short, harsh gasps until Katherine's legs weakened and slid downward, skimming his iron thighs as they went.

Still they clung together, afraid to speak lest their fears be spoken, afraid to move lest the real world find them and drag them apart.

But reality can only be held at bay for a short while.

A shiver seized Katherine, and Travis drew a deep breath and turned, pulling her gently with him toward shore.

The night air felt cool against her skin, and she trembled again, not knowing if the tremor was caused by the aftermath of their lovemaking or the chill in the air. But, regardless of the reason, she seemed unable to release her hold on him, for if her plan worked, she might never see him again after tonight.

The thought made her feel numb and petrified, and she clung to him.

"Get dressed, Katherine," Travis said softly, but she found she could not tear herself from him, and so he finally pulled her arms gently away.

She stood alone now, bereft and chilled. But in a moment he returned with his shirt. Touching the soft fabric to her arms and throat, he gently rubbed her dry before moving the makeshift towel slowly down her torso, caressing her breasts, her belly, the length of her legs.

Tears coursed up from Katherine's heart. He would not say he loved her, and yet she felt it in his touch, in the brush of his fingers, the burn of his gaze against her skin.

"Now what?" Her words were no more than a breath of air as he straightened to look into her eyes.

For a moment he was speechless, but he drew discipline about him like an invisible armor. "We'll be at the ranch soon," he said, a slight tremor in his voice. "You'll be safe there."

Her eyes fell closed, and she weakened. Perhaps it would be worth sacrificing both their lives for a little more time together. "Let me go with you, Travis," she whispered.

"No." The denial was flat and flinty hard.

She swallowed, not opening her eyes. "I don't want to live without you."

"Don't say that!"

"It's true."

She could hear him draw a breath. "I'll be back," he said in a low tone. But she knew he lied. Even if he lived, he would not return for her. She squeezed her eyes more tightly closed.

"I could at least have been granted your child."

"What?" The question was sharp.

Katherine braced herself but refused to look up. "I had hoped I was with child." She bit her lip, realizing it was true.

"Are you?" His voice sounded as if it came from somewhere hard and cold, and she longed to look into his eyes, but dared not.

"No. I know now that I'm not."

His arms did not relax, but remained tightly about her. "You're positive?"

"Yes. I get sick, just before . . ." She winced. "Just before . . . it starts."

His hold on her softened a little. "Sick?"

"My stomach. Perhaps I could . . . " She paused. Lies had become almost indistinguishable from truths. "Perhaps I could rest in the wagon until we reach the ranch."

"Yes." he stroked her hair very gently. "Get dressed now."

They were silent as they made their way back to Blackfeather's crew. The buck Katherine had shot was lashed behind Travis's saddle, but she refused to look at it, concentrating instead on her plans.

The camp fire was bright. Jimmy's harmonica music soared to a final note that hung on the night air when they entered camp.

All eyes turned to them. Travis's shirt was wet, as was her own hair, Katherine knew, but she didn't care.

Saws banged nervously around in the huge pot that hung over the fire. Jacob cleared his throat, locked his gaze on his brother's, and kept silent.

But Finch, being who he was, grinned and asked, "You two get caught in the rain?"

Travis's reply was just about as expected. "Shut up, Finch," he mumbled.

Finch raised his brows, looking from Ryland to Katherine, and back, and, seeing the solemn intensity on both expressions, did just that.

Kat refused to eat. Blessedly, Jimmy's music started up again, drowning the sound of Travis's thoughts, which seemed as loud as thunder from his place so near to hers.

"Can I speak to you?" she asked finally, feeling a tremor shake her hands.

Travis lifted his gaze to her face, and for a moment she thought he might refuse.

"In private."

He nodded finally.

Hidden in the curved fire-shadow of the chuck wagon, Katherine shuffled her feet and took a firm hold on the upper edge of a spoked wheel.

"I was wondering if you could . . ." She paused and cleared her throat. "Please ask the men to let me rest. I need some time alone." She watched the toe of her boot make a sweeping crescent motion.

"Are you all right, lady?"

"Yes." She raised her gaze with a jolt, "I'm fine. Just . . . a woman's affliction."

It was his turn to clear his throat now, and she realized with sudden clarity that his embarrassment might be amusing if the circumstances were different. "Do you need anything?"

Panic momentarily overcame Katherine, for she hadn't anticipated his question. "No." She smoothed her palms down her pant legs and slowed her breathing. "No. I have everything I need."

"I'll bring your meals to you in the wagon."

"No." Again her voice was too sharp. "Please don't bother. I have no appetite during . . . these times."

He frowned, causing her to pray that he knew very little about women and their monthly ailments.

"Please," she repeated, grasping at straws. "I need some time alone."

He nodded solemnly. "I'll make sure you're not bothered," he promised.

Kat held her breath and watched his eyes. For a moment she thought he would say more, but he turned silently and disappeared into the night.

Chapter 30

"Shhh." Katherine was crouched in the darkness, listening for every sound and covering Jacob's mouth with her hand. "Come with me."

His eyes showed white and wide as he turned them toward her.

She motioned wordlessly.

He didn't move, but shifted his gaze to his brother's sleeping form before bending an arm to jab a thumb into his own chest and raise questioning brows at her.

Kat nodded.

It was all the encouragement Jacob Jameson needed.

Silently they crept away from camp and into the heavy timber nearby, where they stopped to listen for any pursuers.

"All's clear," Kat whispered finally, more to herself than her companion.

"Yeah."

His tone was stilted, and she saw him wipe his palms on his jeans as though he felt the tension as much as she.

Nearby, Shadow hid on the far side of a small gnarled pine.

Katherine glanced at the dog before taking a deep breath and scowling. Travis was gone. She'd heard him ride out and knew he would find some lofty place from which to watch for smoke with the coming of dawn. She could only hope he had made certain she wouldn't be disturbed. This would be her only chance to get away unnoticed. The thought increased her nervousness and caused her knotted stomach to roil.

"I need you to do something for me, Jacob," she said suddenly.

"Listen, Miss Kat, I . . ." He took a rapid step backward, with his fingers splayed dramatically across his chest.

"Please." Kat advanced a pace, realizing how much she needed his help. "It won't take so very long. And there will be very little danger to you."

"But . . ." He retreated an additional step. "Ryland said—"

"Ryland's gone, Jacob."

"Gone?" His voice was very faint.

"Yes, but we won't have much time."

At this his brows shot up again.

"I'm not asking you to take me all the way," she added, her mind spinning as she mentally hurried through her plans.

"J-just . . . kissin'?"

For a moment Katherine remained absolutely motionless. "Kissing?" she questioned, blinking once.

Jacob's confusion was visible in the darkness. "Why did you ask me out here, Miss Kat?"

She opened her mouth to speak, but a noise in the underbrush startled her, and she crouched, hoping to hide in the deepest of shadows. The wait seemed interminable as she held her breath.

"Luke," Jacob said finally, rising from the undergrowth, with Kat at his side.

The brothers' eyes met in the darkness.

"Don't go lookin' at me like that, Luke," hissed Jacob. "This ain't what you think. Matter a fact, you should be ashamed of yourself for even considerin' them things 'bout Miss Kat here. She ain't that kind of woman. Fact is," he nodded one jerky motion, "she was a schoolmarm."

Luke's gaze shifted to Katherine, and in that moment she wondered if it might not be true that a quiet mouth hid a deep intellect.

"Please!" Katherine said, then took a deep breath to steady her nerves. "I do need your help."

"How so?" Jacob asked, his voice a bit louder than she would have liked.

She shushed him, motioning down the volume with her hand. "Travis is going after Dellas."

At that news Luke's eyes went wide and Jacob paled noticeably.

"Beggin' your pardon, miss, but what's that got to do with us?"

"I've got to get to Dellas before he does."

The two faces before her showed identical expressions of disbelief, but she shushed them before any objections could be voiced. "Ryland is scouting around to make certain our way to the ranch is safe."

They remained silent.

"Don't you see? He's willing to risk his life for me . . . for *us*. We can't let him do it."

Their jaws had fallen slightly ajar.

"He could have killed you! Remember? You took our money. Were going to take Soldier!" she said, remembering how the two had valued their own swaybacked steed. "He loves Soldier. Why that horse has . . ." Her mind spun. She had to convince them to help her. "He's saved Travis's life on more than one occasion." She nodded abruptly. "That's right. Travis was shot. Through the . . . chest. He fell into the water. And Soldier . . . he . . . he galloped in and dragged him out before he could drown."

"Really?"

"Yes. And there were other times, too. He loves Soldier. And you were going to take him. So you can see why he was so angered. But he didn't kill you, did he? No," she answered herself. "He didn't harm you . . . well hardly at all. And why?" Stepping forward half a stride, she placed a hand to each man's arm. "Because he's a good person."

"He sure as nuts coulda killed us all right," nodded Jacob.

"Yeah," agreed Luke cautiously.

"So it's time for you to do him a good turn," explained Kat.

Their expressions mirrored their uncertainty again. "How would we do that, Miss Kat?"

"By taking me to Dellas."

*   *   *

She would have to leave Moondancer. If the black mare were missing, it would surely alert Travis that she was gone.

The herd of horses milled about as she slunk into their midst, but eventually she caught two dark mounts, one for herself and one for Jacob.

Saddles would be beneficial, but to her knowledge there were no spares.

Cautiously she led the geldings away from the herd, finally slipping into the trees to hand one animal's rope to Jacob. "Here. Take him."

"But . . ." Jameson scowled. "We promised to go honest from now on, and that'd be stealin'."

Katherine ground her teeth, vaguely realizing she had said much the same thing not so many days before. "A man's life is at stake."

"But couldn't we just tell them good-bye?"

"No. We're going," she whispered. "And we're going now."

Chapter 31

"Dear God!" Katherine turned abruptly away from the bloated and burned corpse. "Who was it?"

Luke blanched, leaving Jacob to answer. "It was the fella called Red. He was arguin' with the old man." He swallowed hard. "Guess Dellas don't like to be disagreed with."

"Red?" Katherine tightened her grip on the bay gelding's reins. She could remember Red's voice as clearly as his words. *We ain't quittin' till we drop Ryland's bloody carcass on Grey's doorstep.* He'd planned to murder them. Had been hired by Grey to do so. And there could only be one reason. She and Travis knew too much, knew Mayor Patterson had died of natural causes and that the money had been taken before he met with Ryland.

Thomas Grey had taken the money. Grey, whose mines were running dry. Grey, who hired Dellas and Red to kill Travis.

Her task was clear. She'd find Dellas, take him to Silver Ridge, and convince him to tell the people the truth about Grey. Then Travis's name would be cleared. Dellas would pay for his crimes. And Travis would be safe.

It was all very simple. Just like a dime-novel plot.

Katherine swallowed, refusing to consider the realities of the days ahead. "Do you know where Dellas's horse was tied?" she asked.

"What's that?"

"Finch said Shadow could track a animal anywhere if you gave him a scent."

"Miss Kat, please don't go through with this."

267

"Do you know?"

Jacob stuck out his lower lip. "I ain't gonna tell y', miss. I ain't gonna be responsible fer what might happen."

Katherine tightened her grip on the reins. "Have you ever been in love?" she whispered, almost more to herself than to her companions.

Silence held the place.

"Over by that bent oak." Luke broke his silence and pointed to a tree.

"Miss Kat, please!" Jacob pleaded, but Katherine was already dismounting from the saddle the Jamesons' had insisted she use.

"But Miss Kat—"

"I'm going to make certain Dellas never hurts anyone again, least of all Travis."

"We can't let you do this on your own, miss. You'll get yourself killed."

"I ain't about to let that happen." Luke's tone was deep and definite, and Katherine winced mentally, rethinking her plan.

"We'll have to bury the body," she said flatly.

"That body? But, miss, he was gonna kill us out flat."

"Nevertheless." She kept her voice firm and her eyes averted.

"We ain't got no shovel."

"Then we'll cover him with rocks. It's the Christian thing to do."

"But—"

"You don't want to be like Dellas, do you? Then, get down here. And hurry. We haven't much time."

They did as they were told, but slowly, sliding from their mounts to let their lariats dangle in the dirt, then shuffling halfheartedly off in search of rocks.

"Shadow," Katherine called softly. The dog appeared by her side, as silent as the darkness he was named for. In a few strides they were at the gnaled oak. "Scent, Shadow. Scent," she ordered, nudging the horse dung with the toe of her boot, just as Finch had said to do.

The hound lowered his nose, snuffling up odors in loud breaths before raising his head to sneeze. He emitted a single moaning yelp before dropping his nose again and galloping off, long ears skimming the ground.

There was no time to lose now. Katherine could only pray Shadow had the right scent and that she could keep him in sight.

Running to the bareback mounts, she grabbed up their ropes and led them back to her bay. In an instant she was astride, and was dragging Buck and his companion into a trot behind her.

"Hey!" yelled Jacob, just appearing with a jagged rock in his hands. "Hey! What you doing?"

"I'll tie your horses within a mile of here if you don't try to follow me," Kat shouted.

"Miss Kat, please. You can't go alone."

Ahead was a stretch smooth enough to allow Kat to canter if the Jamesons decided to try to catch her.

"Don't follow me," she warned, "or you'll never find Buck."

Standing in the stirrups, Katherine held the horses at a steady pace to watch the stunned, diminishing figures behind her. "Good luck to you, boys," she murmured, and turned away.

It rained on the third night. Katherine shivered under her damp blankets and prayed.

On the following morning Shadow snuffled worriedly at the ground, then circled back time and again before finally catching the scent.

She'd taken a good deal of dried jerky and sourdough bread from a store box in the chuck wagon. But the food was dry and salty, making her constantly thirsty and finally causing her stomach to ache.

She startled a mule deer from hiding and shot at it, but missed.

The following night was clear. From somewhere too close for comfort an animal howled. Shadow snuggled closer to her side, wrapping his tail firmly against his hind legs and rolling sad eyes to Kat's face. She stroked his head, tried not to think of Travis, of the hunger that tormented her, or of the bloated corpse Dellas had left behind.

Two nights in a row she dreamed she had a child, a little boy with eyes as blue as the heavens and a wayward mane of tawny hair.

At one point she woke to her own scream, clawing away half-remembered images of her child's lifeless form in Dellas's arms.

The next day she shot a rabbit. She skimmed it sloppily, and though she had watched Travis do the same thing, she found she remembered *him* more than she remembered the procedure. Still, she and Shadow thought it a feast.

Billy, the bay she'd stolen and subsequently named, threw a shoe and was beginning to get footsore, which slowed their progress. But if her calculations were anywhere close to correct, and if Shadow was on the right trail, their journey should be very near its end. Though not at all the end she'd expected, for she had thought to find Dellas near Silver Ridge. Instead, the trail had led north and east, toward Latigo's ranch.

Billy's pace slowed even more on the following day, causing Kat to dismount and lead him. They traveled well into the night, and for a moment, from a high, bare knoll on the side of a mountain, Kat thought she saw a flicker of fire far in the distance.

Chapter 32

Katherine's breath came in hard, raspy inhalations. From behind her Shadow whimpered. She prayed he would not break loose and that he and Billy would be silent and remain where they were tied.

Through the trees on the downhill slope Kat caught another glimpse of camp fire light.

For a moment she thought her knees might give way, but they did not. It was her mind that was the traitor. She held Finch's Colt in her right hand and noticed that the barrel wobbled when she lifted it.

From up ahead a voice rose in anger. Kat stopped in her tracks, holding the gun with both hands and breathing hard, remembering Red's bloated corpse. For some time she could not force her legs to move. But in her mind she saw the child she had dreamed of. The blue-eyed angel with the infectious laughter and tawny hair.

She held her breath and crept closer, moving from tree to tree and finally stretching out full length on the ground to stare at the camp before her.

There were four men, two playing cards and two who sat face-to-face, talking in low voices. She couldn't hear their words, nor guess at their emotions. Which man, if any, was Dellas? She waited, feeling her heart rap against her ribs and watching.

"Goddamn you!"

Kat jerked, terror making the slight movement stiff as her breathing clogged in her throat.

"I say you're cheatin'!"

"The hell I am!" came a growled response.

"Damn your—"

"You boys want to kill each other?" A man rose slowly. He was of medium height, with graying hair and a long, wicked-looking knife held casually in one hand. "Or do you want me to do it for you?"

Both men shook their heads, seeming to forget their argument.

"How 'bout you, Cory? You ready to meet yer redheaded friend?"

"I wasn't cheatin', Mr. Dellas. I swear it."

The older man nodded, lifting his lips in a feral grin. "Hear that Duke? He says he wasn't cheatin'."

"But I—"

"Listen, Duke." His tone was very civil. "You wanna die, I'd be more than happy to help, but you've got to wait till we rout Mr. Latigo from his hole!" He pulled his shoulders back one at a time, then realigned his expression into the semblance of a smile. "Then, after Ryland and the girl are taken care of, if you ain't had enough blood yet, we'll see what we can arrange." He laughed, and in the flickering shadows his face seemed to contort into something hideously evil. "Be good boys, now, and go to sleep." He bent, slipping the knife slowly back into his boot, as if loath to feel the weapon leave his fingers. "Tomorrow we're going to go get ourselves some bargaining power."

"I'm tellin' y', it'll take a small army t' get the old man outta that house."

Dellas turned slowly, raising one brow a fraction above the other. "Lucky we have a small army then, isn't it, Selby?"

"It's said Latigo was the one taught Ryland what he knows bout fightin'."

The smile was back on Dellas's face. "Maybe that's why Ryland will come back here, huh? Because he thinks his woman friend will be safe with the old man."

Katherine could not see Selby's expression.

"Hell! Ain't we lost enough men yet?"

"You ever heard of the devil, boy?"

Selby didn't answer, and in a moment Dellas's fist whipped out to grab him by the shirtfront.

"Well, it's me!" he said, and leaning close, he thrust the other man back off the log where he had been perched. "It ain't wise to rile the devil, son!"

Katherine watched as Dellas strode into the darkness.

Sometime during the conversation she'd quit breathing. She drew in air now, but the inhalation sounded frightfully loud, so that she stopped again, watching the men by the fire to make certain they hadn't heard.

"Bastard." The single word was a low growl. But she waited to hear no more.

The night seemed blacker than ever as she crept through the underbrush with the Colt held before her. Her chest ached, and her legs felt wooden and disembodied, but the thought of Travis the boy and Travis the man drove her on.

She saw Dellas in a moment. He was facing away from her, a black shape in the darkness. Her left hand lifted to cover her right, so that she gripped the revolver with all her strength.

"Drop your gun and your knife, or I'll shoot."

Her voice did not shake, but sounded as if it came from a different source. From someone far away.

She saw his shoulders draw back.

"It ain't nice to shoot a man when he's relieving himself."

"Get rid of your weapons." Her voice had come back to herself and quavered from the depth of her guts. "Or I'll put a hole through your head. I swear I will!"

His hands moved, dropping his gun first and then his knife. "You mind if I close up my pants? Wouldn't be proper exposing myself to a lady."

Kat remained silent, every sense honed and focused on the back of the man before her. "Keep quiet, and start moving toward your horse."

He shrugged and took a step.

"Not through camp." Without thought she cocked the Colt. "Silently."

They moved through the underbrush. A twig snapped off to her right and she jumped, jerking her gaze in that direction but not daring to remove her aim from Dellas's back. Up ahead she could see the ghostly outline of a pale gray horse.

"What now, Miss Simmons?" he asked, and laughed, turning slowly to face her in the darkness. The sound shivered along Kat's forearms, immobilizing her body.

"You didn't think I'd know who you are, did you? But then it's a natural mistake to underestimate me. A smart woman like yourself would be inclined to think I chose this profession out of a lack of intelligence." He shook his head. "Did you never consider, Miss Simmons, that I simply might love to kill?"

Her gaze was locked in paralyzed fear on his face, but her hands were steady and her gun was aimed dead center on his heart.

"I'm taking you to Silver Ridge." She managed the words through stiff lips.

"Just you and me on such a long journey?" He chuckled again, low in his throat. "I'm flattered by the invitation, but wondering at the purpose."

"You'll say Travis didn't kill the mayor and didn't steal the money."

"An interesting theory. But how would I know that?" he asked, taking a step toward her.

"Get on the horse," she ordered, her tone brittle.

"But I haven't slept yet." He drew back his lips like the smile of an leering dog. "Maybe you could join me."

"I swear I'll kill you," she rasped.

"I doubt . . ." Dellas began and lunged.

She saw him streak toward her. Her mind begged her to run, but she was frozen in place, her mouth open in a soundless scream. For an instant his face was before her, then her muscles jerked free from paralysis, and the Colt exploded in her ear.

Dellas slammed into her, and Katherine fell, hitting the earth with a jolt. He rose from the ground like an enraged lion and she fired again, scrambling backward. But he hit her with his careening body, knocking her down. The gun fell, unseen.

Kat tried to rise, to wriggle from beneath her captor. His weight lifted momentarily. She jerked her knees up, trying to scramble away as she clawed toward freedom. Hands grabbed at her, and she screamed, terror ripping at her heart. She lunged, fighting her way toward the darkness that could hide her. But someone grabbed her, and she fell back. For just a moment she saw Dellas's crazed face. His smile was set at a twisted angle, and his fist was raised. It seemed to come at her with incredible slowness, and she watched it, entranced, until a low-pitched din sounded in her head, and the world went black.

Chapter 33

It was difficult to tell reality from the nightmares.

They flickered through Kat's head, sometimes jolting her to wakefulness. She had been astride a horse, tied in place. She remembered studying the bonds and thinking she should devise some way to break free. But the hands that pawed and struck her made her shudder and want to wretch. Oblivion was comfortable.

But oblivion was gone now, and in its place sat stark, cold terror.

She was tied to a tree with her back against the trunk. How long had they been riding? Days? Weeks? She had no way of knowing.

A fire blazed less than a yard from her feet.

"I tell you he's out there!" said someone off to her right. "Has been for days. Following us like a damn shadow. No noise. Just following." His tone sounded hysterical. "He killed Duke. I know he did."

Katherine tried to turn her head but found she was immobilized by a rag stretched across her open mouth and tied to the tree behind. She moved her eyes. The effort made her head roar with a dull pain that flooded up like a tide of dark water.

"Maybe our friend Duke simply got lost when I sent him out to watch our trail," Dellas suggested.

"You know he killed him," Cory argued nervously.

"I hear Ryland's not afraid to die," Dellas said, his voice smooth and deadly. "Not like you, huh, Cory?"

"I ain't scared of him. Just wish he'd show his damn

277

face." Katherine could hear him cock his weapon. "I'd blow him clean to hell."

Dellas laughed. The sound was low and made her shiver. "Some say he's already been there, boy. And come back."

"Damn your lies, Dellas!" Cory swore, but his voice cracked and the other laughed.

A guttural grunt sounded from the darkness to Kat's left.

"Selby?" Dellas called. "You there?"

No answer was forthcoming.

Silence settled in, thick enough to cut, but now Dellas was at Kat's side, crouched beside the tree with something poking hard and cold in her abdomen.

"I got your woman, Ryland!" he called, barely raising his voice.

No sound. Nothing except the crackle of the fire.

"Be a shame if she died after trying to save yer hide, huh? You know she plugged me in the shoulder? You got yourself a real spitfire here. I owe her something for my injury, but we've been easy on her so far, cause she couldn't enjoy us anyhow. But she's full awake now. See?" He shook her arm. "She'll feel everything we do to her from now on."

It was hard for Kat to breathe. Terror bound her throat as surely as her hands were tied. Seconds ticked by, echoed by the thud of her heart against her chest.

"Ryland!" Dellas called, his voice louder. "I'm tired of hide-and-seek, so I'm changing the game. And these here are the rules. You lay down your weapons and come on into camp."

Kat could hear nothing but the sound of her own frenzied breathing.

"And you do it before I count to ten." Dellas cocked his weapon, pushing it harder into her middle. "If you don't, Miss Simmons here is going to be mighty disappointed." He drew back his lips in an evil smile. "Cuz it's going to take her a while to die." He shifted closer. "But you know all about gut-shot females, don't you, Ryland?" His gaze skimmed the darkness. "Maybe you thought I didn't recall, huh? That I forgot. But I remember all the people I kill. Like to think about them when I'm falling asleep." He reached out quickly, grabbing her hair to force her head back farther. "And I'll remember her a long time."

"Let her go, Dellas." Travis's voice sounded very close. "And I'll come in. No weapons."

"Afraid I can't do that. We still got us some miles to go to Silver Ridge, and she's my security, huh? But I give you my word not to hurt her so long as you do as I say."

"Let her go." Travis's voice had dropped in pitch and volume, and seemed to rumble from the darkness.

"Are you saying you don't trust my vow?" Silence answered him, and he laughed. "Could be you're smarter than some, Ryland. But it looks to me like I hold all the cards. Or at least I got the queen of hearts, huh?" He laughed again. "Come on in, boy, and I won't hurt her, cuz you see, Tommy Grey, he's a squeamish one. He doesn't like killing women. And he's paying the bills.

"You lay down your weapons out there. All of them, you hear? Because if I find you were keeping any back, the girl will have to suffer, and we wouldn't want that. Lay them down, then come on in nice and slow. We'll ride into town like one big happy family."

"What have you got planned, Dellas?"

"Well now, there's the sad part. Looks like the good folk of Silver Ridge are looking to hang you for murder and thievery."

"And what about you?"

"There's the funny thing. Grey, he paid me to steal his miners' wages. But now it seems it was you who did the thieving. There was an eyewitness and all. I'm just clearing my name by turning you in."

Silence echoed in the forest before Travis's voice came again. "What about the woman?"

"There ain't no reason for her to die, so long as you confess your crimes."

From the woods before her Kat heard a rustle of underbrush. She tried to scream, to drive Travis back into the safety of the darkness, but the gag choked her, allowing only a squeak of protest to issue from her aching throat as Travis came out of the woods.

*　　*　　*

They rode for five days.

Travis no longer slept, but watched Katherine whenever possible. Her face was bruised, and there was a lump on the side of her head. For those wounds he hoped he would be allowed one wish—to cause Dellas's death before he found his own. He took to praying, begging one last favor from a God he had quit believing in long ago.

He did not hope to live out the month. No, he would die. But Katherine must not.

She slept now. He knew by the way she slumped over her saddle horn. The gag had been removed, but she rarely spoke.

It would not be much longer now. Silver Ridge lay ahead, less than an hour's ride, he was sure, and yet his ribs did not hurt. But then, he had been warned of impending danger for years. He could not expect to be warned of his own death, not when he knew it would come.

It was a long, winding descent into the valley. Before them, Travis could see the lights of the boomtown's nightlife. They will stop soon, he thought.

But they did not. There was just the four of them. Katherine and himself, Dellas and the man called Cory. Travis had killed the other two, very silently with his knife. His only regret was his inability to kill Dellas before he had given up his weapons. For now it would be harder.

They rode down the quiet backstreets of the city. A dog yipped, announcing their arrival, but no lights were lighted in the nearby houses.

Up ahead a tall white structure could be seen in the darkness. Shutters framed the windows, appearing as black holes in the building's wide expanse. Grey's house. The horses were halted.

"Get the woman," Dellas ordered. "All right, Ryland. End of the trail."

Soldier braced himself as Travis dismounted and fell, unable to balance without the use of his hands, which had been tied behind his back.

Katherine fell from unconsciousness as Cory pulled her from her mount. Travis heard her gasp of horror as the nightmare of reality found her again.

Cory chuckled, drawing her against his chest and croon-ing, "There now, lady. No need t' fret. I'll give y' what you're needin' soon enough."

"Cory." Travis kept his tone conversational, though his muscles ached with the effort. "Touch her and I'll tear your heart out."

"Big talk from a man who's about to die."

Travis watched him in the darkness. "I'm already dead." Quiet settled in around them. "It hasn't stopped me from killing yet."

For a moment there was no sound. And then Dellas laughed.

"Enough of your lies!" Cory yelled, but he had moved away from Katherine and kept the distance.

They were prodded down the walkway to the front door, where Dellas rapped loudly. The portal opened, emitting a gruff voice. "Who the hell are you?"

"I'm Dellas!" He pushed the door wide, knocking the stunned guard back with the movement. "Tell your master I'm here bearing gifts."

It took only moments for Grey to appear. His silver hair was mussed, and as he hurried forward he tied a quick knot in the belt of his brocade robe.

"What the devil are you doing here?" he hissed.

"Brought you a little something to help you sleep better," Dellas grunted, pushing Travis forward.

Grey took a quick step back. "What happened to your shoulder?"

"Just a little misunderstanding."

Grey grimaced, dragging his gaze from the bloody hole in the other's jacket. "You shouldn't have brought them here, for God's sake. I told you to meet me out at the old mine."

"I wasn't in the mood for waiting," Dellas explained, drawing his revolver and taking two steps to the side to seat himself on a plush, tassled settee. "Besides, you and me, we're partners, so I knew you wouldn't mind my coming straight in."

"You've got to get out of here before someone sees you," Grey ordered, but Dellas only shook his head.

"I come up with a new plan, Tommy. It's real good. You'll

like it. We're going to say Ryland here was the one that stole the payroll at the outset. I heard he was using my name to do his dirty deeds, so I hunted him down and brought him to the good people of Silver Ridge." He chuckled. "It'll do wonders for my reputation. Folks won't hardly blink when you and I are seen together."

Travis watched Grey scowl. "Where's Red?"

Dellas smiled again. "Ryland here killed him." He held his gaze steadily on Grey. "Ain't that right, Cory?"

Behind Katherine, Cory shuffled his feet nervously.

"Ain't that right, boy?" Dellas repeated.

"Yeah. That's right."

Grey's gaze skimmed from Dellas to Cory, finally resting on Travis's face, and for a moment Travis thought he might question the truth of that statement, but he did not. "We'll have to go down to the jail."

"Not her," Dellas said, watching for Grey's reaction. "She'll stay with me." His narrow eyes shifted to Kat, then to Travis. "We got us some unfinished business."

"See here, Dellas, I'm sure we can convince Miss Simmons to see things our way. I won't have her hurt," Grey said.

"Hurt? You talk like I'm some mad dog, Tommy. I won't hurt her. Just give her what she's been asking for."

"I make the decisions here."

Very slowly Dellas turned his gun toward Grey. "I got me a stake in this, Tommy. We wouldn't want folks saying you had something to do with the loss of your workers' money, now would we? The woman's mine."

Hope exploded in Travis's mind. With a roar he charged Dellas, who rose, swinging his gun to bear. But too late. Travis's shoulder hit his midsection and bore him to the floor.

Dellas's elbow smacked against the hard tile, sending his gun flying.

Hands still bound behind him, Travis brought his knee up hard between Dellas's legs. There was a sucking gasp, but already Travis was on his feet.

But there were no weapons, and so Travis drew back his booted foot, aiming for the other's head.

It seemed he heard the crack against his skull more clearly than he felt it. Darkness swelled upward, drawing him down, but he grimaced, fighting it back as he twisted about.

Another blow came, full in his face this time, with something hard and flat, and he fell, hoping Katherine could hear the apology he tried to force past stiffening lips.

"Wake him up so he can see what I do to the woman!" Dellas ordered, and clawed fingers reached for his revolver, but Grey scooped it out of his reach.

"Are you insane? She's our security. As long as we keep her safe, he'll do what we say."

"I'll tell the truth." Katherine could barely hear her own words. She had tried to reach Travis, but Cory held her from behind, and so she locked her gaze on Grey. "I won't let you get away with this, not while there's a breath in my body."

"Ryland is a wanted criminal, Miss Simmons. He'll die one way or the other." Grey watched her solemnly. "He knows he won't live through this. You saw how he attacked Mr. Dellas. He's prepared to die. But you don't have to. Let him claim the crimes. Let him save you. It seems that's what he wants."

"Never," she whispered.

Grey merely watched her. "Cory, put Miss Simmons in the cellar. Lock her in and guard the door. Web, you and Dellas and myself will take Ryland to the jail."

Chapter 34

"Where is she?" Travis gripped the iron bars with both hands as he stared through them at Thomas Grey. At least his hands were no longer tied.

"She's safe."

"Damn you to hell," Travis cursed quietly.

"And she'll remain safe," continued Grey. "Just so long as you do as you're told."

"You'll forgive me for not trusting you."

"I never wanted any of this to happen, Ryland. But my mines were failing. I couldn't afford to pay my employees *and* start up new operations. So I devised a way to rid Colorado of two killers."

"Me and Dellas." Travis supplied the names without emotion. "But what about Mayor Patterson."

"He was a lazy drunk who fought progress at every turn. Silver Ridge is better off without him." Grey scowled. "But I didn't plan on Miss Simmons. I fear she's being difficult."

"Harm her and you'll die in pieces, Grey."

"I have no wish to hurt her. She's an intelligent woman." He paused. "You'll have to convince her to *act* intelligently."

"She's never listened to me yet," Travis said.

"Then, you better try harder, Ryland. If she plays along, she'll be sent back to Boston. But if she doesn't . . ." He shook his head, looking genuinely sorry. "It seems Dellas holds a grudge, and he'll be the one guarding her when you make your statement this morning."

"You're not wasting no time."

"I can't afford a lengthy trial. And luckily for me, the people of Silver Ridge won't want one. They've waited a long time to see you hang."

"Where will Katherine be?"

"I'm afraid I can't tell you that, but she'll be close by. Close enough for Dellas to react immediately if you cause trouble."

"If you let Dellas guard her, all bets are off."

"I'm afraid you have little choice in the matter."

"I'm telling you now, Grey, if you don't want me spilling the truth, you won't let Dellas ever see her again."

"Convince her to keep silent, and I'll swear on my father's grave to protect her."

"And she'll be sent safely back to Boston?"

"You have my word."

Travis glanced toward the window. Dawn was approaching. Impending death felt strangely painless, but the thought of her made his heart ache. "Send her in."

"Travis." She whispered his name through the bars.

"Don't talk." His hands felt warm as they covered hers. "Just listen."

"Travis," she began again, but he gripped her fingers tighter.

"Just this once, lady, please listen. I'm going to die."

"No!" The word was a sob, but she could not help it.

"Yes, I am. But you're not. You're going back to Boston, where you belong."

"No."

"All you have to do is be silent. That's all."

"I won't!"

"Please, Katherine," he whispered. "Please. For me. Don't die. Give my life some purpose."

Her throat felt raw, and her eyes stung. "You never knew how good you were."

"I wasn't good, Katherine. Not without you." Releasing her hand, he reached between the bars to touch her cheek. "All the men I've killed . . ." He shook his head. "Let me save someone worth saving."

"Don't!"

"Let me die loving you, Kat," he whispered.

And she closed her eyes and wept.

They'd cut his arms loose, fed him a decent breakfast, and retied his hands in front of his body. The sun marched up the sky, announcing the coming of the end.

Travis paced the length of his cell. He'd imagined dying, but somehow had not expected it to happen like this—confined to a cage before being hanged by his neck. The townspeople were already beginning to gather. A scaffold could be seen from the narrow, barred window. It was around that structure that the crowd milled.

Travis drew a deep breath. Katherine would be safe. Grey had vowed, and it was the best he could hope for. And yet his heart ached. His ribs, however, were strangely numb, as if it was past time for premonitions.

He paced again, wishing that he had lived his life differently. But how, he didn't know, for it seemed life had a way of leading a body, not letting it choose.

"Come on out." Cory grinned at him. "Grey, he's got him a gift with the people, don't he? He's made them think he's a damn saint, and that you're a devil." He laughed. "Time to make your speech and die, Ryland."

"Where's Dellas?"

"It's none of yer concern."

The key grated in the lock, and Travis stepped forward, bound hands clenched to fists. "Goddamn it! Where's Dellas?"

Cory's gun came swiftly up to settle against Travis's throat. "I wouldn't mind pluggin' you right here and now!" he threatened. "You move out nice and quiet."

Uncertainty caused Travis's chest to ache. Fear was a stranger that came late to visit.

"Are you ready?" Grey stood in the doorway, looking flushed, as if his speech to the citizens had exhilarated him.

"Where's Dellas?" Travis asked again, unmoving.

"He's with my personal physician," Grey said. "It seems his wound has become infected and he'll need a high dose of morphine to have it treated." His gaze caught Travis's.

"Dellas won't be bothering us again. My word is good, Ryland."

Travis held his gaze, searching for lies, but he could not tell. "So is mine, Grey. If she's hurt, I'll find a way to do the same to you. Hell won't be hot enough to hold me. I swear it."

"From what I heard, I didn't think you were the kind to fall in love. Not with a woman like her." He shrugged. "But she's safe."

Travis moved slowly through the doorway. The sun was bright, shining hot against his shoulders and the back of his head. Innumerable faces stared at him, their expressions taut and expectant.

They marched him straight to the scaffolding. It was made of graying wood that was crossed and recrossed in back but open in the front, leaving a clear view for the spectators that crowded the street between the buildings.

He was stopped not far from the structure, and silence settled over the crowd.

"All right." Grey's voice was quiet. "Tell the people what you wanted to say, Ryland."

Travis's gaze caught on Grey's. In the end the words were hard to force from his lips, but Katherine would live.

"It was me that stole the money." His eyes were still locked on Grey's, searching endlessly for a flicker of dishonesty.

"What?" a voice yelled from the crowd.

"Can't hear."

"Get him up on the gallows. He belongs there anyhow."

"Get him up there! So's we can hear 'im."

He was prodded from behind. Not by Cory's hands now, but by many others.

The steps sounded dully beneath Travis's boots. Below him the crowd became hushed again as he turned. The sun was to his right, seeming strangely bright and warm.

"What'd you do with the money?" someone yelled.

Within the midst of the crowd Travis found Grey's face. It looked suddenly more strained and wary.

"Where's the money?"

The crowd went silent.

"I spent it," Travis said, lifting his eyes to the masses before him.

"And Patterson, you kill him?"

Travis waited, wishing he could hold her, just once more. "Yes."

"No!" Katherine tore the gag from her mouth to scream the word. "No!"

Dellas spun about, the devilish light in his eyes bright, his hand uplifted. Kat screamed again, yanking hopelessly at her bonds and twisting about in her chair.

Pain shot across Travis's ribs, but not for himself. For her! He knew it! Katherine was nearby, and he felt her danger. Grey had lied!

"Katherine!" he yelled, his gaze darting to every door.

"Hold him!"

"Watch him!"

"Katherine!" he wailed again, and at that moment he saw the hound. He was pressed against a doorjamb, with one paw lifted to scratch the wood.

Faces lurched toward him, but he was already gone, launching himself from the scaffolding to soar to the ground. Three men went down with him. Travis rolled, braced his weight on his bound hands, and scrambled to his feet.

Bodies surrounded him, but from somewhere guns were fired, scattering the crowd. Women screamed, and men yelled, ducking for cover. Travis lunged forward, all concentration focused on the door ahead. It gave way beneath the pounding force of his shoulder, and he bolted inside as a gun exploded nearly in his face.

Katherine screamed again, but already he had collided with Dellas. Their bodies were crushed together with a revolver in between.

"Damn you!" Dellas cursed. Swinging his left hand, he tried to knock Ryland aside, but in that moment Travis twisted the gun backward and fired.

Dellas's mouth fell open. His hands went limp, and he staggered back a step, dropping his head to gape at the red circle spreading across his middle. "Damn you," he swore again, but weakly now.

Men swarmed into the building.

"Get Ryland!" someone said, but from outside a quiet voice objected.

"I don't think that would be wise, gentlemen. Grey here has something to tell you."

Into the doorway stepped Thomas Grey, and behind him came Cody Blackfeather.

"What's the meaning of this?" Grey asked, glancing over his shoulder, but perspiration had appeared on his forehead and his face was pale.

"Tell the people the whole story, Grey."

"I don't know what you're talking about. Dellas stole my payroll. I hired Ryland to get rid of him, but he killed Mayor Patterson and stole the money."

"'E's lyin'," came a Cockney voice, and Daisy elbowed her way through the crowd.

Chapter 35

"It seems we owe you an apology, Mr. Ryland."

Katherine watched in silence as the man with the walrus moustache spoke to Travis. It was strange how life went on, even when it seemed certain it would not.

Her gaze shifted to Dellas's body, and she shivered, turning back to watch Travis. He was silent and large, looking miraculously unscathed despite it all.

"The citizens of Silver Ridge would like to make amends." Walrus Moustache cleared his throat, seeming to find it difficult to meet Travis's gaze. "We're in need of a sheriff. And we've ahh . . . talked it over amongst ourselves and thought you'd be a good candidate for that position."

"No!" Travis said stiffly.

"But we're in great need, Mr. Ryland. Surely you can see that. What with no mayor, no law enforcement, and now Mr. Grey being incarcerated. . . ." He shook his head.

"My brother and me would like the job." Jacob Jameson stepped into the room. "We ain't had a heap of experience, but we've learned t' be honest and we'll uphold the law. We can promise y' that."

Moustache skimmed his gaze from Travis to Jacob to Luke. "Do you know these men, Mr. Ryland?"

"Yeah." Travis nodded once toward the two brothers who must have ridden like hell to reach Silver Ridge in time to cover his exit from the scaffolds. "They're your men," he said, and turned.

In the corner of the room Daisy spoke to Finch. "But we

need us a mayor. And after you saved the day like you done, turning the hound loose to find Miss Katherine and all. Coo, it was right smart of you. And brave, 'oldin' off the crowd so's Ryland could get free.''

"You think so?" Finch was smiling into Daisy's face, looking rather dazed with the possibilities ahead.

Shadow lifted a paw to scratch at Katherine's pant leg. She lowered a hand to stroke his ear, but Ryland was already outside, and she strode after him.

On the boardwalk, Kat was surprised to learn the sun was high. The birds had not ceased to sing, and apparently the earth still revolved on its age-old course.

Blackfeather sat his horse, his expression unreadable and his rifle resting across the pommel of his saddle. Beside him stood Soldier, who lifted his tawny head and nickered at her.

"Thank you, Cody." Kat's voice was soft, and sounded strange to her own ears.

"I take it you've recovered from the deadly woman's disease."

Despite everything, Katherine blushed. "It was the best lie I could come up with."

"Ryland would have been suspicious of anything more conventional. As fabrications go, it wasn't bad."

Katherine bit her lip with a scowl, not quite strong enough to address Travis yet. "He's leaving, isn't he?"

"You might want to ask him that."

With a lurch of her heart Kat turned her gaze to Travis. He stood stiff and silent. Above his right brow was a blackish bruise.

"I'd only bring you trouble, lady," he said. "Trouble and death." His hands clenched to fists, and for a moment she thought he would say more, but he turned away, striding to Soldier and mounting smoothly.

"Don't go." She couldn't stop the murmured words that conjured up a hazy image of this very scene played out in the dark an eternity ago.

He didn't speak, but sat very still atop the buckskin stallion.

Present and past seemed to meld and swirl in her mind. "Take me with you," she said.

Someone had given him a hat. It hid his expression, reminding her very much of a shadowy stranger she had once met.

"I ride alone, lady."

How many lifetimes ago had she run down this very street after him? And had it truly been she who had caught his stirrup and refused to let go?

"I'm not going to run after you, Ryland." She raised her voice slightly. "Not this time."

His back was very straight as he pressed Soldier away from the hitching rail.

Tears filled Katherine's eyes and spilled down her cheeks. She swiped them aside. Something bumped her elbow, and she turned.

Finch stood not two feet away, extending his Colt to her. "Hold it firm, but gentle," he suggested.

She delayed just a moment, not daring to breathe, before she launched herself from the boardwalk and into the middle of the hard-packed street. "Come back, Ryland!" she yelled.

All eyes watched her, but no one spoke.

"Damn you, Ryland. Come back here." She raised the Colt. "Or I'll shoot. I swear I will."

But Soldier still trotted on.

Katherine bit her lip and aimed. Her first shot spattered dirt not six inches from the buckskin's hoof.

The stallion snorted, twisting sideways, and Travis spun him about to face Kat. "What the hell do you think you're doing?"

"Didn't mean to scare Soldier," she said. "But I'm new at shooting men." She braced her legs wide and raised her brows. "Get down."

"The hell I will!"

She smiled. "The hell you won't, Ryland." Putting her tongue in the corner of her mouth, Kat closed one eye, and cocked. "Sit really still now. I wouldn't want to hit your horse."

"Take a hair off his belly, I'll tan your hide, woman."

Katherine raised her chin and laughed out loud. "You'd

have to come here to do that, Ryland. And I don't think you have the nerve."

She fired again. The bullet slammed between Soldier's front hooves. Travis was out of the saddle and on his feet before they came to a complete halt.

"Woman!" he called out to her. "Me and Soldier been through a lot together."

"And you and I haven't?" she challenged, heading toward him.

"I won't stay with you and ruin your life, lady."

"The next one goes through your right arm." She said the words with flat finality. "I swear it. I don't mind patching you up."

"Don't you know better than to shoot a man when the sun's in your eyes?" Travis scolded. "Ain't you learned nothing. Ain't you learned to stay away from me? That death surrounds me?"

"I think *life* surrounds you," she yelled back. "Only you're afraid to admit it. It's time you faced the facts."

His eyes narrowed, watching her as she continued to approach.

She was directly in front of him now.

"You're about one bean short of a full pot," he murmured.

"Yes."

He clenched his fists. "And I don't deserve you."

"It seems like you make a habit of being wrong." She smiled slowly. "I'm afraid we deserve each other."

"I'm not what you need, Katherine. I'm no knight in shining armor. I'm no hero. No preacher."

"I know exactly what you are, Ryland. I know the man. I know the little boy. And I love them both."

Travis's fists clenched as if he were waging a terrible battle in his own mind. "I couldn't bear to disappoint you, Kat."

She moved a cautious step nearer, her breath held and her gaze fused to his. "You think I'm not scared? You think this is simple for me?" She shook her head. "Did you ever think maybe I'd disappoint *you*?"

"Never." His answer came from somewhere deep inside his chest, and his eyes were hard as steel.

"Then let's give happiness a try."

Travis drew a deep breath, watching her through narrowed eyes. "It won't be no simple 'try' for me, lady. If you was ever mine, really mine, I'd never have the strength to let you go."

"Never?"

He shook his head, saying nothing.

"Then God better save a place in heaven for us, Ryland," she whispered. "Because I'm already yours."

For one painful moment Travis hesitated, and then, taking the Colt from her hands, he drew her into his arms and kissed her.

With the opening scene for MY DESPERADO firmly ensconced in my mind, I told my husband we *had* to go to Colorado to "research" my next historical romance. And so we packed up our two favorite horses and headed for Estes park. After a week I decided riding in the Rockies was the most fun I could have with my boots on. Six months later I knew I was wrong. Writing MY DESPERADO was. Hope you enjoyed Kat and Travis half as much as I did, and if you get a chance you'll drop a note to:

Lois Greiman
PO Box 16
Rogers, Minnesota 55374-0016

If you enjoyed this book, take advantage of this special offer. Subscribe now and get a

FREE
Historical
Romance

No Obligation (a $4.50 value)

Each month the editors of True Value select the four *very best* novels from America's leading publishers of romantic fiction. Preview them in your home *Free* for 10 days. With the first four books you receive, we'll send you a FREE book as our introductory gift. No Obligation!

If for any reason you decide not to keep them, just return them and owe nothing. If you like them as much as we think you will, you'll pay just $4.00 each and save at *least* $.50 each off the cover price. (Your savings are *guaranteed* to be at least $2.00 each month.) There is NO postage and handling – or other hidden charges. There are no minimum number of books to buy and you may cancel at any time.

Send in the Coupon Below

To get your FREE historical romance fill out the coupon below and mail it today. As soon as we receive it we'll send you your FREE Book along with your first month's selections.
